Reader praise for
Tío Emilio
AND THE
Secrets of the Ancestors,
San Diego Free Press serialized edition:

"Richard - a huge thanks for this series here. Love everything you and your characters are saying.... I'm sure you're familiar with the *Peaceful Warrior* series, which has literally changed the way I look at the world. Your work helps to build on that in a new and equally profound way. Let me know if you ever put this into print, I'm buying a dozen copies and getting them out into my community right away..."

—**Dave Rice**, writer and blogger, *San Diego Reader*

"I've read it completely and it's quite good. Rich Juarez is an intriguing writer and the grammar is excellent.... I'm excited at the potential for younger readers, which is obviously who this story will cater to."

—**Annie Lane**, freelance writer,
San Diego Free Press editorial board member

"Very talented writer.... It is powerful, dramatic, and insight into a world few white people know about."

—**Marcia Gewelber**, published writer,
editor, and writing teacher

"Richard Juarez is making me wonder why I'm satisfied reading the average book I check out from the library...."

—**Bob Dorn**, taught writing at UCSD and wrote for
San Diego Evening Tribune, New York Times,
San Diego Reader and *San Diego Magazine*

"Richard, I have been faithfully keeping up with your novel, enjoying it tremendously. As you, I have read the works of Carlos Castaneda, and can see his influence. ...The anthropologist in me appreciates the blending of cultural differences that you illustrate; the conflict between the native Mexican understanding of the spiritual world vis a vis the perspective of the American Catholic, and the degrees of literacy in two languages. Both of these are embodied in the character of Vincent, who finds himself between two worlds. Also, you portray the struggle between behavior choices and social associations that are compelling the 'students'. I think that good fiction dwells in the struggles and conflicts that trouble humanity, and your work exemplifies this quality."

—Jim Kline, retired public school teacher, Blacksburg, Virginia, with an interest in anthropology and religion

"Thank you so much Mr. Juarez, for this beautiful Novel. Its lecture captivated me. I have been myself a Don Emilio's student! And like Vicente and Antonio changed and grew up with his teachings, I did too. I will continue practicing and sharing with all the people that I have the opportunity. I think that your book is not only a Novel but excellent didactic material to raise the motivation of the young people who need to change their habits and give a turn to their lives."

—Vicky Padilla, Latina college student, Costa Rica

"I am really enjoying reading about Tio Emilio and his fledgling students. You have created a very engaging story. I look forward to reading a segment every week! "

—Germaine French, environmental planner, Colorado

"I don't know what I like best, the great story, or the descriptions of food! There also are a lot of visuals -- it would be great to collaborate with an artist/illustrator to get these done as part of the final book. Looking forward to next week, (and the next....)"

—Sylvia Martinez, low-income housing developer, mother of teenage son and daughter

"Rich, this was my favorite chapter so far. I really enjoyed the
'saying grace' section, being mindful and grateful for how we get
our nourishment, down to the plants, animals, growers, pickers
etc. The boys are making good progress spiritually, I'm enjoying
it along with them. I can't wait to see what Nana cooks up next,
the chile colorado description made my mouth water."

—**Becky Mobley**, certified clinical nutritionist

"Rich, Don Emilio and the boys have reminded me that
I need to go back and do more meditation for a calming of my
own 'inner chatter.' I'll be glad when my granddaughters read
the part about thanking the plants and animals for giving us
their energy and strength. We always thank Mother
Earth, but your characters have raised the idea of showing
gratitude to that which we consume and nourishes us."

—**Carolina Juarez**, Spanish teacher,
Claremont Middle School, Oakland, California

"After reading last week's installment, I thought you had
probably read Carlos Castaneda....You have definitely got my
attention with these young boys and their wise beyond belief tio.
I look forward to every Saturday's chapter! Mas, por favor!"

—**Janice Dempsey**, masters degree in
Latin American Studies

"Thanks for the story Ricardo...the Toltec way is the
way to live one's life...your exposure helps to give
the knowledge to a younger generation..."

—**Clyde**

Tío Emilio and the Secrets of the Ancestors

RICHARD JUAREZ

This novel was previously published in a
weekly-serialized format by the *San Diego Free Press*.

Editor: Corinn Codye

Cover Design: Scott Breidenthal
Interior Design: Tricia Breidenthal
www.bookdesigncandy.com

ISBN: 978-0-9997616-0-1

Printed in the United States of America

This book is dedicated to my parents,
Mary Castro Juarez and Jesus Duarte Juarez.
This book would not have been possible
without their belief, support and encouragement
throughout my school years, their support for my
work in the older neighborhoods, and their acceptance
of my need to pursue this other path of knowledge,
the knowledge of our ancestors.

TABLE OF CONTENTS

1

ALONG FOR THE RIDE

"With friends like this, who needs enemies?"

HENRY YOUNGMAN

I didn't want to get in. Tony and I were already halfway home. We didn't need a ride. Not with them. It seemed like every time I was around these guys, something bad would happen. I didn't need more trouble, and I certainly didn't want to hear more yelling from my mother about hanging out with these guys again.

"Get in, *cabrón*!" yelled Eddie, "I ain't gonna sit here all day waiting for you to decide."

Arturo motioned urgently toward the back seat. "Come on, Vincent. Get in!" He was sitting in the front next to his brother. "Eddie doesn't have much time. He's gotta get out to PB."

Eddie should have been a senior but he dropped out in the tenth grade, the same grade the rest of us were in now, and was working the late shift at a taco shop out in Pacific Beach. I didn't see him much now that he had a car. But I knew he liked to drive by school once in a while to check out his old friends and see some of the girls he never sees anymore.

I wanted to just keep walking with Tony. We'd known each other since before either of us could remember. Tony's sister, Alice, and my sister, Gracie, had been friends since kindergarten, and they used to drag us along when they played together. So, we had just always been friends. Tony and I usually walked home after school. Once in a while we took the bus, but we didn't live that far from school, so most of the time we just saved the money, unless we had a big load of books, or Tony had to get to work early at Amador's market.

I wanted to keep going. Even though it was mid-February, the temperature was in the high 60s, so it was a comfortable walk. We were walking along 16th Street through the eastern edge of downtown, with its boarded-up storefronts, old warehouses that badly needed paint, some buildings with small apartments, and a few old houses. A lot of homeless hung out in the area between 15th and 17th Streets. That's why most of the kids at San Diego High from Barrio Logan preferred to walk home along 12th Street, the other main corridor that went directly south past Imperial Avenue and into the barrio. That's where we should have been. Then these guys wouldn't have seen us.

"Ah, come on," Tony said as he climbed into the back seat, "we'll get home faster."

Not that much faster, I thought to myself, knowing the car. The faded grey 1970 Chevy Nova was as old as me, and ran about as bad as it looked. But then again, it ran.

"Hey, man," said Eddie, raising his voice again as I continued to hesitate, "You want a ride or not?" He tightly gripped the leather steering wheel cover with his left hand, while he impatiently tapped on it with his right, waiting for my answer. It looked like he had added some more tattoos on his hands from what I remembered seeing.

"The sissy's mama don't want him hanging with his homies!" Pablito yelled, and laughed from the other side of the back seat. Arturo and Eddie laughed with him.

They all knew my mother didn't want me hanging around with them. I hated it when they started making fun of me because of it, especially Pablito, who only did it when the others were around to back him up, because he knew I'd kick his ass—again. I couldn't let him get away with it.

"Move your butt over," I yelled as I came around and opened the door on his side. "You get to be the sissy and sit in the middle."

He didn't move, so I just plowed into him, like a football player smacking into a blocking sled. Although Pablito was almost a year older, he was about four inches shorter than me and even skinnier, so sliding him over on the grey vinyl seat wasn't hard. Trouble was I knocked him into Tony, who wasn't very happy about it. Tony was just a little shorter than me at about five-eight, but not as thin. He immediately pushed Pablito back. But after a little shoving and elbowing back and forth, we settled down to enjoy the ride, checking out the view as Eddie cruised south down 16th Street toward Barrio Logan. I tried hard not to think about what my mother would do if she found out.

Arturo and Pablito preferred walking through this area after school, where they could check out their potential customers. Eddie seemed to do his business elsewhere, with higher-end customers, but he let Arturo and Pablito handle the small stuff. They would occasionally sell a few joints to these poor guys on the street who were looking for a little high. I don't think they sold much, because they never had much money. But I didn't know for sure. I really didn't want to know. They knew Tony and I didn't want to be involved in that, so they usually didn't sell stuff when we were with them. Before Eddie started working he was always asking if I wanted any weed, to sell to these guys on the street or at school. Although it sounded like it might be an easy way of getting a little cash to spend, I couldn't deal with the thought of getting caught at school, or my parents finding a stash at home. Then I'd really be in for it!

"Hey!" I yelled in panic when Eddie turned and headed east on Imperial Avenue. "We're just a few blocks from home. Where are you going?"

"We're taking the scenic route," said Eddie, laughing with Arturo.

It wasn't really that far out of our way to head east a few blocks to 25th Street, then south under the I-5 freeway bridge and into the heart of Barrio Logan, right next to Chicano Park. Eddie used to spend all day hanging out in the park with his dropout friends. That was before he got his job. But you could never tell what these guys were up to. I sort of calmed down, knowing that Eddie didn't have much time. He didn't have a great job, but it was a job. I thought he wouldn't want to blow it by being late. I mean, what kind of trouble could he get us into in just a few minutes?

As I stared out the side window I noticed that a number of buildings along Imperial, both residences and businesses, had gotten new paint jobs. While they were older buildings, they looked in much better shape than back along 16th Street. This strip along Imperial Avenue used to be mostly Black-owned businesses, and the residents nearby were predominantly Black. But as Black families moved out, and more Mexicans moved into the adjacent Sherman Heights and Logan Heights neighborhoods, more signs in Spanish had been showing up.

"There it is! Just like yesterday!" yelled Arturo.

I turned to see what he was yelling about, just as the car came to a sudden stop. So sudden, I almost hit the back of Eddie's seat with my face. Immediately Eddie, Arturo and Pablito were yelling and laughing. Eddie had stopped just before 25th Street, next to a *Coca Cola* delivery truck that was double-parked. Arturo leaned way out the window, reaching for a case of cokes on the truck. Tony and I looked at each other, and started laughing along with them. I couldn't believe they were doing this. They said they saw the truck making deliveries the day before, and came back to see if it would be there again. Just our luck, or bad luck, it was.

Everyone was laughing and having a great time as Arturo pulled the sodas into the car and slid back down in his seat. Eddie sped off and turned at the corner. There was a horn honking, but no one seemed to be paying attention. As we turned the corner at 25th Street, I saw the post office truck sitting at the light, the driver shaking his fist at us, flailing away on his horn. The guy saw the whole thing. I turned around to see what he was going to do, and by then the light had changed. He sped through the intersection and caught up with us before we had gone one block.

"Oh, hell," cried Tony. "That's Mr. Romero, our mailman. We are screwed!"

2

A WARNING

"Do or do not. There is no try."

YODA

Bam!

The door slammed behind me. She almost hit me with it, but I didn't care. She wanted me out of the house, and I was glad to get out of there. She had been crying all day, just like yesterday and the day before, crying and yelling. It seemed like it went on and on nonstop since two cops and the *Coke* delivery guy showed up. The three of them gave me a long lecture in front of my parents. The *Coke* guy said he would not press charges, but the cops said it would be on my record anyway, in case I ever did anything like that again.

Even though I wasn't actually arrested, my mother cried and yelled about me getting arrested, about robbing a delivery truck, about having a criminal record, about hanging out with hoodlum friends. It just wouldn't stop. I tried to get away from it by staying in my room and closing the door, but she would open it. I went out to the end of the back yard, but it seemed like she just turned up the volume to make sure I heard her. It made me feel so bad to hear her crying, I felt like I was two inches tall. By the third day I was just so tired of it, I wanted it to stop.

I think she was tired of it too, so she kicked me out of the house and sent me up the street to Nana and Tata's house to see her brother, my Tío Marcos. It felt like such a relief to get out of there. But now, I was on to my next encounter and whatever that would get me. Putting two and two together, I figured she and Tata had asked Tío Marcos to come down from L.A. to lecture me about getting into trouble. Who better than him?

As I walked toward the house I could see Tío Marcos in the front yard. I was actually looking forward to talking with him, just him and me. For a long time, I'd wanted to ask what happened to him and Tío Juan. I was too young to know what was going on when they went away. My mother always refused to talk about it, and whenever I asked my father, he said, "Talk to your mother." It was as if she had forbidden him to say anything. Tío Marcos and Tío Juan never talked to me about their past, although I had overheard bits and pieces of it when the adults talked among themselves, in Spanish. My parents were no doubt trying to keep me from knowing what my uncles had been involved in. But with all the secrecy and the time away, I figured they must have been in jail for something.

"Hi, Tío!" I called out as I approached the edge of the yard.

"Hey, Vincent, what's going on, *vato?*"

"Oh, not much," I said as I walked up the steps from the sidewalk and into the yard.

He stared at me with a questioning look.

"Not much? What do you mean *not much*, man?" He pointed to the porch steps. "Go ahead and have a seat." He sat down next to me on the top step. "My sister is mad at me and my brothers because of the trouble you've been getting into. My father is pretty angry too, at her, at us, and you. He's frustrated seeing history being repeated over again with the next generation."

I quickly turned to face him. "You guys don't have nothin' to do with what I' been doing."

"Oh, hell, they know that!" He turned and leaned his back against the wall of the house. "Your ma's just pissed because her 'pride and joy' has been getting into trouble for, let's see, getting arrested for stealing cokes, getting into a big fight, doing graffiti, getting involved with the gang, and I don't know what else. She and Tata think we've been a bad influence on you."

I shook my head. "First of all, I don't do graffiti! It's that idiot, Pablito, one of my homies. He was in the car when they pulled the cokes off a delivery truck. And we didn't really get arrested. The driver didn't press charges. I didn't do anything to help steal the cokes, but I was with them and I did take some home so they wouldn't rag on me."

"Well, they may not rag on you, but now your mother sure is on your case, isn't she! She's been telling us all about it, and crying, saying she doesn't know where she went wrong raising you. After that coke heist, she says she's had it with you. She's also real angry and afraid about you fighting with these neighborhood guys she thought were your friends."

"Uh, yeah, Pablito is the one I had the so-called big fight with." No secrets around here. I guess my sisters told my mother about the fight. "It wasn't no big thing, really. I finally had to stand up for myself after all these years."

"He's your friend and you had a big fight with him?"

"Pablito's just my homie. Tony is my best friend. Pablito and Arturo and the others, they live around here. They're our homies, and we hang out with them sometimes. So yeah, they're friends but they aren't real close friends, like Tony. You've seen Tony. He works part-time at Amador's market."

"And this fight? What do you mean you had to stand up for yourself after all these years?"

"Well, there's this girl Anita who lives down the street from us...."

He looked at me surprised, and let out a loud laugh, pointing at me.

"*Orale vato*, I should've known!" He paused until he could stop laughing. "Fighting over a girl!"

"No, no Tío, it's not like that. Anita is Mona's friend, in her class at school. She's kinda cute and Pablito likes her. I don't. She's too young! Anyway, she told Mona that Pablito said he used to beat me up all the time. That skinny punk never beat me up! He and some of the older guys used to pick on me. I remember many times coming home crying, and my parents never did anything about it or said anything to their parents.

"One day Anita was in front of our house with Mona, and Pablito came by to talk with her. When I saw him there, I went outside and asked why he told Anita he used to beat me up. I said all of them together did, but one-on-one, he never did—and never could! His face got red."

Tío nodded knowingly. "You embarrassed him. I can guess what happened next."

"Yeah, he threw his arms down and motioned to me, saying, 'Come on then, let's see.' I didn't really expect him to try to fight me without his army. But he challenged me, so I had to show him up."

I jumped up into my fight stance to show my uncle, raising my fists up to my chest.

"He came at me swinging. I stood my ground and whacked him with a solid left hook to the side of the head." As I spoke I demonstrated with a quick punch in the air. "He crumpled to the ground, and sat there shaking his head. Slowly he got up, blinking his eyes. He charged again, swinging wildly like before. I faked a right and hit him with another left hook. Pow!

"Down he went, like someone cut off his legs. He looked really surprised that he was on the ground. I was surprised too. I didn't want to hurt him any more, and was hoping he would just get up and go home. No such luck. When he got up, I could see tears in his eyes, but I knew he wasn't going to let them out, not with Anita sitting there. He came at me again, and this time I faked a left and hit him with a right hook to the other side of the head. Bam! Down he went again." I slid back down to my seat on the step.

"He stayed down awhile, first on his hands and knees, then plopping over onto his butt. When he finally got up, he just turned away and walked slowly toward his house. I felt really bad, but I also felt proud that I decked him three times, with just one punch each time. And I don't think he even touched me!"

"So your dad did help take care of it after all!"

"What do you mean?" I asked, my voice getting louder. "He never did nothing! He never protected me. He just let them beat up on me." I paused, feeling that old anger rising again. "Sometimes when I think about that, I just hate him!"

Tío paused, looking at me, perhaps surprised at my saying I hated my father. I probably shouldn't have told my uncle that. I hoped it wouldn't get back to my father.

"But isn't he the one who taught you to box like that?"

"Well...yeah. He bought me boxing gloves and taught me defense, the jab, the hook, how to counter-punch—lots of stuff. He was a pretty good boxer himself. Used to box as an amateur. He said that most guys come at you throwing wild punches, and if you stand in there and hit them with a quick jab or hook, most of their blows will never get to you."

I paused as I thought about what I had just said, and a light came on.

"Oh, so yeah...I guess you could say he helped me after all, Tío. I never thought of it like that."

"*Mijo*, he couldn't go ask those guys not to hit you, or go tattle on them to their parents. He had to toughen you up and help you learn to defend yourself. He didn't want you to be a sissy. He had to do it this way so you could get through it with some respect."

"Respect. Yeah, I guess you're right. As a matter of fact, later that day, Pablito's friends came over and jumped me and knocked me around a little, to stand up for Pablito and help him get back some respect after I embarrassed him so bad. But I didn't get hurt. And we've gotten along okay since then. You could say I gained some respect out of that exchange too."

"So that was the big fight she's been talking about. What about the gang? Did you join?"

"Heck no! She'd really kill me if I did! My father, too!"

I didn't want to get into it any deeper with my uncle, but I was starting to get a lot of pressure from the guys to join. I didn't want to do that and then have to face my parents when they found out. I didn't know what the other guys' parents were thinking or if they even knew or cared. But my parents would probably kick me out of the house. Tony's parents would probably kick him out too, or send him off to live with relatives in the desert.

"I'm glad you haven't joined. So, what's with this other stuff she's complaining about?"

"Well, it's no big deal, and she's getting all bent out of shape."

"No, it *is* a big deal, a *really big deal* for your mother and father to call *me* in to talk to you. Up until now, I've been forbidden to talk with you about my life. I don't know if you knew that."

"No," I said, feeling shocked to find out. "I didn't know."

"When you were a little baby, I loved to play with you. It was like having another little brother. As you got older, I wanted to take you places, show you things, like the guys playing handball and basketball. But I started getting into trouble and got sent to juvie for three months. After I got out, your mom told me to stay away. She didn't want me to be a bad influence on you.

"One night I went to a party and got into a fight with this *vato loco* who stabbed me in the hand, here." He stuck out his left hand and showed me a scar that went all the way across his palm. "I ran out of that party because I didn't want to be there when the cops came. I was on probation and I'd be back in juvie if they found me there, cut up from a fight after crashing the party. It was only about a mile away but I didn't want to go home bleeding. I was afraid my father would throw me out of the house. So, I figured I could get some help at my sister's.

"When I got there, I called to your parents to let me in. Your father opened the door and saw that I was dripping blood onto the porch, and yelled at me to get out of there. Your mom brought out some towels and bandages and was going to help, but your father grabbed them and tossed them to me. He yelled and said they had already told me they didn't want any trouble around you kids. I saw three of you standing in the living room watching what was going on. Your mother was yelling at you to get back in bed, and your father was yelling at me to get out. He was crying as he yelled.

"I squeezed the towel into my hand to stop the bleeding, and just walked away. At first, I was pissed that they weren't going to help me. But when I saw your father's tears, I understood how bad he felt kicking me out. He and I had been close before I started getting into trouble. He was like a big brother to me. You know, *familia* is part of our *cultura*. So I know it was hard for him to push me out that night. I feel bad now that I put them in that situation, where they felt they had to choose between me and you kids."

"But Tío, they didn't do anything for us that night. I think they just sent us back to bed."

"It was more than just that night," he continued. "Your parents tried to create a protective shield around you to keep you isolated from the trouble going on around you in this neighborhood. That night, they chose to try to keep that shield intact. Before then, and since, they chose over and over to protect you. Some years later, a few years after I got married, I got sent away to prison, on drug charges. Do you remember that?"

"Oh my God!" I said, staring at him as my jaw dropped. So that's why they were gone so long. I figured they must have been in jail...but prison! For drug dealing! I had only a vague memory of him being around, and then he and Tío Juan were both gone for a long time.

"No, I didn't know. Whenever I asked my parents where you guys were, they wouldn't talk about it."

"See, that's the protective shield they put around you. They didn't talk about us getting sent to the joint because they didn't want you to know about that part of our lives. When I got out, they repeated to me in even stronger language that I was to keep away from you and not talk about my past. So up to a point, they succeeded in keeping you from this stuff. Now, they say you've been getting into more and more trouble. That shield has broken down."

Man, my parents must have been really desperate to have Tío Marcos tell me all this now.

"Your parents are real concerned about what could happen to you. So they wanted me to load it on heavy and tell you how bad it really is, how you could end up suffering like Juan and I did in prison. We took some pretty bad beatings. Not only from other prisoners, but from the guards too."

I couldn't believe what I was hearing. I could understand fights with other prisoners, but beatings from the guards? I didn't think they could do that, and I told him so.

"Well, that's real life. They say if you don't want to get beat by the guards, stay out of prison. Anyway, your parents didn't want you to know the truth about your neighborhood and your uncles and prison until you were a little older. They didn't want you to know that Juan and I were gang members, or that Juan was the leader, the head guy. They didn't want you making us into your heroes. And I don't either. Being involved with the gang was where our troubles started. We screwed up, man. That's nothing to be proud of. We brought shame on the family, and we paid a high price for it."

I was really surprised to hear not only were they in the gang, but Tío Juan was the leader!

"I don't really want to get into details of it all, because I've tried put all that behind me. But we served four years for selling drugs, and were on probation for three years. Older guys like me keep telling younger guys like you to stay out of trouble, stay in school, and get a decent job so you don't get tempted to go into crime and drugs. But I also know that what I say won't change your mind about your own decisions. You're not going to do nothing stupid like join the gang and then get into drug deals where you might get stabbed or shot. I think you're smarter than that."

He paused and looked me in the eye. He kept looking, waiting for a response.

"Yeah," I said, nodding, "I'm not gonna do nothing stupid."

"You say no, but whether you join the gang or not, if you continue to hang with guys in the gang who are into drugs, one day you might end up in the wrong place at the wrong time."

"But Tío, most of these guys, we've been friends a long time. We see each other in school, we play handball and basketball in the park."

"Okay, okay. I know how hard it can be to make a total break like your parents want. So maybe that will take time. But in the meantime, watch your back. Stay out of situations where they might do something serious and take you along, like your coke heist. Sure, talk with them at school. If you have to hang out around here, make it in a public place like the handball or basketball courts where they can't do anything stupid. But for God's sake, don't hang out at their house, especially the one your mother is so concerned about, this Arturo and his brother..."

"Eddie."

"And don't even think about going inside their hangout up on Logan Avenue. You don't know when the place might get raided by the cops or shot up by some rival gang. You hear me? Be smart. Don't put yourself at risk. Don't go where you could get into trouble."

He paused and stared into my eyes again. I nodded. He kept staring.

"Okay," I said, "I'll try be careful."

"Anyway, that's what I wanted to talk to you about. Your parents wanted me to put the fear of God in you, so to speak. But you're not going to get scared from what I say. You're going to make your own decisions. I just wanted to tell you I made some bad decisions and screwed up my life and my family. Don't repeat my mistakes."

With that, he stood up and walked into the house, giving me a pat on the shoulder as he walked by. I just sat there for a few minutes, taking it all in. He sure put it differently than all the lectures I'd been getting. He simply boiled it down to this: here's what can happen. You choose.

3

THE VISITOR

*"I am not a product of my circumstances.
I am a product of my decisions."*

STEPHEN COVEY

"Vincent," my mother yelled, "did you finish putting the wax on the floors?"

About the only time she talked to me lately was to yell about another chore to do around the house. Which was better than a few weeks before, when she was yelling at me all the time for the great coke robbery, and for everything else she could remember I'd done lately.

"Yeah, I'm just finishing it now," I yelled back as I glared at the floor resentfully. I must have been down on my hands and knees for at least an hour, putting paste wax on the floor in the dining room and living room. My parents were proud of those hardwood oak floors, and made sure they shined. Or, should I say, they made sure *I* made them shine.

"You girls come in here and wash up, and then change your clothes," she called over the squeaking sounds as she cleaned the bathroom mirror. "Tío Emilio will be here soon."

I heard her tossing things into her white plastic cleaning bucket as she moved into the hall. She had been yelling orders all morning while she moved from room to room cleaning the entire house from top to bottom. I could see her through the living room doorway with the white bandana she likes to wear to keep her hair out of her face, scrubbing up and down the pale green wall with a big yellow sponge as she wiped off all the little black fingerprints.

I knew that Tony and the guys were probably playing basketball at Chicano Park. That's where I should have been, but instead, I was doing housework.

"I don't know why I'm the only one who's gotta do this," I said when she walked into the dining room. "I hate being stuck in the house, waxing these *pinche* floors."

"You watch your language young man—and quit complaining!" she snapped back. "Being stuck at home is your own fault. That's your punishment for being so stupid. Robbing a deliveryman! I thought you had more sense than that. But, like I said, I'm not going to say anything more about it. And about having to help with the floors, do you think I love spending my time cleaning this house so that you kids have a clean and safe place to live, and so we don't have to be ashamed of it when we have visitors?" With that she walked carefully over the newly waxed floor and into the kitchen, where she set her bucket down on the brown linoleum floor.

"Hurry and buff the floor," she said loudly, even though I was just a few feet away. "And take out the trash before you wash up and change." Then she started wiping the light pink walls.

While she usually made a fuss cleaning for visitors, she seemed to be going to extra lengths today. Without saying so, she was telling us that there was something special about this visitor.

"Mama, tell us again who Tío Emilio is?" Mona called out, with Gina at her side as they started to walk through the dining room into the kitchen.

"Hey, stay off the waxed floors!" I yelled. "I haven't buffed them yet." They looked at me and then stomped right through. So I threw the dirty yellow rag full of dark brown paste wax.

"Mama!" Mona yelled. "Ugh! He hit me with that yucky rag!"

I thought my mother was going to yell at me again for doing that, but she didn't. She just glared, first at me, then at the girls. She probably wasn't sure who to yell at—me for throwing the rag, or the girls for stomping on the newly waxed floor.

They weren't so little anymore, Mona being twelve and Gina ten, but they still got away with not having to do much around the house, leaving me and Gracie to do most of the work. Gracie was seventeen, two years older than me.

I was about to turn on the buffer but held off making all that noise, because I wanted to hear her answer too. It was not clear to me, either, how we suddenly had a new uncle.

"How come we ain't never heard about him?" asked Gina.

"Stop saying *ain't*," my mother answered with her usual plea.

"Yeah," Mona chimed in laughing, *"ain't* ain't a word."

My mother just shook her head. "Your father and I just never had any reason to talk to you about him, I guess. He's not really your uncle. He's my father's cousin."

"If he's a cousin, why do we have to call him *Tío*?" asked Mona.

"Because it's a sign of respect. He's your elder. Now, for the last time, go wash up and get dressed. Help each other with your barrettes, or ask Gracie. And put on some warm clothes. Your cousins are coming over and I know you'll be running around outside tonight."

I walked into the kitchen where she was quickly wiping the walls. I hoped that without the girls around she might tell me more about this strange visitor.

"Mama," I said quietly, "How come no one ever talks about this Tío Emilio?" Since she mostly wasn't speaking to me, I wasn't sure she would answer. She gave me her stern look, then turned away and started wiping the wall even more rapidly. I could tell she didn't want to talk about him. But I didn't care. I wanted to know more about this new Tío that no one talked about. So I just stood there, waiting.

"Well," she said finally as she moved on to wiping the cabinets, "I guess it's because...." Now she had stopped wiping and turned around to look at me. "Because he is of the old ways, and people don't like to talk about the old ways. Now quit asking so many questions. Hurry up and finish that floor. Your father and Emilio will be here soon."

I walked back to the dining room and turned on the buffing machine, losing myself in thought as the buffing pads did their thing on the waxed floor, the noise drowning out all sounds from the rest of the house. I wanted more answers, but I knew she wouldn't say more. She was keeping this secret inside. *He is of the old ways.* What the heck did that mean … *of the old ways?*

"Vincent!" my mother yelled above the noise of the buffer, yanking me out of my thoughts. "You've been polishing that last spot over and over. You're done!" I switched off the machine so she wouldn't have to yell. "Put that away and go take the trash out, wash up, and get dressed. Then I have one more thing. I need you to go to the store for me."

She sent me to Mike Amador's Market, two blocks away, for a few groceries. For the time being I was restricted to the house, except for these errands she sent me on. Amador's was one of what my Nana called her *tienditas*, little stores that catered to their neighbors. My mother usually drove to the supermarket once a week for most of her groceries, but sent me or Gracie to Amador's whenever she needed a few more things. Mr. Amador had the order in a bag waiting for me when I arrived. She often called ahead and told him what she wanted. I handed him a ten and he counted out my change.

"By the way, Mr. Lopez," he said, raising his voice—he often called us by our last names when he wanted to lecture us— "I'm very angry with you and Tony and your little group. I don't appreciate you guys putting your *placas* on my store wall!"

"I didn't do it! I don't know nothing about it," I whined, raising my voice back.

"Don't you lie to me, young man, and don't you raise your voice to me either! You show some respect to your elders! I already found out it was Pablito who did it. But you're always out together doing these *chingasos.* Why don't you go write on your father's house or your grandfather's? See what deep *caca* that'll get you into. And I don't know why you guys still hang around with that kid Pablito. Hasn't he gotten you into enough trouble already?"

I stood there silently, my eyes lowered. I didn't want to talk with him or anybody about the trouble Pablito had gotten us into. He and Arturo could do some really stupid things at times, too often getting us involved with them, like the coke heist.

"I don't want to see that spray paint on my walls again. You understand?"

"*Sí*," I said meekly and walked out the door.

I knew my father and Tío Emilio would arrive any minute and I didn't want to be late. My grandparents lived on the same street as us. As I got to their house I saw Tata on the front porch, sitting there in the sun, watching the world go by. Tata was tall and thin, and even though he had been retired from the cannery for quite a while, he hadn't put on extra weight from just sitting around eating Nana's food. Although he was old and wrinkled and had a lot of gray hair, it was mostly black, which made him look a little younger than his seventy-five years.

"*Hola, Vicentillo,*" he called to me.

His voice brought me back. Slightly embarrassed, I realized I had been standing there staring at him, lost in thought. Just then, out of the corner of my eye, I saw movement down the block. My father had just pulled up in front of our house and I heard him honk.

"*Mira, Tata, ya vienen,*" I said, pointing down the street.

"*Bueno, mijito.* You go home," he said in his halting English, waving his hand at me in that direction. "Tell your *mamá* we are coming."

Slowly he got up out of his chair and in his slightly stooped, old-man walk, he started for the door. "*Vieja! Están allí. Vamanos.*"

As I walked quickly toward the house I could see my father and a stranger get out of the car. My mother walked up and gave our visitor a hug, and introduced him to my sisters.

"*Y donde está Vicente?*" I could hear him asking as I got closer. In unison, my sisters and mother turned to look in my direction as I walked up.

"Vincent, this is Tío Emilio," said my father, coming around the back of the car.

Tío Emilio stood next to my father. I could see that Tío was a couple of inches or so taller, about five feet ten or eleven. His dark tan, smooth skin, beardless face, and straight black hair made him look very distinguished. He looked older than my mother and father, maybe about fifty or so, but much younger than Tata, his cousin.

"Mucho gusto en conocerlo," I said, using the formal introduction response.

"I am pleased to meet you too," he replied. "But while I know you do not remember, I met you a few months after you were born, when your parents and grandfather brought you and your sister Graciela to our town to introduce the two of you to our *familia* in Mexico."

All that talk about his coming and no one told us we had already met him! Very strange.

"Tío Emilio," said Gracie, "you speak English so well! I thought you would be speaking only Spanish."

"Well, I can speak Spanish if you like, but I learned English in school in Mexico, and for a number of years I lived in Los Angeles. I travel around a great deal, so I have learned to speak both languages, like your parents. ¿Y ustedes muchachos, hablan Español?"

"Sí, Tío," Gracie continued, *"pero no muy bien.* We all understand a lot, but we don't speak it very well."

"Let's not stand out here talking, let's all go into the house," said my mother.

I took up the rear as the family began walking toward the door.

"Por favor, Vicente," said Tío Emilio, "my travel bag is in the back seat of the car. Could you please bring it in? I have some things for you children."

"Here, Vincent," said my father, reaching for the groceries, "I'll take those."

I quickly climbed into the back seat of the car and closed the door. I sat there with his travel bag, wondering who was this guy, this "uncle" that I'd never heard of before. I looked closely at the bag. It wasn't luggage, like my parents' Samsonite. It was a beautiful, light brown leather bag, about the color of my baseball glove. I didn't know much about leather or leather bags. But I had seen some expensive baseball gloves, with quality leather and fine stitching. This bag was better than any glove I'd ever seen. Plus, it had very detailed carvings on it.

I pulled the bag onto my lap to get a better look. Figures were etched into the top and ends, like Mayan or Toltec Indians that I had seen in books at school. On one broad side of the bag was a beautiful eagle in flight, sort of coming down right at me as I looked at it. It must have taken hours and hours to carve each of those little feathers into the leather. On the other side of the bag was a wolf, staring right at me too. Pine trees were in the background. There was such detailed work on this side too, with all the wolf hairs and the pine needles.

I ran my fingers lightly over the bag, feeling the fine work. The leather felt strong, yet soft, like a well-used baseball glove that has become more flexible with use. This was a well-used bag. He said he traveled a lot. Traveled doing what? And why was he here?

Tap, tap, tap.

The sound of little knuckles on the glass startled me. I looked up to see Gina and Mona's noses pushed up against the car door window, their eyes staring at me questioningly.

"You gonna bring in the luggage, or what?" Mona asked. "I wanna see what he brought."

"Yeah, me too!" added Gina.

I opened the door and got out slowly, being careful not to knock the bag against the car. I followed the girls into the house and placed the bag at Tío Emilio's feet. He was sitting on the sofa with my father, with Gracie between them, and my mother in the chair at his side. I joined Mona and Gina on the floor in front of them.

"*Mijitos*, we have a tradition in our family. When we go on a special trip to see relatives, we like to give little gifts so that you will remember our visit. So, I have brought you gifts of folk art from Mexico, made by children about your ages who are being taught these skills by their mothers, fathers, grandparents, or someone else in their villages."

He reached into the bag and pulled out three bundles of cloth, which he slowly unrolled. "Girls, these small blankets were woven by children living in the state of Oaxaca in the south of Mexico." He showed off the designs woven into each as he handed one to each girl. "They not only wove these, they helped to spin the wool into the yarn, and helped to dye the yarn."

"Thank you, Tío," said Gracie. "This will look very nice on my dresser."

"Thanks," said Gina, holding a doll close, already wrapped up in the blanket.

"Yes, thank you very much," Mona said smiling, as she ran her fingers over the weaving, quite pleased with her special gift. "So are you friends with the people who make these?"

"*Sí*, the families of these children are my source for blankets. As I travel around and work with people, I sometimes use a small blanket in a ceremony, and then leave it as a gift."

"What kind of work do you do, Tío?" asked Gracie.

"You kids ask too many questions," my mother quickly interrupted. "Let Tío Emilio show you what else he has in the bag."

Tío looked up at my mother, and I could tell by the look that he had wanted to answer the question. But he could tell from her look back that this was not the time or place to do so. For me, the answer would have shed some light on the mystery surrounding Tío Emilio. Perhaps the answer would tell us something about "the old ways." But it would have to wait.

I knew my turn was next. Tío Emilio reached into the bag and pulled out a piece of leather, about the same color as his bag. It had a very detailed design, like his bag too.

"This is a cover for a three-ring binder for your school work, Vicente." He opened it up to show a single scene engraved across the front and back, with trees, roads, houses, and even what looked like little stores. A bird was flying above the village, like the eagle on Tío's bag. Everything was so very detailed. I was astounded. I didn't know what to say.

"Golly," Gracie said, reaching across and lightly touching the finely carved lines on the leather. "What little kid could do this?"

"Oh, it was not a child. It was made by my friend and teacher, Don José." He reached across and handed me the leather cover. "Vicente, when your parents brought you and your sister to Mexico, your grandfather and I carried you down the street to Don José's house. As we stood outside talking, we heard it calling. We looked up and saw the águila, a little eagle, circling right over us, calling to us. It was an amazing sight. And even though you were just an infant, I saw that you noticed it too!"

I felt strange as he spoke, and had quick flashes of images in my head. I had no idea what they were about, but something felt oddly familiar.

"Don José said this was a good omen and that one day we would learn its meaning. The leather piece commemorates that day. But he instructed me not to give it to you until you were becoming a man, for not until then would you be able to think about this event and find its very personal meaning for you."

"He's not a man," laughed Mona, with Gina giggling next to her.

"No," answered Tío Emilio, "but he is a teenager, and perhaps it is time for him to start thinking about the meaning of life, and about events and omens like this one."

Just then we heard familiar voices, then greetings, as Nana and Tata came in along with Tía Rita and our cousins. Turning back to me, Tío Emilio said, "We will talk more later."

I didn't get to talk with him again that night with so many *tíos* and *tías* and cousins around. Tía Rita, Tía Paula, and Tío Marcos all brought their kids. Visiting with relatives continued the next morning at Nana and Tata's and in the afternoon at Tío Pancho's, so I didn't have a chance to talk with Tío Emilio privately, even though I had many questions. I wanted to know more about the leather gift, and what he meant about an omen. I wanted to know more about "the old ways," and about him, and why he was even here. Certainly he didn't come all the way from central Mexico just to give me the carved binder cover. But he was off to L.A., to visit other relatives and friends, and it would be two weeks before I saw him again.

4

HANGING OUT

*"The City and the State destroyed the heart of the community by
putting a freeway through it. They relocated families, and destroyed the
business district. Then they came back and
put the bridge on top of us, moving out more people."*

THE CHICANO PARK STORY

I had been looking forward to a little freedom hanging out with Tony. Since being restricted to the house I hadn't seen him much except at school. Before leaving for the afternoon my parents told me to get a couple of things at Amador's, so I decided to do it just before Tony got off work. That way we could take the long way home and walk around the neighborhood a little before my parents got back. I was standing just inside in the doorway of the store waiting for Tony to get off work when Pablito walked in.

"Hey, *vato*," he said smiling, "what's going on?"

"You dummy, you got us into trouble," I answered. "That's what's going on! That *placa* you put outside on the wall, don't you ever think about where you're putting that stuff?"

"Hey man," Tony yelled as he walked to the front of the store, "I told you not to put any paint on these walls! That was pretty stupid! Big Mike lectured me and called my dad. When I got home, he yelled at me for an hour! He told me again not to hang around with you guys."

"You snitched and told him it was me?"

"You idiot," said Tony, "everyone knows it's you! The next day my dad made me paint over it while he watched me. It was embarrassing, and I better not have to do that again."

"Or what?" Pablito asked, sticking up his nose and jutting out his jaw. "You gonna mess with me?" Pablito stared at Tony, then quickly glanced over at me, then back to Tony.

"Don't tempt me, pea brain," Tony answered, moving threateningly toward Pablito.

"Cut it out, you guys," I broke in. I didn't need any more trouble. "Pablito, we're serious. What kind of fun is it if you spray paint on someone's property, then we get punished for it?"

"Screw you guys. You got no *huevos,* you sissies," hissed Pablito.

"*Huevos?* You got *huevos?* Just stand right there. Big Mike will be here in just a few minutes so I can leave. I'm gonna watch him kick your ass right out the door."

Pablito suddenly looked very serious. "He's really coming?" he asked.

Tony nodded, smiling, and looked up at the wall clock. "Should be here any minute now."

"Hell, if I had known he knew it was me, I wouldn't have come in here!" He turned and rushed out the door, yelling, "I'll see you guys later!"

"Pablito, wait!" Tony yelled back. "You forgot your *huevos!*"

We had barely stopped laughing by the time Big Mike walked into the store. Moments later we were off, headed east on National Avenue.

We walked past the Logan Heights Family Health Center, and at about the middle of the block we stopped in front of the apartments where Tony's cousin lived. Many of the homes in the neighborhood had one or two apartments in their back yard, but these apartments were different. They were built in a U shape, with two rows of small apartments, three on each side, facing each other, with a small courtyard in the middle, and a larger apartment in the back. The yard wasn't any bigger than ours, so there were a lot of people in a very small space. His cousin said they lived so close to each other they could hear everything their neighbors did-- talking or laughing, coughing or yelling.

There were some courtyard apartments next to my Nana and Tata's house, but they were in much worse shape than these. That owner never took care of them. The paint was peeling off the wood walls and it sometimes blew through the chain link fence onto Nana's plants. Here, at least the owner took care of the place. These had stucco walls, with a fresh coat of light blue paint with white trim on the eaves and window frames, with lots of flowering plants and shrubs, and a little bit of grass.

When my father repainted our house to a lighter green, he made me help him with the white trim. I had to paint the wood around the windows and the wood separating the panes of glass, and scrape, sand and paint the wooden window screens. That was a heck of a lot of work, and I hated it. That's how I spent a lot of my summer last year, while the other guys were out playing around, having fun.

Still, I had to admit, after we finished, the house sure looked good--better than any other house on the street. People walking by would tell my father how good the new paint job looked. He'd thank them and, at least when I was out there, he would tell them that he and I did it together, even though I know he did most of the work.

It didn't look like anyone was home. We called out for his cousin, but there was no answer.

"What do you wanna do now?" I asked, as we both turned and continued up National.

"Arturo's is just up the street. Let's go there."

I slowed to a stop. "I can't. My parents don't want me hanging out at his house."

"Mine neither, because of his brother and their drugs."

"And because we were with him and Eddie during the great coke robbery."

"Man, they're still on your case about that?" asked Tony. "My parents haven't said much."

"Heck, mine ain't gonna let me forget it. We were just lucky the driver didn't press charges or we'd really have been in a mess of trouble."

"Well, you said your parents ain't here. How they gonna know?"

"Easy. They might drive by here on their way home and see us."

"Oh, come on. You said they're gonna be gone for the afternoon. Let's go check out what's happening."

After that lecture from Tío Marcus, and the promises I made to him, I knew I shouldn't even be considering going up there. "I don't know ... I'm already in enough trouble."

Tony started walking again, not waiting for me to finish.

"Well, okay," I said, mostly to myself as I jogged a few steps to catch up with him, "but I'm not going inside!"

We continued east on National Avenue. The next intersection was probably the busiest in the neighborhood, National and Crosby streets. As we were going by, Tony peeked his head into the Ponderosa Market, another small mom and pop grocery store, not much bigger than the size of a house. This one was just one block away from Amador's Market, yet both seemed to do okay. I figured it was probably because the big supermarkets were so far away that people were forced to shop at the little neighborhood markets.

"Hey, Tony," shouted Mr. Gomez from behind the counter, "How's business today?"

"Well, I see you've only got two customers, so I guess we're doing better than you today," Tony called back laughing.

"Yeah," Mr. Gomez responded, "but we have the big spenders over here." He laughed and waved goodbye as we continued on our way.

Across the street we could see some of the firemen out in front of the fire station, which had its doors open. It didn't look like they were going anywhere, just letting in some fresh air. At the end of the next block we came to Chicano Park, built under the pillars of the San Diego-Coronado Bridge. Arturo's house was another block up the street.

There in the park, most of the gray concrete pillars holding up the bridge and its on-off ramps were painted with beautiful murals, with scenes from Mexican history and the Chicano movement. My favorite was the painting of Cuauhtémoc, who at the age of 25 became the last Aztec emperor. The mural shows him dressed in battle gear, pointing his outstretched arm, with huge eagle wings behind him. The Aztec Brewery that used to be a few blocks away on Main Street had a mural inside that showed the Spanish conquistadors torturing Cuauhtémoc by burning his feet.

My father told us many times the story of how Chicano Park came to be. He would get very solemn and would make sure we were paying attention. He told us about how the City and the State had destroyed the heart of the community by putting a freeway through it. They relocated families, and destroyed the business district. Then they came back and put the bridge on top of us, moving out more people. A friend of Nana lived where the bridge is now. She was moved away from her friends, her church, and her *tienditas*—all the things and people who mattered to her. They say she died a few months later, depressed and lonely—she just gave up living.

Then came the ultimate insult. The State tried to put the Highway Patrol headquarters under the bridge, where the City had promised a park. Not that it was an ideal location for a park. But the people had been trying to get the City to help beautify this cold, barren jungle of concrete.

So on April 22, 1970, the Chicano community rose up against the City and the State and stopped the bulldozers that had begun construction of the Highway Patrol facility. A community occupation of this land began that lasted 24 hours a day for twelve days. Students from Memorial Junior High and San Diego High skipped school to participate. Men and women, from kids to seniors, took over the land. They planted flowers, grass, nopales cactus and agave plants. People from all over the state came to help. And the people succeeded in forcing the City to acquire the land from the State, and to turn it into a park, Chicano Park.

"Vincent!" Tony yelled from the corner. "Come on!" His voice pulled me out of my thoughts. I hurried to catch up with him.

"What were you doing staring across the street?" he asked as we continued walking.

"Oh, just thinking about the murals, and what my father told us about when they did the big *movida* and created Chicano Park," I answered.

"The park and murals have been here for over fifteen years. So why the sudden interest?"

"Oh, I guess the murals made me think of my Tío Emilio. When he arrived, he gave us gifts and talked a little about Mexican art and culture, and that's what these murals are all about."

"Yeah, my grandfather told me you had a relative from Mexico visiting."

"We call him Tío Emilio, but...."

"But Tío *Brujo* might be better," laughed Arturo. He was standing at his front gate and had heard us talking as we were walking up to his house.

"So what's a *brujo*?" asked Tomás, one of our homies who was standing there with Arturo.

"*Brujos* are like witches or sorcerers," Eddie called from the porch. He was sitting with his friend Manuel, the head of their gang. "They have strange powers. I hear you have a *brujo* visiting you, Vincent. What strange things can he do? Does he have a magic wand?"

"Or a broom?" asked Manuel. They busted up laughing.

Brujos, witches, and sorcerers? What were they talking about? Were they calling Tío Emilio a *brujo* or a sorcerer? And they were laughing at him ... or at me.

"Leave him alone," Tony said, coming to my defense. "My grandfather said a *brujo* is a very special person, a holy man, with special gifts from God that he uses to help people. He also said some ignorant Mexicans make fun of *brujos* because they think only the priest should bring help from God. Or the idea of *brujos* having special gifts, special powers, scares them."

Eddie jumped up and took a few steps toward us. "What are you saying, Tony, that I'm...."

"Hey you guys, don't get so uptight," said Manuel, looking at us as he reached for Eddie and pulled him back. "We're just kidding! Maybe this *brujo* can help some of the people around here. So, why's he here? Is he moving here?"

Too late. I was already uptight. I really didn't like Manuel asking me questions. I never really talked to him before. I was kind of afraid of him. He was bigger than all the other guys—taller and heavier. And mean looking too. His pockmarked face had a deep scar that ran from the top of his ear down to about the middle of his jaw. I never asked anyone how he got it, and no one ever talked about it—like we were supposed to ignore this big ugly scar. I thought maybe he lost a knife fight to some crazy *vato* when he was younger.

"He's not moving here," I answered, "just visiting. He lives in ... well, someplace in Mexico. He travels around. He's visiting friends in L.A. right now, but he'll be back."

"If he just visited, why is he coming back again?" asked Tomás.

"His teacher made this leather carving about ... well, he's going to talk to me about...."

"So he's coming back to talk to you?" asked Manuel as he walked up closer. "I know your folks are all uptight about your bad boy behavior." That got a laugh from everyone. "Did they send for him to come and put a *brujo* spell on you to turn you into a good boy?" They laughed again.

I felt really uncomfortable with this mean looking *vato* grilling me and laughing at me, and with this talk about spells and a *brujo*. I'd heard of the word *brujo* before, but I didn't really know what it meant. I had asked my mother, but she had just brushed it off with, "That's just old wives' tales, about the old ways."

Oh man! That's it! It suddenly hit me. She said they didn't talk about him because "...he is of the old ways." Dang! They didn't like to talk about him, so I didn't know nothing. But everyone else seemed to know he was a *brujo*. Suddenly I just had to get out of there.

"Hey, man, I don't know nothing about spells, and I gotta split." I turned around and started walking back down National.

I was relieved that I didn't feel Manuel's big hand grab me and yank me back for walking away from him in the middle of his questions.

"Hey, wait up. I'll go with you," called Tony.

I didn't wait, walking quickly down the street. Tony jogged a few steps to catch up with my pace. I wanted to get out of there as quickly as I could. He walked beside me in silence for a short while, and then finally spoke up.

"Are you pissed off because they were making fun of your Tío Emilio?"

"Nah. I'm just surprised and angry that everyone, including you, seems to know more about him than I do. How come your grandfather knows about him? From my grandfather?"

"Yeah, he said that last week your grandfather told him his cousin was coming to visit."

"Did he say that his cousin is a *brujo*?"

"I don't know. That's all he told me. But I've heard of *brujos* before. My grandfather believes in that stuff. He says it's a part of our culture and our beliefs as Mexicans. But my grandmother says that it's just old stories about black magic that uneducated Mexicans were told by the old pagan priests as a way to control them. It sounds like some people are afraid of *brujos* and black magic. But my grandfather isn't. He must think your grandfather's cousin is really special. He even called him *Don* Emilio."

Maybe he is really special, I thought, but why is this all so secret? And how come no one ever told me anything about him?

5

BRUJO

*"The most destructive force in the human condition
is mind chatter.... Stop listening to the mind chatter....
(it) disconnects us from that which we are seeking."*

HANS CHRISTIAN KING

I was trying to make out bits and pieces of the phone conversation my mother was having with Tata. I don't usually try to listen in, but this time she was almost arguing with him, which she *never* does. My sisters and I were playing monopoly in the *sala* on Saturday afternoon. I never liked the game much—it always took too long, and my mind tended to wander between turns. No wandering this time, however. I could tell from the look on the girls' faces that they were as surprised as I was about what we heard coming from the dining room. I didn't understand all of what was said, but I did make out that it had to do with me somehow, and she kept saying no to him, over and over, raising her voice. Then she got quiet, and it seemed like they came to some kind of agreement, as she ended the conversation with a few *buenos*. When she got off the phone she called to me.

"Vincent, they want you over at Tata's. Tío Emilio is down from Los Angeles. You go put on a decent shirt and get right over there. And ... he wants you to bring that leather cover."

Ah, I thought, that's what it was about. Finally, the time had come. I had been waiting, wondering when I would get to talk with him again.

"So much for monopoly," said Gracie in a resigned tone. "And I was winning, too!"

I got changed, picked up the leather binder cover, and headed over to Nana and Tata's. My mind was churning in a jumble of thoughts as I walked up the street. I had so many questions about the mystery of who Tío Emilio really was. If he was a member of the family, why didn't the family ever talk about him? Was he really a *brujo*? And just what was a *brujo*? Did he have special powers? What were they? How did he use them? And why was the eagle on the leather cover so special? What did that mean? Why did he have to wait until now to show it to me? And what was this thing, this omen he talked about?

Coming up the steps, even before I got to the front door, my thoughts were overridden by a wonderful aroma. My Nana made the best *frijoles* and flour tortillas in the world. Many people in the neighborhood now bought their tortillas in the stores, or at the local *tortillerias*. Fewer and fewer people made their own tortillas at home.

"*Hola, Vicente,*" Nana called as I walked in the front door. "*Ven p'acá,*" she said, getting up from her chair in the dining room. I followed her into the kitchen. Nana seemed to fit the image of the typical Mexican grandmother. She always seemed to be wearing a big white apron because she was always cooking something. Usually she wore a bandana over her mostly gray hair. Today it was her light blue one, which matched the color of her kitchen walls. I already towered over her by at least six inches, maybe more. As I caught up with her and gave her a hello kiss, she asked, "*¿Quieres comer?*" Before I could answer, she pointed back to the dining room table, saying, "*Sientate y come.*" She knew I was always ready to eat.

The thought of Nana's cooking almost made me forget why I was there. Tata and Tío Emilio were sitting at the old wooden dining table, eating and talking, and paused only briefly to greet me as I walked into the room. Tata pointed to a chair at the opposite end of the table. I quietly slid onto the wooden chair, trying not to disturb them. Just a few moments later Nana brought me a plate of beans, rice, and flour tortillas. "Mmm, boy!" I thought. She made her beans sort of in-between whole and mashed, with delicious thick bean juice. I loved them that way, especially sopped up with her tortillas! And these were pinto beans, not black beans or kidney beans or some other kind—real Mexican beans. Her Mexican rice was always so wonderful too. I smelled that as soon as I walked into the house—so good!

She soon brought herself a plate and sat down at the table just as Tata and Tío excused themselves to continue their discussion in the *sala*.

"*¿Y para tomar, mijito, qué quieres—agua, leche, Pepsi, limonada?*"

"*¿Tienes Pepsi?*" I asked, somewhat surprised that she offered it. She usually wanted me to drink the other stuff that she said was better for me—water, milk or lemonade.

"*Sí,*" she said, getting up from her chair and picking up Tata's and Tío Emilio's empty plates. She came back with a tall glass of soda for both of us, and more tortillas. After a few minutes she noticed that my plate was just about empty.

"*¿Quieres más, mijito?*" she asked, getting up, knowing the answer.

"Mmmhmmm," I said, nodding my head while chewing a mouthful.

She brought my second plateful and sat down again. Nana was listening in on the conversation between Tata and Tío Emilio from the living room. I tried to listen at first, but my Spanish vocabulary was limited and they were talking about things I didn't understand, words I hadn't heard, and I was losing it. So I just tuned out and focused on the task at hand.

I had gulped down the first plate. With the second plate, I took my time. Nana kept bringing me hot tortillas. She always said I was too skinny, so when she had the chance, she fed me good!

"You're still eating?" asked Tío Emilio, smiling as he walked past. It was more of a comment than a question. I hadn't noticed that they had stopped talking. "When you finish, come out and join me in the back yard."

Suddenly I couldn't eat any more. I didn't have much left of that second serving anyway. But I lost my appetite not because I was full. It was because the moment of truth had arrived! Now, finally, I had the chance to talk with Tío Emilio and to get some answers about the mystery. I put my plate in the kitchen sink and took my glass of soda with me.

"Over here, Vincent," Tío Emilio called, motioning for me to join him inside Nana's garden shed. He sat just inside the entrance on an old dining room chair with weathered chrome legs and a seat with peeling green vinyl. Nana's garden shed was a nice size garden room, about eight feet by ten feet, enclosed on three and a half sides. It had plywood walls going halfway up, with the top half made of crisscrossing slats about two inches wide, spaced to allow some sunlight in. The roof had light green plastic panels you couldn't see through, but which let in light for the plants growing in containers on the shelves.

I walked up to the shed, feeling more and more nervous. Maybe even frightened. I could feel myself breathing faster and starting to sweat. My stomach began to feel woozy. There he sat, this stranger who was a relative I had never heard of, but everyone in the neighborhood knew about. The one they called a *brujo*, with strange powers that people didn't talk about. Yet he was respected by the elders and even called *don*, a title of respect. He was a relative, so I knew I wasn't going to be harmed, but my body was still tempted to run away to avoid this meeting. I had been waiting two weeks, wanting to talk to him, but now, I was … well, chickening out. Suddenly my legs were weak and I had trouble making the last few steps to the shed.

Tío Emilio was holding one of Nana's plant containers, inspecting it closely. As I came closer, I could see that it was one of her aloe vera plants, a big one. The large pointed leaves stuck out in front of him like a bull's horns. Talk about a "moment of truth!" I felt like I was a matador slowly walking up to face the bull who was there waiting for me. Somewhere inside I had the feeling that the "me" I had been up to this point was about to get gored and die. Trying to be brave, I raised my head and chest, and did my fearless *vato loco* walk the last few steps.

He pointed silently to the old wooden chair across from him and motioned for me to sit, which I did. Much to my dismay I realized that I was sitting in the chair with the low bottom. The yellow foam cushion wasn't much support, so I sunk way down. Tío Emilio seemed to tower above me from his chair. I felt very uncomfortable and at a disadvantage. I couldn't think, so I took a big swig of the Pepsi and set it down next to me.

Okay, I thought to myself as I coughed, trying to clear my throat, I don't need to let my imagination run away with me. There's nothing to fear. We're just gonna talk. I had a whole list of questions in my head. I wanted to know so much but didn't want to seem like an ignorant fool, not knowing what a *brujo* was. I decided I would listen to him first, and then ask my questions, starting out with what kind of work he did. One couldn't just venture into forbidden areas and ask loads of questions. I thought it would be best to work my way into it.

He sat there silently, looking at me. My mind was racing. Why didn't he say anything? Was he waiting for me to say something? Suddenly my mind went blank. I couldn't remember any of the questions I was going to ask! Nothing! I could feel wetness on my forehead and above my lip. My hands were sweating. My shirt was wet. My stomach was in my throat.

Tío Emilio was about to say something, but then he stopped. He shifted in his chair and leaned forward, suddenly thrusting the plant at me. Oh God! I tried to jump back from those big horns, but I couldn't move. I closed my eyes and waited....

"Would you please put this plant on that shelf behind you?"

His words seemed to boom and resonate in the empty chamber where my brains should have been. I felt like a big fool, letting my imagination run wild with me. I decided right then that I should cut my losses by just acting like nothing was going on. I took the plant and put it on the shelf. He didn't know that I was freaking out. He might wonder why I was sweating so much, but he couldn't read my mind. I figured I should just ask about the scene carved into the leather cover and why that was made for me. That should be a safe topic to get us started. But even though

I wanted to know about the leather cover, my other curiosity got the best of me, and I blurted out, "Tío, what's a *brujo?*"

He thought about my question for a few moments. *"Mijo,* my cousin Miguel said your *mamá* told you I believe in the old ways of our people. Many mothers and fathers *y abuelitos* want to teach their children our traditions, our culture, and also about the ancient knowledge of our ancestors. But many of them do not really know much about this ancient knowledge themselves, and some have fears of what they call 'the old ways.'

"Brujos are a part of the old ways. Some people use the term *brujo.* Other terms are *curandero,* sorcerer, holy man, or witchdoctor. Many use the term *shaman,* which in Spanish is *chamán.* To some, these words describe a man or woman of honor, and respect, a man of God. Others fear these sorcerers, these witches, as they call them, thinking that they deal with the dark side—with evil. To translate the word *brujo,* I prefer the term *shaman.* Others prefer the term *sorcerer.* I think the words *brujo* and *sorcerer* now carry too much negativity.

"Shamans—they can be men or women—are keepers of a very special body of knowledge about the unseen forces of the universe, and how the energies that make up all things in the universe are connected. Shamans know how to use these forces and energy connections to improve the lives of people they work with, and life in general on this earth."

He peered at me intently. "Now to the other question lurking there ... am I a *brujo?"*

I felt my face flush hot. It was probably red. He knew I had wanted to ask him that!

"Yes, I am. And, as I said, I prefer the term *shaman,* but I do not care what people call me. I just go about doing my work for those who request my help."

He sat there looking at me, waiting for my next question. I was so shocked that he read my mind that it was hard for me to think straight. This stuff was all very strange and didn't make sense. No one had ever talked like this to me before. It was a moment before I could speak.

"Are you saying that you help people?" I asked, finally. As he nodded, I continued, "Then why don't they want to talk about it? Why do they keep it all so quiet?"

"Well, perhaps it is because some people are afraid of the unknown. When the energies and connections between all things are studied and our ability to perceive them nurtured and developed, the result can produce amazing feats of power which some call magic. But the connections are a natural part of the universal energies that exist, so I do not call it magic. In fact, I call it natural! But sometimes, the results shock people who are not ready for such experience. In the past many people turned away from the *brujos'* ways and taught their children not to speak of them, and not to believe the stories people told.

"Your Tata lived most of his life unaware of what a *brujo* or shaman really is, how they work closely with God and the energies of the universe. Even though I am a shaman, because of our age difference, your Tata and I didn't interact much over the years, until a few years before you were born. When he visited, he mostly spent time with my father. As I grew to know my shaman nature and abilities, it took time before I was able to share that with him.

"Years ago, your Tata had his own special connections with animals and crops, which I think helped him to be open to what I have shared with him about my work. Yet he still has his doubts about things that he does not understand."

"You've been teaching Tata about your work?" My mind struggled to keep up with this surprising news.

"Yes, and he wants you to know these things. But he doesn't know enough to teach you."

Just then, I noticed Tata standing just outside the shed, listening. I hadn't heard him walk up. He appeared to be deep in thought. Then he spoke, in Spanish.

"Vicente, I asked Emilio to visit us so that you could meet him. I want him to teach you some of what he knows. I have seen many children grow up in this neighborhood, and have seen many boys get into trouble, mine included. This happens, I believe, because something is missing in their lives." Tata's eyes filled with tears. "If it can help you in your life, then I think you should be made aware of it. Do you understand me?"

I nodded yes, even though I was struggling to keep up with his Spanish. I lowered my eyes, embarrassed by his tears on my account. Then it hit me! That's what this is all about! He asked Tío Emilio to come here to teach me this shaman stuff to keep me out of trouble. My mother thinks a lecture by Tío Marcos will do it. Tata wants Tío Emilio to do it. Hell, I don't need no shaman from Mexico to keep me out of trouble!

"When we look back at our ancient ancestors," said Tío Emilio, speaking English, "we find that from the very young to the very old, people were connected. They had their roles and responsibilities. Every person contributed to the well-being of the village. They lived in a manner that acknowledged their connection to each other, the earth, and God, the Great Spirit. There was a balance in each life and between members of the community, and a balance with the environment around them. There was no need for criminal rebellion among youth." He repeated this again in Spanish for Tata, who nodded his head throughout, indicating that he had understood most of it the first time in English.

Then Tata spoke again, in Spanish: "We must find a way to bring back this balance. I think a way to do this is by teaching the young people about the connection between all living things, their connection to God, and the knowledge of the shamans. If we could do this here, I believe that the young people would find the support and strength they are looking for within the power of our own ancient culture, rather than the negative power of gangs and drugs."

Again, I was shocked to hear Tata talking about this. Tío Emilio just nodded his head in agreement with Tata. Tío Emilio started to speak, and then paused, looking at me.

"Did you get all that?"

I nodded yes, I understood the Spanish. But what were they saying? I'd never thought about these things and I didn't understand them. Why should I care about how people lived hundreds of years ago? They want to get the *vatos* into a culture class? No way!

"Real learning, learning about life, takes place right here in the community," continued Tío Emilio in English, as if in response to my thoughts. "A shaman teaches by doing and his students learn by example, practice, and through deep contemplation or focused attention, connecting with guidance and information from God or spirit guides and teachers."

My head was spinning again. How did he keep reading my mind? Was that part of his power, his magic?

"One of the first things we focus on in our shamanic training," said Tío Emilio, looking directly at me, "is how to increase personal energy. Once a person increases his energy or vibration, and stops leaking his energy, he may begin perceiving more than what most other people perceive. With practice, he may become skilled at extra-sensory perception—being able to read thoughts, anticipate actions, sense events happening in other locations— things like that."

Now I was freaking out. He *was* reading my mind! Yet, he was calmly telling me that this was part of the shaman training.

"I do not want to scare you, Vincent. I simply want you to know that some of what people refer to as power or magic is a basic part of shaman knowledge and our native culture. Your Tata wishes for me to teach you about the spiritual side of our ancient native Mexican culture. That is, if you want to do this. But first your Tata will have to convince your parents. Right now, your mother is opposed to my teaching you about 'the old ways.' She was taught by her *tías* that the 'old ways' are evil or against the teachings of the Church."

Well, if my mother is so against it, I thought to myself, maybe I shouldn't be so fast to say no. What does she not want me to find out? Why has she been so secretive about this relative?

Tío Emilio got up and walked over to me. He gave me a grandfatherly sort of pat on the head. Suddenly, I had this weird tingly feeling and goose bumps all over. As that feeling faded, I became aware that someone else was here with us. I turned around and saw through the shed slats that Gina was standing by the side of the house. Her hand was up to her mouth and she looked afraid to interrupt. Tata and Tío Emilio turned to see what I was looking at.

She yelled to me. "Mama said to come and remind you that you got some chores you're supposed to finish before dinner. She said you have to get home and get started."

"I have plenty of time," I called back.

"Oh yeah," she continued. "Doña Rosa called. She hurt her ankle and can't walk over to the church. So mama wants you to go over there and help her. She needs you to pick up some altar cloths and take them to the church right now, before you come home."

This sure sounded like her! She agreed to a new chore to get me away from Tío Emilio.

"You go ahead mijo," said Tío Emilio. "You have some church business to take care of."

"But Tío," I said, "what about the leather cover? When will we talk about that?"

"We can talk about that story tomorrow," he said. "Come over in the morning after breakfast. I am not leaving until eleven o'clock."

I walked out the back yard and through the alley to Beardsley Street. From there it was just a short walk to the pedestrian bridge over the freeway. Doña Rosa's home was right on the other side of the freeway, just a few doors up the street from Our Lady of Guadalupe church. Doña Rosa and Nana were good friends, having known each other probably longer than I'd been alive. So Nana and my mother didn't hesitate to send me over whenever Doña Rosa needed any help.

I walked up to Doña Rosa's door and rang the bell. She had grandchildren who could have taken the linens to the church, but she probably couldn't track down any of the boys. They didn't let women or girls into the sacristy, past the communion rail, except for nuns and women who did volunteer work for the parish. Doña Rosa did a lot of work for the church, cleaning, starching and pressing the altar linens, laundering the priests' vestments, and growing flowers for the altar.

Her granddaughter Gloria opened the door, grinning with a big smile. I'd known Gloria for years. She was in some of my classes at school, and was taller than most of the girls in our classes, but just a little shorter than me. Her long brown hair was up in a ponytail.

"Hi, Vinnie," she said sweetly, looking intently at me with her big brown eyes. "Come in." She and a couple of the other girls at school liked to call me Vinnie when they felt like making me blush. I think it worked. I could feel my cheeks and my ears getting red. Doña Rosa was sitting on the living room couch. She was about Nana's size, and having been friends for so many years, may have been about the same age, although there was less gray in her mix of gray and black hair. I think she could see I was embarrassed, for as she greeted me, she emphasized my name the way she preferred to say it.

"Vicente. *Buenos tardes*, Vicente. Thank you for coming to help with the altar linens. I hurt my ankle a little, and can't walk over to the church myself."

"I don't know why they don't let girls go onto the altar," said Gloria, jumping into the conversation. "It would have been very easy for me to walk over and put these on there."

"Shhhhh." Gloria's grandmother shushed her. Like many other older Mexican women who are devout Catholics, she didn't like people talking bad about the church's rules, even if they didn't seem to make any sense. She continued with brief instructions, aware that I already knew what to do with the altar linens, having done this for her before. I nodded and reassured her that I wouldn't drop them, and everything would be in its proper place on the altars.

Doña Rosa got up off the couch and walked slowly with a limp toward the dining room table. Gloria quickly walked over to help. There on the table they gently folded the long white linen altar cloths, careful not to make creases after so much work by Doña Rosa starching and ironing them. Together they carried them to me, placing the stack of linens gently in my outstretched arms. Gloria softly stroked the underside of my arm as she released the linens. Doña Rosa didn't.

"*Cuidado mijito*," Doña Rosa cautioned me as they walked me to the door.

"Yes, Vinnie," purred Gloria, smiling at me with those big dimples as I walked past her, "be careful."

I didn't turn around or say anything, just flashed her two red ears. As I turned to walk down the sidewalk toward the church, I thought I heard her giggle.

6
———

THE DREAM

"It's not your work to make anything happen.
It's your work to dream it and let it happen."

ABRAHAM (ESTHER HICKS)

I sat on my bed after dinner, partly listening to my radio, but mostly thinking about the day and about Tío Emilio. After a while, my eyes just felt so heavy, I couldn't keep them open. Maybe sweeping the walks front and back, and sweeping out the patio and wiping down the patio furniture before dinner tired me out more than I thought. Or maybe it was from eating too much. I sat there with my eyes closed, thinking about the leather binder cover and the scene carved on it. Finally, we would get to talk about it in the morning. The thought occurred to me to get up and change into my PJs. But instead, I plopped over on the bed and immediately drifted off into a deep sleep....

I must have been traveling very fast. What a rush, feeling the wind on my face, and hearing it speak to me as it whizzed past my ears. It told me to look up and see the clouds. They looked like huge beautiful puffy balls of cotton floating in the sky. The next thing I knew I was sailing up into one of the lower clouds and could feel the coolness of its moisture. I leaned to the left and curled back down out of the clouds, then sailed right back up into the cool mist. Sometime while sailing through the clouds, I realized that I was a small eagle, flying through the sky.

I looked down. What a majestic sight! I could see mountains, a river, grasses and shrubs of many shades of green and yellow covering

▸ 43 ◂

the open fields, deep brown earth, and trees and plants covering the wetter areas along the edge of the river. Most of the creeks feeding the river looked dry, but the green trees along their edges told of water flowing under the surface.

I could see roads below, and houses. I followed what looked like a main road. It had more traffic than the others and seemed wider. The longer I followed it, the more houses appeared. This road and a few others were paved, while most of the rest were dirt roads. Nearing what looked like the center of town, I realized this place wasn't very big at all.

I felt pulled to a dirt street with a few houses where I saw lines of light leading up into the sky. They came from two men and a baby who were outside one of the houses. A third man walked up and joined them, and as they met, the energies of these four humans joined with the energies of the Earth Mother to make an even more powerful force, a tube of energy that shot up into the universe.

I circled around the column of energy, as my eagle energies intertwined with those of the earth and the humans. I flew, flowing with the lines of energy, spiraling down and then rising again on the currents of warmth rising from the heated ground below. The wind joined in, carrying me up as I continued to circle, it also flowing with the call of the universe. With a gentle shove, it lifted me even higher before falling toward earth to find more heat to push it on its way. I joined with the wonderful majesty of the sky as I soared up through the clouds, and with the astoundingly beautiful earth as I turned back toward the multiple hues of blues, browns, yellows, and greens.

I let out an eagle cry, telling all the world to take note of what I had seen and come to know from this lofty perch in the sky—the four strong energies below, three adult humans and one baby, joined in prayer to the Earth Mother and to the source of all being, flowing an energy strong enough to summon an eagle and the wind. Again, I cried out, "Cheeee, cheeee."

"Cough, cough." Startled, I sat up. It took me a while to figure out where I was and who I was. I could see that I was human and not an eagle. Slowly I realized I was home in my bed in the middle of the night and that I had been dreaming. It was disappointing in a way. I now felt so very confined sitting there in my body, after having flown so far and so free as an eagle. I couldn't recall ever having had such a vivid dream. What an experience! And I could recall it like a movie being shown again inside my head. I didn't want to lose it, so I slowly eased my head back down onto the pillow and watched the scenes repeat as I drifted back to sleep.

At the first light of dawn, I was awake. I hadn't closed the window shades, so the red light of the early morning sunrise splashed my room with ever-brightening hues of color as it slowly pushed away the darkness. Its colors reminded me of the eagle's feathers, and of the sun and clouds at sunset in my dream. It was such a strange dream, but it felt so good! How wonderful it had been flying high above the ground, exploring free, and yet connected to everything below.

Normally, at this time of the morning, I would have just rolled over and gone back to sleep. But today I was just too excited! I got up and stood by my bedroom window, watching the intense colors of the clouds and sky change as the sun rose. After this sunrise, and the sunset in last night's dream, I felt a new appreciation for the beauty of the earth, the sun, and the sky.

It wasn't too long before I finally heard other sounds in the house. Breakfast would be early this morning. For once I was glad because I was anxious to return to Nana and Tata's.

"My, you're up early today," my mother remarked as I walked into the kitchen. I was a little surprised she spoke to me, but there was no one else up yet for her to talk to.

"Yeah, I woke up right when it started to get light." I couldn't wait to tell her about the dream, but as I began, I realized it was so involved there was really no way to describe it all.

"You don't usually remember your dreams, do you?"

"No, I don't. For some reason, this one really stuck with me. I remember it almost like I was watching it again right now." I paused for a moment and thought about telling her more, but decided not to. "Well, so much for my dream. Can I help you with anything?"

"You can wash, peel, and slice the potatoes in the sink for me."

I got busy with the potatoes while she rolled out flour tortillas, which she was cooking on the stove at the same time. After a few minutes of silence, except for the sounds of the knife and the rolling pin hitting the cutting boards, she finally spoke again.

"How was your discussion with Tío Emilio yesterday?"

I thought to myself, it was too short because you made me come home early. But I couldn't say that to her. So I said, "Well, it was kinda interesting. He talked a lot about the work he does and even Tata joined in the discussion. They were talking when I first got there, so we started late. We ran out of time so he asked me to come back this morning after breakfast."

She turned to me with a look of surprise that I would be going back to talk with Tío Emilio. I guess she hadn't expected him to have time to talk with me about his work, and about "the old ways." Perhaps she thought he would limit himself to describing the leather cover. She looked like she was about to say something, but maybe because Tata was involved she chose not to say anything right then, at least to me.

"Well," she said, "you can go right over after we eat. Emilio doesn't have much time this morning. Tata and your father are giving him a ride to the bus station at about eleven o'clock."

It wasn't long before breakfast was finally ready. Once we sat down to eat, I quickly devoured it. Of course, both my mother and father encouraged me to slow down and chew my food. It probably helped me to get in a few more chews, but basically, I inhaled it.

"Why are you in such a rush?" my father asked.

"He's going to see Tío Emilio again before you leave for the bus station," my mother answered for me.

"Yeah," I said as I got up from the table, "we didn't finish our talk yesterday."

I grabbed the leather cover from my room and headed for the door. My father got up from the table and walked me to the door, still chewing his food.

"I'm very disappointed in you," he said in his gruff, somewhat angry voice. Not his real, real angry voice, but angry enough that he got my attention. "I understand you were over at Arturo's again. I thought we had an understanding that you wouldn't go over there."

Dammit! I got caught! All I could do was stand by the door and look stupid. One of his friends must have seen me over there. I knew that was gonna happen!

"Go on now. I know you have to see Emilio. You and I are going to have a talk later. I just wanted you to know that I know."

Walking down the street, I felt a sense of relief that I didn't have to stay home and deal with my father right now. I knew I was in for more punishment, just for being with my homies.

But more important to me right then was that I was finally going to learn about the carving on the leather cover.

7

THE OMEN

"When the student is ready, the teacher will appear."

BUDDHIST PROVERB

As I got close to the house I could see Tío and Tata sitting on the front porch, talking and drinking from their coffee mugs. They both said good morning as I approached the front gate.

"Hola, Vicentillo," Nana called from the living room. She saw me through the screen door as I walked up the porch steps. *"¿Ya comistes?"*

"Sí, Nana, gracias, I've eaten already." I thought about it for a second, but couldn't resist. *"¿Pero ... tienes una tortilla?"*

"Pues sí." She motioned for me to follow her into the kitchen where she immediately lit up two burners on the stove. *"¿Quieres un burrito con frijoles y chorizo?"*

I nodded. I wasn't hungry, but I wasn't stuffed either. She knew I couldn't pass up her flour tortillas filled with chorizo mixed with eggs, and a little of her delicious mashed beans. For burritos, she made the beans a little dryer than her usual juicy beans. Just a few minutes later she handed me the hot burrito wrapped in a paper towel. I dug right in, eating it as I walked back out to the front porch.

"Siéntate, mijito," said Tata, moving his coffee cup off the wooden crate between the two porch chairs. I sat down and finished eating the burrito while they talked.

"So, Vincent," asked Tío Emilio, "how was your night? Did you have pleasant dreams?"

I almost jumped off the crate. He asked the question in such a detached manner, sort of like making small talk. But I saw a gleam in his eye that made me think he knew something. Did he know about my crazy, wonderful dream? Was he reading my mind again?

"Well, Tío, I did have this amazing dream. I dreamed I was an eagle, soaring through the sky." Excitedly I started telling the dream in vivid detail. At some point while rambling, I happened to look down at the leather binder cover I was carrying. Suddenly the shock hit me.

"Oh God!" I yelled, and jumped off the crate with my eyes fixed on the leather binder cover. I recognized the scene carved onto the leather! It was very much like what I had seen from the sky in my eagle dream. The scene from fifteen years ago and my dream last night were the same! I started to freak out again. What was going on? I suddenly felt very confused.

Tata reached over and put his hand on me. "¿Qué pasa, mijito?"

"Th-this," I stammered, pointing at the leather carving. "This is what I dreamed about last night. This is what I saw from the sky in my dream!"

Tío Emilio repeated in Spanish what I said, just to be sure that Tata understood. Then turning to me, he said, "That was a very powerful dream about a very powerful moment. Yes, the scene and your dream are related." This was another answer to a question I hadn't asked.

He paused briefly, looking at me. "Are you okay? Do you want something to drink?"

His calm voice seemed to soothe me a little. "Yeah, I guess so."

"Vieja," Tata called. "Traíganos tres Pepsis por favor."

"Tío," I said, pointing to the scene carved on the leather cover, "how could this be the same thing … how could it be what I saw in my dream while flying around as an eagle? And how could I be dreaming about something I was too young to remember?"

"Well, before we get to that, let me ask about your dream. Was there anything out of the ordinary, anything you did not understand?"

"You mean like how could I be an eagle?"

"No, let's assume that it is not out of the ordinary to experience life from the viewpoint of an eagle, or any animal. Did you experience anything, or see anything that you accepted as an eagle, but that you do not understand from the perspective of a human being?"

I was not sure what he was asking. "I don't think so. I was just flying around the town." I closed my eyes and slowly the picture came back into view. I could see it all again, just like the night before—in full color too. "I can see myself flying around, going up high, circling around, and looking down."

"What did you do next," he asked, "and why?"

"I was attracted to a hill on the edge of the town and landed on a tree at the top of the hill."

"What do you mean you were attracted to the hill?"

"I'm not sure. I guess I was attracted to the tree and felt connected to it." Then I realized I could *see* the connection! "I'm connected to it, Tío!" I said, almost yelling. "I see thin lines of light. Bright lines connect me and the tree, with thinner lines connecting me to other things on the hill. I think I—I mean the eagle—liked coming to this hill and to this tree."

I again experienced sitting in the tree, on a branch near the top, looking toward the town. I felt the warmth of the tree, and could see its life force pulsing through the branch under my feet. "Tío," I said excitedly, "I can see and feel the energy of the tree flowing through its branches!"

"Yes. And what else?"

I hesitated at first. "I think I feel … a lot of love flowing to me from the tree. I feel it in my feet … and I see it in the area of my chest, flowing through the lines of light connecting us."

"Vincent," he said, getting my attention as *Vincent*, rather than as the eagle. I opened my eyes. "Yesterday I mentioned that all things are connected. What you are feeling, and what you saw and felt as an eagle, are those connecting lines of energy. As an animal, you saw the energy lines. A shaman can be trained to adjust his vision to be able to see these same lines of energy."

"Tío, I saw those lines connecting me to everything, even to people! While I was flying around I also saw energy lines coming from a group people and up from the earth under them."

Tío Emilio nodded his head. "Yes, I remember very well seeing the little eagle circling above us, calling out, when your family visited fifteen years ago."

"But how did I dream what the eagle saw fifteen years ago?"

"It was a gift from God, the Great Spirit," explained Tío Emilio, looking at me then at Tata, to see if Tata was following what we were saying. Tata indicated that he got most of it, but Tío Emilio stopped and translated for him, just to be sure. "Last night you were given a vision of a world that few people ever experience. To describe what happened to you, the native Mexicans would say that you shape-shifted. Your conscious awareness traveled to the eagle and you were then able to experience reality from within the eagle's consciousness."

Conscious awareness? Shape-shifted? I had no idea what he was talking about.

"That event was such a powerful omen that Don José and I felt it must be acknowledged and shared with you when you were older. Don José recorded on the leather his impression of the scene from the eagle's view. The gift was given to you in hopes that the scene would stimulate a memory or dream of the event, and it happened last night. It was an amazing dream, or I should say, *vision*. Truly, it was more than a dream. In time, you will discover what it means for you."

Obviously, I was not old enough to understand it yet, as I was very confused. "How am I supposed to figure out what it means? Do you have any idea?"

"I can tell you what I think some parts mean, but visions are very personal. You will eventually learn on your own what it means. The dream about energy lines and the interconnectedness of all things are your first lesson in shamanism. This type of experience is at the core of the shaman's world. We thought that the experience with the eagle might be a sign, or omen, that someday I might share the shaman knowledge with you."

I was blown away! I didn't understand a lot of what he was talking about, this strange person, this hidden relative no one talked about who was able to read my mind and who had shown up at this moment to tell me that I was somehow linked to him and his teacher in Mexico.

"Your Tata would like me to talk with you more about the work that I do, and about this ancient spiritual knowledge of our ancestors." Tío Emilio paused to let that sink in. Tata was pushing it, and seemed to have won the battle of minds with my mother who didn't want me to learn about this stuff.

"If you would like, I can begin teaching you about shamanism when I come to San Diego for visits. You do not need to give me an answer right now. You have plenty to think about with what you experienced over the past two days. Think about my offer."

I didn't say anything. I couldn't! All that had happened left me speechless. I didn't fully understand what he talked about, or my connection with him, but I was beginning to think that maybe this might not be so bad after all.

Right then, our car pulled up in front of the house. Tata had gone into the house and came back out with Tío Emilio's bag. I carried it to the car and again felt the soft leather and admired the detailed carving. Tío Emilio gave me a strong silent hug. He turned to hug Nana, and then quickly hugged a bunch of family members who showed up just in time to see him off. Tío, Tata, and my father then got into the car and headed toward Harbor Drive for the short ride to the downtown bus station.

8
___

DANGER

*"It takes a great deal of courage to stand up to
your enemies, but it takes a great deal more
courage to stand up to your friends."*

ALBUS DUMBLEDORE (J.K. ROWLING)

AA-OOOOOO-GA … AA-OOOOOO-GA.

"Dang, I told him not to honk that horn!" Tony whispered. "My parents are gonna know that it's Pablito's dad's car." Tony peeked into the house and turned back to me.

"Good! My dad's asleep on the couch and my mom's on the phone."

He opened the door quietly and stuck in his head. "Mom," he whispered across the living room to his mother who was seated at the dining room table. "I'll be back in a little while. Vincent an' me are going out for a bit." He didn't want to wake his father and his whispering didn't interrupt her telephone conversation. She was engrossed in her call and could hardly hear him. She looked up briefly, then just waved goodbye. I was surprised his mother was letting him go out. He had been grounded like me, but I guess they loosened up a little. My parents thought I was spending the evening with Tony at his house. I was just hoping Gracie and Alice didn't talk to each other and figure out we were both gone.

We walked to the corner where Pablito was waiting and got into the car. He was sixteen, a year older than me and Tony, and already had his driver's license. But after the trouble he'd been in,

Pablito was only supposed to be driving to take his mother to and from work or the store.

"Hey, dumb ass," Tony said to Pablito in a tone of exasperation. "What good does it do to have you wait down here so my parents don't see you, if you go and blast that horn when everyone in the neighborhood knows it belongs to your dad's car?"

"Hey, bro'," he responded smiling, "it's such a cool horn, ya gotta blow it."

Tony just shook his head. "Pablito, sometimes I just don't know about you. If my dad hadn't been asleep, he would have known it was you. He would have made me stay home and given me a lecture about being out here with you. I wonder what you think sometimes, or if you even think at all!"

"Well, you're here, ain't chu? Your dad's asleep and you guys are here. What'chu bitching about? Let's go get Arturo."

When we drove up to Arturo's, he was standing outside with Eddie.

"Where you guys headed?" Eddie asked.

"Over to East San Diego," Pablito called back. "There's a party I heard about, at the home of some girl, a cousin of this broad I know from school."

"Hey, man ..." I said hesitantly, "it sounds like trouble. That's way outside our area." I'd been having a bad feeling about this ever since Pablito and Arturo invited us. I kept thinking about what Tío Marcos had said.

"It's a free country, bro'," said Arturo as he climbed into the front seat after pulling Tony out. "We can go anywhere we want."

"Yeah, you can go," added Tony, as he got into the back seat with me. "Doesn't mean you're going to live through it. But you can go."

"Don't be so chicken, you guys," said Pablito. "It's just a party, not a gang fight. These folks aren't gonna wanna mess up their own party by starting something with us." He and Arturo were up for it because of the exciting challenge of crashing a party in another gang's territory.

"Don't screw this up for us, you sissies. You can't just sit around here 'cause you're afraid to go out of the neighborhood. We don't expect any trouble, but we need you to go along with us. It's better if there are more of us."

"If you don't expect any trouble, why do you need a show of force?" I asked.

"Hey, if you're too scared, just get out of the car," said Arturo glaring at me.

I put my hand on the door handle. I wanted so bad to just pull on it and open the door.

"Let's not sit here all night talking about it," said Tony. "Let's just go."

East San Diego was an area that had increasingly become home to many Mexican, Black, and Asian gangs. That's why Tony and I were reluctant to go along. But we couldn't just sit at home because some guys didn't want us in their neighborhood. When we arrived, we found there was no parking anywhere near the party. We ended up having to park almost three blocks away.

"I don't know about leaving the car out here so far from the party," said Pablito.

"What are you worried about," asked Arturo. "Look, it fits right in with all the other old cars parked out here. At least here it won't get messed up by people hanging around the party."

It was a long walk, with no moon, and few street lights. So it was dark, very dark, in another gang's turf. Not what I would have chosen to do for my Friday night entertainment.

"Keep your eyes open for trouble," cautioned Arturo as we hurried along.

"Hey man, they *are* open, and I can't see a thing," whispered Pablito.

"Well, the good thing is that they can't see you either," said Tony, "so just keep walking and act like you belong here."

Luckily, we didn't come upon many people while walking toward the party. We saw a few families out on their front porch, with kids playing near the front porch lights. We passed by an elderly Mexican couple walking with a small bag of groceries. The man greeted us in Spanish. A few cars passed by, but none of them slowed down to check us out, so we felt okay.

When we finally got within a few houses of the place, we knew we'd found trouble. The home had a gate, and there were these big, older guys serving as security, keeping out the party crashers. They were checking names on a list.

"Mr. Pablo Sanchez," Tony called to Pablito sarcastically, "I'm gonna assume all of our names are on that list, right?"

"Oh, man!" said Pablito. "I didn't hear nothing about no list."

"Well, no use going up there and getting our asses kicked out," said Arturo. "We don't want to make it obvious that we don't belong here. Let's cross the street and keep walking, then circle around the block and get back to the car."

We started back, walking on the next street over from the party. Nearing the end of the block, we saw a group of about eight guys walk onto the sidewalk from a front yard three houses up from us. We could see there were more guys on the front porch.

"Cross over," Arturo said quietly but with a sense of alarm. We crossed the street and picked up our pace. They started moving quickly down the sidewalk on their side of the street.

"Oh, man!" said Pablito. "We can't go to the car. Even if we get there before these guys, they'll break the windows and slash the tires before we can get it started and get out of here."

"We gotta split up," Arturo said with real fear in his voice. "Four of us are too easy to see if we try to run and hide together." As we came to the corner, he yelled out, "We'll see you guys back at home," and he and Pablito took off, running down the side street.

I was shocked! They just took off and left us alone with these guys coming after us! I was too afraid to move. Where were we going to run to? Where were we?

Tony grabbed my jacket and pulled me with him as he started walking quickly across the intersection. Four of the guys took off after Pablito and Arturo. The remaining four hesitated, then quickly crossed over to our side of the street and started into the intersection right behind us.

Just then, a car came from the direction of the running guys and came screeching to a halt at the corner, its headlights on bright, illuminating the remaining four guys. They jumped back for a moment, staring into the headlights, then backed up few more steps.

It all happened so fast that Tony and I were stunned. We just stood there watching. Then a voice called out, "Vincent. Get in!"

It was Tío Emilio's voice! It was him in the car! We ran to the car and both of us jumped in through the driver's side back door. At the same time, the four guys in the headlights turned and took off after their friends chasing Pablito and Arturo.

"My God, I thought we were goners," said Tony, panting through his fright.

"Me too," I said, shaking uncontrollably, "I thought those guys... were gonna shoot us or stab us." I sat there sprawled out on the seat, leaning on Tony. "I really thought I was gonna die."

Sitting there in the back seat, I realized it was Tata's car. Tío Emilio turned around with a very serious look on his face, maybe an angry look, not saying anything. Finally, his face broke into a hint of a smile.

"I assume you boys need a lift? I would have given your friends a lift too, but they seem to have taken off." He paused, and then added, "They also seem to have attracted all the trouble."

"Tío, I didn't know you were down from L.A."

"I got here late this afternoon."

"What a coincidence he came along when he did," said Tony, looking at me with bugged out eyes and sweat trickling down his face. "He saved our lives!"

"Tío, this is my friend Tony."

"I don't know how you came along at just the right time," said Tony, "but man, I'm glad you did. And am I ever glad to be getting out of this neighborhood!"

"Young man," said Tío Emilio, "in my world, there is no such thing as a coincidence. It was no coincidence that I showed up. Someday, soon, I will tell you more about that." He paused briefly and then came at us just like our parents would have. "You could have been killed or very badly injured," he scolded sternly. "Look at you both, sweating because you are scared to death, just thinking about what could have happened to you. You both had better go home and decide, is this is the way you want to live your life, or end it?"

I was so glad he came by and saved us. But man, I thought, there it was again, another family member giving me a lecture. I didn't want to listen to him. I was too freaked out. I sat there, still shaking, thinking about what just happened. We had almost gotten jumped, beat up, stabbed, or even worse. No wonder I was shaking.

Tío Emilio got onto Fairmount Avenue and drove south out of East San Diego and toward home. He didn't say anything else all the way home. As I sat there in the back seat, I finally stopped shaking. I wanted to escape into sleep, but my heart was still pumping too fast. It was like my whole body was on alert.

We were back in our own neighborhood in just a few minutes. Tío Emilio pulled up in front of Nana and Tata's house and we all got out of the car. He paused in front of the gate.

"Like I said, you boys need to think about what happened to you tonight. You are making choices about your life. You need to ask yourself if you are making the right choices."

"But I didn't choose for those guys to come after us," Tony protested. "I don't mean to be disrespectful, *señor*, but I wouldn't choose to get beat up or killed."

"Yes, you are right. You did not choose for those fellows to come after you, I agree. But you must recognize the decisions you *did* make to put yourselves in harm's way. After all, you did *not* choose to go to a movie, a ball game or a supervised dance."

"I see what you mean," I answered. "We chose to crash a party in another gang's territory."

Tío Emilio turned toward me. "Vincent, I am leaving for Los Angeles in the morning, so perhaps we can talk next time I come back here, probably in a few weeks."

"Sure, okay, Tío."

"See you tomorrow maybe," Tony said to me quietly as he started toward the corner.

"Yeah," I responded, softly as well, moving in the other direction. "Maybe tomorrow."

I stopped and turned back to Tío Emilio. I had to ask.

"Tío," I called out. "If you got here this afternoon, why are you already going back to L.A. in the morning?"

"Because I just finished what I came here for."

With that he turned and walked up the rest of the steps and into Nana and Tata's house. I wanted to yell, "Wait, don't go in yet!" I wanted to know what he meant. Did he mean that he came here just to save us? How could he know? I was confused and angry and still upset about what had happened. But he was right. I was in no shape to talk about it. Right then, I just needed to go home, and like he and Tío Marcos said, I needed to think about the decisions I'd made, and all the trouble and danger I'd gotten myself into. Was that how I wanted to live? Or die?

9

FAMILY TALK

*"Every time you don't follow your inner guidance,
you feel a loss of energy, loss of power...."*

SHAKTI GAWAIN

"Too bad he couldn't stay longer," mused Tío Pancho. "I thought I was going to be able to spend a little time with him today."

I stood on the porch next to Tío Pancho as we watched my father drive off in Tata's car with Tata and Tío Emilio. They were taking him to the bus station, so he could get back to L.A.

"That was a long way to go to turn around and go right back," Tía Paula said as she walked up the porch steps and stood beside us. She lived only a few blocks away, so she had made it over here this morning in time to have breakfast with Nana, Tata, and Tío Emilio. My mother insisted on us doing most of the usual Saturday morning household chores before we came over, so we didn't get there until about eleven o'clock, right when they were getting ready to leave. Tío Pancho arrived just after we did.

"He said he had some important business to take care of here last night, but that he really needed to get back to L.A. before this evening," Tía Paula continued. "He certainly has become a very busy guy for being here for such a short while."

So far, it seemed like Tío Emilio hadn't told anyone about last night. No one knew it was Tony and me he had picked up and brought home. I guess no one in the house heard us talking when we got here. When Tío Emilio said hello to me, he didn't act like he was seeing me for the first time in weeks, but he didn't act like he had just seen me yesterday, either.

His having to be back in L.A. that evening made it even more amazing that he would show up in East San Diego. I would have

▸ 60 ◂

liked to assume, like everyone else, that he had business to handle in San Diego, but I couldn't. I knew inside me that he had come to save us. Somehow, he had known we would be in trouble. Of course, everyone had been telling us we were headed for trouble, but he had shown up in the middle of it and saved our butts. I sure wanted to know how he did that. How could he know we would be in a mess on that day, at that spot? And then to take a bus down, and get over to Tata's to borrow his car, and still get to us in time— it really boggled my mind. Maybe that was part of that shaman stuff he had talked about.

Tata and my father got back in less than an hour, since the bus station was right downtown. Then, with everyone gathered in the house, the conversation, as usual, deteriorated to a focus on me, on the younger boys in the family, and about the drug and gang activity going on in the neighborhood.

"Hey, get off his case," said Tío Pancho, defending me. "He hasn't gotten into any real trouble. All this teenage acting out stuff—you're making it out to be worse than it is."

"Right, he hasn't done anything except hanging out with drug dealers," said Tía Paula. "You call that not doing anything? I know what's going on around here. Don't act like it's nothing." She sounded angry at Tío Pancho.

He came right back with an animated reply. "But Vincent isn't selling drugs. He said he isn't. And he's not a liar. If anything, he's still too much of a mama's boy." Then, turning to me, he said, "Sorry, *mijito*. I didn't mean to diss you."

"*¡Ay, qué tonto, Pancho!*" my mother said as she slapped him on the shoulder. "You just don't know what he's been getting into— stealing, fighting—and those criminal friends of his!"

"Right, and when those guys get arrested, they will all be just as guilty because they're out there together. He could easily be sent off to juvenile hall with those hoodlums." Tía Paula was definitely my mother's sister. They pretty much sang the same song. And they kept at it as they moved into the kitchen and started cooking lunch.

I went back outside and sat on the front porch. I had to get away from it. I just hated this. They were all talking about me, but no one was asking me anything. As far as I was concerned, Tío Pancho was right. I hadn't done anything serious. Tony and I could be in the middle of all this drug dealing if we wanted to, but we weren't. And no one gave us credit for making that decision, for staying out of it. It was hard to walk that line with all the pressures the other guys put on you. But they were also our friends and so far, they respected our decision to stay out of it.

"Vincent," my father called from the doorway, "go home and bring your sisters here for lunch. Tell them to change into some clean clothes, and lock up the house when you leave."

"Okay," I answered as I got up. They could just as easily have called the girls on the phone and told them. But I was glad for the excuse to get away.

The girls didn't ask any questions about Tío Emilio or why he had been here. They looked at me with wondering eyes, but they seemed as confused as everyone else about his short visit. After locking up, I sat in the *sala* while waiting for them to change.

When we got back to Nana and Tata's, everyone was eating. My mother ushered us into the kitchen and began serving the chicken in green chili sauce, rice and beans onto our plates. I could hear from the discussion in the dining room that I was still the topic of discussion. At least two different conversations were going on, in Spanish.

"You kids sit out there in the back patio and eat your lunch. Gina and Mona, you go sit down. Vincent and Gracie will carry your plates out for you."

After bringing out the last plate, I sat down to join my sisters. Gina, who had been staring at me for quite a while, couldn't bear it any longer.

"So, are you going to jail or something?" she asked.

"Not jail," said Gracie, "juvenile hall." Even Gina had picked up on the adult's conversation, even though it was in Spanish.

"Same thing," said Mona. "They lock them up there, don't they?"

"You guys too! What is this, *get on Vincent's case* day? No Gina, I'm not going to go to jail *or* juvie. I haven't done anything to get sent to juvie for!"

"Except for stealing sodas," said Mona.

"And assault and battery!" Gracie yelled.

"Hey, gimme a break. That stuff is over with. I haven't been in any trouble lately, at least not any real trouble. I haven't been caught ... uh, I haven't done anything!"

"You dumb ass ... oops," Gracie quickly put her hand up to her mouth, hoping that none of the older folks heard that. "You dummy," she continued. "Mama and Daddy have been telling you to stay away from those hoodlum friends of yours. They're slime balls."

"Whoa, this really set you off!" I said to her. "I've never heard you use cuss words before."

"Well, I'm sorry," she said with exasperation. "This really makes me mad. Mama and Daddy have tried so hard to keep you out of trouble and you keep hanging out with that idiot Pablito and his drug dealing buddy, Arturo. Stay away from them!"

"Hey, calm down, Gracie," Mona piped in. "Your food is getting cold. Why don't you eat while you cuss him out?"

All of us laughed at that. Gracie never cussed. She was as upset as Tía Paula and Mama. Well ... not as upset as Mama.

"Anyway, I don't know why you would want to be seen around them," continued Gracie. "The girls at school think they're just a bunch of sleazy macho idiots, trying to be bad stuff all the time. They're bad stuff all right. So bad none of the girls even want to be around them."

"Yeah, right," I said, "what girls at school?"

"Well," she said, "Alice and Linda, for two." Those two and Gracie were two years ahead of us in school. Linda was another of Doña Rosa's granddaughters.

"And Anita, too," added Mona. "Pablito thinks she likes him, but she can't stand him anymore, because she sees him hanging around with those other *stupidos*. Besides, she saw you kick his butt good. I think she likes you now."

"She better get in line," said Gracie. "Linda said her sister Gloria likes him." And then, turning back to me, she added, "but not if you're hanging out with those dopes!"

"Woo, hoo! Gloria likes Vincent!" Gina and Mona sang out together.

I could feel my ears getting red, as they repeated it. "Shut up, you guys. She's just a friend in my class." I shouldn't have said anything because I don't think I sounded very convincing.

Mona went back into the kitchen and came out with more tortillas. "They're talking about you in there, Vincent. Mama and Daddy said they don't know what to do. Tía Paula said it's just a matter of time and you'll be in jail, just like Tío Marcos and Tío Juan were."

"They were in jail?" asked Gina with surprise. "When?"

"A few years ago," replied Gracie. "You were too young to remember it."

I finished my plate and went into the house for more food so I could hear for myself what was being said. As I heaped my plate with more of the green chili chicken, Tata started to talk. He spoke in Spanish, so I didn't quite get it all, but he was talking about someone to help.

For some reason, my mother got very animated, shaking her head, saying she didn't believe in the old ways. And she mentioned the Church opposition. She too was speaking Spanish.

Then it hit me. Of course! The old ways! They were talking about Tío Emilio.

"Oh, María," argued Tío Pancho, "you're against it because you think the Church is against it. But none of us really know anything about it. I've never heard anyone connected with the Church say anything against *curanderos* and *brujos*. What he's saying is that Emilio has had success working with young people in Mexico and L.A. So don't be so stubborn. Your father is asking you to give it a chance. If not this, what's your suggestion?"

"Well," she said hesitantly, "I don't have any other suggestions. I ... I've given up. That's why we're talking. I need help. He's out of control, and ... I'm so worried." She began to sob.

That was my cue to get out of sight. I just couldn't take it when she cried because of me. I hustled my food outside and sat down with the girls to finish eating.

"Hey, Mama's crying," Gina called out as she stood by the screen door, looking in.

"So, what are they saying?" Gracie asked.

"Something about old Mexican traditions," I answered, "and about *curanderos* and *brujos*. They're talking about Tío Emilio. I think they want him to come and cure me of my evil ways."

"Wow. They must think you're pretty bad off," said Mona, "if they need to bring somebody else besides themselves to straighten you out. I think a good fat belt ..."

"Hey, shut up, you punk. I don't need straightening out!" I answered, getting angry. "I'm not crooked! I haven't done anything!"

"Right," said Gracie. "You're just an angry young man, with a chip on your shoulder."

"I ain't got no chip on my shoulder," I shot back loudly. "I'm not an angry young man!"

"Yes you do! And yes you are!" yelled Gracie even louder.

"Yes you are!" yelled Mona, trying to be heard over Gracie's yelling.

The three of them laughed.

I wouldn't admit it to them, but maybe I wasn't totally innocent. I knew it was going to catch up with me sooner or later. Last night just came sooner than I thought. Even though I resented the idea of them bringing Tío Emilio here to try to keep me out of trouble, maybe spending some time with him wouldn't be so bad. After all, he had saved me! Somehow, last night, he had saved me. And he *had* offered to teach me about these "old ways," as my mother called them. It was kinda weird what he spoke about. And the dream—that whole thing about seeing the dream carved into the leather was so strange and impossible to understand. But something about it felt right, from the very night I dreamed it. I had a feeling there was a message in it for me somewhere, and perhaps Tío Emilio could help me find it.

10

PATH OF THE ANCESTORS

*"There is guidance for each of us, and by lowly
listening, we shall hear the right word.*

RALPH WALDO EMERSON

As it turned out, our incident in East San Diego didn't slip by unnoticed like we thought it did. One of the neighbors had seen us talking that night in front of Nana and Tata's house. A few days later she asked Nana who had been driving Tata's car and talking to her grandson and Amador's store clerk. Of course it was a total surprise to Nana and Tata that Tío Emilio had been with Tony and me that night. So when they called and asked him about it, he told them the whole truth. And they, of course, told our parents, plus a few others.

Pretty soon everyone in both families had heard at least one or more versions of the story about how Tony and I almost died in East San Diego. In some of the versions, Pablito and Arturo were still missing. You'd think we had been arrested for some serious crime, the way everyone was yelling at us. It was as if it was the worst thing that could have happened. But nothing happened!!

"You keep doing these things!" my mother yelled. "It keeps getting worse and worse. You could be dead already! There's no reason to go talk to him now. He was supposed to help straighten you out. And now it's too late. You won't stop hanging out with those criminals!"

She started in on me again. This had been going on since Wednesday, when Tío Emilio called to say he would be coming down to talk to me.

"Ya Maria!" my father yelled. "Enough already! Let it be!" He paused briefly, then, at a slightly lower volume said, "His life isn't over. Now, more than ever, he should spend time with Emilio. Maybe that will help. Anyway, that's what was already decided, so just stop it!"

He looked at me and nodded toward the door. "Go on," he said gruffly, "he's waiting."

As I walked over to Nana and Tata's, my stomach was churning. My mother and father had been fighting, mostly about me. And I got the feeling she had been fighting with Tata over this too. She still didn't want me to talk with Tío Emilio. But it looked like Tata had already decided what was best for me. I wasn't totally sure about it, but it was either don't do it because my mother said no, or do it because Tata said yes. Even though this whole thing was a little scary, I decided to go with Tata.

Tony was sitting on the curb in front of Nana and Tata's yard, waiting for me. He found out his father and grandfather had talked to Tata and Tío Emilio when he was in town last time. They strongly encouraged Tony to come with me, even though his grandmother was against it. As I started up the steps to flip open the gate, I expected him to get up. But he didn't move. He just kept looking straight ahead.

"Hey, Tony. You okay? You still gonna do this with me?"

He turned toward me, looking a little scared. "Uh … I don't think it's going to do any good. I don't really believe all that *brujo* stuff, even if my grandfather does. But I would like to hear about these powers *brujos* supposedly have. My grandmother says it's black magic. My grandfather says it's not. But he and my father think, black magic or not, maybe this might keep us from getting into more trouble."

Tony stared at me for a few seconds, looking like he was trying to decide. "I guess I'll go with you. I just don't want to get caught up in some black magic problems. I don't know whether to believe my grandmother or my grandfather. First sign of any weird stuff, though, I'm bailing, man. I don't want to abandon you if there's trouble, but I'm not going to stick around and get hurt."

"Hey, Tony, he's my grandfather's cousin. He's *familia*. He wouldn't let anything bad happen to us. And my Tata wouldn't let anything bad happen to us." I don't know if I sounded convincing, but I was worried too. "Anyway, strange stuff or black magic or whatever, we've got to do something. We can't keep doing like we've been doing. I don't want to end up dead or in Juvie. Maybe he can help."

Tony got up from the curb. "Okay, let's go listen to what he has to say."

We walked up the steps into the yard and over to the side of the house, where we paused. Looking into the back yard we could see Tío Emilio sitting in the garden shed, waiting for us.

"*Buenos dias, señores*. Come on, come in." He waved his hand as we walked toward him, motioning for us to join him in the garden shed. "Have a seat."

We both said good morning as we walked in and took a seat across from him on new padded folding chairs that had been placed near the open end of the shed. The ratty green vinyl chair and the old wooden one were gone.

"What a beautiful day," said Tío Emilio. "A great day to be alive, *qué no?*"

Cutting right to the heart of the matter! No beating around the bush. Neither of us said anything. It wasn't really a question, more a vivid reminder of why we were here with him today.

"It is good to see you again, Tony. I am glad you are able to join us. I understand some in your family want you to be here and others aren't so sure. Just as in Vincent's family."

"Yeah, with the trouble we got into in East San Diego and stuff before that, they wanted me to be here too. I think they hope you can figure out a way to keep us out of trouble. But my grandmother is worried, like Vincent's mother and grandmother."

"They do not know what I teach or what I do to help others. People fear what they do not know. You do not know how I was able to be there the night I rescued you. That has *you* a little worried. But your parents and grandparents are willing to set their concerns aside at this time if what I have to share will help you. The primary concerns of your families are the bad choices you have been making and the trouble this has gotten you into. What I have to share with you is more than being in the right place at the right time. It is about choosing to live well rather than choosing badly. A bad choice was your attempted suicide that night in East San Diego."

We both chuckled at his little joke, calling our close call an attempted suicide.

"You can laugh, but I am serious. It was an attempted suicide, even though unconsciously you left it up to someone else to do the damage. There are no accidents. We choose our life actions, and doing so, we choose the consequences too. If we choose not to die, we do not put ourselves in danger."

Tony responded, "I still say I didn't ask for those guys to jump us. But, I have to admit, I knew it was a stupid and dangerous thing to do."

"And you have to take responsibility for the decisions you made to put yourselves in that dangerous situation, yes?"

We both nodded.

"Well, your actions have your families very concerned. So, they have asked me to try, as they said, to 'straighten....'"

"Straighten me out!" I said, yelling, before he could finish. "I hate that! I ain't crooked!"

"I prefer to call it helping you choose a better path. Both of you have to choose between becoming more like your two friends, or taking a different path."

"Hey, man," whined Tony, "we ain't becoming like Pablito and Arturo. I don't wanna be like them."

"No," said Tío Emilio, "but right now you have one foot on each path, and the paths go in different directions. You cannot follow both. You are kidding yourselves if you think you can be involved with gangs and drugs and not fall into further danger."

"Our parents want us to stop seeing our friends, but that's impossible," I said, with some exasperation. "We see them all the time––on the street, at school, the park. Tony and me, we don't like the drug dealing and other illegal stuff some of the guys do, but except for that, hanging with our friends is hard to give up. I mean we grew up with these guys. We've known them all our lives."

"I am not saying that you should not do things with friends," said Tío Emilio. "But perhaps the time has come to not simply follow others, and instead, go a different way. I am offering you the opportunity to take a completely different path than most people. It is an ancient path, the path of your ancestors, a path connected with nature and the earth, connected to God and the energy of the universe. It is the way our ancestors used to live."

"Aha, *los conquistadores!*" said Tony with a smile.

"Yeah, right," I said, smiling back at Tony. We had heard enough conquistador bashing around here and in school to know he didn't mean them.

"I am talking of a way of life still lived by many native groups on this continent and elsewhere," he continued. "This way of life goes back way before the *conquistadores*, before the formalized practice of religion lost much of its true connection with God and with the energies of nature and the earth. It goes back before the Aztecs, Mayans, and Incas, and before them the Toltecs, before them the Olmecs, and back to their ancestors. It has its roots in the spiritual practices of the ancestors of all native cultures in the world."

"That's some pretty old stuff," said Tony. "But haven't we learned a lot since then?"

"Yes, we have learned much since then, but the knowledge is, how do you say, lopsided. We have had 500 years focused on advances in technology, but in the process, we separated ourselves from our spiritual nature, our connection to the earth and all living things. The elder shamans and their guides say the time has arrived for the shift back to a better balance, a more spiritually connected existence. They say we must now share the secrets of our ancient spiritual ways to help others learn a different way of life. If you allow me to share this knowledge with you, and as you experience this other way, your spirit will recognize the path. You will open up and let your full self, your higher self, guide you on a path of personal growth and spiritual awareness. This path of spiritual awareness will last your entire life and beyond."

I didn't want to stop him because what he was saying sounded really interesting. I wasn't exactly sure what he meant by things like higher self and spiritual awareness, but I thought I would let it slide for now and find a better time to ask.

"I will teach you about the sacred ways of your ancestors," he continued, "and about how to live in a sacred manner, connected to the earth, to all living things, and to the spirits who guide and protect us. It is not so much a matter of *doing*, but an awareness of that connection, and living or *being* in that awareness. Your ancestors knew these things. If you decide to enter this training, and if you practice this way of being, you will *be* a different person."

Tony raised his hand, and Tío Emilio nodded. "What do you mean I'll be a different person? Different how?"

"You will see things differently. You will think about the world differently. You will *feel* more connected to things, people, God. You will know things ahead of time, where to go, how to be in the right place at the right time. You will have an inner knowing that is not available to you right now."

My hand shot up. I had to ask, "Is that how you...."

"How I read your mind? Yes, that is how I sometimes know what you are thinking and what you want to say. My connection with you is very strong, and as long as I am in that connected place, the information I need flows to me, and I am aware of it. As you learn the secret teachings, you will find that information flows to you too, along with the good things you want in life. You will learn that the bad things that have happened were created by you, and you will learn how to stop that from happening. I will even show you how to get high without drugs or alcohol, using the spiritual ways of your ancestors."

Tío Emilio's words gave me a glimmer of hope for finding a way out of the garbage pit of life I had been slowly sliding into.

"Count me in. If this can help keep us out of trouble, and help make things better in our lives, then it's gotta be worth it."

The look on Tony's face told me he still wasn't convinced. "I'm not so sure about the *brujo* stuff," he said, "and I don't want to get involved in any black magic spells that might cause us trouble. But I do want to know more about this secret you mentioned. If this can help make good things happen, I'm all for it. Lately it seems like it's been bad stuff happening to us."

Tío Emilio turned in his chair and looked directly at Tony. "I want to put your mind at ease right now. As I said to Vincent, there are *brujos* who misuse these powers and work with what some call black magic. I am not that kind of *brujo*. That is why I prefer the term *shaman*. I want you both to know there are no spells or black magic in the work I do. Nothing we practice will cause either of you any troubles."

I was glad to finally hear him say there were no spells. Although I didn't think there would be, I had to admit I had been wondering about it ever since Manuel asked if the *brujo* would be putting a spell on me.

"Your first step in this process is to agree to participate as opposed to being forced by your families. This is very important. It is a statement of your intention and your desire. You must be very clear that this is what *you* want to learn and experience. Your intent is what will open the door to create changes in your lives. Now, do you freely choose to participate in this effort?"

I nodded again in agreement.

"My mother and grandmother don't want me here," said Tony. "But they said it was up to me to decide. So, I guess I'll give it a try. By the way, what should I call you? You ain't my tío."

"Well, now that you have asked," he paused for a moment, "some people call me *Don* Emilio, as a sign of respect for the work that I do. So, as a sign of respect for this sacred journey we are beginning, you can both call me Don Emilio. And, as a mutual sign of respect, I will call you Vicente and Antonio, your formal names in Spanish. Is this agreeable to you both?"

We both nodded.

"Very well then, I will begin now by talking about the teachings of the ancestors in general terms, and in later sessions will cover these topics in more detail. Our first topic is spiritual energy. According to recent discoveries in the field of physics, everything that exists in this universe is made of energy—it is everywhere and is in everything. Centuries before the scientific discoveries, the Toltec shamans were aware of an indescribable energy, that they called *Intent*, which permeates the universe. They taught that this energy is alive, and has consciousness. Every thing in the universe, from a pebble, to a tree, to a star, to a galaxy, are all a part of that one living energy consciousness, and therefore all are alive and have consciousness. That one living energy consciousness is here on the physical plane as well as the non-physical plane.

Don Emilio looked at Tony, then at me. We must have looked clueless. Despite the blank stares, he continued. "I know much of this may sound strange to you, but I will explain these terms as we move along. As you become familiar with the words, the concepts we discuss will begin to make more sense to you. For now, ask any questions and stop me whenever you want clarification. And you do not need to raise your hand. You are not at school."

"Okay, why do you call it spiritual energy if it's just energy?" I asked.

"Because it is not *just* energy. I am not talking about strength energy or a caffeine energy jolt. I am talking about the energy essence that permeates all things, the life Force of the universe."

"Force?" asked Tony. "Like in *Star Wars* and *the Force be with you?*"

"As a matter of fact, yes. As everything in the universe is made of energy, that Force sustains us and connects us to all things in the universe. Our personal life force is a part of the larger Force of the universe.

"Some shamans live a life focused on keeping their spiritual energy levels high. Those who commit to this path of increased spiritual energy call themselves spirit warriors. They become very aware of persons, actions, or events that result in a loss of energy—much like the abilities of the Jedi knights in the *Star Wars* movies.

A spirit warrior aims to stop living by the whims of whatever or whoever comes along to impact his energy, and instead live a life dedicated to taking every opportunity to increase this energy.

"Our initial objective is not as intense as that. I want both of you to simply become aware of your personal spiritual energy level. When you have that awareness, you can then begin to understand what happens to cause you to lose some of that energy, and what you can do to stop losing it. I will also show you how to increase this energy. Does that sound simple enough? Are you ready to begin?"

I nodded. Not because it sounded simple. I wasn't sure about what he was saying. But I was ready to hear more about this Force.

"So, let us start with a simple exercise that will help raise your energy level, as well as help stop the mind chatter that is constantly going on in your head. In this exercise, we focus our attention on an object as a way to calm the mind and stop that internal dialogue. Some call it meditation. It starts with relaxation and deep breaths.

"Start now by closing your eyes. This is the first step in turning away from the outer senses, and opening up to the inner world. Sit back and relax. Move a little in your chair if you need to, so you are comfortable. Move your head … relax your face muscles … shoulders … arms … legs. Let your whole body relax. Take a deep breath in, and then let the air all the way out, while you seem to sink into your chair. Slowly, take another deep breath, and then let it all out as you relax even more. Now breathe normally, but be aware of the air as you breathe in, then as you let it out. Keep your attention focused on each breath, in … and out. This deep breathing helps you release your thoughts and worries, and helps you relax. You might hear each other breathing. Ignore that and focus on your own breathing."

I focused on each breath, listening to my own sound. I could hear Tony letting his air out. Don Emilio was right. Closing my eyes and breathing deeply did help me to slow down and relax a little. The outside world seemed far away even though I knew it was just on the other side of my eyelids.

"If your mind wanders, do not worry. When you become aware you are thinking about something else, stop, and then focus again on each breath, as you inhale and exhale."

It was a relief to know I wasn't screwing up, because my mind was already wandering. Once in a while Don Emilio would remind us to focus on our breath. Sometimes when he spoke I was still aware of each breath, and other times I was off somewhere in other thoughts. When I heard his voice, I just came back and concentrated again on my breath. It felt very relaxing to just listen to the in and out, in and out. And sometimes it was an effort to keep from going off on some thought that popped in. After a while, there was just quiet....

"Vicente and Antonio." The voice sounded so very far away. He spoke again, slowly and quietly. "Take three deep breaths now ... move your body a little ... and when you are ready, open your eyes."

When he said *move*, I had to think to get anything to move at first. Everything felt heavy and a little numb.

"Are you back now?"

With heavy eyelids, I looked at him and slowly nodded. I realized that when he called our names and started talking to us, I was no longer aware of my breathing. I had lost track of it entirely. I think I had lost track of everything.

"You both relaxed so well that you fell asleep. When you get this relaxed and you shut down the mind's control, your body can do what it needs to do to restore itself. It can build its own energy, which is good. Apparently, you both needed some total rest."

"Yeah, I guess I dozed off," said Tony, stretching and yawning. "I know I lost track of my breathing for a little bit."

"I felt so groggy when you called our names," I added. "I must have dozed off too."

"You both followed your breath off and on for four to five minutes. Then you were out, fast asleep, for at least ten minutes."

"No, you're kidding. Ten minutes?" Tony seemed as shocked as I was.

"An afternoon nap! I can't believe it," I said. "I can never take naps during the day!"

"That is because your mind has been in control, and would not let your body do what it needed. Meditation shuts down control by the conscious mind and sidetracks it into concentrating on something simple, like following the breath. Try this same exercise at home this evening. As we did now, listen as you breathe in and breathe out. Your mind will wander, but do not worry about it. Just stop and come back to being aware of your breath.

"In addition to doing the breath meditation this evening, I would like you to practice it at least once a day, for about 20 minutes. Try to get into a habit of doing it at the same time each day. It was easy for you to do that meditation, at least before you fell asleep, because I was here to talk you through it. Since you will do this on your own for the next few weeks, you may find it more difficult to stay focused on your breath. Your mind will wander. Just know that the more you practice, the easier it will be to let those thoughts pass without giving them too much attention, and then to refocus on your breath. As you practice staying focused on your breath, you will eventually experience less mind chatter. We will talk about your experiences when we get together again in four weeks.

"For our future sessions, we will meet for a couple of hours or so on Saturdays, and occasionally on Sunday as well. We will have four to six weeks between most sessions to give you time to think on what we talk about and to practice what you experience. That will be the method we use for all our sessions. You will experience some of what I talk about, and you will practice those experiences on your own until the next time. I will sometimes specifically mention something I want you to practice, but usually I will not. It is up to you to pay attention, and then practice on your own. You can ask at any time for clarification. As our sessions add up, you will find you have a lot to practice. So that you do not feel too overloaded or stressed out, you will choose what to practice based on what best helps you to increase your energy and minimize your internal chatter. As you practice, your experience will help you to choose."

With that, he ended the session and sent us on our way. We left through the alley and walked to Amador's, where we sat on the wall behind the market for a few minutes, thinking and talking about this first day with our own private shaman.

"This could be kinda interesting," said Tony. "What he said about secret teachings, learning to make good things happen in our lives, and reading people's minds—that's what I want to hear more about."

"Yeah, I'm really interested in those secret teachings too. What if they really turn out to be something special, like information that really makes our lives better? Then everyone will want to know more about it—our friends, and even our parents."

"But I'm still concerned," said Tony. "He said there wouldn't be any black magic stuff. Do you believe him?"

"We don't have any reason not to believe him. Not yet anyway. Let's listen and think about what he says. And like you said, you can always bail later if something gets too weird."

"Yeah, I guess there's no sense worrying about that unless something happens. You know, this might not be so bad after all. I kinda like your Tío … oh, excuse me, *Don Emilio*."

"Yes Antonio," I clowned in a deep voice. We both laughed. "I kinda like him too. When I first heard about him coming here, my mother didn't want to talk about him. That seemed really weird. I was worried about who this guy was, but not anymore. I think he could really help us. If nothing else," I said grinning, "we get to take naps in the afternoon."

11

HOOPS

"Change your thoughts, change your life."

JAMES ALLEN

One immediate result of the sessions with Don Emilio was that no one in the family bugged me or gave me a hard time anymore. From sisters, to parents, to grandparents, no one asked what I was doing, or where I was going, or who I was going with. When I asked if I could go to the library after our session with Don Emilio last week, to do some research on a school paper, my mother surprised me with her response.

"You don't have to ask if you can leave the house anymore," she said. "I should keep you on restriction, but your father and I promised Tío Emilio that we would let him deal with you. So you are now off restriction and in his hands. Don't go and blow this, and embarrass him and your Tata. Tata is the one who really wanted Tío Emilio to help you. I was opposed to this, but Tata insisted, and ... well, he's my father. You don't have to ask any more, but use your common sense, and let me know when you'll be gone, so that I don't have to worry about you."

When I called Tony and asked if he could go over to Chicano Park to play basketball, I was surprised he could go, but he told me that the same thing had happened at his house. It felt strange, walking out of the house and not having to ask first. It felt even stranger to see Pablito again for the first time since that Friday night three weeks before. So much had happened since he and Arturo took off running. I hadn't seen either one of them at school.

"Hey, bro', I see you're not dead after all," I called out to Pablito as I neared the gate to the basketball court in Chicano Park. Pablito was coming from the opposite direction, walking onto the court just ahead of me. Tony, who had phoned Pablito and asked him to come play with us, was already there taking shots at the basket. There was no one else on the court, so we had the whole place to ourselves, although we were going to use just one of the four baskets.

"Did you hear some bad rumors about me being dead?" Pablito asked as he chased down the ball. "Hey, who was that guy who walked into his own funeral?"

"Tom Sawyer," said Tony. "The Mark Twain book we had to read last year."

"Oh yeah. That was a way cool book. I didn't get around to finishing it though."

"How did you do the book report?" I asked.

"Hey, I didn't say I got a good grade!"

Tony and I laughed. Of course. I didn't expect that he had gotten a good grade. Why would I think he had read the whole book?

"We thought for sure you two were in for it when all those guys ran after you out in East San Diego," said Tony.

"Oh, what a *pinche* situation that was. I thought we left you guys in the dust to deal with those guys, and then it looked like all of them were on our tail. How did you do that?"

"Hey, they didn't want to mess with us, *cabrón*," Tony said, puffing out his skinny chest.

"Yeah, right," Pablito said grinning and shaking his head. Turning toward me, he asked, "So what really happened?"

"Man, you won't believe it!" I was eager to tell the story. "When you two took off, some of those guys ran after you, and four of them started to come after us. But they stopped cold when this car came screeching to a stop right in front of them at the corner, with its headlights lighting them up. When the driver called to us, those guys turned and took off after you and their friends. It was my Tío Emilio in the car! Can you believe that?"

"What a coincidence that he would appear right then, out there," said Tony. "He said it was no coincidence. Somehow, he knew we were gonna be in trouble, and somehow, he knew where we'd be. It was amazing!"

"What's amazing is that we got away from those guys," said Pablito, taking a shot at the basket. "I thought we were gonna die. Those guys chased us for about four friggin' blocks. I was running as fast as I could the whole time, in my good party shoes. I don't think I could have run any farther. Luckily, we caught up with a bus on University Avenue and jumped on just as the driver was closing the doors. As the bus pulled away we could see those guys out the back window as they ran after the bus and one by one gave up as we got farther and farther away. We rode over to North Park and stayed at Arturo's cousin's house. We didn't wanna get too far away because we had to go back for the car in the morning. His cousin dropped us off at the car."

Pablito stopped talking and chased down the ball again after Tony took another shot. He seemed to ignore what we had said about the "coincidence."

"I didn't know your Tío was back in town," said Pablito, before tossing up a skyhook that didn't come close. Tony caught the air ball on the fly.

"Neither did I. He just showed up."

"Hey, Vincent, you gonna take a few shots to warm up?" asked Tony, throwing me the ball. "Or are we just gonna start?"

"Just let me take a couple," I said as I swished the first one from the free-throw line and then bounced the second shot off the front of the rim.

"Okay," said Tony, grabbing the rebound, "let's go. Horse. Free throws to determine what order we shoot in, okay?"

We nodded. We knew the routine. In the game of HORSE, you make a shot, and the next guy has to make the exact same shot you did, no matter how weird. If you miss, you get a letter, starting with H. When you have missed enough to spell HORSE, you're out of the game.

As usual, we were pretty intense about our shots for the first six games. Tony won three, I won two, and we sort of let Pablito win the last one. Then we got creative and tried some really impossible shots. At that point in the game, when one of us would finally make it, there was almost no chance that the next guy would. So from then on, we didn't really keep score, except to joke around that so-and-so had something like HORSSSSSSS.

"Hey Vincent," Tony called out, pulling up his shirt and wiping the sweat off his face, "we should tell Pablito about this new stuff Don Emilio was telling us."

"Don Emilio? How come you're calling him *Don?*" asked Pablito.

"He's our teacher now, so we gotta call him Don Emilio," I answered as I chased down the ball, "as a sign of respect."

"What exactly is he teaching you?"

"He's teaching us to be *brujos,*" Tony said, emphasizing the word *brujo.* "We're gonna learn how to cast spells. Next time you ditch us and leave us to fight off a gang by ourselves, I'll put a spell on you so that you won't be able to run. Your feet are gonna be dragging." Tony walked around very slowly, acting like he was trying to run but was barely able lift his feet. "And they're gonna get closer and closer, and finally they'll catch you. And wham!" He pounded his fist into his palm with a loud pop. "Then we *really* will have your funeral after all."

All three of us busted up laughing.

"Is he really teaching you *that* kind of *brujo* stuff?" Pablito asked, with what sounded like fear in his voice.

"He's going to teach us about his work and about the spiritual side of our culture, our native ancestors' culture," I said. "And it ain't about spells. It's about connection with God and the earth and all living things. About energy and stuff like that."

"Oh, man, I don't believe it. You guys gonna get religious." He raised his hands toward the sky, laughing, while he yelled out, "You gonna get saved, hallelujah!"

"Well, I've already been saved," I said. "Don Emilio saved our butts from those guys. I want to keep learning from him. He's going to show us how to make good things happen in our lives, and how to get what we want. As far as spending my time, I think it's better than just hanging around doing nothing. And maybe it will help keep us out of this gangbanging, drug dealing pit that guys are falling into. You should join us, Pablito. Maybe you'll live longer."

"Hell, I don't think I'm gonna live to be 21. I'll be lucky to get to 25. But I'm not gonna wimp out. I'm gonna go out with a bang. Sounds like you guys are wimping out. We gotta be tough, man. We got this area to protect, people to take care of. That religious crap, where's that, man? How's that gonna take care of your homie or your babe?"

Listen to him, I thought to myself, skinny wimp that he was, talking about wimping out. Protecting your babe. Heck, he ain't never had a girlfriend, that liked him back anyway. What babe did he think he was taking care of? It wasn't any use talking to him about it. He just didn't have a clue.

"Hey guys, I gotta be getting home," Tony called out, taking one last shot. I knew he didn't want to carry on this conversation with Pablito anymore either.

"Well, I guess I better get home too," I said. "That's enough running around for today." It had been hotter there on the court than I thought. My shirt was soaking wet, and sticking to me.

"I'll catch you guys later," said Pablito. "I'm gonna head over to Arturo's. And don't get into any trouble on your way home," he laughed as he started toward the fence gate. He stopped and turned around. "You're not really gonna do none of that *brujo* stuff to me, are you?" He paused and looked like he was thinking about his own question, then said, "Naaaw," waving both hands at us and shaking his head. "Later, you guys." And he turned and walked off the court and out into the park.

I could tell that the gulf between us and Pablito, and the others as well, was beginning to widen. He didn't pick up on any of the positive stuff. He only talked about the imaginary spell Tony made up.

"You know," said Tony as we walked away from the basketball court, "Pablito can really be a jerk sometimes. And the trouble is, he ain't acting. That's how he is. He's a jerk and a loud mouth. He and Arturo take the stupidest risks. And too often we're the ones who end up paying for their stupidity. I'm glad we have a chance to take a new direction, to do something different instead of hanging with them all the time."

"It's definitely different," I said. "Like Don Emilio said, this could change our lives. Man, I'm ready for a change."

"Me too. But like we talked about, I don't want to just move on and forget about our homies, even if some of them are real jerks. If there's something in the teachings that will help us, maybe it can help them too. I mean, we've known them all our lives. They *are* our friends, even though sometimes they don't act like it."

"Well," I said, "Don Emilio did say that our homies could choose this too. I don't mean I want to go in a new direction and just forget about them. Maybe we'll be able to convince them to join us. Maybe they would if we have something to offer."

"Speaking of something to offer," said Tony, stopping to sit for a minute on a bench near the park *kiosko*, "what about the daily breath meditation? You think we could get the guys to do that?" He was grinning because he knew the answer.

"Don't think so," I answered sitting down next to him. "Too boring for them. You know, I didn't think it was going to be so hard to keep my attention focused on my breath. Mostly my mind kept wandering. And when I can't get it to stop thinking all kinds of things, I feel like stopping the exercise. And when I look at the clock, sometimes I still have ten or fifteen minutes to go."

"Yeah, the first few times I didn't finish," said Tony. "I couldn't sit there for the whole twenty minutes. I would find myself breathing faster, trying to drown out the thoughts. I'm glad Don Emilio said not to worry about it and just practice, because it's gotten easier. Some days I can keep my mind on my breathing more."

"For me too," I said. "And the more I practice, the less bor-ing it becomes. When I'm not thinking about stopping and doing something else, it actually feels good to finally get into a groove and just kinda space out, thinking about nothing but each breath."

"I'm glad we still have three more weeks before we have to tell Don Emilio how we did," said Tony. "I'd like to keep practicing and see if I can get a little better at it before then."

<u>12</u>

THE OLD WAYS

*"We are not human beings having a spiritual experience,
we are spiritual beings having a human experience."*

PIERRE TEILHARD DE CHARDIN

We were both so eager to start our next session with Don Emilio that the month just seemed to drag on and on. When the time to meet with him again finally arrived, Tony met me at my house and we ran to Nana and Tata's.

"Good morning," Don Emilio called to us we bounded up to the garden shed.

"Good morning, Don Emilio," I answered as I stepped in and took my seat, breathing a little hard from the short run.

He was inside looking at the potted plants at the west side of the shed. There was a worktable there with most of Nana's pots and flower trays on top, and underneath, her storage area. She had quite a few potted plants, as well as trays of little plants ready to be dug into the garden. Her table looked really nice with all the red, pink, purple, yellow and white flowers, and multiple shades of green leaves. I could see that some of the flower trays had been moved back and to the side to make a clear space in the middle of the table.

"So, Don Emilio," said Tony as he just sort of waved his hello and began right in, even before he sat down, "now that we're learning this ancient spiritual stuff, when are we going to learn how to do mind reading, and being in the right place at the right time?"

"The ancient secrets we will be talking about involve much more than that," he answered, wiping potting soil off his hands. "But before we talk about anything new, I want to know if you had any questions about the breath-focus exercise you practiced."

We both had lots of questions, mostly about falling asleep and wandering thoughts.

"Most beginners have the same problems," he reassured us. "The problem with sleeping will lessen if you get enough rest at night. Also, do not do this exercise right after eating, as a full stomach and relaxation tends to induce sleep. As for wandering thoughts, once you are aware that you are thinking about something else, you simply go back to following the in and out breaths. You may have to shift back and forth quite a few times at first, but with practice it becomes easier to ignore the thoughts floating by and keep focused on the breath."

"I assume you will want us to keep practicing this for a little while more," said Tony. "How many weeks will we have to practice before we can keep the stray thoughts out?"

"While dealing with your thoughts was a major issue for both of you over these past four weeks, that is not the end purpose of this exercise. That was just the first step. Once you get your thoughts under control, you will be able to enter a place of silence where you can connect with the energies of the earth and the universe, and connect with your higher self and other guides. Eventually, you will *want* to make this connection every day because of how you benefit and not because you have to do an exercise each day."

"So, this breathing exercise we practiced, we just do that and then can see into the future and read minds?" I asked.

"No, I am afraid it is not that easy," chuckled Don Emilio. "It is just a beginning point for learning how to work with energy. We will discuss other ways to increase energy, move energy, and stop leaking energy, which help to increase your vibration and your awareness. When you vibrate at a higher rate and have a higher level of awareness, you may have a sense of what a friend may be thinking, or have a strong feeling about what is going to happen.

Tony sat there with a big grin on his face. "Man, that would be really cool if we could do that! But I don't know, this is some pretty strange stuff."

"What I have to share may seem strange at first," said Don Emilio, "but there is nothing to be afraid of. It is simply an ability to see more and be aware of more. I have access to more information and power than you do. Not because I am special, but because your eyes and minds are partially closed to the possibility of this additional information. I say partially closed because part of you *is* aware and wants to share this with the rest of you that lives in ignorance."

"Oh, come on," said Tony. "Why would we choose to live in ignorance?"

"It has been an unconscious process, from the time we are very small until we die. We are pressured by society into believing that *good* people believe only in certain ways, and that other ways of acting and beliefs are wrong. That is why some people believe that only *their* religion is the right religion, or that only *their* way of government is good. An unstated pressure toward conforming results in people just following along, not asking questions, and not following their own intuition. This conformity process goes way back. It was used forcefully by the Spaniards to conquer and convert the native peoples here in the Americas."

"You mean the Spaniards tried to keep the Indians from knowing about their connection with God?" asked Tony. "Why would they do that? I thought they were trying to teach the Indians about God, and to educate them, not keep them ignorant."

"Yes, they were trying to teach the Indians about God," Don Emilio responded, "but about their own version of God, and their own version of religion. The government of Spain and the Catholic Church set out to destroy the culture and spiritual practices of the native people, and to replace these with Spanish Catholicism and Spanish culture. They did this as the most efficient way to conquer and control the diverse populations. In this process, people were punished or even put to death for spiritual beliefs that were contrary to the teachings of the Spanish Church. So the practice of native spirituality, 'the old ways,' had to go under-ground. It had to be hidden from the eyes of Church and gov-ernment officials––hidden so well, in fact, that over time many families lost the knowledge of this ancient spiritual way of life."

Tony and I looked at each other. He seemed as shocked as I was. We had heard about the conquest, but not much about the dirty details. "Is this why you called it the secret teachings?" I asked. "Because it had to be hidden?"

"Yes, and if some in your family believe they should not talk about the 'old ways,' it is because they were taught that you do not talk about these things, either because their families did not believe in them or because it was not safe to do so. I know that your Nana and Tata, Vicente, left Mexico at a young age, before anyone had a chance to teach them more about the old ways. They only learned the first part––that you do not talk about it."

"*'Because he is of the old ways, and people don't like to talk about the old ways.'* That's what my mother said when I first asked about you."

"Well, that is what she was taught. It was not on purpose that your mother or grandparents or great-grandparents kept their families in ignorance. Originally it was for protection; later it was simply from lack of knowledge, and it became one of the many traditions passed down blindly to each generation. Now I am here, at your grandfather's request, to help break that tradition of ignorance and to support the spiritual part of you that knows the truth."

Tony looked confused. "I still don't get it. How can part of me live in ignorance and part of me know the truth? What parts?"

"You have probably been taught that you are a physical being who is born, grows up, lives, dies, and then your soul goes to heaven. But in truth, you are a spiritual being existing in the non-physical void connected to and a part of that one living energy consciousness, and just a portion of you is temporarily occupying your physical human shell.

"The spiritual entity that you are, sent a portion of your consciousness, which some call a soul, to temporarily occupy a physical body. In fact, that spiritual entity, or Higher Self, sends multiple souls out to experience life on earth. The soul of your current human shell carries within itself the knowledge of its Higher Self consciousness, and of its many experiences on earth. It knows that the physical part is only temporary, that it will die away, and that the soul will merge again with its greater or Higher Self.

"During the time that a portion of consciousness exists here on earth within a physical body, the mind usually forgets that there is the larger consciousness of which the being is a part. People come to believe that they are only this physical being they see each day in the mirror. Further, the mind has them believe they are separate from other physical beings and objects in the world, and separate from All-That-Is or God. So part of our work will be to help you reconnect with your Higher Self.

"Now, all persons and objects are not only made of energy, but are surrounded by a field of energy. They appear as balls of energy to some Toltec shamans and others who can see the lines of light energy. We are much more than the physical body that you see.

"Increasing the amount of spiritual energy that you hold in your personal energy field is the first step in connecting with your Higher Self and with that greater energy of which we are all a part. It is through this connection with your Higher Self and with the greater energy consciousness that you will make the changes in your lives that you desire."

"Oh man," said Tony, "like a split personality––definitely not what we've been taught."

"Yeah, but somehow, it feels right. My brain is a little confused, but it sorta makes more sense than what we've been told."

"I understand what you are going through, as I experienced the same thing myself," said Don Emilio. "It is difficult to put this information into words or instructions. Much of this information is non-linear; it comes through the right side of the brain, the side that accesses information differently, not in words, but in images, intuition, or concepts, from other levels of awareness. Some of what you learn will not be words or instructions. You will just 'get it.' This is a lifelong learning process. My intent is to help you get started on that spiritual learning path by showing you some of what you can expect to encounter along the way."

"You don't expect us to learn it all? You're not going to give us a test on ancient spiritual truths?" Tony asked, smiling.

"I hate to disappoint you Antonio," answered Don Emilio smiling back, "but no test. My intent is to expose you to what you already know deep inside. I will show you how to bring your energy up, and to increase your spiritual power, so you can begin to access the ancient truths inside of you."

13

ENERGY CONNECTIONS

"The seer sees that every man is in touch with everything else, not through his hands, but through a bunch of long fibers that shoot out in all directions from the center of his abdomen."

DON JUAN (CARLOS CASTAÑEDA)

Don Emilio rose from his chair and started slowly pacing in front of Nana's worktable. He looked deep in thought for a few moments before turning back to us and continuing.

"I want to talk more about these energy connections. As a human race, we need to reconnect with the earth and all of her energies. It is one way to strengthen our connection with spirit, with God. We have a lot of machines and technology, but we have moved further away from what is real, from what is important. Coming from the native Mexican-Indian culture, we have a tradition of connection with the earth, and with all the powers of the universe."

"Oh, wow!" I blurted out. They both stared at me, surprised at my outburst. "Just a minute. I've got something like that," I said excitedly, as I reached into my back pocket and pulled out my wallet. "Mr. Marin at school has a poster in his office, with a quote by an Indian, a medicine man, I think. I liked what it said, so I copied it down." I unfolded a small piece of yellow lined paper and read it out loud.

"The first peace, which is the most important, is that which comes within the souls of people when they realize their relationship, their oneness, with the Universe and all its powers––Black Elk." I stood there, staring at the yellow paper in my hand.

"Yes, native cultures have known this for centuries and centuries," said Don Emilio. "But it is not just a concept or a nice idea. Black Elk and the ancients knew this as a fact. We are actually literally connected to all things around us."

"Actually connected? What do you mean?" asked Tony.

"Some of our people, especially some shamans, can see the luminous fibers, lines of energy that make up our energy field, and which extend beyond that to connect us. You may even learn to see these lines." Don Emilio looked directly at me.

"Lines of energy?" I asked.

"Yes," he said, smiling. "Very thin filaments of light. They are like invisible lines, like a web of energy connecting all living things." He paused, looking at me. "Everything is connected by this unimaginable maze of energy pathways." Don Emilio kept looking at me.

Then it hit me. "Oh, of course! No wonder I liked that poster. My dream!"

In my dream, I saw the lines of light connecting me, the eagle, with everything else. In the dream, I really felt a connection with everything! I was surprised that such a significant event in my life as that dream faded away so that I didn't even remember it until Don Emilio coaxed me with his pointed looks. It had been about two months since I had that dream.

"How come I didn't remember?" I asked, somewhat embarrassed. "I know about the lines of light, from my dream. How come I forgot?"

"You did not forget," he responded. "Not totally. Perhaps your mind pushed this information away, as it is not part of the worldview it is comfortable with. But it seems that another part of you attempted to bring the information to a conscious level through the poster."

"Sounds like a chess game is going on inside there," said Tony.

"A whole lot more is going on inside you than you are aware of. But let us get back to the strands of light energy, the connecting rays. This light energy is the essence of our existence, the basis of all life, and it helps us to understand how we are all connected. Light energy is not only sunlight warming the earth. It is light transformed by plants and animals into food energy. It is the energy that runs through the earth's own electric and magnetic grid lines, some of which runs through our individual human energy system. It is a great inter-connected grid of energy. We are all connected––and all a part of each other."

"Can we feel this energy flowing?" asked Tony.

"Yes, you can. Energy flowing from our bodies travels along those luminous fibers. It also can be seen or felt as energy radiating from our bodies, in what is called an *aura*. Some people can see auras. Energy also flows off our hands and fingers. I will show you what I mean." He started rubbing his hands together. "Bring your hands together and rub your palms back and forth quickly, like this, for about ten seconds. Then, slowly separate your hands, moving them away from each other. Now slowly bring your palms toward each other again, until they are almost touching."

I could feel warmth and a tingling in my hands as we did this.

"Now, move them apart a few inches, then back, then out and back again." He paused. "What did you feel?"

"It felt like I was sorta squeezing something between my hands!" Tony said with surprise. "Then it felt like I was stretching it when I moved my hands away. That's weird."

"Rather than weird," he corrected Tony, "it is simply natural to become aware that you have an energy field around you, and it extends beyond your hands. It has mass. You can squeeze it, let it expand back out, and send energy out through it. It is a very powerful force, yet very much a part of our daily lives. Energy is not something that runs only in the electric wires. It circulates through us and around us. We can get it moving within us at a greater intensity through yoga, martial arts, or other energy-moving disciplines.

"As I mentioned, energy also runs between beings by means of those invisible luminous fibers. All matter is basically energy that is interconnected by these thin lines. This is what the medicine man Black Elk was referring to when he talked about our oneness with the universe. We feel we are one, we feel connected––and we actually *are* connected. On an energy level, you and I and the trees and the rocks are each a ball of energy, with many fine lines of energy coming out of the balls of light, connecting to everything in the universe."

He paused to let that sink in. As we sat there in the quiet, I had a flash of inspiration.

"Don Emilio! I was just trying to imagine everything connected to everything else, and it was really hard to think about how that could be. But thinking back to my dream, I could see it!"

"Yes, the dreaming side of you knows the truth, that everything is energy and everything is connected. As with the electricity in the wires, all energy and all matter vibrate at a certain frequency, and the higher the energy level, the higher the rate of vibration. We are connected to everything, but our connection with other people and things is stronger when the other's vibration rate is similar or close to ours.

"Your first major task then, is to learn how to increase your energy. When your energy is higher, you vibrate at a higher rate. In this state of higher energy vibration, you will then find that you move beyond day-to-day concerns, things will seem to go well in your lives, and things will come to you at the right time."

"Things we need coming to us, and life going well––I could go for that," said Tony.

"As we discussed before, according to the ancient shamans there is an amazing, indescribable energy that permeates the universe, which they called *Intent,* and which others refer to as the *Force.* Everything in the universe is connected to everything else by means of the thin filaments of energy. When we have sufficient levels of personal energy and then focus our attention on what we want, the Force uses those connections to make things happen to bring those items to us. This is the magical nature of the universe."

"Now we're getting somewhere," said Tony. "This stuff about balls of energy and vibration is sort of confusing. But if this is how to get the life we want, that's what I want to learn about."

"Okay," I said, "so if we work on increasing our energy and our connection with this Force, we will get what we want, like good grades, a job, money, a new car?"

"It is not quite that simple," said Don Emilio, "but yes, that is the general process. Take the example of a new job. When you consciously increase your energy, you open yourself up to receiving insights about what you need to do to make that new job happen. Maybe you get inspired to go over to the youth center, and while there you see a job notice on the bulletin board. On the other hand, if your energy is low, you may be less able to receive the insight, and it may never occur to you to go over to the youth center. So you end up missing that opportunity.

"You have to be clear about what you want, and aware of your spiritual energy level. Now about what I called "spirit warriors," we use the term *warriors* because, as in a military campaign, we make a commitment to be constantly on duty, maintaining our focus on saving, increasing, and using our energy to strengthen our connection with spirit."

"Oh man! Constantly on duty?" Tony asked. "Constantly working on increasing energy? Why would someone want to do that all the time?" It sounded like these warriors really got a raw deal.

"As I said before, you will at some point decide how important it is to you to continue working with this spirit power, this awareness. Each of you will decide if you want to live this life of spiritual awareness, and if so, what you will do to incorporate this knowing and power into your life. Let me point out that it is not necessary to be a full spirit warrior or a shaman to benefit from what you will learn. As we get a little further into the teachings, you will understand why a spirit warrior chooses to constantly be aware of opportunities to increase his or her energy."

We stopped there for the day. As we left, Tony and I walked along the side of the house. When we reached the front yard, we were both surprised by Tata's voice.

"Hola, Vicentillo y Antonio." He was sitting there alone on the porch, taking in some sun.

"Hola, Señor Castro."

"Buenos días Tata. How are you feeling today?" I knew Tata had been sick lately.

"Oh, not very well," he said speaking in Spanish. "But I am better right now, sitting here enjoying the sun. And you two, how go the classes with Emilio? What are you learning?"

Tony and I looked at each other. Where to start?

"There is so much to learn, Tata," I answered in English, hoping he could understand me. "I'm beginning to understand some of it, like he says—that everything is energy, that everything in the world is connected, and how we have to raise our energy level. There is just so much! And we've just started!"

Tata just looked at me with a blank stare. I could tell he hadn't understood all of what I'd said. And I couldn't say it in Spanish. I looked at Tony. His Spanish was a little better than mine.

"Hey, don't look at me," said Tony. "I barely know what this stuff is in English."

We both looked at Tata sheepishly.

"Está bien. Yo lo entiendo un parte. I understood a part. *Bueno, váyanse."*

As we walked away, Tony said to me, "It must be pretty hard on you, not being able to understand your Nana and Tata all the time. I'm lucky. My grandparents speak more English than yours, and my Spanish is better than yours."

"Yeah, it's especially hard because I'd like to talk to Tata about this stuff we are learning, and he seems to want to know. But I don't know how to get it across to him, in English *or* Spanish."

"Well, I can hardly grasp it myself, much less talk with anyone about it," said Tony. "Eventually, though, we have to figure out a way to make it easier to understand if we're gonna talk about any of this with the guys. They're gonna ask us about this stuff sooner or later."

"Yeah, you're right," I said, not really focusing on what he was saying. I was still thinking about Tata, and that I'd have to figure out a way to tell him what I'd learned—after I'd learned it.

14
___

BASEBALL AND ENERGY CONNECTIONS

*"Intuition is really a sudden immersion of the soul into
the universal current of life."*

PAULO COELHO, *THE ALCHEMIST*

"Hey man, take a look at this!" Tony was looking through his binoculars toward the Padres' bullpen. "Look at the guy in the stands next to the bullpen pitchers' mound. He's talking to Luis DeLeon, one of the guys warming up. And he was just shaking his hand. Doesn't he look familiar?" He handed me the glasses.

"Here, hold my hot dog for me," I said, "and don't eat any of it. I don't have much left." Tony had already inhaled his hot dog. I looked through the binoculars and found the bullpen. "No way! It can't be. That looks like Don Emilio! But I don't think so. I knew he was still in town, but he never said anything about going to a Padres game or even liking baseball."

"Let me look again," said Tony reaching for the binoculars as he chewed on something. I saw fresh mustard and ketchup on his face. "Yep, that's him. I recognize his blue windbreaker."

"Look at him," I exclaimed, "talking up a storm with DeLeon like they were old friends."

"DeLeon just shook his hand again, then went back to warming up," said Tony. "Don Emilio's waving goodbye and walking up the aisle." Tony put the glasses down. "Well, I'll be! All the years we've been coming, and we've never been able to shake anybody's hand."

"That's because we sit out here in the cheap seats," I said. We were seated in the middle of a general admission section, five rows up, and about 15 feet above the center fielder's head.

"I wish we were sitting up close to the action!"

"You should try increasing your energy and your vibration," I said grinning.

"I have! I've been focusing on my breathing all week, and on being closer to the action at this game, but it didn't work. I really wanted to see this game up close because the Dodgers are my favorite team after the Padres. I was hoping I'd be able to come up with the extra seven dollars to get a field level seat near the bullpen."

"And an extra seven for mine. See, that's why you didn't get it, you were only thinking about yourself. You weren't putting that energy into a good seat for me too."

"Well," responded Tony, "one day I'll have a job that pays decent money and I'll be able to afford good seats. Two of them."

We continued watching the players warming up, as the Dodgers came off the field, and the Padres went on for infield practice. Tony looked back toward the bullpen with his binoculars. "Don Emilio isn't back in his seat yet. I wonder where he went?"

"*Hola mijos!*" Don Emilio called out to us as he stood at the end of our row of seats. "Nice night for a ballgame, *que no?*"

"Hey, Don Emilio!" Tony shouted, waving my empty hot dog wrapper. Our teacher made his way past an elderly couple sitting at the end of the row, squishing their peanut shells as he stepped in front of them. "How did you find us?"

"And how did you even know we were here?" I asked, as he sat down next to Tony. "We saw you through the binoculars, sitting over by the bullpen."

"Oh, I had a feeling you'd be coming to the game. I thought about coming, but was not sure I would be able to until late this afternoon. Then I had no way of contacting you after you left home. Did you ride the bus?"

"Yeah. We rode the Padre Express from Horton Plaza Park downtown," I said.

"So how did you know where to find us?" Tony asked again.

"Well, I had narrowed it down to the outfield bleacher seats. I figured you did not have much money to spend on tickets, because I was sure you would want to save some to spend on food. Nothing like good hot dogs at a baseball game, *que no*? Even in Mexico, I like to eat hot dogs at the games."

"Yeah, Tony *really* likes ball game hot dogs," I said sarcastically. "He had two of them."

"But you must have walked right to our aisle," Tony persisted, ignoring my hot dog whining. "We saw you leave your seat just a little while ago, so you didn't have time to search for us in all the aisles and seats,"

"I did not search for you. My life as a shaman is about energy work. I followed our energy connection. Other than the pitcher Luis DeLeon, you are the only ones here that I have a strong energy connection with. I picked up your strong enthusiasm for the baseball game, so I focused my energy on our connection and allowed my body to follow that connection. I walked along the main walkway up there, and turned down this aisle because it 'felt' right. As I walked down the aisle, I did not have any intuition about you sitting at the top and I did not feel any connection on the right side of the aisle either. So I looked over to the left side as I continued walking down the aisle, and there you were."

"He's amazing," Tony said as he turned to me. We both just shook our heads.

"Well," Don Emilio continued as he stood up, "the game will start soon. Come on!" He was looking straight at Tony.

"Where to?" Tony asked.

"Next to me, over by the bullpen. I have tickets for both of you, complements of Luis. If we hurry, maybe we can see him before he leaves the bullpen pitching mound."

Tony and I just looked at each other in surprise. Then off we scrambled, following Don Emilio. We reached the seats just in time for Don Emilio to introduce us to DeLeon, a relief pitcher for the Padres. And we got to shake his hand before he sat down with the other pitchers in the bullpen.

"Man, what a night," said Tony. "Great seats, and we finally got to shake hands with one of the Padres. Amazing!"

"Yeah, and you got to eat two hot dogs."

Tony laughed, and turned toward Don Emilio. "I've been wanting this for a long time."

"You have been focusing energy on that thought, and made it happen," said Don Emilio.

"Well, yes I have been. But that didn't do it," Tony protested. "You're the one who..."

"Do not sell yourself short on your ability to pull in some magical powers from the universe. I think you are the reason I had the urge to go to this game, and the reason Luis had the thought to leave tickets for us, just in case. I had previously told him I occasionally come to San Diego to work with you. You see, that is how it works. That is the magic of the universe. You just worked some magic.

"The examples of energy connections are all around us," he continued. "Many, many people, who know nothing about what you are learning, have experiences where they 'sense' what someone else is thinking, they know what someone is going to say before they say it, or they know when and where a friend is going to be. It is real. And the key to consistently being able to know such information, or getting what you want, is to keep your spiritual energy at a high level, constantly striving to increase your energy and to plug your energy leaks."

"With it being all around us like that, maybe this shamanism stuff is not so weird," said Tony. "It's sorta normal."

"It *is* normal," said Don Emilio. "The only thing different about the shaman's approach is that your ancestors made a science of studying this phenomenon. Shamanism is the science of working with energy, spiritual energy. And because everything in the world is energy, and since all things are related and connected by energy, we know that we are dealing with our connection to Spirit, to God. For us, working with energy is a spiritual practice.

We know that at the core of our beings, humankind innately strives to move closer to the light, closer to union with the Spirit. We know we can do that by working on increasing our spiritual energy. We know that everything we do, think, or say can have an energy-building or energy-depleting consequence.

"That is why in native cultures they refer to the shaman as the holy man. When an older shaman has spent his life striving each day to increase his energy connection with Spirit, he is full of this spiritual energy and is able to do things such as physically heal others by correcting a person's energy imbalance, read minds, or hear messages from animals, trees, water, or the wind. He may achieve a level of spiritual energy where he is truly connected and able to communicate with spirits of nature, his own spirit guides and teachers, and maybe with the saints and angels.

"You do not need to try to become like that holy man. You are simply trying to be as full of spiritual energy as possible. As beginners, you are breaking out of old habits of thought and action that deplete your energy. And you are learning what to incorporate into your daily practice that will help build your spiritual energy and move you closer to a union with Spirit."

15

POWER ANIMAL

"You become what you think about."

EARL NIGHTINGALE

The more that time passed, the more I found I really looked forward to spending time with Don Emilio. The stuff he had talked about so far was not the typical boring stuff we trudged through in school. Some of it sounded strange, but in a good way. I didn't really understand it yet, but I knew these ancient teachings were really important stuff, and that I would eventually want to share it with others. I was glad that Don Emilio and people like him were making an effort to see that this knowledge was preserved.

"Let us talk about your energy practices over the last four weeks," said Don Emilio. Tony and I were happy to be back in the garden shed, ready for another session with him after the break. "Did you get used to feeling the energy between your hands?"

"Stretching the energy and pushing it back was kind of fun," I said. "Each time I felt the energy between my hands it reminded me that we're learning how to move it and use it in ways that most people don't know anything about."

"I found out something really weird," said Tony, looking anxious to share his news. "One night I was in my room and I was doing that pushing and stretching of the energy, and realized that I could hear it! There was like a soft buzz or vibration whenever my hand got close to my face or my ear. And I accidentally found out I could throw the energy off the tip of my fingers."

103

I looked at Tony in great surprise, because he hadn't said anything to me about it.

"I know, I know, I didn't tell you," he said, looking at me. "It freaked me out at first, so I wanted to do it a few more times on different days, just to be sure I wasn't imagining it, or dreaming. I wanted to ask Don Emilio about it first, to be sure. But I know what I heard."

"Tell me what you did," I said as I put my hand up to my ears, trying to hear something. When I cupped my hands on my ears, I could hear a sound.

"No, not that ocean sound. It's more like a low vibration when my hand is flat, or my fingers point straight in. I have trouble hearing it outside during the day—there is too much other sound. At night, inside, when it's quiet, I can hear it."

"Tell us how you discovered you could throw the energy," said Don Emilio.

"I was listening to the sound of the energy coming from my fingers, and was testing to see how far away from my ear my fingers could move before I could no longer hear the buzz. And I discovered that when I flicked my finger I could hear the buzz again for a brief moment. I played with moving my fingers farther away and flicking or pushing the energy toward my ears."

"That is so cool," I said laughing, "I can't wait to try that tonight."

Don Emilio smiled. I could tell by his look that he already knew about this, but he was enjoying hearing Tony explain his great discovery.

"I have a question," said Tony. "If this is throwing energy off finger tips, is this similar to how Kung Fu masters send energy from their hands and knock an opponent back?"

"Yes, it is, but it takes a lot of practice to build up and store the tremendous amount of energy required, and a very forceful release. That is quite a way from flicking energy off fingertips, but it is similar. Energy responds to our intent and our action."

"Hey, Tony, this is right up your alley." Then, looking at Don Emilio, I added, "Tony has been taking karate lessons at the youth center, for a long time. He's really good at it."

Don Emilio nodded. "I am not surprised you made this discovery, Antonio, and that you thought it might be related to energy in martial arts. Perhaps you will be able to find a way to combine your knowledge of martial arts with what you will learn in our discussions on energy."

We talked some more about our practice exercises, with both of us reporting better success staying focused on our breath, and reducing the mental chatter. But we still had a lot of thoughts going in and out. Don Emilio told us again not to worry, that with practice we would improve.

"Before I talk any more *about* this path of our ancestors, this way of being," said Don Emilio, "I want you to actually *experience* a small part of it for yourselves. Both of you relax there in your chairs, like we did before. Close your eyes and take a few deep breaths, exhaling fully."

I sat up straighter and adjusted my feet so I felt more comfortable, and took some deep breaths.

"Breathe normally for a few minutes, focusing on your breath." Don Emilio spoke slowly. His deep resonating voice was calming and relaxing.

"We are going to shift now," he said softly as drumming music started playing, "from focusing on the breath, to a different focus—an inner journey." He paused briefly while we listened to the beating of the drums, which relaxed me even more.

"Imagine yourself now in a beautiful mountain setting, perhaps in a place familiar to you or one you can imagine, with lots of tall trees, colorful flowers, and lush green grasses. You are walking along a trail in this beautiful setting, and you come to a small clearing, where you stop for a few moments to enjoy the surroundings." He paused.

"Now you notice a path leading away from the main trail, a path that goes up the side of a hill, higher and higher into what looks like a layer of white clouds. You leave the main trail and follow the path as it gently climbs up into the clouds. You find it refreshing as you move into the coolness of the cloud mist.

"As you continue walking you see an animal emerge from the mist. You keep going and you recognize this animal, because it is one you are interested in, your favorite animal! Now, remember, this is a non-physical journey, so the wild animal cannot injure you. Keep walking on this path until the animal comes up to you." He paused again briefly. "Finally, the animal comes close, and you meet your power animal, an animal spirit that has chosen you for mutual learning. Go up to the animal, greet it, touch it, and get to know it."

Don Emilio asked us both to nod yes if we had met our animal yet. Keeping my eyes closed, I nodded. After a few moments, he continued.

"Most likely, you do not really know much about your power animal. Just like a human friend, you will want to get to know it—where it lives, its behaviors and strengths, how it views the world. But you cannot really get to know your power animal unless you can become one with it. Your power animal is prepared to let you do just that, to merge with it, to do what we call *shape shifting,* so that you can see the world from its eyes.

"So, thank your animal friend in advance for this great favor, and now, merge your awareness with it. Do not look at two objects merging. Rather, *be* your awareness on that path in the clouds. See yourself moving closer as you go inside and finally merge with your power animal. See and feel yourself become this animal.

"Look out from that animal's eyes. See what your skin looks like, what your hands and feet look like. Discover how it feels to be that animal. Move around, the way your power animal moves around. Look around the way that animal looks around. Spend some time *being* this animal. Let it take you to where it lives. See where it rests and sleeps. Be aware of where it takes you and how you get there. Get to know its territory, and how it moves about there."

He paused to let us be with the animal. After a few minutes of quiet, he began again.

"Now, while you are merged with your power animal, I want you to leave this forest path and transport yourselves back to your human home, Barrio Logan, San Diego. Start from any location here." He paused for a few moments to give us time to find ourselves in Barrio Logan.

"Begin to move away from your starting point so you can see more of the neighborhood and perhaps the surrounding community. Move about just as your animal would move…. Examine the area you can see. Make a note of items that catch your eye."

He paused again so we could follow his instructions and look around.

"Continue your movement. Maybe you want to move out farther. What do you see? You see a lot, but what do you really notice that you didn't notice before? Keep looking with your animal's eyes and instincts. Move out farther, or closer if you need to, to see what your animal wants you to see. Notice anything that catches your attention."

He paused again for a while, and I continued to experience the strange sensation of looking out of different eyes. I could feel myself moving back and forth, from an awareness of myself as my animal, to an awareness of myself, and back. It was strange to be doing that. Physically it felt strange too, like an electric charge going through me.

After what seemed like a long period of silence, Don Emilio's voice brought me slowly back from what felt like a deep dream, as he spoke softly.

"Okay, I want you to slowly separate from your power animal now. Thank your animal spirit for allowing you to merge with it, and allow it to leave. Take a few seconds to come back. You may want to just wiggle your fingertips and your toes, or move your hands or feet just a bit to help yourself come back to the garden shed this afternoon. Now, slowly open your eyes."

"Hey, trippy, man," said Tony, sounding groggy. "I feel like I'm a little high."

"I really zoned out," I said. "I was totally gone, but your voice shocked me when you spoke. It was like I was dreaming and you woke me up."

"Yeah, it was like a dream," said Tony, "but one that I could change."

"Not everyone can follow a guided journey the first time and go that deeply into a trance state," said Don Emilio. "Some have difficulty visualizing. That was good. Let us talk about it. What animal did you become? Antonio, you first."

"Well, I've always liked the wolf, *el lobo,* the grey wolf. I have a poster of one in my room. It felt comfortable for me to be a wolf. I was really able to imagine myself as one, to walk like a wolf. Vincent," Tony said, turning to me, "I bet you were an eagle."

"No brainer, I've always felt a connection with the eagle. Especially after that dream I had. So, I sorta know what it's like to be an eagle. When you had us move around like the animal, I was immediately flying."

"Describe your animal's actions, Antonio," Don Emilio continued. "Describe what you saw as you moved around the neighborhood. What caught your eye, or rather, your animal's eye?"

"The wolf ... well, I stayed in Barrio Logan, circling around the neighborhood, going back and forth, seeing what was there, realizing that no one could see me. I looked at businesses, homes, cars, yards with plants and flowers, yards full of weeds and trash, and graffiti on the walls. With each step I felt the earth, listened for danger, and watched, always on the lookout, watching people going about their business.

"Next, I found myself inside the youth center watching a karate class. I started stalking again, watching the instructor going through his moves, then moving to the back of the room, watching the kids as they practiced the moves. I saw some were just going through the motions, not really caring if they were doing it right. Others were trying hard to get it right."

Tony paused, and seemed ready to ask a question, but Don Emilio spoke first.

"I know you have a lot of questions Antonio, but first, let's hear what Vicente saw." They both turned to look at me.

"It felt so great to be back in the sky again, flying free. I felt full of power and so happy. After a while I realized I hadn't gone anywhere but up, so I started to move outward and could see long distances because I was up so high. I was up so high that I noticed things more on a large scale than in smaller details. I saw the freeways, major roads, the bay, the green of Balboa Park, the business district downtown, then the houses up in Hillcrest and North Park. I noticed the business district strips along University Avenue and El Cajon Boulevard, with groups of houses and apartments on both sides.

"As I looked to the east I could see San Diego State. Suddenly I was flying out over the college, circling around it, looking at all the buildings, the traffic, and all the people moving around. That's where I was when your voice came in, Don Emilio, and then it all faded away."

"Well done. You both saw a lot of detail, which is very good for the first time. You discovered your 'power animal,' as we call it, and experienced what it felt like to be that animal. Then you saw what your power animal wanted you to see. You successfully completed half of the exercise. The second half will be equally important. Your task is to figure out what this journey meant. What was your animal spirit trying to tell you? Why did your animal notice what it saw?

"Antonio," said Don Emilio with sudden authority in his voice, "tell me quickly, and do not worry about what anybody would say or think. Say the first thing that comes to mind. Why do you think your power animal took you to the youth center?"

Tony hesitated at first, and then quickly responded.

"Well, I'm taking a karate class there, but I didn't recognize the kids or the instructor."

"What did you notice? What struck you about what you saw there?"

"I was surprised at how different the kids were in their ability to follow the instructor, or maybe about whether they cared to follow and do it right."

"And does that mean anything to you?"

"Well, I could see that some were doing it wrong and I wanted to go up there and help them do it right, but I knew they couldn't see me. It was like I wanted to help teach the class. I think I'd like to do that in the future."

"And you, Vicente," Don Emilio said with that sudden authority again, "tell us why your power animal had you looking at freeways, roads, parks, business districts and housing areas. When have you thought about that before?"

"I went to some meetings with my father where city planners from downtown put up maps for Barrio Logan showing those kinds of things. I remember thinking that I might like doing studies like those planners to improve the community. When I saw the city from the eagle's view, it was a lot like looking at those planning maps. But I don't know why I was looking at San Diego State. You think maybe I'm gonna go there and star on the baseball team?"

I looked over at Tony, and he just rolled his eyes.

"Do you think so?" Don Emilio asked.

"Nah, I was just kidding. I can't hit a curve ball. My career is over." Tony and I both laughed while Don Emilio smiled, doing all he could to keep from laughing.

"So," he said, trying to stay on the subject, "what else about San Diego State?"

"I don't know. I haven't thought much about college."

"Not to butt in or analyze what's being said," Tony added, glancing quickly at Don Emilio, "but I read last month in the *El Sol* newspaper something about a city planning program at State, and about students doing internships around the city, including Barrio Logan."

"So maybe my eagle is telling me to go to San Diego State?"

"Or perhaps to look into it," said Don Emilio. "In Antonio's case, his power animal seemed to encourage him to pursue thoughts he already had about teaching karate. In your case, Vicente your eagle spirit gave you new information, perhaps encouraging you to go to San Diego State."

Tony had a confused look on his face as he motioned to Don Emilio.

"Yes, Antonio?"

"Hold it a minute. What is going on here? How can this wolf know what I was thinking, when I was barely thinking about it? If it was reading my mind, how did Vincent's eagle come up with information that he wasn't even thinking? Where is the eagle getting this information?"

"Those are good questions. The Toltecs and other native cultures of the Americas believe that the spirit of an animal has chosen to be one of your guides and helpers. On a spirit level, you have agreed to accept its help. This animal spirit has been with you for some time now and knows your thoughts, dreams, and your subconscious thoughts. It knows other information, too, from its observation or other sources, and it can try to share that information with you."

"But what if I have trouble believing that?" Tony asked.

"Well, another belief is that this power animal spirit is really an image created by your own Higher Self as a way to provide you with new information and inspiration."

Oh man, I was having trouble following this before. Now he was losing me. "I remember you mentioned this before, but we didn't go into it much. What's my subconscious, and how did information about San Diego State get in there? And the Higher Self--that's what our soul is a part of?"

"I have the same questions," said Tony. "How is talking about things like a Higher Self going to help us? And this stuff about animal spirits, how is thinking about or dreaming about a wolf or eagle spirit going to help us?"

"It is important to know how these can help you," Don Emilio explained. "My intention is to walk you through a number of experiences and techniques that can help you to increase your spiritual energy and awareness, and open up lines of communication with nonphysical guides who may be of help to you, such as angels, spirit beings, your Higher Self, or power animals.

"The power animals have a unique way of accessing information, based on their own animal nature. As you learn to connect with your animal spirit, and get more in tune with its nature, you will more easily access information not available by other means. How you approach certain situations, or the actions you take, may reflect your animal's knowledge or nature."

"Uhh," Tony grunted, still looking confused. "Can you give me an example?"

"Well, say for example you were learning the next level of karate moves. Approaching it from your wolf nature, instead of just standing in a line with the other students and practicing the moves, you might want to observe the teacher in detail, seeing the move from every angle. You might even want to watch a video to learn different techniques. Part of your wolf nature might be to eventually teach it. Many native cultures view the wolf people as the clan of teachers. The individual with the wolf nature returns to the clan to share what he has learned.

"Okay, I see what you mean," said Tony. "It's true; I think I learn best by watching the instructor doing each move. Just practicing it after a short demonstration doesn't work as well for me. I need to see it done, over and over, so I know I've got it right. And I think it would be pretty cool to teach karate."

"What about the eagle?" I asked. "How can the eagle help me?"

"First of all, understand that you both have access to the help of both animal spirits as you focus on them, get to know and understand their nature, and take time to connect with their spirits. But each of you has a stronger connection to the spirit of the animal you already identified. Now, regarding the eagle, because it soars so high in the heavens and has such great vision, native peoples associate the eagle with the Great Spirit. Eagle vision helps you to take a broader view of issues you encounter, and to find answers without getting bogged down in the fine details. This ability to see beyond the day-to-day issues is also related to being able to dream or envision the future, being a visionary."

"Now, back to the previous questions. The *conscious self* is your everyday awareness through which you perceive the world. Your *subconscious* deals with the functioning of the body, instinct, emotions, and access to memory, including thoughts hidden away. It is through our Higher Self that the conscious self and subconscious self are able to receive insight and inspiration from spirit guides and angels. We will discuss these more in a later session.

Tony shook his head and blinked a few times. "I have more questions, but I can wait."

"It is important that you know about this," Don Emilio continued. "That is why I am telling you a little now, but I do not want to overwhelm you. I think this has been plenty for one day."

16

CAGED BIRD

*"You don't have to work at being in the high vibration
that is natural to you. But you do have to stop holding
the thoughts that cause you to lower your vibration. It's a
matter of no longer giving your attention to things that don't allow you
to vibrate in harmony with who you really are."*

ABRAHAM (ESTHER HICKS)

Tony was waiting for me at the bus stop bench by his house. We had decided to take a trip to the zoo, which Don Emilio had suggested might be a good way to learn more about our power animal. He also encouraged us to do some research in the library if we had a chance. So I had gone to the downtown library, and brought along my notes to share with Tony.

"I want to hear what you've got. I've got my notes too," said Tony, as he pulled a sheet of paper from his back pocket and unfolded it. "Let's read them while we wait for the bus."

"Okay, I'll do mine. *The eagle is thought of as a sacred bird because it flies the highest and closest to the Great Spirit. It also has really powerful vision, able to see long distances. Native Americans say eagle medicine connects us with the Great Spirit and helps to awaken our inner vision and intuition, and also helps us to see our outer surroundings with greater clarity and insight. They also say that the fearless eagle, flying so high and free, gives us the courage to face our problems, and encourages us to spread our wings and break free from limiting thoughts."*

"Hey, that was pretty good," said Tony, "especially that part about awakening inner visions, and courage to face problems. Very much like what Don Emilio told us."

"Yeah, and I like the part about spreading our wings and breaking free. And the wolf?"

"Wait, before I read mine—you didn't get that out of an encyclopedia, did you?"

"No, I got different parts of it from books on Native Americans and animals. And you?"

"Oh, I just used an encyclopedia and *National Geographic* in the school library. I got some good stuff too. Listen to this: *The gray wolf looks similar to a German shepherd dog, with a thick, shaggy gray coat, mixed with black and brown, erect ears, and a bushy tail. The typical adult male weighs 100 to 120 pounds. They can run short distances at more than 30 miles per hour. They live and hunt in packs of 6 to 10, and can cover 12 miles or more in a day. They are territorial by nature and can be aggressive towards other packs, using their high-pitched howl to warn other wolves not to come into their territory.*"

"Hey," I said laughing, "that last part sounds like gangs protecting their turf."

"Yeah, it does. Maybe we should practice howling along with everything else we practice."

"Aaoooooo!" I responded.

"No, really, I'm serious," said Tony. "I saw a kung fu movie on TV, and the good guy used a high-pitched howl to shake up his opponents. I think it might be good for me to incorporate a blood-curdling howl into my karate moves, to bring the power and spirit of the wolf into my moves. Don't you think that would be pretty cool?"

"HAAOOOOOOO!" I screamed.

"HAAOOOOOOOOOOOOOOOOOOO!" screamed Tony, sounding really menacing. I thought he must have already been practicing.

Thank goodness the bus arrived just in time to save our vocal cords. We rode into downtown and transferred to the route 7 bus that went up Park Boulevard and into Balboa Park. After a short ride we got off and were walking toward the zoo when we heard a familiar voice.

"Hi guys!"

It was Gloria. She and her sister Linda were coming from the main part of the park, walking toward the zoo entrance.

"My, what a surprise meeting you here," Linda said, with a hint of sarcasm in her voice.

"Yeah, what a coincidence," I said, looking at Tony. I remembered that during the week, I had mentioned to Gloria that Tony and I were going to the zoo on Saturday. She seemed curious why we were going. I just told her we had to do some research for our work with Don Emilio.

"You girls want to go into the zoo with us?" Tony asked, knowing they didn't.

"Uh, no," said Gloria, "Linda and I were just getting some walking exercise."

"Uh ... yeah, walking exercise," said Linda. Clearly, Linda hadn't wanted to do this.

"We're waiting for my little sister," Gloria continued. "She's taking a guitar class over at the Centro Cultural. We gave her a ride and decided to walk around a little."

"Nice place to get some exercise," said Tony.

"She wanted the exercise, not me," Linda chimed in. "But since I've got your attention, what in the heck are you two fools doing still hanging out with your hoodlum buddies? I've been telling Gracie and Alice that you two had better watch it with those guys. But they said you don't listen, and that everyone has been telling you the same thing."

"Linda!" said Gloria, surprised by her outburst.

"Well, it's true!" Linda insisted. Then, looking first at me, then at Tony, she said, "Anyway, what's this about a—*ow!*"

Gloria elbowed Linda and cut her off in mid-sentence, saying to me, "We heard you've been over at your grandfather's house meeting with his cousin from Mexico every week."

It sounded like Nana had been giving Doña Rosa the full blow by blow.

"They say he's teaching you some things about old Mexican ways. But I was wondering ... I mean, we were wondering, how come you want to study with a ... a...."

"*Brujo*!" Linda blurted, like she couldn't wait to get the word out. "We heard you're taking lessons from a *brujo*." Her voice escalated. "That could be as bad as your other trouble, or worse, you know! Gracie said he's your relative and he's a good person, but I don't know. I've heard a lot of bad things about *brujo*s. When our Nana heard about you studying with him, she crossed herself and started praying for you." Gloria elbowed Linda harder, trying to make her stop.

"Oh, we don't meet with him every week," I said.

"Right now, we're just practicing a few ancient pagan rituals," Tony added enthusiastically, "using chickens and...."

"I knew it!" hissed Linda. "Nana said that *brujos* do these pagan rituals with chickens. She was right! That's what he's teaching them!"

"Come on, Tony," I begged, "cut it out! They're gonna think that's what we're learning."

"So ... you're just kidding ... right?" asked Gloria, not sure of the answer.

"Of course I'm just kidding," Tony answered. "You don't really think Vincent and I would be doing ritual sacrifices with chickens right there in his grandmother's back yard, do you?"

"Well, no," said Gloria, "but I...."

"We do that in *my* grandmother's back yard, with *her* chickens!"

"EEK!! screamed Linda, as Gloria stood there with her mouth open, staring at Tony.

"Oh ... you guys!" said Gloria, as she laughed weakly, finally getting the joke. She turned toward her sister, who wasn't laughing, and said emphatically, "Hey, they were kidding!"

"Really, Linda," I said. "He was kidding. Don Emilio isn't the kind of *brujo* who deals with black magic and rituals with animals. He's teaching us about connecting with God and other spirits, and about the energies that connect all things in the universe."

"Then you guys aren't really studying anything about animals like we heard?" Linda asked.

"I don't know what you've heard, but we did learn about our power animals," said Tony.

"We learned how to connect with the spirit consciousness of our power animal—the eagle for me, and the wolf for Tony."

"Power animals? Spirit consciousness? What in the heck are you guys talking about?" Linda asked.

"Well," I answered, not wanting to get into too much detail for fear of screwing it up worse than we had so far, "after we've learned a little more, maybe we can tell you about it."

"Hey, I feel really connected to the eagle," said Gloria. "Is that my power animal?"

"Could be, just like me." I answered, smiling at her, and thinking to myself that teaching her about this stuff would be a great way to be able to spend a little time with her.

"Well, I still don't think my grandmother or my mother would want us involved with any of this *brujo* stuff," Linda quickly interjected.

I could feel my smile fall right off. Gloria saw my expression change and quickly reached up and gently pinched me on the cheek. "We'll see, Vinnie," she said smiling, "we'll see."

Ah, those big brown eyes of hers, and that smile! She put a big grin right back on my face.

Linda looked at her watch. "Gloria, we better get going."

"You guys have fun," said Gloria, waving goodbye. "See you around."

"And leave those chickens alone," Linda called out laughing as they walked away.

After they got far enough away, Tony said, "I think she's in love with you."

"Aw, Tony, come on. She's just a friend. She's not *in love* with me."

"Well then, she's definitely *in like* with you. And she's gonna want to know more about what we learn from Don Emilio. Heck, she's gonna have to learn enough from you on the sly to be able to get her mother and grandmother to back off."

"I sure hope she succeeds," I said with that big grin still on my face, "because I wouldn't mind being able to spend more time with her. I wouldn't mind that at all."

Inside the zoo, it was like another world, with its many colors, sounds and smells. The first thing one sees is the flamingos exhibit, with many of these beautiful pink birds just standing there motionless on one long leg. There was constant chatter above, from the soft chirping of small local birds flying freely, to the loud *caw, caw,* from larger exotic caged varieties.

"Let's go check out our power animals," said Tony. "Yours is closest."

We walked toward the bird section, weaving in and out of the crowd of slower moving people, which thinned out as we moved away from the main entrance. On the way, we passed the monkey enclosures, and could hear lots of monkey chatter, including the loud *whoop, whoop, whoop* calls. When at the zoo, I usually stopped to watch the monkeys chasing each other, swinging around their enclosures, hanging by arms, legs, or tails. But not this time. I wanted to get to the birds, which were just past the monkeys. Once there, I immediately went to the eagle exhibit. Talk about sad. In my dream, I saw the eagle flying free, able to sail with the wind through the clouds. This poor guy was all alone in a cage that was only about 20 by 20 and 15 feet high.

"Man, this isn't the place to get to know my animal. I should get my parents to take me out to the zoo's Wild Animal Park. I understand eagles fly out by that area."

"Well, we're here," said Tony. "So do your exercises, and then we'll go see the wolves."

"Yeah, you're right," I said. I sat down on the bench in front of the eagle cage. An elderly couple was standing up close to the cage, blocking my view. I figured they'd eventually leave, so I closed my eyes and took a few deep breaths, relaxed my body, and then just focused my attention on my normal breathing, in ... and out ... trying to reduce the voices in my head, and to block out the monkey chatter. When I opened my eyes, the couple had gone.

The eagle was in the back of his cage. I closed my eyes again, and now, in a light trance, I projected myself in my mind out toward the eagle, like I had done on the shamanic journey. I imagined myself right inside the cage with the eagle and focused on sending him my energy, right out from my heart. I did this for a few minutes with my eyes closed.

When I opened my eyes, the eagle had moved closer to the front of the cage and was looking at me! I was starting to feel really good about being here, but as I sat there watching him, I suddenly had this very bad feeling, like a deep sadness. I closed my eyes, and immediately I was thinking about my dream. I was sailing around, flying free, and I wanted to be back there.

Suddenly the loud ruffling of feathers brought me back. I opened my eyes just in time to see the eagle slowly bring his outstretched wings back close to his body, as if again realizing he was in this small cage, and wasn't going to be flying out of there anytime soon. That's how I felt sometimes too, confined by the cage of everyone's rules and expectations, telling me what to do and when to do it, where to be and when to go, what to study and when to learn it by, and what kind of grade I had to get. I often wished I was older, past my teens. Then I would be able to make my own decisions, and do what I wanted to do.

I closed my eyes again and tried to see if I could sense any kind of message from the eagle. But I couldn't get anything. I just continued to feel really bad about the small cage, like the walls were right on top of him. Eagles need to fly free. What was an eagle doing in such a small cage?

"Hey, Vincent, look at what it says here," Tony called out. "The eagles here have been found injured. They take care of them here until they've healed, then they take them out near the Wild Animal Park and let them go. How great. They don't have to be in a cage like this forever."

That made me feel a little better, but I was still irritated at the thought of the eagle being confined in such a small space. I thought perhaps that's why I didn't get any message, or maybe my own feeling of sadness for him got in the way. Anyway, I wanted to get away from there.

"Okay, I'm done," I said. "Let's go see the wolves."

The wolves were kept on the upper mesa, near the western edge of the zoo. The two grey wolves were both female. I sat on a bench away from Tony so he could do his thing. While he was concentrating, both wolves left the back of the enclosure and came up near the front fence. They paced back and forth along the fence, carefully checking out Tony, and looking over at me. They were aware of everything going on around them. They even looked closely at the people walking behind us who didn't come up close to the fence. Eventually they tired of this and strolled to the rear of the enclosure.

When he was done, Tony got up and stretched. I was dying to ask him what he had felt or seen, but decided to wait and let him open up if he wanted to.

"You wanna see anything else?" he asked.

"Not really. Earlier I thought about seeing the snakes, but I've seen enough for today."

We left the zoo and walked out to Park Boulevard to catch the bus, neither of us saying anything the whole time. On the bus to ride home, I finally asked Tony if he had picked up anything, or felt anything as a result of sitting there with the wolf.

"Well, I noticed as we walked through the park and over to the bus stop, I was much more aware of the people around us than I had been before. I was really looking around, like a wolf would. I was noticing things, and people. Normally, I don't think I would have been looking around so closely at everything. I was looking all around me, just like when we did that power animal exercise with Don Emilio. How about you and the eagle?"

"I didn't get anything. I was so irritated about the cage the eagle had to live in that I didn't sense any kind of message. Even so, it felt good connecting and merging my awareness with it."

It was good practice for what was to come.

17

INCREASING ENERGY

"Modern science confirms that everything in the
universe–all sound, light, and matter, including you–
is simply pure energy vibrating at different frequencies."

B A R B A R A   D E   A N G E L I S

Tony was fidgeting so much it was obvious he was anxious to talk about what we had done during the month. We had arrived a few minutes early and were already seated as Don Emilio walked in. Once he was seated and ready to begin, he asked us how our practice exercises went.

"My shamanic journey practice went well," said Tony jumping in immediately. "I got even more information than the first journey. The wolf that came to meet me went through a whole process of getting to know me—looking, smelling, and listening until he trusted me as a friend. I felt comfortable with the wolf, and felt like we really connected. That was cool. Then we took a trip to the zoo, to try to connect with a real animal. At first, I wasn't sure I got anything out of sitting there watching the wolf in its enclosure. But as I sat there for a while, I really got into watching it move around in its enclosure, seeing how it closely observed all that was going on around it. When we left the zoo, I was surprised to realize that I was sorta acting like a wolf, looking back and forth, trying to be aware of everything around me."

"Your wolf nature stayed with you after you left the zoo," said Don Emilio.

"Yeah, for a little while anyway. But even after that, when I think about it, it seems natural for me now to look closely and be more aware of what's around me, like the wolf."

"Yes," said Don Emilio, "the more you connect with your wolf, the more it will feel normal for you to be in your wolf nature."

"HAAOOOOOOOOOOOOOOOOO!"

Don Emilio almost fell out of his chair, and quickly reached over to Tony to make sure he was okay. I started laughing. I couldn't help it. I didn't know what was funnier, the surprised look on Don Emilio's face or Tony doing the howl. Don Emilio looked confused and concerned.

"That was my wolf howl," said Tony, "to connect me with the power of my animal." He explained what he had found about how the wolf scares away intruders. "I think I will use that with my karate moves." He demonstrated once more, a little less blood curdling the second time, and the three of us had a good laugh.

"I like the idea of incorporating that into your karate moves, at appropriate times," said Don Emilio. "It will help move the energy ... as well as scaring off other wolves."

"I didn't get much from my power animal journey," I said, feeling a little frustrated. "I kept losing track of the eagle, thinking instead about how good it felt when we did the journey with you and when I had my eagle dream. I didn't get a chance to be with this eagle enough on the journey, and didn't get much out of the zoo experience except feeling like the eagle didn't belong in that little cage. It needed to be free to fly. I thought I was supposed to have some kind of special relationship with eagles. And now I'm not so sure. I can't seem to connect. I think I need to go see some eagles out in the wild."

"Well, that sounds like an excellent idea," said Don Emilio. "I will see if I can arrange to do that sometime soon. But don't let a few problems with these practices negate what you know in your heart about your connection with eagles, or negate what you experienced in your dream and in the first power animal journey. Those were too powerful to now act like they were nothing. Which felt the most connected to the eagle," he asked me, "your experience being the eagle in your dream, or being with the eagle in the cage at the zoo?"

"Oh, no question," I answered, "flying like an eagle in my dream."

"If you want to nurture your connection with your power animal," Don Emilio continued, "live in the power of those moments when you felt most connected, rather than wallowing in the frustration of those times when you had trouble connecting. Does that make sense to you?"

I nodded my head, and as I thought about it, it certainly did feel more powerful and more energizing to remember being connected to my soaring eagle than trying to merge with an injured, captive eagle in a small cage. No wonder I couldn't connect.

"So," he continued, "how about your progress with the breath exercise?"

"Like before, sometimes it was easy and sometimes hard," said Tony. "At first, it was simple to listen to myself inhale and exhale. But after a few minutes, my mind would wander, thinking about all kinds of stuff, and I realized I wasn't aware of my breathing anymore."

"Yeah, same for me," I added. "Sometimes I spent most of the time thinking about all the stuff that popped into my mind when I was supposed to be listening to my breath."

"As I said before, this is all normal," said Don Emilio. "It will take a lot of practice to be able to shut down the constant mind chatter. When you realize you are no longer aware of your breath, simply come back and put your awareness on your breath as you inhale and exhale.

"Overall, I would say this was a good month for both of you in terms of progress with your exercises. And Vicente, even though you haven't been able to connect well with your eagle, at least you have an idea to follow—to try going out in nature to connect."

I nodded my head in agreement.

"Let us now focus on today's lesson," said Don Emilio, "about other ways to increase personal energy. As you recall, increasing our personal energy and stopping the leakage of energy is just the starting point for increasing our awareness. What are other ways to increase our energy? One way is to connect with the Great Spirit in a manner that allows the energy around us to come naturally into our bodies and be made available to us.

"Light energy is pouring down on us constantly," Don Emilio continued, "from the sun, the stars, from All-That-Is. This energy is always available to us, if we ask for it and allow it in. So now, I am going to give you a way to consciously connect with this energy. This method is very powerful and easy to use at any time of day, no matter what you are doing." He told us to take three deep breaths, and to relax all our muscles, from head to toe.

"Now see a constant stream of energy coming down on you, like rain, entering into the top of your head. Let this energy flow through your whole being. Take it in, knowing that your body and spirit are being refreshed and revitalized with this infusion of light, this energy." He paused to allow us to experience taking in the energy.

"Simply be aware of this rain of energy from the heavens, and let it pour down on you, onto your head and into your whole body. Let this light fill up every space within you. Feel it filling up your feet and legs … up through your stomach and your chest … it fills up your hands and arms … your neck … then it fills you up to the top of your head. You can stop when you feel totally full of healing light energy, or you can continue and let the healing energy run a little longer through a hurt muscle or other ailment."

Don Emilio let us experience the feeling briefly. I just sat there, letting it run through me. It really did feel good, like having an internal shower of energy!

"Don Emilio … what happens to … the extra light … after we get all filled up?" My question came out so slowly it surprised me.

"It just keeps coming, like it did before you started focusing your awareness on it. Once you feel full of light energy, you can do something else with it. You can share it with others. Remember, I said one of our goals is to increase the amount of energy within our personal field of energy. When we increase our light energy, we vibrate at a higher rate, which helps us bring good things our way, and to those to whom we send this energy. You can do this right now. Think of someone you want to send this light energy to.... Now send out this energy from your heart area. See a beam of energy traveling out in front of you. For a few moments, keep thinking about that person, and in your mind's eye, see your light energy flowing into them."

He was silent as we sent light energy on its way. I visualized sending it to Tata

"Keep sending that energy. Doing this strengthens your connection with the person receiving this flow of energy. It raises their vibration rate. When a person is sick or feeling down, their energy is low. The energy you send will help them, even though they do not know you are sending it. While you send energy out, keep aware of always filling yourself up with energy. See new energy flowing in, as you are sending energy out, in a balance of inflow and outflow."

He paused again as we practiced filling ourselves with energy and sending it out.

"When you are ready, you can open your eyes. We have completed that exercise for today." Once Tony and I were both "back," and alert, Don Emilio continued.

"You can send energy out from your heart area, as you just did, not only to someone who is sick but to any persons, or animals and plants. Sending energy in that manner increases your connection with them, and also carries a level of communication between the two of you."

"Communication?" asked Tony. "Are we supposed to talk to them when we send energy?"

"No, the communication is not of words, but rather sending good feelings from the heart. If we had to translate into words, it would be sending feelings of love and joy. These feelings are encoded in the energy sent from the heart. And when the recipient–person, animal or plant receives the energy, its energy level in increased, and its heart center decodes the information or good feelings being transmitted."

"You can repeat these exercises on your own. Know that anytime you think about light energy, it is immediately drawn to you. You can take a few brief moments during each day to think about light, and as you become aware of it pouring down into the top of your head, it will fill you with energy and raise your vibration."

He paused to see if we had any questions, but neither of us did. So he moved on to the next topic for the day.

18
─

ENERGY FROM PLANTS AND ANIMALS

*"Everything is energy and that's all there is
to it. Match the frequency of the reality you want
and you cannot help but get that reality. It can be no
other way. This is not philosophy. This is physics."*

ALBERT EINSTEIN

Don Emilio stood up and, as he had before, looked out into the garden where Nana's crops were still growing even though it was the end of August. She had some tomatoes ripening, lettuce, cilantro and other herbs, as well as zucchini squash, although most of what remained were the few she left on the vine to get bigger—for large stuffed zucchini.

"There is another way that we increase our spiritual energy, and we make use of it every day," he said, still looking out at the garden. "We accept the gift of life-giving, energy-giving sustenance from our animal and plant brothers. They give themselves up to be consumed by us, letting go of their energy, so that others can benefit. We humans consume plant life—vegetables, fruit, nuts, and so on—as well as animal life. Our bodies transform what we eat into energy."

I thought it seemed appropriate to talk about plant and animal life while sitting in the shed next to the flowering plants and

▸ 128 ◂

vegetable garden. Plus, Tata used to raise chickens and rabbits in the back yard.

"This exchange of energy is a sacred ceremony, a ritual, the giving and receiving of life," Don Emilio continued. "People were more in touch with the sacred nature of this sharing when they lived as hunters and gatherers, coming face to face with the beings who sustained them. Or, as farmers, tilling the soil and carefully tending the precious growing beings in the fields, and at the end of their growing cycle, holding harvest ceremonies to celebrate life.

"Most of us are no longer that close to the actual taking of the animal's or plant's life, but we still participate in the transfer of that life force into our bodies through buying, preparing, cooking, and eating food. To gain the most benefit from this chain of transforming energy, we must be aware of the exchange between ourselves and the food we eat. We can treat that exchange with respect, by increasing our spiritual awareness of the magic of the moment. This is one reason for prayers before meals. Do you and your families say prayers before your meals?"

"At home, we say prayers before we eat dinner," I answered, "but after what you just said, those prayers don't seem to be enough. I mean, we thank the Lord for the food, but in that prayer we don't thank the animals or the plants."

"At least you pray before the meals," he said.

"Yeah, but we just sorta say the words quickly to get through them, so we can eat," I said.

"If you make a commitment to connect with your food and its source before you eat, not only will the food transform more effectively into usable energy, you will also strengthen the connection with each being that you consume, and with each person who has been involved in the process of getting the food to you."

"All that just for saying grace?" Tony asked.

"The words of the prayer are not important," Don Emilio answered. "What is important is being grateful for what you are receiving, connecting with the spirits of the people responsible for getting the food to you, and with the spirits of your brothers the plants and animals, thanking them for giving their life force so that you may continue your earthly life."

"Wow," said Tony, shaking his head, "that makes eating seem to be really heavy. It's like you can't take a bite to eat without involving everyone, everywhere."

"You are right," said Don Emilio. "Eating *is* really heavy. It is a spiritual experience that many people miss in their rush to eat the food. Make a habit of giving proper thanks when you eat, and it will change your life."

"So, Don Emilio, what prayer should we say?" I asked.

"Your prayer should always come from your heart. Say what you feel in your heart. But I can provide an example, a structure, if you like. I first thank the Great Spirit, God, for providing the food. Then I thank the plants and the animals for giving up their lives so that we can be nourished. You can be very specific and thank the carrots and the chicken, for example."

Tony laughed. "Thank the carrots and the chicken? Everyone at the table will laugh."

"I would hope not," answered Don Emilio, "not if you have been saying your prayer in a devout, thoughtful, spiritually-connected manner. This may all seem a little strange to you at first, but I think you will find yourselves building a strong spiritual energy connection, a positive connection with the Great Spirit and the spirits of all whom you acknowledge when you do this regularly and sincerely. Others will feel it too, because your words will come from your heart.

"Third, I thank the people involved in getting the food to us. You can be specific here, too, if you wish, and thank the people who raised the crops or animals, the fieldworkers, the meat processors, the food packagers, and so on. Fourth, I give thanks for those who honor us by preparing our meal. Lastly, I like to add thanks for other blessings and people in our lives.

"On some occasions, you may wish to give a full, heartfelt thanks out loud, so that all present can share in the blessing with you. On other occasions, when you are alone, you may wish to say a shorter version to yourself. Whether your prayer is short or long, silent or out loud, it should be with real feeling of connection to those you are thanking or blessing."

I had a feeling we would have that chance real soon. I'd been hearing Nana moving around in the kitchen the whole time we'd been there. "Speaking of food," I said, sniffing the air, "If I'm not mistaken, that's my Nana's special *chile colorado*. Man, I'm getting hungry!"

"That smells really good," said Don Emilio. "I saw Julia toasting the *guajillo chilies* earlier before making the red chili sauce. Very authentic—no bottled chili powder for her. I understand why you are distracted, but hold on a little while longer. I wanted to mention that where we place our attention when we eat is also important. We must be mindful of what we are doing, and remain connected to our brothers the plants and animals while we eat. We must be aware that a sacred transformation is taking place, changing this food into life-giving energy. Slowly and thoroughly chewing our food while we think about this will help increase our level of energy.

"Practice this mealtime contemplation at dinner, at least one time per week, along with saying your prayer before eating. If your family uses another prayer, just silently practice your own prayer. Say yours for the family if you want to."

"But Don Emilio," I protested, "I … I never…."

"Do not get upset thinking about having to perform," he said, stopping my whining. "It is just a prayer. Write it out beforehand and read it if you want to. I can assure you that your family will appreciate your contribution. Work on these exercises as well as the previous ones."

"Man, our list of exercises is getting pretty long," said Tony.

"Well, just do what you can. What you practice, you will learn. What you don't practice, you will have difficulty remembering."

"Just like practicing hitting baseballs or shooting hoops." I added.

"And you need all the practice you can get hitting baseballs," said Tony laughing.

"Yeah, like I said, it's those curve balls."

Don Emilio glanced into the house, and then turned back to us. "I believe Julia is ready for us now."

Nana must have heard us moving our chairs around in the shed, because as we walked into the house, she was already heating a pile of flour tortillas. She invited us to sit down at the dining room table, and soon brought out big portions of that *chile colorado*, big chunks of pork in a dark red chili sauce, served over a bowl of Mexican rice and her delicious soupy beans. Lucky me! Nana and Tata had already eaten so it was just the three of us at the table. We said a prayer of thanksgiving, Don Emilio leading, with Tony and me adding a few words of thanks to it. The prayer turned out to be pretty simple—and short.

After passing around the tortillas, and a dish of oregano, cilantro, and chopped onions, we finally dug in. I didn't hear anything for a while except a few *mmmm's*, and a few slurping sounds. About halfway through my bowl, I came up for air, and I had to ask him.

"Don Emilio ..." I said, dipping the tortilla into my bean juice, as I struggled to find the right words, "it seems like you have been telling us a little more about energy each time we meet. You said if we did these prayers at meals, our lives would change, and if we did the exercises we could stop the talking in our head, and start hearing intuition or guidance that could change our lives. And that if we practice connecting with our power animal, it will help us."

Don Emilio looked up from his food, and nodded.

"So when will all this help start? How long do we have to practice?"

"I have the same questions," said Tony, chewing on a mouthful and holding up the last piece of his tortilla. "I know you said this was a lifelong process, but how long in this life do we have to wait before we start seeing results?"

"You are correct," said Don Emilio, "we have focused on energy so far. My first goal has been to show you how to increase your level of energy. This is the starting point for increasing your awareness, so that you can begin to hear messages from your Higher Self and spirit guides, and be able to access the ancient truths inside of you.

The energy practices are tools to help you increase your awareness of higher energy. As you do, it will become easier for you to hear messages that come to you. And as this spiritual awareness increases, you will begin to understand and perhaps see and feel your connection with all things.

"At that point, you will understand that you have the power to make anything happen, the power to create the change you are looking for, and to create the life you want. You have that power right now, but you do not believe it. You have already had some successes, but because you do not believe in your own power, you dismissed your successes as not related to your studies."

"Yeah, I know," said Tony, "like the baseball game. I'm still not so sure about that one."

"Antonio," Don Emilio continued, "you fulfilled a long-time desire to get close-up seats for a Padres-Dodgers game. You think I was the one who did it for you, but I did not know you had that strong desire, and I had no plans to go to the game until very late in the day. I know that the inspiration came from your energy, your messages."

"What were the other things you mentioned?" I asked.

"The amazing work that both of you did with your power animals," he answered. "You both did much more than others typically do on a first power animal journey. Plus, Antonio connected so deeply with his animal during your visit to the zoo that he took on its mannerisms without consciously trying. That was also quite an accomplishment.

"Other more subtle changes are happening as well. How you spend your time, relationships with family and friends, your outlook on life, thoughts about your future—these are all changing. You are not fully aware of the extent of these changes because it is hard for us to see day-to-day changes in ourselves. But when you spend time meditating—focusing on your breath or filling up with light, you are changing your focus from this physical world and connecting with your spiritual guides, and your Higher Self. You are a spiritual being, a part of your Higher Self, which has taken on a physical body at this time on earth. The more you allow yourselves to *be* in that greater spiritual awareness of who you really are, the more it will change the physical person here before me."

"So let me see if I understand this right," said Tony. "These meditation exercises are not just to stop mental chatter, or to increase energy. They are also to allow us to spend time with our Higher Self, and to hear messages from it?"

"That is correct," said Don Emilio. "When you focus your attention on something, or meditate, you shut out the distractions of this physical world. You allow yourself to take in the flowing energy, increasing your vibration. As your vibration increases, you become more aware of your Higher Self, and learn to hear, or just *know*, your own guidance. It all starts with very simple meditation exercises and an awareness of increasing your energy.

"Change in you is happening. Your families have already noticed. But other than the baseball game and your experience with your power animals, you wonder when *you* will be able to see it. Over the next few months, believe me, you will begin to notice significant changes.

19

MOVING ENERGY

*"I cannot tell you any spiritual truth that deep
within you don't know already. All I can do
is remind you of what you have forgotten."*

ECKHART TOLLE

That last session with Don Emilio kept me focused on the positives during the four-week break that followed. I stopped moaning about having to sit and meditate for twenty minutes each day, struggling to keep stray thoughts out, and realized those twenty minutes were a chance to connect with a more powerful me who was waiting for the little me to get my act together. But Don Emilio wouldn't be so judgmental. He'd probably say my Higher Self was happy to see that I was becoming more aware of myself as more than just this physical me. I also found out that when I was meditating on the rain of light and connecting with my Higher Self, it really seemed to help keep the mental chatter down, better than when meditating on my breath.

It was the last Saturday of the month, time for another session with Don Emilio. I had a little extra time, so I met Tony at his house and we set out to Nana and Tata's house from there.

"Hey dudes, where ya been?" Pablito called out. He was on the corner at Beardsley and Logan, leaning against the wall of the pump equipment company. Pablito had spray-painted this wall a number of times, although today you couldn't tell, as it had a new coat of paint. Most of the businesses in the neighborhood knew

▸ 135 ◂

that it was best to paint over the graffiti right away or they would soon have a wall full of it.

"Don't see you guys around much," he said, as we got closer.

Tony was a little ahead of me as we walked up, and he immediately got into it with Pablito. "I've been busy, man, doing things like studying with the *brujo*, working lots of hours at Amador's, yard work at my house. What else you wanna know? You just been hanging around as usual? I heard you had to take some summer school classes. Are you keeping up?"

"Heck, I ain't even cracked the book yet!" Pablito said, laughing.

"Man, you're not taking care of business," Tony continued. "Pablito, you're...."

"Hey, homie," I said, walking past Tony, "good to see you, man!" I did the Chicano handshake with Pablito, then took another step forward and gave him a hug.

Surprised, he stepped back, looking confused, with one guy tearing him down, the other acting like he was a long lost relative. I reached out again and patted him on his shoulder.

"I been wondering what you been up to, man," I continued. "Haven't really had much time lately to hang out with you guys. Everyone doing okay?"

He nodded his head. "Yeah, the guys are good. But ... listen up man. Some of them have been saying stuff about you two, wondering how come you don't spend time with your homies no more."

"Your dad working?" I asked, ignoring his warnings about the other guys. I knew they had been having problems at his house because his dad had been laid off a while back.

"Yeah. They got a new Navy contract at Southwest Marine, so he's working now."

"That's great," I continued. "Hey, we were just going over to my Tata's house for another lesson with Don Emilio. You wanna come?"

"No way, José!" he snapped. "It's okay with me that you guys got religion or *brujo*-ism or whatever, but it's not for me, man. But ..." he paused, as if hesitant to ask, then blurted out, "so what have you been learning?"

"Remember what I told you last time?" asked Tony. "Well, we've just about got it down. I've been practicing this one for you. Let me show you."

Pablito backed up two steps and moved toward me. I didn't want to bust up laughing, so I turned away and looked down the block.

"*Uno, dos,* calling in the ghost," began Tony. Then louder, "*Tres, cuatro,* send it to Pablo." The volume increased a bit more. "*Cinco, seis,* in his face!" Tony raised his hands high and stepped toward Pablito, who was turning white and shaking slightly. Tony yelled loudly, "*siete, ocho,* now do the ..." He paused. "Darn. I can never remember the last part."

Tony and I both started laughing. Pablito looked back and forth at both of us, then relaxed his very tense body, heaving a loud sigh of relief and smiling weakly.

"Oh, man! You got me again, *vato,*" Pablito said, giving Tony a playful shove.

"We gotta get going," I said, taking a couple of steps away and stopping. "Hey, you guys enjoy that Padre game this afternoon. Only about a month left in the season. Don't forget to take binoculars. It's a long way to home plate from those bleacher seats."

"How did you know we were going to the game? And how did you know we were gonna sit in the outfield seats? I just talked with Arturo this morning."

"That's part of what our lessons with Don Emilio are about," I said. "We gotta go see him now, but we'll talk about it sometime. We waved to him as we headed down Beardsley Street.

"What was that all about?" Tony asked after we walked far enough away so Pablito couldn't hear. "How did you know about the game and the seats? And what was all that handshaking and hugging?"

"When I saw you jumping on his case, I decided to try out what we've been learning. So, I focused on energy entering the top of my head. Keeping my awareness there, I wanted to reinforce my energy connection with Pablito. So we did the Chicano handshake. But that didn't do much for a personal connection, so

I hugged him. And when he backed off, I reached out and patted him on the shoulder. Don Emilio said we are all balls of energy connected by energy fibers. So I imagined Pablito and me connected by an energy fiber. As I was talking to him I let my energy flow to him through that connection, and I waited to see what information might come through. While you were doing that *'uno-dos'* thing on him, suddenly I got a really strong sense that he couldn't wait to get out of there and get going to the Padre game."

"How did you know where they'd be sitting and who else was going with him?"

"I never said who was going with him. I just said 'you guys' because I know he never goes anywhere without his homies. And he never has much money, so I guessed he'd be sitting in the cheap seats, just like us."

"That was good, logical guessing. But you *did* read his mind about going to the game. It looks like you *are* starting to get this stuff."

He slapped me a high five.

"Yeah, this stuff is working," I said, "just like Don Emilio said it would."

"You're really going to have Pablito and the guys talking now," said Tony. "I bet he's really freaking out, trying to figure out how you knew."

"Just like I always say about Don Emilio, 'How did he do that?'"

We walked down the alley and up to the back gate of Nana and Tata's yard. Because of the delay with Pablito, we got there a little later than our usual time. I noticed that the car wasn't in the back yard where they usually park it. We walked up to the shed and didn't see Don Emilio in there, so I figured he must be inside. As we walked toward the back door of the house, we heard music start. It sounded like an Indian flute and drums, with a good beat. I walked ahead of Tony and was surprised when we got to the kitchen. I could see into the living room, where Don Emilio had moved the big chair out of the room. He was dancing to the beat of the music!

His eyes were closed, and he moved to one side of the room, then back, his body moving to the beat, his arms swaying above his head. It was beautiful. He looked graceful, like a deer when it runs. But he wasn't jumping like a deer. Just moving. I didn't think about old guys dancing like that, moving so freely and into the music.

"Wow," said Tony when the music stopped, "that was pretty cool. You really got the beat down on that one. What was that, a special Mexican-Indian dance?"

"It was just free-form motion, moving to the beat," he said as the next track started up. "This is another way to raise your energy level." As he talked, he moved to the beat of the music, but not as fully as before we had walked into the room.

"Movement like this is good for your physical system as well as your energy system," he said. "The movement gets things flowing. Our bodies have a tendency to get sluggish when we do not use them. We sit all day and the systems slow down. So it is good to get up, get the blood flowing faster, and get the air moving through the lungs. This kind of movement is good for the body and the life force, what the Chinese call *chi*. It keeps everything tuned up. Dancing like this increases the flow of energy.

"Come," he said, waving his hands, motioning for us to join him.

Tony got right into it, waving his arms in the air and moving his butt from side to side. I didn't move. Don Emilio waved again as if pulling me toward him in the center of the room.

"I can't," I said. "I ain't got no rhythm."

"Ahhh, ahhh, ahhh," Tony laughed or chanted in beat to the music as he looked at me, while continuing to bounce around like he'd been doing this all his life.

"Oh … how do you say it," said Don Emilio, "oh, baloney. All Mexicans have rhythm. It is in the blood. You are just thinking too much. Your body wants to move, but your mind…."

"It's embarrassed," Tony cut in, "or afraid of looking silly."

"Which you do!" I shot back.

"Come on, do not think," said Don Emilio. "Focus on your breath and stop your internal judgment of yourself. Once you start to move, you will be fine."

I took two steps forward and started to move, tentatively. I closed my eyes so I wouldn't see Tony looking at me.

"Do not worry about what you look like. No one is here to see you. That is why the house is empty. I asked them to give us some private time here."

Neither of them commented on my dancing. All three of us continued to move as the music went on to the next track. I finally started getting into it. After a while, Don Emilio spoke. "Continue to move as I speak. Now, movement of this type can bring forth what some people call a peak spiritual experience. Others call it an ecstatic experience, a trance, or simply 'spacing out.' In other words, you may lose awareness of what your hands and arms are doing, and lose track of whether your feet are keeping the beat. The music may seem to take you somewhere else. A portion of your awareness may leave this level of consciousness and go to a higher energy level. When this happens, you are truly dancing with the spirits. You may have a strange feeling inside of you, a lightness, a glow, a feeling of being connected to a higher force."

Just then the drumming stopped abruptly. I opened my eyes.

"You may not want it to stop," he continued, "but sometimes the music cuts out, like that, and brings you right back to earth." When the music began on the next cut, Don Emilio began performing some karate moves. "Martial arts movements are also good for getting energy moving and increasing it."

"I mentioned that I've been taking karate classes for a couple of years," said Tony.

"Yes, and it would be good for you to take karate too, Vicente. Karate is excellent for building strength, flexibility, and self-confidence. All of these contribute to increasing your energy." He continued with the moves. "Then there is *tai chi*, which is for any age, and it works well for us older guys." He started doing what looked a lot like karate moves except in slower motion.

"Tai chi looks similar to martial arts, and preceded many of them. But tai chi can be used for energy work instead of self-defense. Some tai chi movements are in fact very similar to an ancient Toltec system of physical movements, used by Toltec sorcerers," he said, shifting to another position and beginning a different set of movements.

"Is that the Toltec stuff or the tai chi?" asked Tony.

"The Toltec. I wanted to show you a few movements of each type. These movements are a physical regimen for maintaining the body and mind in peak condition. They are also a means of circulating energy through the human energetic field. The Toltec sorcerers found that doing these movements helped them achieve inner silence. The Toltec sorcerers used movement to access states of heightened awareness. They could see energy flow and could access other realities."

Don Emilio continued doing Toltec energy movements as Tony and I attempted to copy him. He was so smooth and fluid, so light on his feet. Tony leaned over toward me and said very softly, "Not bad for an old man, huh?"

Not bad, I thought to myself. I hoped I could move like that when I was fifty years old.

"You guys take this energy and body movement stuff seriously now, and when you are my age, you will both be able to move like me. Maybe even better."

"Man, reading our minds again!" I said, looking at Tony.

"Okay, we briefly reviewed free-form, karate, Toltec, and tai chi movements," Don Emilio continued. "We did the free-form movements together. For the rest of the session we will spend time doing karate, Toltec and tai chi movements. Antonio, I would like you to lead us through a series of karate movements, if that is okay. Basic movements, so Vicente can keep up."

"Oh, great!" Tony said excitedly. "I already taught him a few moves, last year." Then turning to me, he said, "I'll go slow and demonstrate if you don't remember all of what I showed you before."

For the next fifteen or twenty minutes Tony led us in doing karate moves. By the time Don Emilio had us stop I was feeling a little tired physically, in my arms and legs. But I was energized. I could feel that my energy level was up. I thought we were going to take a short break, but Don Emilio moved right into the Toltec moves he was doing before, but did them slow so we could follow along. We did those for about fifteen minutes too. We finally took a very short break, then spent the rest of the session doing tai chi moves. Don Emilio showed us only a few of the basic moves so that we could repeat them on our own. Once I got the foot positions down and learned to keep my body centered over my feet and legs, I did okay. I could feel energy building up in my hands on some of the moves. My hands got warm, and I could feel them tingling after a while. On other moves, I could feel my feet getting warmer as we visualized moving energy down through the legs and feet and into the earth.

By the time we finished, I was buzzed. I could feel the energy in my hands and arms, my legs and feet and head. Don Emilio had us lie down and rest, and said to let the energy flow, from the top of our heads down through our feet and into the ground. We did that for a little while, and I became more and more relaxed, and a little spaced out.

The music player started up again, this time with the sounds of a gong. Don Emilio told us to focus on the music, and just go with it. Simple enough instructions, and before I knew it, I was traveling inside the sound, deeper and deeper into wave after wave of sound and colors. It was really an amazing experience. I don't know how long we did that, but eventually I heard Don Emilio's voice lightly calling us back, from someplace way out there, to the room in Nana and Tata's house. I had forgotten that was where we were.

"Man, that was trippy," said Tony, once we were fully back and sitting up. "You said you would show us how to get high without drugs. That was it!"

"Hey," I said, "can we get a copy of that gong music?"

"Not yet," answered Don Emilio. "If I gave it to you now, you would be frustrated that you could not repeat this experience. The intense movement exercises before meditating with the gong sounds raised your energy vibration significantly. That is what allowed you to be transported by the sounds. That was a taste of what we can work on in future classes."

"Okay," said Tony, "I look forward to doing this later. That was some trip."

"Moving on, I understand you compared notes about your daily energy practice."

"Yes, we did. It really helped to talk together. I think I learned some things from Vincent."

"And I learned from Tony."

"That is the advantage of going through this learning process with another person," said Don Emilio, "because as you move into the next phase of learning, the focus will be about your own experience, rather than new information I may share with you. It helps to talk with someone who is learning the same thing and going through the same experiences you are."

"Yeah," Tony responded, "I felt like I needed to talk to you about this stuff, but then I realized what I really needed to do was just practice the techniques on my list. Just do them. Then, when Vincent and I talked, it really helped me to understand better."

"It sounds like your energy practice is going well. Tracking each other's progress is good because I will not always be around to answer your questions. As you raise your energy, you will have fewer questions for me. You will begin to believe in your own knowledge, and recognize that you have many answers already. It will continue to be helpful for you to speak to each other—as you said, confirming each other's insights, and helping each other learn. You are reaching the stage of actually teaching each other."

"Don Emilio," said Tony, "you said something about the next phase of our studies. There's a second phase?"

"Yes, we are coming to the end...."

When I heard him say "the end" I almost jumped out of my seat in panic. "What? Wait a minute! I thought we were just going to start some new material, not end the sessions. We can't stop now!"

"Calm down, Vicente," he said reassuringly, "We are not at the end of the first phase yet. But even then, that is not the end. We will start the next phase when you are ready. But first you have to live it. You have to incorporate into your life what you have in your head. It has to drop down to your true knowingness. That takes some time. Slowly you will realize that you just know it. You will become comfortable admitting to yourself that you know. More and more, those magical events will take place and you will see what you needed to see. You will get what you asked for, and things will start falling into place for you. At first you will be surprised, and later you will simply expect it to be that way."

"That sounds pretty cool," said Tony.

"Then, when things start to *not* go so smoothly," Don Emilio continued, "that will be a message to you that you have slipped, that you have an energy block somewhere. I cannot do this part for you. It is a path you each must walk for yourselves. When you slip, you will know that you need to refocus on your energy practice."

"When we get into that groove, Don Emilio, what then?" I asked. "It's not just about making our own lives easier, is it? That's not what you do."

"No, it is not just about the self. But it has to start there. You need to have internal awareness and internal knowingness first. Then you can move on to other things."

"What other things?" asked Tony. "What else is there?

"We have only scratched the surface. There are many paths that a person can take. Among them are healing physical conditions energetically, using plants to help heal physical conditions, using dreaming to travel and learn, creating positive changes for your life and for your family, working with groups and communities to create change on a community scale, and developing psychic abilities to help others with insights about their lives. And most important, helping others to understand the implications of the fact that we are all spirit entities, all connected, and a part of All That Is."

"We're supposed to choose one of those paths?" I asked.

"Or maybe when we become more psychic, we'll be able to see our own future," said Tony smiling.

"You are joking, Antonio," answered Don Emilio, "but you are not that far off. As you continue to do your energy work, you will know which path or paths you prefer. And you will also get messages from your guides who will be helping you on the path."

Our list of energy practices kept getting longer, but neither of us was complaining too much just yet. School had started and we now had homework to do, but we were mostly keeping up. I wasn't able to do all the practice exercises every day, but I was doing most of them. Starting a karate class was going to take up a good chunk of my time, but Tony was already doing that, so I couldn't complain. Plus, I had wanted to take a karate class for a while now.

I think Tony and I both knew that all this energy practice would help us understand what Don Emilio wanted us to know about increasing and moving energy. We were beginning to get the point. And the more we understood, the more both of us could sense the change that was starting to come over us.

20
———

THE OTHER SIDE

*"The dream state...can bring you in contact
with wisdom you have been denying yourself."*

SETH (JANE ROBERTS)

It was still overcast when we walked over to see Don Emilio. The overnight fog must have been pretty heavy for it not to burn off by late morning. That made it cooler than usual. A shiver ran through my body as we walked into the yard, from the cold, I thought. Or was it because of today's topic? A couple of weeks back, when Don Emilio was visiting, he told me he was going to talk to us about dreaming and trance journeys next. I wondered if he was going to talk more about my dream, or about something scarier.

I could hear drumming music coming from the shed as we got closer. We stopped at the entrance to the shed and could see that Don Emilio's eyes were closed. It looked like he was in a trance. But as I stood there looking at him, I noticed he was not moving at all. It seemed to be a deeper trance than other times. I guess he heard us as we walked in and sat down, because he started to stir, but it took him longer than usual to come out of it. Finally, he stood up and started to pace in the small area in front of our chairs.

"I have to move around a little to come back, so I can focus on this side." He took a few deep breaths as he paced, then went back to his seat and started up again. "Today I want to talk about contacting the other side, or traveling to other levels of reality."

"I read something about that in the library," said Tony, "in a magazine article about shamanism. It said that a shaman goes into a trance and that his spirit travels to an underworld where he meets various beings, evil spirits, or animals, or maybe like monsters—strange and scary beings. I don't want to meet up with scary beings and evil spirits!"

"I don't think I want to go on that kind of a trip either," I said. "Is it necessary to visit this underworld? Will we be safe in those other realities?"

"You are not going to go into an underworld of scary monsters and evil spirits," Don Emilio assured us. "That is for people of other belief systems. Different realities exist, different from what we are experiencing right now. We can tune into an alternative reality by going into an altered state of consciousness. You do this when you dream or when you go into a trance, where your consciousness leaves the body, or a large part of it does, and goes to a different level of reality. I say reality because it is a *real* experience. Part of your consciousness is experiencing that moment, just like your consciousness is experiencing this moment. The trance journey and the dream state are nothing to be afraid of. Both are altered states of consciousness and ways to access information not readily available in our normal waking, conscious state."

Tony looked relieved to learn that we were not going to be involved with some scary underworld. "Oh, so is this like the exercises where we met our power animal and moved around like we were that animal?"

"Yes, on that power animal trance journey you traveled to another level of reality where you became your power animal, looked out from his eyes, moved like him, and thought like him. You saw things from a perspective you could not see from your physical body form. Those were powerful shamanic journeys. There was nothing scary about that, was there?"

We both shook our heads. Now I understood why he had us do the power animal journeys so early in these lessons. It made more sense now as he talked about trance journeys.

"You mean that experience was real, that we were in a different space and time than this life here on Earth?" asked Tony.

"Did you think it was real at the time?" Don Emilio asked.

"It seemed very real to me!"

"Yeah, mine felt real too," I answered, "but I thought that maybe, like you said, it was just our higher self showing us some things."

"Whether you believe it was your power animal or your higher self is not important. You were getting information from a dimension you do not normally perceive. The information came from a different level of reality. Same physical space, but a different level of awareness."

I was listening real close, and trying to stay with him. But this stuff Don Emilio was saying was hard to understand. Even though I was having trouble getting my mind to understand what he was saying, I knew it was real because I experienced it in my dream. Somehow I was in another place and time in that dream. So I thought I should just stay with it and let it sink in for a while, and see if it would eventually make sense.

"On a shamanic trance journey, is the shaman awake, or dreaming?" Tony asked. "I remember I was a little out of it when we ended our journey. Were we dreaming it?"

"Entering a light or deep trance, an altered state of consciousness, we escape the chatter of our mind, the doubts and fears of the ego, and leave the conscious mind behind, put it to sleep so to speak, as in the dream state—although we are more awake and aware of this world than while dreaming. In the trance state as well as in the dream state, we filter information through the subconscious mind. The subconscious is the doorway through which we can access information from our spirit guides, guardian angels, animal spirits, and other nature spirits, like the trees, plants, wind, and water."

"From the wind?" I asked, as I got up and walked to the back of the shed. "From trees, and plants? Like these?" I picked up one of the plants from Nana's worktable, an aloe vera plant. It looked like it might be the one Don Emilio handed to me the very first time we talked in here.

"Yes, from trees and plants. You will see for yourselves soon enough, believe me." Don Emilio paused and looked at us like he was about to say something, but maybe changed his mind. He then continued with the lesson.

"The focused attention exercise or meditation is another way to access that information. The goal is to stop the internal mind chatter, and get the conscious mind to shut down for a while, allowing access to the subconscious mind. Now, as you recall, we did the focused attention exercise prior to that power animal journey. And I did that just a short while ago, before you walked in. It is one way to slip into a trance state. The trance state is the vehicle for travel, a way to escape the overpowering control that the ego has on the self. And, as I said, another way to connect with alternative levels of reality is through the dream state."

Tony shook his head. "Wait a minute. Through dreams? I hate to keep being the doubting Thomas here, but I think most people believe that a bad dream or a nightmare, or even a good dream, is just something that happens in our minds, and we just watch it. How do we connect with something while we are asleep watching a dream?"

"We can control our dreams, even though most people do not consciously do so. There are people who have developed their dreaming skills to access many kinds of information. One of those skills, being consciously aware that you are dreaming and then choosing what you want to do and where you want to go in the dream, is called *lucid dreaming*. Related to that is what people call an *out-of-body experience*."

"What do you mean people choose what they want to do and where they want to go in a dream?" asked Tony. "How do they do that?"

Even though it sounded like Tony was pestering with all his questions, I was glad he was asking. I had no reason to doubt the truth of what Don Emilio was telling us. It was just getting harder and harder to grasp, as we had never heard about it before. Yet he was talking like it was everyday stuff.

"Lucid dreaming is choosing to dream differently than most people dream," said Don Emilio. "Typically, people just watch the dream and passively let things happen to them. And usually, the scenes jump around. There may not be much logic to them, and the person has to struggle to figure out what the jumble of different images mean, if they even try. In lucid dreaming, on the other hand, you can be watching your dream and then consciously decide to move in a certain direction, or to do a certain action. Or you may just want to explore the dream landscape, to explore dream reality and become more familiar with it, especially if you are new to lucid dreaming."

That all sounded very strange, and a little scary, I thought to myself. But it also sounded pretty cool–to be able to move around and do things inside your dream. "How do you do it?" I asked. "How do you switch from just watching the dream to being part of the action?"

"The first step is to realize you are dreaming while you are having a dream, rather than after you wake up. Usually you dream and experience what is going on, but do not realize it is a dream. The first thing to do, when going to bed, is to tell yourself that you want to become aware in your dreams. Second, make it a habit to look for things in your dreams that cannot happen in this physical world, like traveling at high speeds without a vehicle, or maybe playing basketball and slam-dunking. You have to try to realize that your experience is out of the ordinary, that you cannot dunk, so you must be dreaming. Third, once you realize you are dreaming, you try to remember to take some action."

"Yeah," said Tony, "like I wanna go back and slam dunk some more!"

"Right. In your dreams is the only place you'll ever slam dunk," I said, laughing.

Don Emilio smiled and paused briefly, trying to stay serious. "All three steps take a lot of practice. It is not something you will be able to go home and try and then come back with success stories right away. But it is something that you can practice. Get a notebook and keep a dream journal. Write down your dreams and what you were able to do about those three steps."

"What about the out-of-body thing," asked Tony, "how do you do that?"

"The easiest way for me is through a trance state, as if I were going on a shamanic journey, because, well, that is what I am doing. But rather than going to meet my power animal, I use the trance to travel to the other side. First, I get very relaxed, as we have done in our focused attention exercises. And I allow myself to go really deeply into that calm state. The deeper I go, the slower my brainwave activity. The deep trance slows down my brain activity, and I move from conscious mind, where the brainwave activity is called the *beta* wave state, to subconscious mind, where the brainwave activity has slowed to what is called the *alpha* wave state. And as I go even deeper, the brainwave activity slows down to what is called the *theta* wave state."

Beta, alpha, theta? I shook my head and looked over at Tony just as he spoke up, sounding a little frustrated.

"Oh man, do we have to remember this alpha beta stuff?"

"No," Don Emilio answered. "I do not want to confuse you with the terminology. I just want you to know that you are going to progressively more relaxed states, both in your body and in your brain. I start by relaxing my body from the toes on up, the reverse of what we usually do. I try to feel each of the muscles, and then relax them—the toes, the feet, the lower leg, and keep going up, relaxing all the muscles. As I move up, I let the muscles I have passed totally relax; I let them drop as a dead weight. By the time I get up to my head, I do not feel the lower parts of the body. It seems as if my consciousness is focused in a point of awareness in my head, unconnected to my body.

"By changing my brainwave activity, my consciousness moves away from my mind and physical body awareness into an inner world awareness, accessible only when I can first put the mind to rest, distract it, and give it something to do while I get away, like focusing on its body and relaxing each muscle. Once in the *theta* wave state, in this inner world awareness, I am ready to travel."

Oh wow, I thought, how cool is that? That made more sense. Slow down, relax, and get ready to travel!

"Now, some people get to this place not through a trance state, but from the sleep state. They might do the same relaxation process just described while they lie in bed, and then allow themselves to drift down deeper and deeper into sleep. In this way, they are also stepping down their brainwave activity, so that when it reaches the *theta* level, they too can take the inner journey.

"The trick in this method is to catch yourself before you slip down to the extremely slow *delta* brainwave level, which is the deepest level of sleep, beyond dreaming and traveling. Look for clues while dropping down to the *theta* level--for example, a feeling of numbness, spinning, falling, vibrations, or sounds. Use any of those feelings as a reminder not to go deeper into sleep but instead, as with the trance state, to move into an awareness of a feeling of one point of consciousness, unconnected to the body. You may feel yourself, as this one point of consciousness, pop free of your body and actually see yourself as separate from it, or simply find yourself traveling."

"And where do you go when you actually do it?" asked Tony. "Where do you end up? And how do you get back?"

"Let me first say, to allay any fears, that you get back very easily, by simply deciding to come back, at any time, no matter what is happening wherever you are. Now, I can go in different directions. I can enjoy a favorite pleasant place where I can meet my power animal or my higher self, a place I created in my mind. Or I can travel within a spiritual, aura-like version of the physical world, its duplicate, along with a duplicate of everything in it. There I can visit people and places anywhere on the Earth or beyond.

"I can also move on to other levels of reality or of what some people call the astral plane. There, I can explore landscapes, events, and interactions that I myself create, just like I do in my dreams. Or I may meet up with a relative who has passed away, a fellow traveler, a teacher, or guides in a setting created by them. For those of us who have worked to increase our energy, and our spiritual development, we can move to higher levels within this otherworld and meet spiritually advanced souls and teachers. We can participate in classes and learn more about our spiritual natures, and about existence in these other realities, and about many wonders that we cannot even begin to comprehend."

I could feel my jaw drop open as Don Emilio paused to let us take all that in. I looked over at Tony who was looking back me with wide-open eyes and his mouth wide open too. Don Emilio had done it again. He blew our minds talking about these strange concepts, but speaking like it was everyday common knowledge. My mind was spinning with thoughts of advanced souls and teachers, classes in other realities, records of other lifetimes, and different levels in this other world.

"Don Emilio," I asked when I could finally speak, "do many people know about this, about traveling to all these places?"

"Many people do lucid dreaming and other-worldly travels. Some do it as a group. The Yaqui Indians for example. Part of their culture, the way of their society, is group dreaming. Together they are aware in the dream. There are other cultures that do this as well."

"What?" I asked, shocked again at yet another surprise. "You mean people are actually together in their dream or in this inner traveling, doing things together? And they all remember the dream?"

"Jesus," said Tony shaking his head, "more hocus pocus."

"Not at all," said Don Emilio. "We all dream together, and we travel in these other-worldly landscapes, even though we may not be aware of it. You could say we dream our existence into reality. On another level of consciousness, in the dream state, we meet with others and make decisions about things and events in our lives. We work out agreements at that level and set things in motion, so that what we have chosen for our lives materializes in this physical reality. We dream our individual lives, and we dream our group lives as well. The problem is that 99.9% of the time we have no recollection of this, but it does take place. Strange and hard to understand perhaps, but it is part of the magical nature of the Universe."

This was just amazing! Too amazing, and hard to believe. I thought that outside of this universe there was heaven. Now he was talking about different levels, multiple realities, people dreaming this life into existence. It was really mind-boggling. I had no reason to doubt him, but wow, what a whole new world.

"Man! This is so much new stuff," said Tony. "I … I can hardly keep it all in my head."

All I could do was nod in agreement.

Don Emilio looked at us and realized we had heard enough. He had given us plenty to think about for a while. He asked how our exercises were going. We talked about them briefly, and then ended the session.

Rather than leaving with Tony I went into the house to see Tata. He had not been feeling well and had spent the last few days in bed. My father had stopped by to see him also and was already with him in his bedroom, so he was able translate for me. Tata asked me what we had learned today, and I told him our topic was traveling to the other side.

"Ah, yes, perfect," he said in Spanish. "That is what I want Emilio to teach me. I want to learn how to travel to the other side. He used to tell me about his travels. How magnificent." Then he got a very sad look on his face and continued, speaking in Spanish. "But perhaps it is too late. I am very old, and I am not well. I wanted to travel, but now I'm afraid."

"Tata," I answered, "Don Emilio says not to be afraid of evil spirits and that kind of stuff when you travel to the other side."

"No," he said, "I mean I'm afraid that if I travel to the other side, they may not let me come back."

2

HOOPS TWO

*"Those who say it cannot be done should
not interrupt the one doing it."*

CHINESE PROVERB

"About time you guys got here. We're already warmed up and ready to trounce you."

Pablito was shooting off his mouth again, acting like the great basketball player that he wasn't. For some time now, the guys had been bugging us about not hanging out with them much anymore. So we agreed to get together with them to play some basketball in Chicano Park.

"Hey 'Turo, wha'sup?" Tony called to Arturo, who was at the foul line shooting.

"Yo, *carnal*, not much. Just trying to improve my game."

As I ran under the basket waiting for his shot he called to me. "How's it goin', Vincent?"

"Things are good," I said, reaching for the ball as it bounced off the rim. I tossed it back to him. "So good I got an A on both those exams last week." The four of us were in a History class and an English class together this year.

"Yeah, I aced 'em too!" said Tony, as he shot the ball he brought. "How 'bout you, Pablito?"

"Don't talk to me about no *pinche* tests! I can't believe they're giving exams already. We just started the school year."

"In case you hadn't noticed," Tony answered, "we've been back about five weeks."

"He didn't do too well," said Arturo, laughing.

"Let's not talk about school. Let's talk about this game," called Pablito as he chased Tony's ball. "You guys finally pulled yourselves away from the *brujo* man long enough to spend a little time with your friends. You ain't been spending no time with your homies, man, and that ain't good. They don't like it." He took a shot from the corner, and swished it. "All right! All right! I'm hot!"

"Is that the first one he's made?" Tony asked sarcastically, smiling at Arturo.

"Hey, he's hot today, relatively speaking. He's been making quite a few. He was out here practicing way before I got here. You two go ahead and take your warm up shots."

"Just the four of us today?" I asked.

"Yeah, the other guys couldn't make it," said Pablito. "We'll go against you two."

"Today we were going to spend time with our homies," said Tony, "and they don't show. If anyone complains they don't see us, remind 'em they were the ones who didn't show, okay?"

Tony and I took our warm up shots and they chased down the balls for us.

"You sure you don't wanna shoot for teams?" I asked.

"Nah, that's okay," Arturo responded. "We can switch later."

Tony and I looked at each other and smiled. Perfect. We had been hoping it would work out this way. Pablito had been trying to ask us about the mind reading thing I did about the baseball game, but I always managed to avoid being around him long enough to talk about it. We knew they'd want to talk about it today. On the way over, Tony and I had worked up a scheme to make them think we were reading each other's minds. We had set up two simple plays for no look passes using hand signals that they wouldn't notice.

As expected, they started right in. They took it out first, and Arturo scored on a layup around me. Second time down, Pablito was dribbling and started asking about the baseball game incident. He asked that same question I had been asking Don Emilio: "How did you do that?"

"That's part of the stuff Don Emilio has been teaching us about. I asked if you wanted to come and sit in with us when we go see him. You should come and see for yourself." Offering him the opportunity to sit in with Don Emilio seemed to make Pablito jittery. He shot the ball and missed—air ball. Tony got the rebound and went right to the top of the key as planned.

"I think that was just a lucky guess," Arturo said. "The Padres were playing an afternoon game, and you just guessed that we'd be going, that's all. That mind reading stuff is just B. S. You were faking it and trying to make it look like you do it all the time."

"Is that what you think, too?" I asked looking over at Pablito. Tony stopped dribbling and gave the signal.

"Yeah, man," said Pablito. "I bet you can't...."

I faked going to the outside, cut back in to take the pass, turned and laid it into the basket.

"Pablito, you paying attention?" Arturo asked. "Tony just threw that ball without looking. Watch the ball, bro'."

"Hey, he's your problem. I'm covering Vincent," Pablito responded.

"Not very well," Tony added.

Tony took the ball out and tossed it to me. I went to the top of the key and gave the signal. Tony grabbed my pass and hit a short jumper as Arturo lunged at him trying to catch up.

"Hey, Arturo, you watching the game here?" Pablito said sarcastically. "He just threw that ball in your direction without looking."

We did two more of those and were up 8-2. They started looking for blind throws and didn't guard us closely, so we went back to our normal game and had very easy shots. We were up 20 - 6 when they started asking about mind reading again.

"So what does the *brujo* tell you about mind reading? How do you do it?" asked Arturo.

"It's not just mind reading," Tony answered. "It's about *knowing* in general, like knowing where the ball is going to be, or knowing that you should go to a certain place and then you find something there that you need. It's all about energy, keeping a high level of spiritual energy, and living right. And if you keep that high energy level, you start to become aware of more things, more than other people. You just *know.*"

"And it's about connections between people," I added. "It's about both the personal connections and about the spiritual energy connections that exist between us."

Tony threw another no-look pass over his head to me and I laid it up again.

"How did you do that?" Pablito asked with frustration in his voice.

We did that one more time, then went back to our regular game because we didn't want them to catch on. We ended up winning 30 to 10. We mixed up the teams for the next two games, and since we were on opposing teams we didn't do that trick again. But I think they kept wondering if they'd see anything else. After the third game, they decided they'd had enough for the day.

"It was good seeing you guys," Arturo said, walking off the court. "Don't be so scarce."

I could tell Pablito was still thinking about the mind reading as he paused to watch Arturo cross the street and walk toward the cluster of murals in the park.

"This stuff is useful for basketball and knowing who's going to a baseball game. Is it good for anything else?"

"Pablito, I tell you, you oughta come sit in with us," I said. "It'll blow you away."

"Like ... poof!" Tony added, throwing his fingers at Pablito like a magician.

"Yeah, yeah. Well, maybe sometime. See you guys later."

Once they were both far enough away, we busted out laughing.

"Man, that act really worked great. We really had them fooled," said Tony. "They thought we were reading each other's mind!"

We sat for a little while to rest, watching the other people on the court. Luckily it wasn't crowded yet. A mix of small kids and older guys were playing at two of the other three remaining half-courts, with one vacant, so we didn't have to share our half-court.

"Are you keeping up with all these energy practices?" I asked Tony as I got up and took a shot from the top of the key and missed.

"You're kidding, right? Now I understand why he has these sessions spaced out with at least four weeks in between." Tony drove to the basket and made a layup. "I'm not complaining about how much there is to do, I just can't do all of them every day. But I do as many as I can." He ran down the ball and bounced it my way. "My goal is to do them all at least a few times before we meet with him again. But I make a point of doing one of the two meditations every day."

"Yeah, he did say to do what we can. I can't do them every day either, but I've mostly been keeping up. Lucky for me the new karate classes don't start for a few weeks. I thought I would be able to do everything, but it's tough. I'm not complaining either, because I'm beginning to understand why it's important that we practice this stuff. I like your idea of at least doing everything a few times during the month. And right now, I'm also doing one of the meditations every day, and building energy and sending it out once or twice a week." I dribbled down the right side and shot a jumper—and missed.

"I like building the energy up and feeling it in my hands," said Tony, "and sometimes throwing it. Tai chi is good for that. Hey, are you giving thanks at one meal a day?"

"Yeah," I said, bouncing the ball back to him, "and trying to eat mindfully too, at least once during the day. Not always at the same meal, but I do try to get those in."

"Let's do another game of *around-the-world*," Tony called out as he went to the foul line to shoot for first up. He was about to shoot the ball, but then stopped suddenly, staring up the street. He kept looking and looking, trying to see who was walking toward us on Logan Avenue.

"Hey, speaking of things we'd like to have in our lives, isn't that Gloria walking this way?" he asked, still holding the ball.

"Whoever it is, is over a block away," I answered, "and I can't ... yeah, I think you're right. I think that's Gloria. So stop staring man, and just shoot the ball!"

"You think she's walking over here by accident? Or did you tell her we were gonna be here? Or maybe you've been sending energy her way?"

"Tony, stop staring and shoot the ball!"

He finally shot, but it missed, just short of the front of the rim. I picked up the ball and went to the same spot. I dribbled the ball a couple of times, then held the ball, lining up my shot. Then I dribbled a few more times, held the ball, and looked at the basket again.

"Well?"

"Yeah, I talked with her yesterday and mentioned that we were gonna be out here this morning playing basketball. But she didn't say anything about coming over here to see us."

"To see you, not us! She's not coming here to see me. And for Chuey's sake, shoot the ball!"

"Hey, don't rush me, man," I said, as I dribbled again then took take aim. "I don't want to look foolish and throw up an air ball like you. She's getting closer. I gotta make this look good."

My shot hit the backboard and bounced straight down into the net, so I moved to the first spot on the key at the side of the basket.

"Okay, folks, he's looking good, but he's gonna choke on this one." Tony tried to psych me into missing, but I didn't let his chatter get to me. I made all four shots without missing, and was back to the free throw line just as Gloria came up alongside the court.

"Hi, guys!" she said, walking onto the court. "Can I play?"

"Well, I guess that's about it for me," said Tony.

"You don't want to play another round?" I asked, knowing he wouldn't.

"I can count," he said. Three's a crowd."

"Oh, come on, Tony," Gloria implored, "You just don't want me to beat you."

"No, really, I have to go. I have to work at the store for a few hours. Here," he said, passing the ball to Gloria, "you two can keep playing. Bring it to me later today, Vincent."

After Tony left, we took a few shots at the basket, but it was soon obvious that Gloria wasn't there to play basketball. She wasn't even trying—just sort of killing time.

"So, Glo, what are you doing walking around over here?" I asked. "Had to run an errand for someone?" I pointed to the brown paper bag on top of her purse.

"My nana asked me to go to Porkyland," she answered, motioning up the street. "She likes their tortillas."

Doña Rosa was like my nana. They prefer to make their own tortillas, but if they don't want to go to all the trouble, or want some right away, Porkyland tortillas are about the only ones they'll buy." The Porkyland tortilleria and restaurant was two blocks up Logan Avenue.

"I need to be getting back home to give those to her. She's making burritos for lunch."

"Yeah, so I guess you better get going then."

"Well, before I do, I ... uh ... I wanted to ask you ... about your *tío*."

"Which one?" I knew very well who she wanted to talk about. She didn't have any interest in my other *tíos*.

"Emilio."

"He's not my *tío*, he's my grandfather's ..."

"I know, I know. You said what he's been teaching you is to think about light touching your head, saying prayers before meals, and dancing?"

"No, not just dancing ..."

"Okay," she said quickly, cutting me off again, "movement."

"Yeah, movement. That includes karate, tai chi, Toltec movements, *and* dancing."

"And thinking about sunlight?"

"Not just thinking about it. Focusing attention on the light energy, or *meditating* on it."

"Oh, yeah, I've heard about meditation. But what's the big deal about learning from a *brujo*? I could go to the YWCA and take classes on different types of movement and dance. My Nana always leads our prayers before we eat. And lots of people meditate."

"I never said it was a big deal. And I don't know why people are so concerned that Don Emilio is a *brujo*. Well, I do know. It's because people have these strange ideas about *brujos*. That's why Don Emilio doesn't even like the word *brujo*. He prefers the word *shaman*. *Brujo* makes people think about black magic and strange rituals."

"Like the chickens," she said smiling.

"Yeah," I said with a laugh, "like the chickens!"

"Linda and I still laugh about that one. You guys got her good that day."

"Got her?" I asked. "Just *her?*"

"You don't think I believed you guys were doing rituals with chickens, do you?"

"Oh, no, no. Ah, what kind of rituals did you think we were doing?"

"Come on, Vincent. I only know what you've told me. That's why I'm asking questions and trying to understand what you are learning. When my nana or mother say something about your *tío* or about *brujos*, I want to be able to inform them if they have some wrong ideas."

"Do you think they're going to change their minds about *brujos* because of what you say?"

"Well, I hope so, because they don't like me seeing you or talking to you, because they know you're learning from a *brujo*."

"What the heck is this?" I said, raising my voice and starting again to feel the pressures of everyone trying to tell me what to do and what not to do. "Why should I care what your grandmother or your mother think about Don Emilio?"

"Because ... I don't want them to tell me not to see you." She turned her head and looked down, avoiding eye contact. "I like being around you ... and talking with you." She paused, and neither of us said anything for what seemed like an eternity. I guess she was waiting for me to tell her the same thing. Finally she looked up at me and said, "Well, Vincent, don't you?"

"Yeah, I like being around me," I said with a big grin.

"Vincent! You're impossible!" she said, slapping me on the shoulder. "Be serious!"

"Okay, okay. I like being around you too," I said, quickly running on to my next sentence, "but what else can *I* do to get them to change their minds about Don Emilio?"

"Nothing, I guess," she said reaching out and taking hold of my right hand with both her hands. Then, moving a little closer said, "Just keep helping me understand what you're learning, so I can tell them they don't have anything to worry about."

"I hadn't mentioned this to you before," I said, "but Tony and I have talked about wanting to share this stuff we're learning with the guys ..."

"And girls," she quickly added. "You *were* planning to share it with the girls, too, right?"

"Uh ... well, yes, of course. That's why I'm mentioning it. It was a struggle for us to understand a lot of it at first, but I think it's beginning to come together now. I'd like to figure out a way to share what I've learned with you ... and others. This stuff Don Emilio is telling us is too important for us to just keep to ourselves."

"Well, I can't wait until you guys figure it all out. Just keep telling me as much as you can, and I'll keep talking to them and hoping they don't forbid me to see you."

"Hey, if it's any consolation to you, my mother and my nana don't like me studying with Don Emilio either. For the same reasons, I guess. They don't really know what he teaches."

"But, they're letting you?"

"Tata insisted."

"And they're still against it?"

"I guess so. But we haven't been meeting with him very long. It's only been about four months. I guess they're still waiting to see what happens—whether he straightens me out, or ..."

"Or what?"

"Or turns me into a sorcerer's apprentice."

We both laughed. But I think she wasn't so sure if it was a joke.

22
——

THE SECRET LIFE OF PLANTS

"The clearest way into the Universe
is through a forest wilderness."

JOHN MUIR

I was so excited about this trip to the mountains that I arrived early, and waited for Tony and Don Emilio. When we were finally ready to go, I jumped into the back seat of Tata's car. Tony sat up front. We took Interstate 8 east, out to Cuyamaca State Park, about 50 miles away. It was a nice drive, watching the scenery change from the dry, mostly golden colors of the lower elevation brush and dry grasses, to the greens and browns of trees at the higher elevations.

Don Emilio pulled into at the Paso Picacho campground and parked in the picnic area. It felt good to get out and walk around after sitting in the car for an hour. And it was great to breathe in the clean mountain air with its pine tree fragrance. It was a beautiful sight looking across the green and mostly yellow meadow to the green hillside camping area thickly covered with pine and oak trees, and manzanita shrubs. Although the late October morning was cool, I knew it would warm up during the day.

"Are you boys ready to start our session?" Don Emilio led us over to one of the wooden picnic benches. The dark brown paint looked recent, but I could tell that the benches had been there a long time. The edges of the wood had been worn smooth by many years of use. People had carved their initials on the table, some barely visible under the paint, and some so deep into the wood that the paint couldn't cover them up.

"Man, I was just getting into walking," said Tony, sounding a bit disappointed. "Afterward, are we gonna have time to walk around, take a hike, stuff like that?"

"Not after––*during.*" We will walk through the forest, and by the time we leave I think you will feel you had quite an interesting hike out in nature. Then, as I promised, we will hike in another location and see if we can find eagles in their natural habitat."

"Yes!" I blurted. "That's what I've been waiting for! Last night I meditated on my eagle power animal, and like you said, I asked him to join us today. Before going to sleep I even tried the power animal journey. I was able to connect for a little while, but I was too excited about doing the real thing to get much out of that attempt. And during the night I even dreamed again about flying as an eagle. I just know I'm gonna see eagles today!"

Don Emilio looked at me and smiled. Then he said our usual opening prayer, and after that closed his eyes and sat in silence for a little while. Finally, he opened his eyes and spoke.

"We are here to connect with Mother Earth and the spirits of nature. So, to begin, we are going to do a different type of focused-awareness exercise today. This one is to ground you, to help you feel more connected to the earth, and to allow you to be a connection between the earth and the sky. Close your eyes and relax your body as usual. Take in a few deep breaths."

He waited for us to take in those deep breaths. Tony remarked how good it felt to breathe in the cool mountain air. I nodded in agreement, not wanting to speak as I sat there very relaxed.

"Breathe normally now, as we begin the rain of light meditation," said Don Emilio. "Do as before and focus on the rain of light energy entering the top of your head. As you breathe in, feel it begin to fill you up. Now, imagine that you have long thin filaments of light, like roots, extending out from your feet, and penetrating deep into the ground. On a few out-breaths, send energy out through your feet and through those thin filaments, into the earth. Besides feeling physically better yourself, you can feel good knowing that you are serving as a connection for the transfer of healing light between the Great Spirit and the earth. Continue visualizing this exchange of energy from the universe through you into the earth."

Don Emilio paused while Tony and I did as instructed, pulling in light energy on our in-breaths, and sending it into the earth on out-breaths. I was so focused on it that I was a little startled when I heard Don Emilio's voice.

"As you come back," continued Don Emilio, "I want you to keep your awareness on the light energy raining down upon you and entering the top of your head. Stay seated for a few moments and maintain that peaceful, centered feeling. Your mind has been quiet for the past few minutes. We will maintain that quiet, peaceful feeling while walking."

"We're going to walk with our eyes closed?" Tony asked.

"No," he chuckled, "but you will walk with your *mind* closed, keeping out your usual mind chatter as much as possible. You can open your eyes now."

He pointed across the meadow to the base of the mountain. "We will start over there." Tony quickly got up and led the way on the trail through the meadow, walking very quickly, and I was right behind him.

"Slow down a little," Don Emilio called out. "We are not in any rush. Let us take today's experience slowly, as it may be difficult to maintain focused-awareness while walking fast. Are you both still aware of the energy pouring through you, entering the top of your head?"

"Mm-hmm," I said, nodding my head. Tony nodded his head too, but only after raising his eyebrows and putting his hands to his mouth with an expression of "oops." Don Emilio smiled but didn't say anything about it.

"Now as we hike," said Don Emilio, "we will walk slowly and focus our awareness on each step, and where we are stepping. This is another focused-attention exercise that helps to stop the mind chatter. You can stop thinking about the energy coming down on your head now. I thought since we are walking you might like to try this walking meditation technique. Do not *think* or start up that mind chatter again. Just be aware as you walk. If you notice a pretty rock or flower, just acknowledge the thought and move on. Stay present and aware of what you are doing in the moment. Maintain your awareness of each step, as you lift one leg and put it down, then lift the other and put it down, step, by step, by step."

"You know," said Tony, "it is real hard to stay in that quiet and peaceful place, and listen to what you are saying, plus walk, without thinking about it! It's like I'm losing some of it as we walk, and I'm not hearing all that you are saying."

"Yes, I know this is difficult," said Don Emilio, "because I am giving instructions for a process that requires not so much thinking but awareness, while processing instructions usually requires thinking. Do not worry."

I felt the need to check what he was expecting us to do. "So we need to keep that calm, peaceful feeling, and be aware of our steps as we walk on this trail."

"Yes. Be aware of each step that you take. That awareness will help maintain and enhance that peaceful feeling inside."

Don Emilio stopped talking and looked at us. He was waiting to see if we had any more questions. I didn't say anything. I was anxious to get hiking. Tony was quiet too. So Don Emilio nodded his head in the direction of the trailhead. We started walking side by side, but Tony was soon walking ahead of me. I was trying to be aware of each of my steps, so I needed to go slower. Tony hesitated when he noticed he was getting farther and farther ahead.

"It is okay to walk at different speeds," said Don Emilio. "Walk at whatever speed makes you comfortable, while still being aware of your steps. If your mind starts to wander, bring your focus back to the act of lifting up your foot and placing it down."

It wasn't long before Tony had slowed down to my pace. After a while, Don Emilio spoke loudly, so we both could hear.

"You may find it easier to focus on either your left or right leg, as you walk, unless you are walking really slowly. At the pace you two are going, I would suggest that you pick one side."

That was an interesting walking experience. I had to be constantly aware of the movement of my right leg as I lifted it and placed it down, and lifted again, but this eliminated most of my internal talking to myself. We had been walking for maybe thirty minutes when we came to a spot where the trail curved around the side of the hill and presented us with a view of a small valley. Don Emilio walked a few feet off the trail toward some boulders.

"This looks like a good place to sit," said Don Emilio. "Let us talk about what you have been experiencing. Does your body feel any different from when we started?"

"I feel a little light-headed," Tony said. "It went away as we talked about everything and started the walk. But now I feel it again."

"I feel like that, too," I said, "and sort of energized, like I could just keep on walking."

"How did focusing on your steps compare to focusing on the light energy?" he asked.

"I was surprised," I said. "I didn't think I would be able to do as well while focusing on my walking, but once I got used to concentrating on my right side, I got into a rhythm and most of the inner chatter stayed away, maybe even more than with the raining energy."

"Yeah, for me too," added Tony, "maybe because it takes more concentration."

"Anything else you are aware of right now?" he asked.

"Just that it feels really good being out here with all the trees and plants and flowers," said Tony. "It's really beautiful."

"Yeah," I said, nodding my head. "It really is."

"Have either of you been here before?"

"A few times," said Tony.

"Me too. I've come here with my family, during summer, for many years."

"And how did it look to you last time you were here?"

"Well, now that you ask, it seems more beautiful now," I answered. "The colors of the flowers seem brighter today, and the greens of the tree leaves and pine needles seem greener."

"If you have been here many times before, how is it that the forest seems more beautiful and greener today?" asked Don Emilio.

"I don't know," said Tony. "Everything just seems different to me too, so bright and so alive. I think the change has to be in us. What's making us see things this way today?"

"Very good, Antonio. The difference *is* in you. These focused-awareness exercises have helped cleanse your perception. While you focused your attention first on the rain of light coming down and entering your body, and then on your walking steps, you were in a state of heightened awareness. You were still right here, but your awareness shifted over to a place where you could see and understand more than you usually do. You are much more aware of the beauty around you today. You both have done well. While you are in this heightened awareness would be a good time to talk about auras."

"Auras? We talked about auras before," I said. "That's the energy around the body, right?"

"That's like the halo they show in pictures of Jesus and the saints," said Tony.

"Yes," said Don Emilio, "but more than just a light around someone's head. The aura is the energy body, which extends beyond the entire physical body. Every living thing has an aura."

"And since everything is alive, everything has an aura," chimed in Tony.

"Exactly," said Don Emilio. "But the amount of life force energy in objects differs, so the auras will be different."

"Come this way," he said, rising from his boulder and walking a few feet to a spot where we could see across the valley. "We are going to look at the aura of trees. Focus your gaze on the tops of the trees on that small ridge across from us. As you continue to stare your eyes will tend to go cross-eyed. Don't try to correct that too much. Let the double vision come, but keep your attention above the tops of the trees. When your vision changes from precise to slightly double you may see a layer of perhaps blue light extending along the tops of the trees."

"Wow, right when you said blue light, I could see it!" I said.

"Hey man, I don't see nothing but the trees," said Tony, sounding a bit frustrated.

"Try something different," said Don Emilio. "Try focusing on the next grouping of trees in the distance behind those trees. When you do that, the trees in front will be slightly out of focus."

"Yeah, got it!" Tony exclaimed. "Now I can see the blue light on the trees. I see the aura!"

"Okay, so now you can both see auras. You each focus a little differently to see the aura. If you practice this more, you will begin to see auras of people, and then later you may see the various colors within those auras. This will take much practice, however. You can practice on your own at any time by doing just as we did now. Perhaps you can help each other when either of you get stuck and cannot get it. Now let us continue our walk."

We walked on the path for perhaps another ten or fifteen minutes, during which time Don Emilio continued to periodically remind us to be aware of lifting and placing our foot. While admiring the beautiful variety of plant life alongside the path, Tony and I both noticed a grouping of small yellow flowers within a growth of weeds. But what really got our attention was a fluttering within those weeds. The fluttering motion was a butterfly, the same pale-yellow color as the flowers. Slowly, we moved up closer so we could see it better. What we found within that growth of weeds was a whole little world of very small flowers, small plants, butterflies, bugs, and new shoots of trees and plants that looked like tall trees.

"Whoa, is that amazing or what!" exclaimed Tony. "It's almost like the butterfly was fluttering its wings so we would notice it and come take a look at its home. Look. It's not moving much now."

"It's so amazing to see all these little players in this miniature forest, somewhat separated from the rest by these weeds," I said.

"It looks like they're protected by the weeds," said Tony, "since the weeds both surround them and provide some cover over them."

"Those are not weeds at all," Don Emilio added, "but other plants, now dead or dying, all of which are an essential part of this interconnected family of plants and insects that coexist in this little part of the forest."

"Yes! Everything is alive and interconnected. And those weeds, like you said, they aren't weeds; they're other plants that are part of this family." I was talking loud and fast, I was so excited about our find. "I remember one day I was complaining about having to pull weeds in my yard. Tata and my father were there, and Tata talked about the connection between the insects and the birds and the weeds, but I didn't understand what he meant. I heard the words but I didn't get it. Now I get it! I really understand that they are so alive and interconnected. And this is just a smaller version of how the rest of the forest and the rest of the world is interconnected. I don't know how I understand it, but inside of me I seem to *know* it. I can feel it!"

"This really is amazing," said Tony. "I think now I also understand these connections. But it seems to be more than just being told, and then believing it. *Feeling* it seems to be the right word. Vincent, that quote you have about when people realize their oneness with the Universe and all its powers—man, that makes a lot more sense to me now."

"Yeah, I always liked what it said. And now, like with my eagle dream, I can *feel* what it really means."

Don Emilio looked at us and smiled. "This is what I meant when I said that this information is not something that can be taught, and that at some point you would just get it—that you would feel and understand it inside your being, not just through your rational mind."

After being with this miniature forest for a while longer, we continued along the forest path. As we walked, I kept silently apologizing to the grasses in the path as I stepped on them. I had a new awareness of the life within each blade of grass and within all the beings in the forest, and a new awareness of my connection to them all. I continued to hold this awareness as we moved along the path. I heard the crickets chirping, saw the lizards and squirrels scurrying by, heard the birds calling, and saw amazingly beautiful plants and flowers. And I felt like I knew them all for the very first time, and knew them as a family, rather than just as individual beings.

After walking a while longer on the trail, Don Emilio called for us to stop. He walked off the trail a few feet and went up to a tall wide oak tree. He put his arms around the tree and hugged it for a few minutes. Tony and I just stood there on the trail waiting for him.

"I sure hope he isn't going to tell us we have to start going around hugging trees," Tony said quietly. "We'll never live that down. I can just see us, hugging a tree on the way to school! Wait 'til the guys see that. Wait 'til the girls see that! We'll be finished, man!"

Don Emilio turned around, looked at the tree, looked up at the sky, and then looked around on the ground on both sides of the trail. He pointed to a couple of small boulders about twenty feet away. "Sit over there, facing the old oak tree." He followed and stood behind us as we looked toward the tree.

"I want you to take three deep breaths, and relax. And while you are sitting there relaxed, I want you to look at the tree. Notice its beautiful shape, the deep green of the leaves, and the unique texture of its gray-brown bark." He paused to give us time to admire the tree. "You saw me hug the tree. I want you now to reach out with your energy and hug the tree from where you sit. Send energy out from your heart area to the tree, and just hold it in the warmth of your energy."

We did that, and waited for Don Emilio to continue.

"This old oak tree has something to show you. Look at the tree's branches, where you can see blue sky in the background. Pick out a thick branch and focus on that area. Look at that branch as if you were trying to see its aura. That is, stare at it and allow your eyes to go a little out of focus, like you were trying to focus at a point in the sky behind...."

"Oh my God!" Tony shouted. I knew what he was shouting about, because I saw it too.

"What is this?" he asked in a very animated manner. "I don't believe what I'm seeing."

I kept looking at the tree, because what I saw was just amazing. In my peripheral vision, I could see Tony dancing around excitedly with his hands raised in the air.

"What am I seeing?" he shouted. "Oh heck...I can't see it anymore." He had stopped his antics and was trying to see it again. "Don Emilio, how come I can't see it now?"

I had blinked my eyes in wonder but was able to keep that 'out of focus' vision on the thick tree branch. I could see a kind of green stuff flowing along *inside* the tree branch, and somehow, I knew this to be the life force of the tree. I stood there in awe, speechless, watching the flow. Suddenly I remembered seeing this before. It was in my dream.

"You are proving to be very powerful apprentice shamans, if I may go so far as to use that term. Not only have you proven yourselves able to see into another level of reality, but when you do not believe you can see what you are seeing, Tony, you are able to stop yourself from seeing it." Don Emilio chuckled at his joke. "That is pretty powerful. And you, Vicente?"

"This is amazing. I'm just watching this bright green stuff flowing inside the branch. I saw this before, in my dream about the eagle. Is this the life force of the tree?"

"You are asking my confirmation for something you already know inside. That is one reason to have a teacher—to make you feel better about what you are experiencing, to ease your doubts. But you will get to a point where you just accept what you know, even if you wonder how you know. You just know. Yes, you are seeing what you know you are seeing."

"How come we are able to see it now," said Tony, "and we've never seen it before?"

"Your preparations have brought you gradually into a state of heightened awareness, because we have spent time in both sitting and walking focused attention. Plus, we are here among these grand pines trees and wonderful old oak trees. They too are sentient beings, aware of the spiritual nature of your journey, and they are helping you. Also, our spirit guides and our higher selves have been communicating with the spirits of the forest. We have a lot of helpers with us right now."

"I'm feeling strange, Don Emilio," I said. "Part of me is thinking all this is very weird and scary. And another part knows it is not weird. It's almost like I feel happy to see this, to feel connected to all this. I kinda feel caught in the middle of two sides here."

"I'm not caught in no middle," said Tony. "This *is* all too weird. Having x-ray vision to see this green stuff flowing inside a tree. No one would ever believe I saw it. I'm not sure I saw it."

"These questions, these doubts, are good signs," Don Emilio answered. "Your conscious self is remembering its connection to all things, and is asserting its knowing of what is true. You are beginning to learn that your mental side is not all there is to you. But the mental side is now trying to protect its dominance by telling you not to believe what you saw, what you call this weird, scary stuff. As you practice what we are learning here, you will become increasingly better able to differentiate between what that voice in your head tells you, and what your true essence knows is real."

With that, Don Emilio turned and led the way as we walked back to the trail and continued our hike. As we walked through the forest, we continued the walking meditation. I found it amazing how easily the mind chatter stayed off as long as I was aware of lifting and placing my foot as I walked. As before, Tony and I moved out ahead of Don Emilio. After a long walk we came to the edge of another meadow, and Don Emilio called to us. He had walked out into the transition between the trees and the meadow and stood between two tall pines. In front of these pines were a variety of flowers and green plants. He waved us over to where he stood.

"I want you to tell me what kind of plants and trees you see right around us here."

"Pine trees, oaks, and junipers," I answered.

"Cedars, cottonwoods, manzanitas, and ferns," said Tony.

"Flowers, lots of different flowers, but I don't know their names," I added.

"Okay boys, we are now going to do our final exercise, called the *un-naming* exercise. I want you to pick any one of those beings you just pointed out, and *be* with it. But erase the name from your memory. It is not a pine tree, not a fern. Just as your name is not 'human being,' its name is not 'oak tree.' Give each being the respect of not calling it by a generic name. By not calling it by a generic name, it stops being just one of thousands. Rather, it is the unique being right here with you. Pick one being and sit there with it."

Don Emilio opened up his backpack and handed each of us our lunch bag.

"You can eat your lunch there. After you have spent a little time with this being, send energy out through your heart area and connect with it like you did when you practiced sending energy. Spend some time experiencing that heartfelt connection between you and this being. Once this being has had a chance to receive your energy and decode your feelings message, see if it has any information to share with you. We will get back together in about thirty minutes."

With that, he swung the backpack onto one shoulder and walked back to the edge of the trail, where he stretched out on a large flat boulder under an oak tree.

I didn't have to think much about which being to choose because I seem to have a real attachment to pine trees. I went over and sat in front of one of the big pines at the edge of the meadow and started in on my lunch. Once I was done eating, I did what Don Emilio said and sent energy out from my heart area to this being. Then I sat there for a while just feeling that connection.

Don Emilio knew what he was doing when he assigned this exercise. He didn't tell us what would happen; he just set the stage. I hadn't really expected to get any message. I didn't hear specific words. But I knew what its message to me was. Like Don Emilio had said earlier, I just knew. The more I observed this being, the more I became aware of how intricate the life connections around it were. This was not a solitary being on the edge of the forest. Yes, it had other nearby trees, but it had so much more. Two squirrels ran up and down its trunk and below it on the ground, sometimes reaching for a pinecone that perhaps one of them had broken apart. They seemed to be picking out seeds from the pinecone. Later, a blue jay came up to the same pinecone to see if it could get any seeds, and then flew up to a nest high in the branches.

I could see that the decay from chewed-up pine cones and leaves, twigs, pine needles and branches had created a thriving living environment for a variety of flowers and small plants, all within the shade of this being. While I was watching, two butterflies came frolicking through, jumping from one flower to the next under this being before moving on to their next destination. I pushed my finger into the ground and realized it was more decaying plant material than dirt. I had to push farther in to get to actual solid dirt. In the dirt and decaying matter were little bugs in the process of making the ground suitable for growth of the flowers and plants, and occasionally making a nice lunch for the birds that lived above.

I thought about this magnificent being, and how it could only stand in one place all its life—stuck there in the ground, looking out over the meadow—how it wasn't free like me to go where I wanted, to see what I wanted to see, to do what I wanted to do. Then something reminded me: I liked being up here, next to the trees and trails. Right then I noticed the being's long branches seemingly reach out to show me the environment encompassed within its outstretched arms. That's when I got the message. This being had an extended family made up of many species, not just trees. It was like a caretaker for these many little beings that lived within its immediate environment. It loved being what it was, and loved being connected to so many other life forms. And I knew that this being would not want to trade places with me. It would not want to be a human. It was totally and completely happy just *being.*

When Don Emilio came back, we told him about our experiences. Of course, he was not surprised. Tony's experience was similar to mine.

"Today you were able to experience plants, flowers and trees, and birds, butterflies and insects very differently than you ever have. When you sent out energy from your heart area and connected with the being that you chose, you discovered that a wealth of information could be communicated to you, information about its connection to all things in its environment. When you paused to be with the old oak tree and you sent energy out from your heart to that wise old being, it shared an amazing sight with you. The beautiful little butterfly so enchanted you that you unconsciously opened up your heart energy and connected with it and its family. They showed you a hidden miniature environment, and you were able to understand the extent of the many energy connections in that little web of life.

"You learned to talk with your brothers of the plant and animal kingdoms by sending energy from your heart. While the mind needs words and sound to talk, you experienced more in-depth communication than can even be expressed in words, and you did it through heartfelt sharing of energy. This has been a good day, and we are not finished yet!"

Don Emilio turned and started walking back on the trail toward the car. He was right. It had been a good day. We had a lot to talk about, but my attention quickly shifted. As we followed behind him, I called out excitedly, "Are we going to go see the eagles now?

23

CALLING EAGLES

*"Look deep into nature, and then you
will understand everything better."*

ALBERT EINSTEIN

We drove north from Paso Picacho past the turnoff for Stonewall Mine, and past the Boy Scout summer camp. I had gone to that summer camp a few years back. I really liked walking around there under the pine trees and out in the meadow where we played games, and hiking up Stonewall Peak and Cuyamaca Peak. We continued driving, past Cuyamaca Lake and then into the little town of Julian. Although mining was the major reason for the town's early existence, it had become mostly a tourist attraction, a mountain get-away with little shops selling antiques, gemstones, arts and crafts, and its well-known apple pies and apple cider. While on our camping trips, my parents liked to take us into Julian to walk around the town, and sometimes get an apple pie and some cider to take back to camp or to take home.

Don Emilio told us we were going to meet someone in town. He parked the car on Main Street and we walked about a block to the Julian Town Hall building. As we approached, a woman sitting on the porch called to Don Emilio, and they greeted each other with a hug.

"You guys must be Vicente and Antonio," she said as she stepped toward us.

And you must be his friend, I thought. Don Emilio said he would be meeting a friend, but I thought it would be a guy—and someone his age. While this woman was older, she wasn't as old as Don Emilio. She looked to be about forty, and pretty good-looking for an older lady.

"Elizabeth, this is Vicente," said Don Emilio, pointing to me, "and this is Antonio."

"But that's not what you call yourselves, is it?" she asked. "I know Don Emilio likes to use our formal names. Tony and … Vince?"

"Tony and Vincent," I answered.

"My, that's still pretty formal. Not Vince or Vinnie?"

"Yeah, Vinnie. You'se can call him dat," said Tony cracking up at his own attempt at a New York mafia accent.

"Hmm," she said, "Vinnie … "

I could feel my ears getting red. "I prefer Vincent, or maybe Vince."

"Well, Vincent, you can call me Liz, even though Don Emilio calls me Elizabeth."

"Elizabeth and I work together with some youth groups in the L.A. area," said Don Emilio.

"He's also working with me on shamanism and energy work," she said, "like with you."

"Have you been waiting long?" Don Emilio asked.

"No, not really," she said. "I came up early to walk around and see Julian. Then I came here and have been reading and watching the tourists come and go. I really haven't even been waiting for you. I figured you would get here when it was time to get here." Then her smile got brighter, as she said, almost laughing, "And I was right. Here you are!"

"Okay, so I guess we are ready to go," said Don Emilio. "I would like to visit the town myself, but we had better go before we run out of daylight."

The four of us walked down Main Street back to Tata's car.

"I'll sit in the front so I can navigate," said Liz. We all climbed into the car and started down the hill away from Julian.

"When Don Emilio said you wanted to see eagles in their natural habitat, I volunteered to come and help out," Liz said, turning in her seat so she could see us. "Did you already tell them?" she asked Don Emilio. He shook his head.

"Anyway, I have this friend, a Native American, and he showed me a place up here once, quite a few years back, where eagles nest. Although it has been a while, I think I should still be able to find it. It's hard to lose a mountain. However, I should warn you. You won't always see eagles here, even though this is their nesting area. They may be gone temporarily, flying around another part of the mountain range, or they may not be using this area right now."

She turned back to look out the window, and then checked the map spread out on her lap. We hadn't gone very far when she motioned for Don Emilio to turn left down a paved road. That road went for quite a way, maybe about two miles, and then the pavement ended.

"Let's see," she said, pointing to the map. "We continue on this road after the pavement ends for about one-and-a-half miles, until it comes to a T." A few minutes later, we arrived.

"Turn left, then look for a parking area a few feet up this way," she directed Don Emilio.

And sure enough, there was a parking area with two other cars there.

"All right!" she exclaimed, seeming a little surprised that she had found it. She turned around toward the back seat and offered her raised palm. Tony reached up and gave her five.

"Yes! I knew I could still find it!" she said, sounding a little relieved.

We parked the car and got out our daypacks and water. We also put our jackets in the packs, in case it got cool on the way back, although the temperature was still very comfortable, even a little bit warm. We then walked a few feet to where the trail started. Well, actually two trails. Liz led the way and took the one on the left.

As we walked, she called out, "Up that way, behind that hill, is where the eagles are."

This appeared to be a popular area for hikers, because the paths were so well worn and not overgrown with weeds or plants. The trail was mostly a gradual climb, with a more strenuous elevation change in only a few spots, at least in the early going. Twice our trail was crossed by other trails, both of them wider and well-traveled. And at these junctions, our trail seemed to appear narrower and less used. I thought that was a good sign, because I didn't think that eagles in the wild would be too happy next to a very busy trail.

Soon the trail got steeper and steeper. We had to stop a few times for water and to rest. The trail seemed so unused in places that we had a hard time finding it after it crossed large areas of rocks. But we kept finding it again, and kept climbing.

Liz and Don Emilio chatted away the whole time. I had never seen Don Emilio so talkative or enthusiastic. He really seemed to come alive around Liz. It was good to see him happily interacting with someone else other than Tony and me.

While they talked, I got quieter and soon was totally in my head. I could feel the connection with my eagle spirit getting stronger. Because I had done a power animal journey the night before, and had another eagle dream, I was really feeling connected with the eagles. I felt confident that I was finally going to join them in their natural habitat.

After hiking up the hill for quite a long time, we came to the crest of the trail and discovered we were just a few yards from the top. We walked hurriedly the rest of the way up the trail, anxious to see what lay beyond the large outcropping of boulders at the top. Tony and I ran toward the boulders, but Don Emilio and Liz called to us to slow down and move quietly, since eagles might be up at the top. But when we arrived, all we saw was a beautiful view into a little valley, and across the other side of the valley, another peak.

"Heck, I don't see any eagles," said Tony.

"Remember, Elizabeth said we might not see any today," said Don Emilio.

"I have good news and bad news," added Liz. "The good news is that I see some eagles...."

"Oh, where?" Tony hollered.

"There, across the valley, at the top of that other peak."

I could see them now—two large birds circling near the top of that peak.

"The bad news," she continued, "is *that's* the peak we were supposed to climb. I guess at the trailhead, we should have taken the trail on the right."

"Look," said Don Emilio, "more eagles have joined them."

"Can we hike over there and get a closer view?" asked Tony.

"That is still quite a distance," answered Don Emilio. "I do not think we have enough daylight left to get over there and still find our way back down the mountain."

I don't know why I did what I did next. I didn't think about it or plan it. But I walked away from them as they talked and climbed on top of the boulders. As I stood there on a flat area, the highest point on this peak, I closed my eyes and bowed my head, then spread my arms out, like wings. After taking a few deep breaths, I sent energy from my heart out to the eagles.

The wind picked up. I could hear it rushing past my ears. A strong gust pushed on my wings, almost lifting me up. I bent forward, turning my feathers into the wind, and jumped off the rock, while I batted my outstretched wings, catching the wind as I sailed off the peak. The steep mountainside dropped away rapidly as I flew over the void toward the opposite mountain where the eagles circled. One by one they flew toward me, then past. I turned back and followed them. We circled over a group of people at the top of the peak. Then I heard a distant sound, a very faint sound. It was one word that seemed to move toward me, until I could almost make it out. I closed my eyes as I strained to hear the word, and also heard a very faint whooshing sound.

Vincent....

The faint word hung there in the blackness. For a moment I seemed to be caught there in the void, alone with that one word.

"Vincent," Liz called softly, "look up!"

I opened my eyes and slowly raised my head, with my arms still spread out. Then I saw them—four eagles circling right above me, just a few feet over my head. Right where I knew they were. They were almost close enough to touch.

<u>24</u>

CREATING WHAT WE THINK ABOUT

*"You create the world that you know. You have been
given perhaps the most awesome gift of all: the ability
to project your thoughts outward into physical form."*

SETH (JANE ROBERTS)

"That was one weird trip, my eagle friend," said Tony as he sat down across from me. We had agreed to meet in the quad at school during lunch on Thursday to talk about what happened on the mountain trip. I had wanted to talk with him sooner, but with classes, homework, him working at the store, and all our energy practice, it was tough to find time to get together. It was probably better that we had to wait a few days anyway, to let it all sink in.

"It was weird, all right," I answered, "but weird good. It was magical. Better than Disneyland."

"Yeah, it definitely was magical. You know, I had my doubts about whether any of the stuff Don Emilio was telling us was going to be of any use. I thought it might be a waste of time, but at least it was getting my family off my back for a little while. My biggest concern was what weird *brujo* stuff he was gonna dump on us. And just when I was thinking it wasn't too strange after all, we do the mountain trip and find out about the secret world of trees and plants and butterflies. We're talking to trees and they're talking back. Then, using x-ray vision, we see a tree's life force flowing. And on top of it all, you call your eagle friends over to fly with you."

We both laughed at first, then shook our heads in wonder, as neither of us could ever have dreamed up what happened on that trip.

"You know of course," I said, "no one will believe any of this when we tell them."

"Well, I've been thinking about that. Maybe we just tell what they might believe, like if we told someone about the auras of the trees. They might not believe us at first, but we could show them how to do it."

"Okay, then what? Show them how to talk to a tree?" We both laughed again.

"No way," said Tony as he bit into his roast beef sandwich. "Too weird."

I opened up my bag and pulled out the tuna sandwich. "We don't have to tell anyone right now. We still have more things to learn from Don Emilio, and we can talk to him about this. Maybe right now the point is to figure out what this means for us—what did *we* learn, and how can *we* use it. And for now, perhaps we put this stuff on that list of things we want to share with the guys after we have finished these sessions with Don Emilio."

"Yeah, I guess you're right." Tony took another bite of his sandwich as we both tried to finish our lunch before we ran out time. But even in the silence it was clear neither of us could stop thinking about those magical moments.

"That was really something," Tony said finally, "looking into that tree branch like we had x-ray vision. Like superman."

"We can't leap tall buildings in a single bound," I added, "but you and I saw inside that tree! That was real!"

"And called eagles to come and play," Tony added.

I sat there in silence, except for the sound of me finishing my sandwich, replaying over and over in my head the almost unbelievable events of that day in the mountains. I looked at Tony, but he was staring right past me, zoned out like he was also looking back at those events in his mind rather than seeing what was in front of his eyes.

The next few weeks passed so quickly I didn't have enough time to practice everything I wanted to. Not that I spent all that much time working on them. I guess I needed to get into a habit of doing them, and not stop before I was finished. But Don Emilio had said not to beat ourselves up about it, and just do the best we could. So that's what I did. But I was anxious to have another session with him to see what was next. This stuff he was teaching and showing us was getting to be so amazingly great.

When the day finally came for our next session, we met at Tony's house before heading over.

"Hey, have you tried to see any auras?" I asked, as we walked out of his yard. I was curious how he was doing with the new exercises, or if he was even practicing any of it yet.

Tony looked at me, surprised that I asked. "Man, auras and all that other stuff? I haven't even thought about doing those yet. Have you been practicing any of that?"

"No," I answered, "not with everything else we have to practice. I guess I could start doing the walking meditation, and maybe even looking at auras."

"But talking to trees, and looking inside! Man, that's just so weird it scares me," said Tony.

"Scares the part of you that doesn't want to believe this stuff is real." I remembered he had erased it from his sight because he couldn't believe what he saw.

"Yeah, I know. I guess I'm slipping back to that place of being comfortable with what I've always known, rather than moving on and reminding myself that we know what we saw, and we know we can see with x-ray vision into the tree, and we know we can talk with trees and plants."

"If our energy is up," I added, "and we are in ... what did Don Emilio call it?"

"A state of heightened awareness."

We turned at the alley and walked toward Nana and Tata's yard. I mentioned that lately I had been keeping my energy up, and as a result, I was becoming more aware of my intuition and getting messages.

"Oh yeah? What kind of messages?"

"Oh, I'm sorta reading minds," I said nonchalantly as we walked into the yard. "Let me see." I put my hand to my head. "I think Nana wants to fix me a burrito."

"Yeah, right. Mind reading," Tony said laughing. "That's wishing and hoping. I'm hoping she has one for me, too!"

Don Emilio came out of the house as we walked up to the back door.

"*Hola mijos.*" How are you two doing today?"

"Oh, fine," I said.

"Fine, my eye. I just got very hungry hearing Vincent talk about his Nana's burritos."

When it really came down to it, what Tony and I both liked best for lunch or a snack was my Nana's bean burritos. She had made a big pot of beans the day before, so I knew there was a good possibility we could get a burrito. I looked at Don Emilio, then into the house toward the kitchen, then back at Don Emilio. "Do we have time?"

"Yes, yes," he responded, "go ahead. Your Nana has some food waiting for you. She has a way of knowing when you are going to be coming around looking for food."

"*Siempre busca por comida,*" Nana said to Don Emilio from the kitchen doorway. "*Todo el día tiene hambre, y siempre está comiendo, pero no sé a donde se pone la comida. Mira no más, qué flaco.*"

She insisted to anyone who would listen, that I was too skinny. That's why she kept pushing food my way, which was just fine with me. I just loved to eat Nana's food.

"*Hijos, vengan aquí para comer,*" she said motioning for us to come inside and eat.

"I just ate," Don Emilio said to us as we walked into the house. "You boys take your time. Remember, a prayer before meals, and then think about what you are doing, what is going on, as you chew. Come out when you have finished."

We said a silent prayer before digging into our big, delicious burritos of mashed beans with melted jack cheese and a little red chile sauce. I quickly gulped mine down, as did Tony. Nana wanted to feed us more, but didn't want to keep us from Don Emilio, so she wrapped a second burrito for each of us in paper towels and sent us outside.

"Don Emilio," I said as I sat down in the garden shed, "Tony and I were talking about the mountain trip. That was one heck of an amazing experience." I unwrapped the burrito and took a big bite, looking at Don Emilio.

"I agree, it *was* very amazing," Don Emilio answered smiling, probably not surprised that we got out of the house with a second burrito. "I was very pleased with what you both were able to do that day. Your energy vibration was so high, you were both in a state of heightened awareness much of the day. What you experienced was certainly extra ordinary, way beyond what you can usually perceive. I am sure it left you somewhat unsettled and unsure of what you experienced. But I assure you it was all very real.

"Yeah, unsettled may be a better word," said Tony, also chewing on his burrito. "I was thinking fear. I think I'm afraid to try looking into a tree again, or trying to talk to one. So I haven't practiced that yet."

"I did not assign that as an exercise because you first need to be in a high energy, high vibration state. Let us leave that for the advanced level, and for now practice what your small self, your ego, can experience without being fearful of what it does not understand. I could say do not fear, just trust your Higher Self. But the mind does not give up control so easily. It tries to protect you by sending up a red flag, a warning, which you perceive as a sense of fear. So we need to approach such experiences differently, under conditions of high energy vibration, where the self experiences these out of the ordinary events in a safe environment and with less of a shock to the mind."

"Okay, so we won't be doing that again anytime soon," said Tony. "Anyway, how does seeing into trees or talking with them help us?"

"Or flying with eagles?" I added.

Don Emilio got up from his chair and stood in front of the worktable. He clasped his hands in front of him, almost as if he was going to pray.

"Mijos, this is really important," he said, looking at us intently. "Those experiences showed you that the limits you have placed on what you think you can do, are no longer valid. You can do much more than you ever dreamed possible. But not while stuck with what the mind thinks is possible. On the mountain you were able to quiet the mind to some extent, and entered a state of heightened awareness. In that state you saw the aura, or the energy, emanating from living beings. You saw inside a tree and saw its life force flowing. You heard the thoughts of plants and animals, and understood the complex web of life and the energy connections among them. In your previous vision experience, Vicente, you even saw the lines of energy connecting you with all things. Then, at the top of the mountain, you sent those same lines of energy out to your eagle friends, and joined them in flight. You both sent lines of energy out from your heart area, and were able to connect with the web of energy, the Force, that connects those beings there on the mountain.

"That web of energy exists not just on the mountain among those plants and animals. It exists everywhere, all around you. Just as you sent out your energy to connect with those plants and animals, you can connect with anything and anyone, right here. Our previous sessions and your exercises prepared you to know energy and move it, to stop energy leaks and increase your energy, and to send it out to connect with others. By moving into a state of heightened awareness and directing your energy out into that web of energy connections, you have the power for more than just seeing into a tree or flying with eagles. You have the power to create whatever you desire. Let me say that again. Using the techniques I am sharing with you, you can create whatever you desire and focus on––anything you want to have, to do, or to become."

"I'm all for that," I said, with a certain amount of doubt. It sounded almost too good to be true that we could create whatever we wanted. But with all the amazing stuff we'd seen and done with Don Emilio, I figured I might as well keep on believing.

"I don't know," said Tony. "If I told any friends or family members what you just said, they'd say I was crazy. But it's been crazy good so far, and it feels like we're getting closer. So now what?"

"Now we will go right into the topic for today," said Don Emilio, "which is *creating what we think about.* We discussed this topic briefly before, and now we will go into it more deeply."

"Great," said Tony, "I've been wanting to get back to that. As I remember, you said that this Force responds to where we focus our attention, and makes things happen to create what we think about. So how do we do it? How do we use this Force to get what we want?"

"Well, let me begin by restating a few basic points." Don Emilio moved back and leaned against the worktable. "One, everything is alive and has consciousness. Two, everything is made of energy, and on an energetic level is actually a ball of luminous energy fibers. Three, everything is connected by these thin luminous fibers of energy. Four, there is a massive, living, thinking web of energy permeating the universe. This energy, which some call the Force, and others call Intent, responds to the focus of our attention and makes things happen that match our thoughts. The luminous fibers are key. They connect us to everything, *including our thoughts,* which are alive and have their own consciousness. These thoughts do not have a physical mass that we can see, but they are alive. They are energy, and they exist within our energy field, our ball of luminous fibers. Are you following me so far?"

We both nodded.

"Let us use the example we used before: the thought of wanting a better job. Even before the thought of a better job was completely formed, you began to build up more and more emotional energy about wanting more than a job working in the store. Eventually the thought that evolved in your head was you wanted a job teaching karate.

"What happened on the energy level was that the idea became fully formed and popped out of your enegy field as a separate thought bubble, still connected to you. A large amount of energy then traveled through the luminous fibers to that thought bubble. This living entity, your thought bubble, became more refined as you imagined yourself teaching karate, and it grew stronger and stronger as more energy was sent to it. When this thought bubble had accumulated a sufficient amount of energy, your Higher Self took over and, using its infinitely numerous lines of energy fibers, sent that thought-energy out into the Force, broadcasting the information about your desire.

"As a result, the karate instructor got an inspiration to hire someone part time to help with the younger kids. When they posted the job notice, you responded to an urge to go to the youth center. While there you saw the notice. You applied and, since you had the required training, you were hired."

"So what *seem* to be coincidences can be the result of messages being sent out and responded to?" I asked.

"Yes, information coded into the energy in the Force gets broadcast to those who need to receive it," Don Emilio answered. "This is a simplified version of the process. You start by defining what you want, and you focus your attention on it, thereby sending it energy. Then you maintain a strong and enthusiastic belief that it is on its way to you. Intent, this Force, then in some mysterious way, arranges for all the players to somehow come together in a magical dance, responding to the song that you broadcast over the energy waves. The clearer your desire and more energy sent to the thought, the greater the possibility that clear communications will be received by those who need to hear it.

"How many times can we do this sort of thing, like make a job happen?" asked Tony. "How many times can we create something we want?"

Don Emilio moved away from the worktable, stepped over to his chair and sat down in front of us. He looked directly at both of us, making sure that we were paying close attention.

"Again, this is really important," he said. "This process I have been talking about, this creation process, is how we make anything and everything that happens in our lives. Whether consciously, or unconsciously by default, everything in our lives has been brought to us through this process. I used the example of wanting to teach karate, but it could be anything. The higher your energy level and the clearer your desire, the better your connection will be with your Higher Self and with the Force, and therefore the more successful you can be in creating the world you want. Or perhaps more correctly, co-creating your world along with your Higher Self, the Force, and all the connected entities, physical and non-physical, who play a part.

"Your personal energy levels have a great deal to do with how quickly you manifest your desires. Self-doubt and not trusting your ability to create are linked to low levels of energy. If your energy level is constantly at a low level, you cannot transmit much energy to the thought bubble, and likewise, there will be less energy behind the effort to send the thought out into the Force. If you consciously or unconsciously choose to remain at low levels of energy, you are, by default, choosing for things to remain the same."

"Oh, now I understand why we've focused so much on increasing our energy," said Tony.

"So now tell me how you deplete your energy," said Don Emilio.

"By not meditating," I answered, "and not giving thanks for our food, and...."

"Okay, good," said Don Emilio interrupting. "You remember what we talked about. But I mentioned those more as ways to increase your energy, to help keep it up. It is not necessarily true that if you do not do those things, you will deplete your energy. I want to talk about how you actually cause a loss of energy. What things do people do to lose energy? How do they go from a high energy state, feeling connected to God, with everything going their way, to a low-energy state where everything seems to go wrong?"

"Getting into a fight." said Tony.

"Or even just getting angry at someone," I added.

"Doing something that gets my parents angry at me is another downer," said Tony.

"I think being jealous or resentful about something would cause a loss of energy," I said.

"Thinking about something that makes me sad can make me lose energy," said Tony.

There was a pause as we both thought what else to say.

"Oh, I know," I added. "Being angry about having to do yard work makes me lose energy."

"I get down about having to work extra time at the store when I want to be somewhere else. And another downer would be if I ask a girl out and get turned down."

"Uh … Tony," I said grinning and turning to look directly at him.

"Okay, okay. I think that if I ever asked someone out, getting turned down might bum me out. That better?" he asked, smiling back at me. We both laughed. "But, hey, you should know about that, Vincent. Didn't you want to go to the Homecoming Dance with Gloria?"

"Um, well, yeah. Talk about getting bummed out and depleting my energy."

"What happened?" asked Don Emilio.

I really didn't want to bring this up with Don Emilio. This was a bad result from taking these lessons with him. I didn't want him to feel bad about something like this happening to me. But since Tony brought it up, I had to tell him.

"Well, I've been talking with this friend, Gloria, who is in a number of our classes. We've known her since grade school. I walk home from school with her occasionally, and sometimes we eat lunch together. And once in a while we even talk on the phone."

"He's beating around the bush," said Tony. "He likes her."

"Well, yeah. Anyway, I've been telling her a little bit about what we've been learning from you. At first she seemed really interested. Then she told me that her grandmother and mother warned her about what I was saying, and about what you have been teaching us. They told her something about it being contrary to the teachings of the Church. By the time I got around to asking her to the Homecoming Dance, the first time I ever asked *anyone* to go out, she said no! Her mother and grandmother didn't want her to go out with me. She cried when she told me."

I had to stop talking. In my mind I could see her tears. It was all I could do to hold back my own tears. I got all choked up.

"That is a real bummer," said Tony. "Those two ladies don't even know anything about what you're teaching us, and they don't like it."

"These family beliefs about 'the old ways' run very deep," said Don Emilio, "especially when they think their Catholic beliefs are threatened."

He looked at me and put his hand on my shoulder.

"Are you okay *mijo*?" I nodded my head. "I have heard some talk about this," he continued. "Is this the grandmother who is a friend of your Nana?"

"Yeah, they're good friends," I said, nodding again.

"Yes, she mentioned this situation to me."

"Well, aren't we just the talk of the town," said Tony, grinning.

"So," I said, trying to move the conversation off me, "that was how I lost some energy. What about things like lying, cheating, or wishing for something bad to happen to someone?"

"Yes," he answered, "those are good examples. So you can understand how these deplete our spiritual energy, and move us away from a strong connection with God."

"I think I'm getting it now," I said. "To keep our energy up, we need to be aware of things that cause us to *lose* energy. Plus, we need to do things that *increase* our energy. We have to do more increasing than losing, so that we can have more energy. With more energy, we can change our thought bubbles into reality and create what we think about."

"Yes, this is how the process of creation works," said Don Emilio, nodding his head in agreement. "This is the magical nature of the universe, and the core of the secret of your ancestors. That is why up to now we have practiced the focused-attention exercises and other techniques for increasing your energy. But, as we discussed, you cannot just increase your energy on one hand and then lose it on the other. It is very important to be aware of *how* you lose energy, and to stop doing things that cause you to leak energy.

So, for the next few weeks, keep a daily record of each time you do something to deplete your energy. Be honest with yourselves and write down everything that happens that causes you to leak energy. Write down what you did and make a note of how you felt afterward. Write it as soon as possible after any event, so you remember how you felt at that moment. Then total up the number of times it happened each day. As each week progresses, see if you can reduce the number of times it happens each day."

"And write it down with a pen, not a pencil," I said to Tony, "so you can't cheat."

"You don't cheat, neither," Tony shouted, laughing. "Just be sure to write down all the times you leak, you cheat!"

"Let us stop here for the day before you feel too overloaded," said Don Emilio smiling at our antics. "This is a very active assignment, and it will require your attention during each day. Make this task a priority, along with your focused-attention exercises, and do as many of the other energy practices as you can. We have more to cover on creating, so we will continue this discussion next time we meet, which will be the first weekend in December. Oh, and as we discussed before, remember to say a prayer of thanks at your meal on Thanksgiving day."

As anxious as I was to hear everything he had to teach us, I appreciated the fact that he was still spacing our sessions out to give us time to practice these assignments. While the list continued to grow, Don Emilio seemed to be trying to keep it from being too much of a burden on us by telling us to focus on some and to do as much of the others as possible. That way we couldn't complain about the amount of exercises we had. And that made one less thing to leak energy over.

25

SENDING ENERGY TO THOUGHTS

"You create your reality through your thoughts, emotions, beliefs, and intent, which determine your vibration and thus the people, objects, events, and circumstances you attract to your life."

ORIN (SANAYA ROMAN)

"Welcome back, *mijos,*" said Don Emilio, as we walked into the garden shed. He was seated next to the worktable.

"Good morning, Don Emilio," I said cheerfully. It had been three weeks since our last session, and I was anxious to get back to our discussion on creating.

"Happy Thanksgiving, Don Emilio," added Tony. "Did you celebrate Thanksgiving?"

"Happy Thanksgiving to you both. I like to eat turkey, so I celebrated while I was in Los Angeles. Were you able to say a prayer at the meal with your families?"

"I wrote mine down," I answered, "and it turned out to not be such a big deal after all. Gracie asked me if the prayer was from you. I told her it was generally what you told us, but that I added my own stuff. She said she liked giving thanks to the food and to the people who helped get the food to us."

"I said mine too," said Tony. "No one made a big deal about it, although I got some looks when I went on about thanking the vegetables and the turkey. But they didn't say anything."

"Another accomplishment that seemed a difficult task when you first feared it, but it turned out to be fairly simple, *que no?*"

We nodded. He then asked about our experience keeping track of energy losses.

"Do you want to know the number of times we screwed up and lost energy?" Tony asked.

"No, it is not that at all. There is no judgment here."

Well, that's a relief, I thought to myself, because on some days I had a long list. But other days, it was pretty short. "So you want us to focus on progress, not numbers?"

"Yes. This exercise is about becoming aware of what brings your energy down. Before we started these sessions, you never thought about these situations in terms of energy loss. When you write down an incident of energy loss, you are forced to think about what caused it."

"This was difficult at first," I said, "because I had to slow down and think about what I was doing, and I had to remember to write about it when I lost energy."

"What were the main things that caused you to lose energy?" asked Don Emilio.

I looked my notes, and grinned. "Dealing with my sisters and having to do yard work. The yard work was a triple whammy, because I lost energy just thinking about having to go out there and do it, I lost energy doing it and complaining to myself, and then I lost even more energy when I listened to my father tell me how I needed to do it better."

"No problem there," said Tony grinning. "You ought to be able to stop losing that energy when you turn twenty-five and move out of the house." Tony laughed at his own joke.

"Shouldn't take me that long to stop losing energy over yard work. I'll move out when I'm twenty-one." We laughed together. "Naw, not really," I said, turning to Don Emilio. "Over these weeks I learned to control my reaction to things my sisters do that bug me. And I don't have to make such a big deal about doing my weekly chores in the yard. The number of times that I lost energy on these has been less each week."

"Very good, Vicente. And you, Antonio?"

"Oh, some of the same stuff. Reacting to my brothers and sisters. But I'm learning to control how I react to them. The next big place where I lose energy is when Big Mike tells me to do something in the store that I don't really want to do. But I'm learning not to react so negatively. I remind myself that I'm lucky to have a job and earn money for doing those things."

"Very good!" said Don Emilio. "You both learned when and how you lose energy. You noticed that your internal resistance to certain situations could bring your energy down quickly. I want you to continue practicing this energy awareness."

"Right," said Tony. "Why work on raising our energy if we turn right around and lose it?"

"This is called stalking," said Don Emilio, "like an animal stalking its prey. But instead of stalking prey, you are stalking or watching yourself. You step outside yourself, so to speak, so you can be more observant and aware of what you do, think, or say to leak energy. There is much more to the concept of stalking, but we will save that for advanced sessions.

"Now, let us return to the topic of creating. We will begin an exercise that we will not finish today. You will continue it on your own until we meet next time. Relax now, and take a few deep breaths. For this exercise, close your eyes, and think of something you want."

He paused briefly. "Okay, did you both think of something?"

"Uh, wait … not yet," answered Tony.

"Just something simple," Don Emilio continued. "It does not have to be the final greatest thing you ever wanted, okay?"

We both agreed. He gave us a little more time, and then began again.

"This thing you have in mind, imagine it as a thought bubble located inside your energy fields. I want you to spend a little time now thinking about and refining this thought, clarifying what it is that you want." He paused again. "When you think you are very clear on what you want, imagine this invisible thought bubble popping free and floating out on its own, but remaining connected to your energy field by a thin fiber of light energy."

"It sounds like the word bubbles in comic books," I said.

"That is a good image," said Don Emilio, "perhaps with a much thinner line connecting you with the bubble. See the image of the item you want, or a symbol that represents this item for you. Connect with the image inside its energy bubble and feed it as much emotional energy and enthusiasm as you can. What is happening on an energy level is you are pushing this emotional energy from the center of your energy field, up that thin energy fiber to this little thought bubble."

Don Emilio paused briefly, then told us to open our eyes.

"That was pretty easy," I said. "I could understand what you were talking about. While you were explaining about the light energy fibers, it reminded me of my eagle dream, and the strands of light I saw. That helped me with what you were saying."

Tony looked a little confused as he stood up and moved around, shaking his head.

"It may have been easy for you because of your dream," he said looking at me, "but this stuff was really strange for me. I mean I understood what I was hearing, but I had trouble thinking about me pushing energy up a fiber that's connected to me."

"I understand," said Don Emilio. "This information about the energetic nature of reality can be difficult for the mind to grasp. I want you to know that you do not have to use thoughts of energy bubbles and fibers of light. Some people find it easier to simply think of sending light energy from the region of the heart to the thought image or symbol that represents the thought, consciously making the symbol brighter and brighter as you work with it."

"Okay, that sounds easier," said Tony, nodding. "I'll try it that way."

"As you practice this exercise," continued Don Emilio, "fill yourself with energy as you just did, and enthusiastically push that energy to the thought or symbol. As you see the image or its symbol in your mind, know that it is real and alive out there in the web of energy, transforming from thought energy to physical matter, with all the necessary connections being made for it to come to you. Do not worry about how it will get to you. Do not wish you could have it in some future moment. Know that it is yours, right now.

"Now, since this is all new to you, there will be doubt, and your mind will likely revert to its old patterns, telling you this exercise you did is not real, and that you are not going to get it. I suggest that you repeat the process as often as you can for a few days, to lessen the power of these old beliefs.

"After a few days, when you clearly see this item in your mind as real and yours, move to the second stage of the creation process. Think about the item out there in the web of energy, now moving toward you. Think about it with grateful expectation of its arrival—not doubting its arrival, but rather with enthusiastic anticipation, as if you were waiting for a special visitor to arrive. Appreciate it with feelings of joy, enthusiasm and gratitude. Being enthusiastically grateful is one of the keys to the creative process. Do something to demonstrate your belief that this item is on its way, perhaps making room in your closet for the new pair of shoes, for example. Now, is all this making sense to you?"

"Yeah, I think I get it now," answered Tony. I nodded in agreement.

"Do not make your request so specific that you miss other opportunities to fulfill your desire," added Don Emilio. "Do not insist on a full-time job when you would be okay with part-time. Do not focus on a brand new racing bicycle if you would be fine with a basic model. Be open to what comes your way. The Force will not reinterpret your desire by saying he did not really mean that; here is what he meant. You have to clearly imagine what you mean, and that what you put in that thought bubble is what you really desire. That is why the first part of the process, the refinement of your desire, is so important."

I looked at Tony and smiled. This was what we had been asking––how to use the secret of the ancestors to make good things happen in our lives. Tony didn't smile back. He was still having problems with it.

"Don Emilio," he said, "this was a lot to think about. I hope I can remember it all."

Don Emilio looked at his watch, then at us, and said, "Yes, this was a lot. It was important information, and there is so much more. I know you are feeling a bit overwhelmed right now. Let us give it some time to sink in. How about if we take a break for now and walk over to Amador's market. I will buy sodas for all."

Within moments, the three of us were on our way to the corner store. Don Emilio urged us to walk in silence while we reviewed in our minds what we had just covered. We didn't really have a lot of time to think about it, since the store was less than a block away.

Big Mike was in the store, so he and Don Emilio got a chance to talk. They sounded like good friends, so I got the impression that they had talked many times since Don Emilio first arrived. While they talked, Tony and I walked around near the back of the store. It felt good to move around a little since we had been sitting for so long in the garden shed.

"*Hola,* Doña!" we heard Big Mike call out to a customer. I looked over and was surprised to see Doña Rosa standing in the doorway. As she came in and walked toward the two men, I could see that someone was behind her. I wondered if it would be...yes! It was Gloria!

I know I blushed. I could feel my face getting warm, and my ears too.

"Hey, your face is pink," whispered Tony. "You still have time to go bright red."

Big Mike introduced Gloria and Doña Rosa to Don Emilio, and the four of them carried on quite a conversation. Don Emilio really turned on the charm, getting broad smiles from Doña Rosa. After a while Gloria noticed Tony and me hanging around the back area, so she excused herself and came over to say hello.

"What a coincidence to see you guys here."

Tony and I looked at each other and smiled, knowing that Don Emilio didn't believe in coincidences. He had looked at his watch just before cutting off our conversation and suggesting that we walk over Amador's. Well, as far as I was concerned, it didn't matter to me if it was planned or if he simply had gotten an inspiration to go to the store, for there I was, standing in front of Gloria.

"Yeah…and we were just talking about you," said Tony. "Ain't that a coincidence." He stood there looking at me and tapping his foot, waiting for me to make my move.

"Hey, Gloria…uh, good to see you." Suddenly I didn't know what to say. "Uh…you look nice today." I didn't have the slightest idea if what she had on looked good or not. It just popped out of my mouth. But she always looked good to me. Today she had her long hair up in a ponytail twisted up into a bun. I liked that look on her. It showed off her face and her neck.

"Oh, brother," Tony mumbled almost too low to hear. "I mean, hey bro, I have to straighten a few things out in the back room while we're here. Don't leave without me." Tony disappeared into the back room, leaving me with Gloria.

"I'm glad my grandmother had a chance to meet your Tío. It sounds like they're having the grandest time up there. I didn't think you guys would be done with your lessons for today."

And I didn't know she even knew we were having a lesson today. I think women in this neighborhood have this communication system that us guys can't even begin to understand.

"We aren't quite finished. We decided to take a break and come here for a soda." Suddenly I wondered why we didn't just go to Nana's refrigerator and get sodas from there. "We still have more to cover, so we'll go back to my Nana's in a little while, after they finish talking."

"Well, before they finish talking, I better go grab a few things we came in for." She stroked my arm, then turned and started walking through the aisles. I stood there watching as she walked away.

In the back room Tony was sitting in the corner office with his feet up on Big Mike's desk.

"I thought you had some work to do."

"Nah, I don't have to work today. I just said that so I wouldn't have to hear you blabbering like an idiot." We both laughed. "Hey, at least your face isn't so pink anymore."

"Well," I said, "that was pretty cool, and quite a surprise, getting to see Gloria. At least I was surprised. I bet Don Emilio wasn't surprised."

By the time we got back to Nana and Tata's the three of us were getting hungry. So Don Emilio suggested we stop for the day and continue the discussion the next morning.

26

CLEARING BLOCKS

*"The greatest discovery of our generation is that
human beings can alter their lives by altering their
attitudes of mind. As you think, so shall you be."*

WILLIAM JAMES

"That was a great session we had yesterday," I said to Tony as we walked over to see Don Emilio. "I'm glad we finally got into the meat of these teachings."

This time we were walking from my house, so it was a short walk

"I'm glad too, but I'm having a hard time keeping up. It feels like he's really piling it on."

"Yeah, it's a lot, but I'm feeling really good about it," I said, as we started up the front steps into Nana and Tata's yard. "I want to hear what else he has to say about creating so we can start getting things we want."

"I've got a lot of questions I need to ask him about creating," said Tony as he walked behind me toward the garden shed.

As usual, Don Emilio was already sitting there in his chair. He greeted us and pointed to our seats, likely aware that we wanted to get started right away. Once we were settled, Tony spoke right up.

"Don Emilio, you say we created what's in our life by what we have thought about and focused on. But what if we thought about something and really wanted it, but it didn't happen? Why do we get some things and not others? Is this Force only able to make it work sometimes but not others? And what about all the bad stuff that has happened. Why does it seem so easy to make bad things happen, and so hard to make good things happen?"

Tony was really on a roll. He paused, like he had more to ask, but then settled back in his chair to give Don Emilio a chance to answer.

Don Emilio didn't respond right away. Instead, he seemed to be thinking about what he was going to say. After what seemed like a long silence, he answered.

"Let me say this again. You have created everything that is in your life, by what you focus on, consciously or unconsciously. Let us say a student likes math and believes math is easy, and that he knows he is going to get an A. He will get an A because of his positive focus on math, his delight in learning math in class and as he reads his textbook, and his unwavering belief that he will get that A. If a student has been sick the first week of school in the past, and then all summer hopes he does not get sick the first week of school, he will be sick that first week...."

"Whoa, wait a minute," said Tony, jumping in before Don Emilio could finish. "I can see the first one, because he likes math and finds it easy and believes he will get an A. But the second one doesn't want to get sick. See, bad things happen even though he doesn't want it to happen."

Don Emilio didn't answer immediately, meaning he was giving us time to figure this one out. So I thought I would try.

"You said we get what we focus on. In these two cases, is it because of what they focused on? The first one enjoyed math and focused on getting A's. The other guy focused on sickness."

"Correct." said Don Emilio, "In both cases they got what they focused on. One student focused on liking math, expected to do well, and therefore got an "A". The second student thought about sickness all summer. The first week of school he got what he focused on. You need to be careful what you focus on, and be aware of where you put your attention."

"But I thought the second guy didn't want to be sick," said Tony.

"Probably not, answered Don Emilio, "but the focus of his attention was sickness. He can change that by thinking about being healthy, giving thanks for being well during the summer, and imagining how great it will be to enjoy the first week of school with all his friends, all healthy and happy starting the new year. In addition to worrying about getting sick, he may have had a belief that he gets sick at that same time each year. He needs to change that belief.

"This illustrates another factor in the creation process––how your underlying beliefs may block you, and not just your conscious beliefs. There may be some beliefs you are not even aware of that prevent you from getting what you say you want."

"Wait," said Tony. "Something I don't know I believe could be blocking me?"

"Yes. It is one reason people do not always get what they think they want. They pray to God over and over and still do not receive what they are requesting, and wonder why."

Suddenly I was feeling very confused. It felt like all my positive energy had just leaked right out. I looked over at Tony. He was shaking his head, apparently just as confused.

"Oh man," he whined, "how can we tell a belief is blocking us if we don't know we have that belief?"

Don Emilio didn't answer right way. He got up from his chair and walked slowly back and forth in front of the worktable, eyes down, not saying anything.

"Okay, okay, I get it," I said. "You're waiting for us to answer the question."

"I don't think that's going to work this time," said Tony. "I am so confused. I don't have a clue how to find out something I believe, that I don't know I believe."

"I know you boys are feeling frustrated right now," said Don Emilio, now looking directly at us, "so I will help you. A Shaman who wants more easily to control his creating process does what is called a *clearing*. Some call it a *recapitulation*. He identifies emotional energy blocks and negative beliefs. Once the negative thoughts and beliefs have been cleared, the things that he focuses on, without countering beliefs, will show up more quickly."

"Okay, that sounds great," said Tony. "Tell us how."

Again, Don Emilio didn't say anything. He was waiting to see if we had any suggestions.

"Okay, wait," I said. "Let me see if I can guess. Maybe we should meditate, with the thought that we want to know why we aren't able to attract what we wanted. Maybe we will get some inspiration or message that tells us what is blocking us."

"Hmm, that's good," said Tony, "I think." We both looked at Don Emilio.

"Hmm, sounds good to me too," he said. "By going deep inside, you give your inner awareness a chance to identify potential hidden blocks. If meditation puts you too deep to keep focused on this problem, you might get the answer by just sitting very still, quieting your mind, asking for some guidance on this question, and allowing the information to come through."

"But what if we don't get the answers with meditation or quiet sitting?" asked Tony. "Are we just stuck? Is there another way to find out what we believe but don't know about?"

"The second approach to clearing would be a *complete* assessment of your beliefs, to see what thoughts might be blocking you."

Oh my God, I thought to myself, did he just say a *complete assessment of our beliefs?*

"As an example," he continued, "let us say you want a new job that pays more money. So you start by looking at your beliefs about money. You can write down or mentally list beliefs you have about money. The act of thinking deeply about an item, and listing what comes to mind allows the information we have below our surface awareness to come out. Using the money example, Vicente, are there any negative beliefs you have about money?"

"Let me see...how about...I never have enough money."

"Money is hard to come by," added Tony.

"I have another one," I said. "You have to pinch your pennies to save up any money."

"If you have a lot of money you must have cheated people," said Tony.

We quickly ran out of negative things to say about money. When you don't have any, there's not a whole lot to say. Don

Emilio asked us if we wanted a few more minutes to see if we could think of anything else, but we both felt like that was about it.

"Now I want you both to get into a very relaxed state. I am going to have you start meditating on your breath, but only for a short time to help you get very relaxed." Don Emilio paused for a few moments as we sat quietly, focused on our breath. "As you continue to be aware of each breath, think again about money, and see if any other thoughts about money come up. If so, do not speak out loud yet. Wait and see if more thoughts come up, and when we stop we will hear about any thoughts." He paused again to let us proceed.

As usual, Don Emilio was right. I didn't think I had any more to say about money, but in that quiet space, new thoughts did pop up, for both of us. I started off first.

"*Not* having money is the *real* root of all evil."

"Time is money," said Tony. He looked over at me, and then decided to go ahead with another. "Money can't buy happiness."

"Yeah, and like the Beatles said, money can't buy me love."

"Okay," said Don Emilio, "that is enough to show that as you go into the silence, some additional beliefs show up that you were not consciously aware of. A person's emotions and opinions can also give you a clue to beliefs that may be causing blocks. Perhaps he gets irritated when he sees someone with a new car, and he says they are just showing off, trying to make their neighbors think they have lots of money."

"Yeah, I've heard comments like that," said Tony.

"The person making those comments has an issue with money that needs to be cleared," said Don Emilio. "A person cannot desire more money, and also have a negative belief about people who have money."

"Some kids in school think the ones who get A's are trying to show off," I said. "And they don't want anyone to think they're showing off, so they don't get good grades."

"Yeah, and if those kids suddenly needed to get A's and B's to raise their grades to a C average to qualify for sports," said Tony, "you're saying it ain't gonna happen."

"Correct. It could be very difficult for such students to get good grades while having a negative perception of anyone who gets good grades. Now, as I said, you could do this for many areas of your beliefs."

"But Don Emilio," I whined, "couldn't there be a ton of beliefs, a hundred or more?"

"Yes, and I see you realize it could take quite a bit of work to completely clear using this method, depending on how many countering beliefs and thoughts one holds, known and unknown. But that is just what many shamans do to clear those blocks."

The thought of doing what we just did for a hundred or more beliefs floored me. "We might as well stop there," I said, "'cause neither of us is gonna do that! It would take forever!"

"Now, now, do not worry. I will not ask you to go through all possible beliefs to look for blocks. As I said, a shaman looking to clear all his blocks, would do so. But that is a very intense course of action. Since you are just starting out on this path, a more efficient process is to deal with blocks as you become aware of them. If there is something you have focused on, and it is not coming to you, stop and try to identify beliefs that may blocking you. For you it is better to deal with what is, rather than a long list of beliefs that might come up later."

"Yeah, I agree," said Tony, sounding greatly relieved.

"Let us end here," said Don Emilio. "I know this is a lot of information to absorb. Your practice for next time is to continue with the creation process you began, focusing on your desired outcome and its thought bubble. Push energy out to it, with emotion, helping it to move toward manifestation. Do this in the two stages we discussed, and identify at least one belief or thought that might block your success."

As Tony and I walked out of the shed we saw Tata sitting there in the shade of the patio with his eyes closed. He slowly opened his eyes as he heard us walk toward him.

"*Hola, mijitos.* Tell me, what did you study today?"

Tony jumped right in and told him in Spanish a little about what we had covered today.

"Very good," answered Tata in Spanish. "I hope Emilio will be able to teach you boys how to create better conditions in this neighborhood. Get rid of these junkyards. Create jobs for the young people. Get rid of the drugs and the violence."

Tony looked over at me to see if I had understood.

"Yeah, I got it," I said. "He's right. What good is raising our energy to do a power animal journey, or making up some little thing for a thought bubble, when we have to live here with all these real-life problems?"

"Well, if you want to do something about those problems, why don't you raise your energy and focus on getting a job working on neighborhood problems."

It was strange that Tony said it that way. I had often thought about Cesar Chavez and those who work with him, who have done so much to help farm workers. What we need are people like him in the cities, working on these neighborhood problems.

Tony interrupted my thoughts, saying, "You're thinking about something. Is it something you want me to tell him for you?"

"Naw. Let's just go." I gave Tata a goodbye hug and went into the house to give one to Nana. I came right back out, and as Tony and I walked through the yard and toward the front gate, we called out a final goodbye to Don Emilio, who was still sitting in the shed.

As we walked down the steps, I turned to look at Tony and grinned. "I think we're getting closer to understanding this stuff so we can really use it."

"Yeah, he really poured it on yesterday and today, and last month. Everything he's been telling us up to now has been leading up to these sessions on creating. But do you think we can really create what we want in our lives?"

"Well, it's what he and his teacher have been using in their lives, and it's what he teaches others," I answered. "I guess if we learn it right, we should be able to do what he teaches, don't you think?"

"He did show us how to get our energy and vibration high enough to get x-ray vision, talk with trees, and fly with eagles. So I guess, why stop there, huh?"

27

CREATING CONSCIOUSLY

"Recognizing the power to create your reality is the key to turning the page and beginning a new chapter in your life story."

RASHA

The holidays came and went, and I was back to focusing on the creating exercise, plus as many of the old energy practices as I could. Near the end of the six-week break I felt like I was finally getting the feel for the whole package, except I had some major issues with the creating exercise. I kept changing my mind about what I wanted to put in the thought bubble. I wasn't so sure it would work for what I really wanted. But I remember Don Emilio said something like don't try to do the greatest thing ever, just do a simple object. So I was glad to finally get to the second weekend in January for a chance to sit down with him again.

After greetings and a little small talk about the holidays, Don Emilio started the session by asking about our main assignment.

"You were to put a mental symbol of what you wanted to create into a thought bubble, and then direct your energy to it, feeding it with a lot of emotional energy and enthusiasm. Did you do that each day?"

"Well, for a while," I answered, "then I kinda got stuck."

"I did it almost every day," said Tony. "And when I pretty much had a clear image of what I wanted, I tried to do some things to reinforce my belief that I would get it."

▸ 211 ◂

"Good, Antonio," said Don Emilio. "Let us talk about what you wanted to attract, and about any blocks you identified."

"Well, the item I put into the thought bubble was a new base-ball glove. I wasn't particular about the brand, but I pictured an infielder's glove, not an outfielder's with the longer fingers. And I definitely felt enthusiastic about it, since getting a new glove would be great. Then I adjusted the image to me *playing* with a new glove. At that point, I knew it was a very clear image, and that all the necessary messages had probably been sent out into the universe. So now," he said with a big grin, "I am enthusiastically anticipating its arrival!"

"That's pretty good," I said. "I almost expected you to say the glove arrived last week."

"Yeah, but if you had been paying attention, you would know I wasn't through. The next step was to reinforce my belief that the glove was already mine. So I stored my old glove in the garage. The next day I got out some leather oil, so when the new glove came I could oil it and break it in. On the third day, I got out a baseball to put into the oiled glove to help shape the pocket. I couldn't think of anything to do on the fourth day, but on the fifth day, I remembered I had an elastic bandage from when I sprained my ankle. I got that out to wrap around the glove to keep the ball in the right place in the pocket."

"You did a great job formulating the thought, imagining your-self playing with the glove rather than imagining a new glove in the store, and sending strong emotional energy to the image," said Don Emilio. "And that was a great follow up, doing some-thing on the following days to reinforce your belief that the glove is coming."

"Yeah, I was a great success at everything except getting the glove."

"But maybe the glove just hasn't had time to get here yet," I suggested.

We looked at Don Emilio, expecting to hear his comments. But he looked at us, looked around the shed, looked outside, and back at us. He was stalling again.

"I don't know if it's coming," said Tony, sounding a little dejected, "but probably not right away. It may be too soon. I looked inside to see if I had any beliefs blocking me."

Don Emilio nodded his head and smiled.

"As I was putting the old glove away, I was thinking that it was a pretty good one, with soft and flexible leather. It just looks a little ratty because the leather is rough in spots where I've scraped it scooping up grounders. I realized I have a belief that I'll be happy using the old glove if I don't get a new one. Also, I think it's too much money to spend on a glove when I already have one. I think these beliefs might be blocking me."

"Man, he's not getting a new glove," I said to myself, but out loud. Those sounded like good reasons why his family shouldn't buy a new glove. "So he's done? Should he just switch to another desire?"

"That is a good question," Don Emilio answered. "What do you think, Antonio?"

"Well, going through the exercise really helped me see how the creation process works, even though it didn't create a new glove yet. And it helped me see how thoughts that we're not fully aware of can block the process. So maybe for this example, we can say that I should give up on the glove." He paused, and then smiling, added, "Maybe I should go for a football."

Don Emilio didn't say anything right away. Since we had already suggested abandoning the glove idea, and he didn't say he agreed with that, I knew we needed to look at alternatives.

"Okay, let's think about this," I said, while I delayed, waiting for some inspiration. Then it hit me. "Oh, of course. That's why you're waiting for us. We didn't do the last part."

"What's that?" asked Tony.

"Now that you have identified the beliefs that are blocking your desire, you need to see if you can change those beliefs."

"Very good, Vicente. You guys are doing great."

"Well, I kinda did that quickly and thought nothing could change," said Tony. "My parents have higher priorities for their money, and I agree with that. Also, my old glove is good enough.

That's not going to change. It will always be good enough, even if it sits in a box."

"Hey, we gotta think *outside* the box," I said to Tony. "What if we were on the varsity team, or even summer American Legion, and the coach said everyone will get a new glove, even though your old ratty looking one works fine. You'd want to have a new one then, wouldn't you?"

"Yeah, sure I would."

"Well," I said, "what's wrong with getting a new glove even if no coach tells you to do so. Repeat after me, and say it each day: I'm a great guy, and I can have a new glove if I want one."

"I'm a great guy, and...."

All three of us busted up laughing about that one, even though Don Emilio tried not to.

"And for this exercise," said Tony, after we calmed down, "let's assume I will make the American Legion team, and the coach will get a sponsor to donate gloves for the team, so my parents won't have to spend the money. Or maybe there's another way the glove will get to me without my parents having to pay for it. So I just wasn't looking closely enough at alternatives."

"And he doesn't really need to worry about the alternatives, right Don Emilio? He just needs to trust that within the Force all the necessary energy connections will be made, and the right people will take the necessary actions."

Don Emilio nodded his head in agreement.

"Hey, we cleared the blocks!" said Tony excitedly as he high-fived me.

"Mine was interesting but...uh, difficult," I said, as they turned to listen to me. "I started out fine, but then changed my mind about what to put in the bubble. I'm not sure that some things can be done this way. Maybe we can't create some things we want."

"He's beating around the bush," Tony said to Don Emilio. "He tried to put his greatest number one wish into the thought bubble."

I knew I should have just made up something simple, like a football, or a new jacket, or a shirt. But I didn't. And now I had to fess up.

"The thing I wanted to attract, the image I put in the thought bubble, was...um."

"Oh, for crying out loud," said Tony, laughing, "just tell him, or I will."

"I want Gloria to be my girlfriend," I blurted out. I didn't want Tony to tell him, and I didn't want to keep thinking about the best way to say it. "I know it's not a thing, like a glove. Is that okay?"

Don Emilio nodded. "It is a thought, a desire."

He didn't say anything else. He just looked at me. So I thought I better keep explaining.

"I thought maybe I should put a more precise thought in the bubble, like I want her to go to the Junior Prom with me, or I want her grandmother and mother to change their minds about me, or maybe just an image of the two of us standing together, holding hands."

"This is a good first step," said Don Emilio. "It is important to refine the image. Tell me, which of those statements created an image in your head, and feelings or emotions that represent your intention."

I knew immediately. "The image of the two of us holding hands. When I think of that image, I feel sort of tingly, like what I feel when I'm near her. The others are just words, with no feelings."

"If an image you put into that thought bubble can generate strong emotional energy," said Don Emilio, "that image has a better chance of quickly materializing."

"You mean I have to be in love with my new glove?"

"No Antonio," said Don Emilio, grinning, "but really wanting it, and being very grateful for what is coming to you will help. Generating strong emotions speeds the creating process." He paused and turned back to me. The smile went away and his look turned serious.

"Some of our thoughts involve only our own desires and choices. Other thoughts can involve one or more other persons. We cannot make other people choose what we want them to do. You cannot stop your friends from involvement with drugs just by putting that in your thought bubble. You cannot make someone's mother like you. That person is the one who will choose what happens in his or her own life."

I could tell he was trying to let me down gently and not embarrass me for choosing such a dumb thought. Of course I can't make Gloria's grandmother and mother like me just by putting that in my thought bubble. I already knew Gloria liked me, but that doesn't do any good if she's not allowed to see me.

"Okay then," I said, "I want to switch to another thought, getting a new jacket. But I'll have to start over and refine the thought, look for blocks...."

"I did not mean to scare you away from your desire," said Don Emilio. "I wanted you to be aware other people are involved, and there are many decisions to be made. If that is what you have your heart set on, do not give up so easily."

"I don't want to give up. But I think I need to refine the thought, or make multiple thoughts, and then see what beliefs I may have that might be blocking me."

"Do not make it too complicated. You know what you want. And the situation may be easier than you think. From my conversation with Doña Rosa a few weeks ago at the market, I think she may have a better opinion of you, and of me, than you think."

"Don Emilio," said Tony with a look of surprise on his face, "if we create by this process, and if we can clear the blocks in our way, well then...we can create anything, anything we want!" He looked like the light just went on inside.

"Duh, genius," I said. "That's what Don Emilio has been saying all along."

"I know, I just never really understood it until now." He paused briefly, turning to look straight at me. "Do you know what that would mean? That could be like letting a little kid lose in a candy store. People would go wild, grabbing at anything, creating anything they dreamed up."

"Except for the blocking beliefs," I reminded him. "You just tried to do a simple exercise for getting a glove and found out that some hidden beliefs stopped you."

"Yeah, but we found the blocking beliefs. So now I'm gonna get my glove."

"We can look at anything we have, good or bad," I said, "and see what beliefs helped bring that into our lives."

"So it turns out," said Tony, "that analyzing our beliefs is just as important as focusing on what we want. And that's as important as storing and using energy to make all the connections."

"Right," said Don Emilio grinning.

"Man," I said, grasping at what felt like major revelations, "when something bad happens to us, there is no more blaming Pablito or anyone else. We have no one to blame but ourselves. Same thing when something good comes into our lives. We know we attracted it."

For a moment there was just silence, and then a soft "whew" from Tony, as he and I tried to register the significance of what had just blown through our minds.

"I feel like the whole world just exploded before me," said Tony, "and now there is a clean slate. I can create what I want—as long as I increase my energy, focus my attention, and clear blocking beliefs."

"Don Emilio," I said, "I feel a sense of responsibility now. It's like I can't just sit back and let things be as they are."

"Be careful, boys. Do not think that you now have to go out and create an entirely new world tomorrow. Give yourselves at least a week!"

All three of us started laughing, which was good, as things were getting way too serious.

"I know you will feel a sense of responsibility," said Don Emilio, trying to wipe the grin off his face. "That always follows once we understand that we are responsible for the world we create. That is what we do, all the time—we create. Since you are now more aware of that, you will want to create more consciously, and more responsibly. That desire will drive you to keep looking at your beliefs, and to maintain your energy levels because focused energy drives the creation process. It is all related. But be aware that you are just beginning to understand this process of creating.

Consciously creating is more difficult than simply understanding the steps. But as I said, you create every day, so you might as well do it consciously."

<u>28</u>

FLOWING ENERGY

*"And it's everpresent everywhere, and it's
everpresent everywhere, that warm Love."*

Van Morrison

"Don Emilio," I said, "I understand better now. When we first talked about different ways to increase our energy, it seemed like it would be a lot of work to keep practicing all the techniques. I thought that spirit warriors had to do way too much energy work, and because of that, couldn't have much of a life. That didn't seem very appealing at all. But now, I realize that keeping a high energy level is so important to creating the life we want!"

"I'm feeling the same way," said Tony. "I thought it was going to be a real chore to list all the things we had to do each day, then having to check them off and report back to you. Right now, I don't feel like it's a chore that I *have* to do. Instead, I *want* to look at my list and see what I can do to increase my energy so that I can create the next thing in my life."

"You both had quite an experience. I want you to remember this feeling and your appreciation for energy and its importance in helping you create your lives, because this feeling will come and go. Humans are creatures of habit, and you have had many years being unaware of your role in creating your life. Right now, you have a heightened awareness and appreciation. It will pass, and you will revert, to a large extent, to your old ways of thinking. But the feeling and the understanding will come back again and again as you work with energy and continue to successfully create what you focus on."

"Don Emilio," said Tony, "You're not teaching us this stuff so we can have more *things*, are you? We started out talking about increasing our energy and quieting our mind so we could have a better connection with our higher self and with God."

"Yeah, you told us about the connection between creating and what we did on the mountain," I added, "seeing with x-ray vision, talking to trees, and flying with eagles. But I got so focused on learning the steps to this creating process that I guess I lost some of the big picture, how it's all related. I know it's got something to do with my eagle dream and all the energy connections I saw."

He rose from his chair and began slowly pacing in front of the worktable.

"I have been expecting these questions. We talked before about how the ego resists new information that is not consistent with its view of reality, so you tend to forget. That is why it is so important to practice as often as you can. The repetition helps make it a part of your core belief system. And yes, it does have something to do with your dream of the energy connections. You sent those energy connections from your heart area when you visited your power animals at the zoo. In the mountains you sent energy down into the earth, and you sent it to the tree you talked to. You sent that energy to the eagles you flew with. In your creation exercise you sent energy to the item you held in your thought bubble. And from there you sent that energy out into the web of energy connections that make up the Force."

He stopped pacing and turned to look directly at us.

"You are consciously connecting with God, All-That-Is, when you are directing your energy out into the web of energy connections, and allowing that energy to flow back to you. By using the techniques you have been practicing, you have the power for more than just seeing into a tree or flying with eagles. Through your conscious connection with the Force and All-That-Is, you have the power to attract to yourself whatever you want in life. In our creation discussion I used simple items for the purpose of explaining the steps in the process. But remember, you have created every-thing in your world, mostly without consciously thinking about it. The spirit warriors you mentioned know that they are con-stantly creating their world, and they strive to do their creating consciously. Their focus is to stay filled with high spiritual energy, stay consciously connected to the Force, and consciously use that energy to create their world."

"Man, that's what I want to do," said Tony. "I want to be sure that what happens in my life is what I really want, not something that happens because I wasn't paying attention or wasn't thinking about it."

It sounded really good. I could go along with the idea that everything in my life is here because of my thoughts, whether I did it consciously or not. And it was a no brainer that we should do it consciously. But I wasn't sure Tony and I could do that, every minute of every day, thinking about what we were bringing into our lives. I didn't want to say anything negative though, as Don Emilio was on a roll. But I figured he would be reading my mind anyway.

Don Emilio walked over to his chair and sat down with us again. He closed his eyes.

"Visualize in your mind how, as a spirit warrior, you might connect with energy during the day. Close your eyes and become aware of the connection with energy coming down to you, enter-ing the top of your head and filling you up.... While you are becoming filled with this energy, be aware of the many thought bubbles floating above you. These represent not one thing you want, but all the things you think about and desire, what you want next week, next month, next year. All that you want, con-sciously and unconsciously, to come into your life is there, and these constantly get refined, as we discussed before. Remember, all these thoughts are energy and are alive. Can you visualize these many thoughts there with you?"

That was a bit of a surprise, to visualize the space above me filled with lots of thought bubbles, for everything that I may want or think about. But of course, that made sense if we are creating everything that comes into our lives.

"Isn't that a lot of thoughts to think about and manage all day long?" asked Tony.

"That is a good question, and I want to clarify one thing. Whether it is one thought or many, your task or the task of a spirit warrior is not to think about all the items in the thought bubbles or to somehow try to manage them. Your task is on an energy level, to take in the energy and allow it to fill you up and raise your vibration. As you do that, be aware that some of the energy you take in is constantly flowing out to those thought bubbles.

"Feel the energy flowing out from you, and feel it being replenished by the light energy flowing down into you. Many of the desires in the thought bubbles are clear and refined. See and feel your energy flowing to those thoughts, and from them out to the Force, going out to the people and places necessary to bring those items into your life.

"You visualized the energy flowing out into that web of energy connections. Now visualize the strands of light energy flowing straight back to you from the Force. You are a magnet, attracting to yourself what you desire and focus upon. These strands of light are the leading edge of the energy of those objects you desire. As you allow the strands to come to you, feel the energy getting stronger and stronger. That is where your joyful anticipation begins. You feel the energy of the items. You feel them coming. You joyfully await their arrival, without doubt or hesitation.

"There are many strands of energy flowing straight to you right now, connected to the next things that will show up in your life, in the next minutes, hours, days. But you are mostly doing it unconsciously. The spirit warriors are doing it consciously. If you choose to live a better life, choose each day to do it consciously, as often as you are able. Be consciously aware of the back and forth flow of energy between you and the Force."

Don Emilio stopped and told us to open our eyes. I looked over at Tony and his eyes were closed. He must have still been looking for the leading edge of his glove.

"Don Emilio," I said, "I really liked that, being aware of the flow of energy as we create what will come into our lives. But that seems like a whole lot of time focused on thought bubbles and their energy. One minute I get enthused about doing this, like you said, choosing to do it consciously. But then I realize it would be impossible for us to do it all the time."

"Yes, I know. That is why I said imagine how a spirit warrior would do it, not how a high school student would. You can choose to create your life consciously as often as you are able. The more you do so, the more your life will reflect what you have chosen. I provided that image of a spirit warrior to show you the simplicity of a life focused on a conscious connection with the web of energy that permeates everything in the universe. It is up to you to decide how much of that life you can live right now. You have to decide how much time you will spend consciously directing the energy of your desires to that web of energy and then greeting the energy of those desires as they return and begin to flow into your life. If it is something you really want to do, I think you will be surprised at how often you can find a few moments during each day to focus on consciously creating the life you want.

29

THE HIGHER SELF

*"Understand that you are offering a signal, and
the entire Universe responds. And when you finally get that,
and you begin to exercise some deliberate control about the signal
that you offer, then it really begins to be fun, because then you recognize
that nothing happens outside of your creative control. There are
no things that happen by chance or by circumstance."*

ABRAHAM (ESTHER HICKS)

"Before we leave this topic of creating," Don Emilio continued, "I want to clarify the role of the Higher Self. As you recall, I said we want to quiet the mind and stop the thinking process, so that we can enter into the quiet space where we perceive guidance from our Higher Self and our guides. But I also said we get what we focus on, what we think about."

Don Emilio paused and looked at us.

"Uh, I think there's a problem here," said Tony, realizing Don Emilio was waiting for a comment about those two statements. "How do we keep thinking about what we want and also practice stopping the thinking process? Do them at different times?"

Don Emilio didn't answer right away, so I added my two cents worth. "I don't think it's that simple. A Spirit Warrior would always be focused on increasing his energy and quieting his mind as much as possible, and he would always be aware of what he was consciously creating."

"Oh, I know!" said Tony, almost yelling. "You said the Spirit Warrior had these thought balloons over him, but he wasn't

▸ 224 ◂

thinking about them all day long. Instead he was sending energy to them. He had already thought about what he wanted to create but didn't keep thinking about it."

Don Emilio smiled. "That is an important distinction. You have an idea about what you want and you think about it, refining the thought until you have a clear picture in mind. Once you have clarity you send energy to that item in your thought bubble. You think about it and become enthusiastic about it coming. The anticipation starts to build. Through these feelings you are directing more energy to the item. Soon you will have internalized your belief that the item is yours, and that it is on the way. At that point, you do not have to keep thinking about it. Subconsciously you just know this item is coming.

"It is through this subconscious knowing, information coming from your subconscious self, that your Higher Self is able to filter this desire out from the many partly formed images of desire you have created in your mind and your thought bubbles. Because your Higher Self is connected to all other Higher Selves, when your Higher Self sends this fully formed and internalized thought out into the Force, the information gets to all the necessary players.

"We do not usually acknowledge our connection to our Higher Self. So it is important to practice being the Higher Self. That will help you to trust that you, as your Higher Self, will send those energized internalized thoughts out into the Force, and that the necessary connections will be made to bring to you that which you have chosen to come into your lives."

"Whoa! Wait a minute," Tony interrupted. "I've been trying to follow you on this Higher Self stuff. But I thought we were trying to *hear* what the Higher Self spirit wanted to tell us, rather than trying to *be* this spirit. Cripes, isn't that like trying to become our own guardian angel? And if I really believe that this Higher Spirit exists in a spirit world connected to other Higher Spirits and to everything else, then I'm *really* gonna be freaking out. You really want us to practice being out there in a spirit world connected to everything? Or are these just mental exercises? And are we just pretending or imagining this stuff?"

Good questions, I thought to myself, and I jumped in before Don Emilio could answer.

"Are we trying to get some spiritual benefit from imagining things like light energy raining down on us or pretending that we are our Higher Self?"

"I do not say pretend or imagine," answered Don Emilio. "I prefer to say visualize. There is no need to pretend that you are your Higher Self. You are that Higher Self, the spirit entity or soul that has sent a portion of its self here to earth to experience this life you are living. You need to visualize it because you have forgotten and now do not believe it. From where you sit, it seems impossible to grasp the idea that you could be much more than this physical shell walking around. But if you were to suddenly die right now, and if we could continue this conversation, you would say, 'Oh, I understand now. I can see my body lying there, but I am still conscious, and aware that I am more than that shell of a physical body.' You would suddenly be aware of yourself as an immortal soul connected to the other souls who make up the essence of you, the over-soul or Higher Self. In that higher state of awareness, you would also be aware of the lines of energy connecting you with other Higher Selves."

Don Emilio paused, giving us time to try to grasp all that. After a few brief moments of silence, he asked, "Do you understand? I know it is difficult to believe, but it is what it is. You are what you are, even if you have trouble letting go of what your physical body's limited mind tells you. That is why it is important to quiet that voice in your head so you can hear the truth."

All I could do was nod my head as I tried to make sense of what he had said.

"Okay," said Tony, "Let's say I believe what you're saying. I guess I need to let it sink in."

"To help that sink in," said Don Emilio, "I will lead you in an exercise to practice being your Higher Self. You already know the process, since it is similar to the power animal trance journey. Begin by relaxing your entire body as you have done before.... Sitting in a comfortable upright position, with your back straight, slowly take several deep breaths.... Now breathe normally, and become aware of the rain of light beginning to fall. Let it fall onto you and enter through the top of your head, filling you up with light energy."

Don Emilio paused to let us meditate on the rain of light for a while. Very soon I lost an awareness of anything but the light falling down on me.

"Now, in this light trance state, see the rain of light begin to fade as you become aware of a beautiful shimmering light in the distance. The light is moving toward you. It is your Higher Self. Like you did with your power animal, greet your Higher Self and encourage it to come closer.... As it continues to move closer, you see lines of light emanating from your Higher Self reaching out and embracing you. Likewise, you send your energy out to embrace your Higher Self. Now allow your Higher Self to merge with you. Feel your vibration increasing as you merge with this powerful energy and become one.

"Take a few deep breaths as you sit in the moment and experience being one with your Higher Self. Remember now that you have always been one. There never was any separation. Just as your arm is a part of your body, you have always been a part of your Higher Self. But you forgot—you lost that awareness. So as you sit here, experience the higher energy vibration and awareness that is yours.

"Now, if there is an issue about which you as your smaller self desire guidance, bring that issue into your wise Higher Self awareness as you sit in the stillness. Take your time as you experience the light and energy flowing to you. Be aware of any guidance from your Higher Self that may come to you through your intuition, gut feelings, or internal knowing." Don Emilio paused, and there was just the silence for what seemed like quite a few minutes.

"You may want to sit there a while longer," he said softly, "and then slowly come out of this state of awareness. Do not rush. When you have finished, thank your Higher Self for allowing you to experience the awareness of being one."

When we were both finally back and alert, Tony spoke up first.

"Man, I feel spaced out. I could sit like that for hours. But I'm not sure I got a clear message because I started wondering if I was making it up or hearing from my Higher Self."

"Yeah, me too," I added. "How do I know if it's really information from my Higher Self?"

"Through a combination of higher energy and practice. This is an exercise you will want to practice as much as you can. The more you practice being your Higher Self, the easier it will be for you to move into that place of awareness of who you really are, and into an awareness of messages, intuition, and just knowing what is real and what is mind chatter. But you also have to work on quieting your mind and on increasing your energy levels. You cannot really move into that state of heightened awareness if you have a very low energy level that keeps you stuck in the more dense energy of day to day problems, concerns and the incessant voice in your head."

It seemed like there were already too many exercises, but as Don Emilio explained the newest one on our Higher Self, it seemed to be an important one to add. And whenever he added on exercises, he also reminded us to keep practicing the previous ones.

"Back to the subject of the creation process," he said as he paced slowly in front of us, "I want to share with you information from the Hawaiian or Polynesian tradition, even at the risk of confusing you more. In that tradition, the *kahunas*, their shamans, taught that a person's middle self, which we call the physical or conscious self, is the part that chooses what the person wants. The middle self sends that message to the lower self, which we call the subconscious. Using the person's excess spiritual energy, which they called *mana*, and utilizing strong emotions, the lower self takes that message and sends it to the individual's high self. This high self is connected to the high self of everyone else, and in that way connects the individual to other people, facilitating the inspiration and actions by others which are needed to bring about what was desired."

"Oh wow," I said, "it sounds very similar to what you already told us."

"Yes, it is similar," he said as he stopped pacing and faced us directly. "I especially wanted you to hear what they say about how energy is sent out through the higher selves to all who need to receive the information."

"So this new stuff is from the kahunas, and not our ancestors?" asked Tony.

"It is all from our ancestors. But some of them traveled to distant lands where the teachings were modified some over time. But at their core, the basics of native spirituality have remained fairly consistent."

"Do we have to remember all of what you said about lower self and middle self and *mana* and such?" Tony asked.

"You can choose to disregard it. Or you may find that it helps you to make sense of these different approaches to creating. You may want to do more research into Huna, the Hawaiian mysticism. A man by the name of Max Freedom Long wrote about this is his book *The Secret Science Behind Miracles*.

"You might also want to look into information that has been received from nonphysical entities, such as the material provided by an entity called Seth, as channeled by the author Jane Roberts."

"Okay, wait a minute," said Tony. "A nonphysical entity? What's that?"

"You mean like a spirit, or a ghost," I asked.

"Yes, a spirit. The Seth entity did experience previous lives on earth, but at the time of providing the information was not a physical being."

"What did you mean," Tony asked, "about information being ... what was the word ... channeled?"

"Channeling means the person, in this case an author, hears the information, or perceives it as an intuition, or even speaks the information while in a trance state. In Jane Roberts' case, she went into a very deep meditative state and into a trance to allow the Seth entity to 'enter,' so to speak, and take over her body, so that Seth could speak the information out loud and have it written down by Jane's husband."

"Ah, yes," I said, "we talked about doing a focused attention exercise or meditation to go into a silent space where we quiet our mind in order to hear our intuition or maybe hear a message from our higher self, or from our guides. Is that how she did it?"

"Yes," he answered, "but she went one step further. Her Higher Self, in communication with the Seth Higher Self, agreed to let Seth use her body to communicate the information."

"What kind of information did this Seth give?" Tony asked.

"I knew we would be covering this material so I brought some notes to read to you." He took some paper out of his pocket. "This is from her book *The Seth Material*. Here is what Seth said through her:

'We are individualized portions of energy, materialized within physical existence, to learn to form ideas from energy, and make them physical....' and further he says *'... the object is the thought, materialized.'"*

He looked up from the paper. "Sounds familiar, yes?"

"That's just like what we were talking about earlier," Tony answered.

"There is more: *'You make your own reality. There is no other rule. Knowing this is the secret of creativity.'"*

He stopped again and looked up. "Here is another one: *'The entity is the basic self, immortal, nonphysical.'"* Don Emilio pointed out that *entity* referred to the Higher Self, the larger soul. Then he continued: *"'It communicates on an energy level with other entities, and has an almost inexhaustible supply of energy at its command. The individual is the portion of the whole self that we manage to express physically....'"*

I was amazed to hear him read these words that were very similar to what he told us came from our Mexican Indian ancestors and from the Hawaiian Kahuna ancestors. But I wondered about the source of this latest stuff.

"Don Emilio, it's great to hear that this kind of information is coming from so many different sources. It sorta helps make it more believable. But I really wonder about a spirit that takes over a body and teaches this strange new information. I'm not sure anyone would believe me if I told them about it. It's kinda weird."

"Yeah," said Tony. "Can we really believe that dead people can take over a body and dictate strange concepts?"

"Well, first of all, not just any dead person, but a very special being who, according to Seth, has been physical on earth in the past in order to share this kind of information. I say again that you should think about what I share with you and decide for yourself what you choose to believe. But I will point out that whether the tradition is Toltec, Huna, or Seth––what we are talking about is going into the silence or second attention, moving out of the mind chatter and normal thought process, and shutting down thought. In the process, we go to a different level of awareness and open up to receiving information that we could not access before. We go into that other place and hear a few words or get a thought inspiration. In the case of Jane Roberts, she got more than a few words or inspirations. She got a whole book, or in fact, multiple books. The best one, in relation to what we have been discussing, is her book *The Nature of Personal Reality*. If you do research into the Seth information, that would be a good place to start."

My head was spinning. All this new stuff––but it wasn't really new. It was like what he had already told us, just that it was coming from some spirit that dictated books.

"I think that's really cool that this spirit is teaching the same stuff that our Toltec ancestors taught," I said. "If I wasn't so overloaded right now, I'd like to read up on this Seth guy."

"Yeah, I'm so overloaded I couldn't add another thing right now," said Tony. "But I definitely would like to know more about this Seth person and what else he has to say."

"There is no need to do additional research right now. You can learn more when you have the time. You might also be interested in another spirit entity that goes by the name Orin, channeled by a woman named Sanaya Roman. They also produced a number of books. The one I would recommend starting with is *Spiritual Growth: Being Your Higher Self*. What Orin provided on the Higher

Self is similar to the Huna information, and very similar to what we just discussed because I use some of their concepts."

"You don't use just the Toltec information?" I asked.

"I do not limit myself to just those teachings because, as I mentioned, when the ancestors moved to other locations, the information they taught was modified somewhat. It is said that the Huna shamanic teachings are the most intact because of the long isolation of the people in the Pacific Islands. But whether it is Orin, Seth, the Toltec or the Huna teachings, the core concept is to quiet the mind and listen for guidance from the Higher Self. What I teach is what I have been guided to use."

Don Emilio paused and correctly sensed overload. It had been a long session, with a lot of information.

We will stop here," he said. "I am sure you are both quite hungry by now. Enjoy the rest of your weekend, and I will see you again in four weeks. As always, practice as many of the exercises as you can. And be sure to practice being your Higher Self."

30

Dealing with the Gang

*"Worrying is using your imagination to
create something you don't want."*

Abraham (Esther Hicks)

"Hey bro', how ya been?" Tomás came up to me at my hall locker at school.

"Hey, Tomás. I'm doing pretty good. Busy as hell, and trying to keep up, but things are going good. What's going on with you?"

"Oh, same ol' same ol'. Not much different happening. But..." he paused, "there's a lot of folks wondering about you. I don't know if anyone has told you yet, but the guys have been talking about you and Tony leaving your homies."

For months now, the guys have been bugging Tony and me about the fact that we hadn't been hanging out with them much anymore.

"Well," I said, picking out the book I needed for my next class, "I don't think either of us said anything about leaving, but I know I have been swamped with loads of other things. A while back we came out to play basketball like we all agreed, and most of you guys didn't show. Only Arturo and Pablito were there. But I can't just hang out like I used to. You still spending all that time over there?"

"Probably not as much. But when my homies call, I go on over. It's my duty. But we ain't seen you around when they call. And

▸ 233 ◂

some of the guys don't like it. They figure you just decided to quit. And some are saying...they ain't just gonna let you walk."

Damn! I silently shouted to myself. I knew this was coming! We shouldn't have ignored what we'd been hearing. But what the hell could we do? I pushed my locker door and it slammed shut, making much more noise than I meant to.

"Tomás," I said as I turned to look directly at him, face to face, "we've all been friends for so many years. I don't want these guys telling me where I need to be when I've got some other stuff going on. It's bad enough dealing with my parents telling me where to be and when."

"Hey, man, I'm just telling you...as a friend. Guys are talking. Some want to just let you be, cause they know you been busy working with the *brujo*. But some others are saying that it don't cut no ice, that you're just like everyone else. And a *carnal* can't just walk out on his homies. They say you gotta pay."

"And what do you think?"

"I don't know, man. We got rules, you know. I gotta follow them. Maybe everybody needs to follow them. I know you got this special thing going with the *brujo,* but some of the guys say that it's not real shit, that it's just a plan by your folks to get you away from your homies. You better talk to Tony and do something, soon, before some *vato loco* does something stupid."

"Yeah, I will," I said as he turned to walk away, "and hey, thanks for the heads up."

I knew we had to talk with Don Emilio about this. Luckily we only had to wait another week to see him. Tony and I were both so busy we didn't have a chance to talk before then. The week seemed to go on forever, and the whole time I felt really confused. On one hand, I kept worrying about what the guys might be planning to do to Tony and me. And on the other hand, I thought about all the sessions we've had with Don Emilio as he talked to us about these teachings he called the secrets of the ancestors. In the last few sessions, he really focused on the process of creating what we wanted in our lives. In that last session, I finally *got it*. I saw how all the pieces fit together. But I kept thinking about the warning from Tomás, and what might happen. And the biggest question was how did that fit into what we create in our lives?

When I got to Tony's house he was sitting on his front porch steps. He started right in before I had a chance to say anything.

"I am really ready to talk to Don Emilio! This stuff seems to be flowing easy right now. I'm really jazzed about being able to focus on creating what we want, even though I know we can't just spend all day imagining what we want and sending it energy. I know we have to do all the other things to get our energy up. But I've been so excited that I've even been waking up early. With the extra time, I've been able to get in a few minutes of meditation before leaving for school. Sometimes if I'm walking to school alone, or on the way back, with nothing to do but move my feet and look out for traffic, I've done the thought bubble exercise. A few mornings, when I didn't get a long enough meditation at home, I even did a walking meditation. At lunchtime, it takes less than thirty seconds to give thanks for my food. And for a few seconds more, I can add on gratitude for all things in my life, now and for what's coming."

"Hey, Tony, that's really good. I was doing really well too, for most of the month. I could tell something was different. I didn't struggle to find time to do the exercises. I didn't even look at them as exercises I'd been assigned to practice. They were the things I did during the day, whenever I found a few minutes. I did them because I wanted to, not because I had to report to Don Emilio.

"But then I talked with Tomás last week. He said the guys were angry that we haven't been around." I told Tony the details of what Tomás said. "Now I'm afraid something's going to happen. And it's getting in the way of being able to concentrate on my exercises. I mean I'm still doing them, but sometimes my heart isn't into it. I've tried to meditate and get those thoughts out of my head, but they just won't go away."

"Maybe like we said before, we need to start figuring out how to share a little of what we've learned with the guys," said Tony. "I think that might help. What do you think?"

"What?" I looked at Tony and shook my head, surprised he suggested it right now. "I know we talked about doing that eventually. But they're thinking about punishing us right now, not about learning what Don Emilio's teaching us."

"Man, that conversation with Tomás really has you freaked out. I mean, I've been worried about what to do too, but not like you. I'm glad we're going over to talk to Don Emilio. Maybe he can help us figure this out."

He peeked into the house. "Whoa, I'm glad I looked at the clock. It's almost eleven. We better get over there."

We didn't have to run hard, but we definitely walked fast down the street, picked it up at the alley, and jogged into the yard. When we got close to the garden shed I heard slow meditation music playing, so we had to quickly shift gears. As we stepped into the shed I saw a thin stick of incense burning. It had almost burned down to the end. The thin line of smoke was gently rising, gliding from the front table to the back of the shed and out into the yard. Don Emilio sat there with his eyes closed, enjoying the quiet. Well, quiet until we arrived. Slowly I slipped onto my chair. Taking a few deep breaths and inhaling the aroma of the incense helped to calm me immediately. The music helped too.

Don Emilio didn't say anything, letting us get adjusted to the atmosphere he created. He hadn't used incense to start our sessions before, and rarely had meditation music playing. As I sat there waiting for him to begin, I listened to my breathing going back to normal, getting slower and slower. Soon I realized I had started meditating without really thinking about it. It didn't last long though, as he finally stood up and walked over to the table. He turned off the music and snuffed out the incense stick.

"Let us begin today with any questions you may have about our last session or your exercises."

"Don Emilio," I said, "we need to talk with you about our, uh, club."

"Your 'club', eh?" Then walking and talking in a perfect *cholo* style, he said, "Sooo... wha'sup, *ese?*"

Tony and I both laughed. "*Orale,* Don Emilio," said Tony, going through the motions, mimicking him back. "You got that down pretty gooood, *ese!*"

"It's about leaving the gang," I said, getting back to business. "We haven't had much time to be with the guys and have mostly just ignored what's going on with them. We haven't shown up when they've gotten together, things like that. They know we've been busy working with you and doing karate and Tony's work and all. So they let it slide for a while. But..." I paused to think how best to say it, "they don't just let you quit."

"It's like being a Catholic," Tony added. "The nuns told us, 'Once a Catholic, always a Catholic.' Well, these guys say once a *carnal*, always a *carnal*."

"Hmm. I thought I heard that your uncles were involved with this gang, Vincent, and that Juan had been head of the gang. They are not still part of the gang, so what is this about 'always'?"

"Well, I don't know." I said, "But they've been talking about what to do about us. They know we won't be back. We still hang out with some of the guys, but we aren't going to go back to being part of the larger gang. And we were never really initiated as full members. That's not something either of us has any interest in doing. We used to hang out with them sometimes and act like part of the gang because there wasn't much else to do, and being part of the gang was cool. It brought a sense of safety in numbers."

"But now that we've had a chance to step back from it," added Tony, "we don't want to be involved in the drug stuff many of them are into. And you feel safety in numbers, but you also need it because you become a target of other gangs."

"So they're talking about how to punish us, to make an example of us for leaving." I paused, then added, "Like beat the crap out of us!"

"Like a rite of passage out of the gang," said Tony.

Don Emilio didn't respond right away. He stared at Tony for a few seconds, and then at me.

"I hear fear in both of your voices, and I see it in your eyes."

"Darn straight!" I shouted. "I'm scared as hell of what could happen."

Don Emilio rubbed his chin, then leaned back in his chair. "You are afraid of what your life-long friends might do to you."

I nodded, even though that sounded pretty stupid.

"Are you sure their objective is punishment, or are they looking for some formal closure and a means for them to save face with your leaving?"

Tony had a puzzled look, and I'm sure I did too.

"What do you mean?" Tony asked.

"Well, there seems to be some ways to leave that are okay. We talked before about older boys getting a job, or getting married."

"Yeah," said Tony, "the older guys can't be as easily intimidated. Man, if I was 6'4" and 240 pounds, those skinny wanna-be-somebodies who are talking up punishment wouldn't have the *huevos* to say anything."

"Then there *are* ways to leave that are okay, right?" asked Don Emilio.

"Well, yeah, I guess so," I responded. "But just for the older guys."

"But Vincent," added Tony, "some of the guys our age have moved away with their parents to another part of the county and dropped out, and it's been okay."

"So, Don Emilio," I said, "what you are getting at is that there may be other alternatives here. That getting beat up may not be our only option."

"There are always alternatives," he answered. "We have spent a lot of time talking about how we create what comes into our lives, how we get what we focus on. You create those alternatives, consciously or unconsciously, and in the end you choose one and make it happen."

"Oh boy, here we go again." Tony stood there looking at the ground, shaking his head. Then looking up at me, he said, "You're the one who's freaking out here."

"I'm creating the alternative of getting beat up?" I asked. "No way! Why would I want to get the crap beat out of me?"

"Well," said Don Emilio, "if you focus on your fears and create thoughts in your mind about a bad outcome, and if because of your fears you send emotional energy to this imagined outcome, by definition you are creating it. Now, it may be that on some level you agree with this rite of passage into and out of the gang. Perhaps you believe that if you go through it, you will be able to hold up your head when you see these guys on the street, and they will acknowledge you for having had the courage to go through this 'rite of passage' out of the group. Then again, you might be able to come up with a totally different rite of passage that leaves your face intact."

"But *they* are gonna decide how to deal with us," I said emphatically. "*I* ain't got much choice in the matter, do I!"

Don Emilio didn't respond to my statement. He kept looking at me.

"Do I?" I finally asked, making it a question.

"When things get difficult, there is sometimes the tendency to let someone else do the decision-making," said Don Emilio. "It is 'group think,' or the old 'going along with the guys' routine. Remember when you tried to crash the party in East San Diego? You said you did not want to go, but you went along with the guys anyway. Arturo and Pablito made your decision for you."

"Yeah," I responded. "They were talking the tough guy crap, accusing me of being afraid. Then the first thing they did was run away."

"They went out to that party knowing the risk," said Don Emilio, "knowing they were looking for trouble. They chose to put all of you at risk. When they ran off, they fully expected that the two of you would get beaten up, or worse. But I came along and changed that, because you and I are dreaming a different dream. Vicente, the events of 16 years ago when you were brought by your Tata to meet me were meant to end up with me teaching you about the ancient spiritual power of your ancestors. You were not supposed to end up dead in East San Diego. So I had these very, very strong messages that caused me to get to San Diego when I did, and to drive your Tata's car out there to find you. Our connection had more power, more energy, than Arturo's decision to look for trouble and to let you take the fall."

"Looking back on it now, it seems like a miracle that you showed up when you did," said Tony. "It *was* a miracle!"

"Yes, it was a miracle. It was magic. It was part of the magical nature of the Universe. Your guardian angels and guides, and mine, were communicating loud and clear and helped save you from what could have been a real disaster. The two of you had a lot of help that night coming from the spirit level, looking out for you and protecting you. You got your own messages, but you went anyway.

"Now with that as an example of the extraordinary measures your guardian angels and guides will go to in order to keep you safe, what makes you so certain that there are no options other than getting your faces bashed in by your 'friends'? Do you think your protectors are simply going to abandon you this time? Sure, your 'friends' are not planning to kill you, but how maimed do you plan to get?"

"Man, I don't even want to think about how maimed," I said.

"Okay, but do not ignore it and allow it to happen."

"All right, then," said Tony, "so what can we do? How do we, as you say, create a new alternative?"

"Well, I cannot create it for you. It has to come from within you. If you look to your own inner messages, and as you think about what we have discussed over the past year, I think you will find your answer."

Don Emilio paused, and walked back to his chair. He sat down and took a deep breath. Certain we were finished with that issue, he began again.

"Now, as I said earlier, I want to hear any questions you have about the last session or about any of your practice exercises."

"The one I'm having trouble with is dreaming," I said. "I've been trying to become aware in my dreams. I'm remembering a lot of my dreams, and writing down as much as I can, but I can't remember to do some action in the dream. A few times I realized I was dreaming, but I guess I got so excited each time about getting to that point that I woke up before I could take an action. But mostly I just kept on dreaming. I couldn't do anything. It's getting frustrating. How do I stop and do something else and not keep dreaming?"

"You have achieved a lot! Congratulations! There is no need to be so hard on yourself. To repeatedly be aware that you are dreaming is a great start. Just keep it up. Keep trying to be aware in the dreams and keep writing down your dream experience. Soon you will be comfortable with the idea that you are aware that you are dreaming. Then it will be easier for you to take some action. Let me suggest that you decide on one action you want to take—like clapping your hands—or one place you want to go in the dream. And whether you try a dream or out-of-body experience, do the same thing. When you go to bed think about doing that one thing. And with enough repetition, you will eventually remember it in the dream. And when you remember it, firmly will yourself to do it or to go there."

"What do you want to do or where do you want to go?" Tony asked me.

"Well, Tata has been sick again, so I've been thinking about him all the time. I think I'd like to go check up on him and see how he's doing. You said we could travel to places and see people. Can I do that?"

"Sure," said Don Emilio. "That would be a good action for you to take. And since you say it is something that is always on your mind, it could be easier than most anything else for you to remember. Now when you arrive at your Tata's house it will be late and he should be sleeping. I would suggest you wish yourself to be at his bedside rather than in front of the house. And although he will be sleeping, remember that just as your consciousness is awake, his spirit self may be awake and aware of your presence and may want to communicate with you. So be aware, and listen for communication from him."

Wow, this is really cool stuff, I thought to myself. Who would ever have thought we would be talking about flying at night to visit Tata. "This flying stuff, Tony, the guys could really get into it! Think about the possibilities! We'd better practice dreaming more."

"Yeah, so maybe I can join you when you visit your Tata. How trippy."

"That is part of what this is all about," added Don Emilio. "Have fun, expand your awareness, learn more, check up on your loved ones. Yes, think about the possibilities. I would like to emphasize that insights into the answers you seek will come from your shamanic energy practice. As you have already discovered, you can get messages. You can know things ahead of time. You can get into the flow. But you need to consistently work on increasing the amount of energy you have in the luminous egg that is you. You need to light up your being, and to plug your leaks. That comes from practice.

"Each day, do the exercises that best help you to increase your energy level. The techniques you practice will evolve over time. Your commitment to daily practice is the key, not only in dealing with your friends, but in all aspects of your life. Increasing your energy each day is the key to living in the flow of the universe, connected to all things. Daily practice ingrains this way of being into your mind, and into your entire consciousness. Daily practice helps you remember who you are."

We ended the session and said goodbye to Don Emilio. Out on the front sidewalk we talked briefly before going our separate ways.

"I appreciate what he's telling us about raising our energy and trying to get our own answers," I said, "but Tomás was really serious. We don't have much time left. I'd really like to know what our homies are planning for us."

"If only I could read a few minds right now," added Tony.

We both laughed, but it was an uneasy laugh. We knew the time for dealing with them was coming real soon. So we agreed to talk about it again after school on Monday.

31

THE PROPOSAL

*"Courage is resistance to fear, mastery
of fear: not absence of fear."*

MARK TWAIN

"I'm glad I'm finally getting out of there," said Tony as he walked up to me. "I've been waiting all day to talk to you."

We had agreed to meet just off campus to walk home.

"We could have met at lunch time if you were so anxious."

"We tried that before. It was hard to find a spot where there weren't many people around. I thought it would be better to wait so we wouldn't have to worry about someone sitting near us hearing what we were saying."

With so many students getting out at the same time and heading home, there was a pretty big crowd walking down 12th Street. But we could either walk faster and get ahead of them, or slow up and let the crowd thin out as we walked, so they couldn't hear us clearly.

"What are we gonna do?" I asked as we started walking. "We gotta think of something before they come after us."

"Okay, okay," said Tony. "First, we have to figure out what to do about some of them wanting to beat us up. And we also have to think about how to tell them what we've learned from Don Emilio. I know you don't think we should be doing that yet. But remember, he said the answer to the getting beat up part might have to do with what we've been learning."

"I don't know how we're going to get them interested in what we've been learning when what they want to do is beat the crap out of us."

"Well, hell," said Tony, "I don't know, I ... ah...."

He slowed down, looking up into the sky. Suddenly he stopped and pounded both fists into the air. He stood there smiling at me with a big look of relief on his face.

"I know what we should do!" He sounded so sure and yet so surprised. "It just came to me!"

"What? Tell me!" I pleaded.

"Well, you know how we've been telling Don Emilio we can't just ditch these guys and act like we don't know them anymore, 'cause they've been our friends for years?"

"Yeah? So?"

"So," continued Tony, "rather than quit and try to stay away from them, which we don't want to do, why don't we share some of what we're learning and help them. Before now, we haven't been able to figure out what would make most of them interested in this stuff. I think we could start out teaching them karate, even if it's just to help them fight better. I know most of these guys are pretty pathetic when they fight, even when they're just playing around. We could show them how to fight better with karate, then show them other energy movements. After that we could teach them other things about energy."

"Tony! That's it! Karate is pretty popular, but I don't think any of them have ever taken karate lessons because most of them have some sort of arrest record, so they're not allowed into the Youth Center. But how does that get them to stop their plans to kick the hell out of us?" Suddenly Tony's great inspiration didn't sound so great to me.

"From what Tomás told you the other day, it sounded like some guys want to fight us, and some don't. But they agree they gotta do something if we're quitting. It's the rules. And like Don Emilio said, maybe they just need to save face. They can't just ignore our quitting. So maybe we propose teaching them karate and some simple energy stuff as an alternative that helps them save face, and that benefits each one of them. We could 'graduate' to becoming their personal teachers, and maybe they'll forget about wanting to beat us up."

"That's a pretty big maybe."

"I know we aren't ready to teach them all this stuff yet, but we could start with what *I* know best. Vincent, you could help me. I'm not saying I can teach everything about karate and hand out black belts or certificates. But we can show them different movements and how to get their energy moving. That's all we're interested in for now. We just want to get them started."

Tony paused, but I didn't want to say anything else. He was on a roll and I didn't want to interrupt him. I knew there was more. I could see him thinking about what he would say next.

"This fits in with our creation exercise and what I really want in my life right now," he continued. "I know it's what Don Emilio used for the practice exercise, but I want to do it for real. It's what I've wanted to do for a long time. Like Don Emilio's example, I want to get a job at the Youth Center or at the Boy's Club or somewhere helping to teach karate to younger kids. That's what I put into a thought bubble recently. But this is even better, even if it's not for pay."

"Did you give up on the baseball glove?" I asked.

"No, I'm still expecting that to show up, and I'm still sending it energy, but it's teaching karate and energy movement that has me most excited, so I've been mostly focused on sending energy to this new thought. Maybe it's about to really happen!"

"Sending energy rather than sacrificing chickens. Well, that sounds like an improvement!"

Tony and I stopped in our tracks and turned around, surprised to hear Linda right behind us, laughing.

"Stop with the chickens," pleaded Gloria, laughing with her. "They were kidding!"

I thought we left a lot of space between us and any other kids walking home. I guess we got so involved in our discussion we didn't notice them gaining on us.

"What a surprise to see you here," said Tony sarcastically."

I elbowed him in the ribs.

"You guys look a little sweaty," said Tony. "Been running?"

"Oh, we always walk fast on our way home from school," said Linda, also sounding a bit sarcastic. "Let's see, to get more exercise, or...so we don't get hassled by homeless guys, or...."

"Hi Vincent, Tony," said Gloria, as she waived a light tap at her sister to get her to stop. "Did you say you're going to start classes on what you're learning from your Tío? Sorry, I just overheard a little of what you said."

"We'd like to start some classes teaching the guys about karate and energy movement first, then some of the other things Don Emilio has taught us," said Tony. "We're gonna talk to them about it."

"Vincent," said Gloria moving up closer to me, "don't forget, you said you would include some of the girls."

"I'm not going to no classes with those hoodlums!" Linda said emphatically.

"And they won't want to go to any class with you," added Tony, laughing.

I looked at Tony and smiled. "Yeah, we already figured out we'd have to do separate classes." The girls smiled and nodded. "But we're planning to start with the guys. We have to do something for them before they come after us for not hanging around them much anymore."

"Hm," said Linda. "Maybe you guys aren't so dumb after all."

"They're coming after you?" asked Gloria, sounding concerned.

"There's been talk about it for a while now," Tony answered. "So we're gonna go propose doing some classes for them, in exchange...."

"In exchange for not getting our faces bashed in," I added.

32

THE SHOWDOWN

"Nothing happens unless first a dream."

CARL SANDBURG

A meeting had finally been arranged for Tony and me to go before the guys and talk about our situation. It was just getting dark when I went to Amador's Market to get Tony so we could walk over there together. But when I got to the store he had bad news for me.

"You go on over, I'll be there soon. This shouldn't take but about half an hour more."

A big order of food arrived late, and he had to help get it priced and up on the shelves. As I walked the four blocks to the meeting, I thought to myself that if I didn't know better, I would have thought Tony had made up an excuse to stay away from this showdown with the guys. I know he didn't have any control over the truck showing up late. And I know that when these orders arrive, he always has to help with printing the price tags, sticking them on, and stocking the shelves. I just wish I could have been the one to find an excuse to avoid facing the guys.

The meetings usually take place in a building on Logan Avenue that has vacant shop spaces on the ground floor and apartments on two floors above. My father said that a small grocery store used to be there, but I only remember it being vacant with boarded up windows. It belongs to one of the guys' family, so we get to use it as an occasional place to hang out, our clubhouse. There are a lot of these vacant storefronts, former businesses that died when the freeway and the bridge came through the neighborhood, tearing out the heart of the business district.

As I walked down the last block on Logan, I had a very uneasy feeling. The whole street looked strange for some reason. There were parked cars, but there was no traffic on the street, and no one walking by on the sidewalks. It was just past sunset, and I guess because the high fog had rolled in, the streetlights seemed to give a weird color to the sky.

My heart was pounding as I approached the old building. It showed its age, with peeling paint and sagging window frames. This building had seen better days. I'd seen better days too, and I knew that this was not going to be one of them. Slowly I opened the door and looked in. It was dimly lit inside. I saw that there were about 15 guys already in the room, sitting in chairs or standing in groups, talking. About a third of the guys were about Tony's and my age, or just a little older, the guys we hang out with. The rest were older members. A few heads turned toward me as they heard the old door creak. I turned back to look down the street, hoping perhaps to see Tony walking this way. It was already too dark to see very far down the street. Anyway, I knew it was way too soon for him to have finished yet. There was nothing left for me to do but suck it up, walk in, and get on with it.

From the time I walked into the room, it seemed like I was in a fog. People started yelling at me, talking about Tony and me abandoning our homeboys, and turning on them.

"But we haven't turned on anyone," I insisted. "We're still your friends. We just don't have much extra time any more to hang out and...."

"Shut the hell up. We'll do the talking here," said one of the older guys.

"Yeah, we're not here to listen to your lame excuses. It's too late for excuses."

"You vowed to hang with us forever, you *pinche* bastard, and now we can't find you...."

"You never show up when you're supposed to."

"You think you're better than us...."

I tried to speak up and defend myself, tell them we weren't abandoning them, but nobody wanted to hear anything. This was their time to let it all out, to justify their actions that I knew would follow. Before, I couldn't imagine how friends could beat up on friends, the punishment for leaving the gang. Now I could hear it in their voices. They had created an imaginary hurt, and built up an anger that each spoke, an anger that grew as each listened to the others. As they continued to speak, the volume got louder and louder, and they got angrier and angrier.

Oh damn, where's Tony, I thought to myself. If I have to take this beating all by myself, I'm in real trouble. There is so much anger here, they'll beat the holy crap out of me. Not that I wished hurt on Tony, but if we shared the blows, and if we could give some back together, rather than all of them pounding on just one of us, me...we could get through it.

Manuel, mister scarface himself, finally got up out of the large upholstered chair he liked to sit in. He had been listening to what everyone else was yelling, but he remained calm, and never spoke himself. As he stood there, he stuck out his left arm, like he was parting the waters, and the noise receded. Everyone deferred to him, and the room fell silent.

"Where is your partner, Vincent? I understand the two of you wanted to talk to us today."

"Tony should be here soon. They got a load of food in at the store just as he was about to leave. He had to unpack, price, and shelve the food. He should be done any minute now."

"So go ahead. Tell us what you wanted to say. Or do you need Tony to back you up?"

"No, I...uh, can start...I guess."

Tony and I had already told Arturo, Pablito, Tomás and a few others what we were proposing, that we could start teaching them the basics of karate, and then some of the energy movement stuff that Don Emilio had taught us.

"Well," I began, "we want to share some of the stuff that my Tío Emilio has taught us, but we want to begin by teaching the basics of karate, which he said is a good way to start moving energy...."

A low rumble in the crowd slowly erupted into shouts, for and against. A few voices were pulling for us, but it was clear those against us were yelling louder.

"What's this karate crap?"

"They quit. They gotta pay."

"Let 'em work for us. Let 'em teach us karate."

"Kick their ass if they wanna leave."

"We don't need no damn karate classes."

"Let's get it on! I wanna pop the mother upside his head!"

"Yeah! Let's do it!"

It was getting louder and louder. These guys were getting out of hand. I thought most of them were on the verge of getting very violent. It was getting so loud that I could hardly think. I knew I was done for.

"Shut the hell up!" yelled Manuel. "Shut the hell up! I'll handle this! And someone turn on that fan! It's getting goddamn hot in here."

Manuel reached behind his back, pushing his loose-hanging Pendleton shirt out of the way. My knees suddenly got very weak.

Oh my God, I'm dead, I thought to myself, I think he's got a gun.

"All right!" someone yelled, laughing. "Do it to him!"

Just then all the lights flickered, then went out.

"Hey! What the hell!"

"Who turned off the damn lights?"

"The fuse blew!"

"Hey man, I can't see a thing!"

Everyone was yelling again. I couldn't see a thing either, but it didn't sound like anyone was moving. This was the break I needed. I knew now was my chance to get out of there, but I also knew that if I ran out the front door, the light from the street would light me up and make me an easy target.

While they yelled at each other in the dark, I slowly and quietly started to make my way toward the back storeroom and the back door. I walked in the darkness with hands out in front of me, hoping I wouldn't bump into anything or anyone. When I got to the side wall I turned toward the back and walked quickly. I knew it was a clear shot out the first door, into the storeroom, and then out the back door. As I expected, once through the first door, the dim alley light shining through the window lit the storeroom just enough for me to see as I ran through that room and out the second door. I could hear them yelling.

"He's getting out the back!"

"Turn on the damn lights!"

"Someone go flip the switches in the damn fuse box!"

"Run after him, dammit!"

When I reached the alley, I started to run toward Chicano Park. Just then a figure jumped out of the darkness and started running ahead of me, scaring me so much I almost pissed in my pants. But I quickly realized it was Don Emilio.

"Jesus, where did you come from?" I yelled to him.

"From the Great Spirit," he yelled back as we ran. "I was told you were in great danger again. I stood by the back door and heard what was going on. When the lights went out I had a feeling you would run out this way."

I looked back and could see that four guys were running down the alley after us. When we got to the corner, I saw three more running parallel to us half a block over on Logan Avenue, heading us off from going that way.

An elderly man was standing there on the alley corner, watching what was going on. He held a Mexican cowboy hat like Tata's, which he was whipping on his leg, as if cheering for us in the race. I noticed that he looked *very much* like Tata. As I ran by, he shouted, "Vicente, don't worry about those guys. And try to come and visit!" But I could have sworn I did not see his lips move while I heard those words. How did he know my name, and why would he want me to visit? And how could I not worry about those guys? They're right on our tail! This was really weird. But I didn't have time to think about it, because after running across the street, Don Emilio continued down the alley.

"Don Emilio, no...." I slowed down a little. I didn't want to follow him in this direction, but I didn't want to leave him alone either. "This alley turns back onto Logan!" I yelled as I ran a little behind him. "Those guys are gonna cut us off and jump us there!" The freeway off-ramp at the edge of Chicano park cuts off this alley with a tall concrete wall.

Don Emilio slowed up so that I was again running next to him. He grabbed my hand.

"Think about where you would rather be," he yelled. "Wish it with all your might!"

God, I'd rather be home, in bed, I thought to myself, safe and warm under my covers, with my father in the front room to protect me from these crazy *vatos*. Sometimes I can't stand being around my father, but right now I'd give anything to be with him.

As I was thinking this, Don Emilio yanked on my hand as we ran alongside the concrete wall. He turned as he yanked, and we both went crashing into the wall....

I remember everything disintegrating, in slow motion, breaking up into smaller and smaller bits, including me, until there was just blackness and space, with white lights scattered throughout the blackness.... And I knew that I was connected to all of those white lights, and to the darkness between them. It was me, and it was everything else, and I was connected to it all.

33

THE ALTERNATIVE

*"We warriors of light must be prepared to have patience
in difficult times and to know that the Universe is conspiring
in our favor even though we may not understand how."*

PAULO COELHO, THE ALCHEMIST

"Mijo," I heard my father call from somewhere far away. "Tony is here."

"Huh?" That was all I could say. I was coming back, but I couldn't form any words.

"Go on in there," he said to Tony. "Looks like he was pretty sound asleep."

I could hear it all, but it was slow to make sense, and slowly I was able to focus my eyes on the objects in my room. I could see that it was still light, but beginning to get dark.

"What the hell are you doing taking a nap?" Tony asked. "Get up! We've gotta go meet with the guys, or did you forget? You're not gonna try and tell me you're sick and can't go, are you? Come on. Get your butt up."

I was confused, and couldn't remember how I got into bed. "Gotta...gotta quit having these weird dreams...." I said when I could finally talk, sort of. "They're killing me. For real.... I can't figure out what's real and what's not."

Don Emilio popped his head into my bedroom doorway and said, "It is all real. Your dreams are as real as this life. Maybe even more real."

▸ 253 ◂

I now realized I had heard his voice and my father's. They had been in the living room talking. And dream or not, Don Emilio seemed to be aware of the experience I just had.

Don Emilio came into the room and sat on the bed after I got out from under the covers. I saw that I was fully dressed, including my shoes. I couldn't figure out why I would have gotten in between the sheets wearing my shoes. I just don't do that. I sat there on the bed with him. Tony sat on the floor across from us.

"Well, come on. Tell us about the dream," said Tony.

So I told them about it as best I could. I was still having trouble connecting my thoughts and my words. I gave them as much of the details as I could, including crashing into the wall and disintegrating. Tony thought that part was especially funny.

"Kinda like Humpty Dumpty falling off the wall," he laughed, "except you put all the pieces back together again."

"Not all the pieces," I said. "It feels like I'm still not all the way back together again yet."

"Part of your consciousness is still in that other place," said Don Emilio. "I know you feel uncomfortable, because it is different from how you normally are, but it is not necessarily a bad place to be. You will be your regular self soon, but I want you to know that a person can adjust and learn to speak and think normally as I am now, and yet maintain a connection with the other side. And in that manner, be able to access information and guidance not readily available to people in their everyday state of awareness. That is how a shaman functions to help with healing someone. He walks between the worlds—enters into his subconscious level to see or perceive information he needs about his client or patient, or he communicates with other beings or spirits on that other level who tell him what he needs to know."

"I wonder what that old man who looked like Tata was trying to tell me?" I responded.

"I wish you had found out some information we need to know about this meeting we have to be at in a little while," Tony said getting serious. "Hey, you know, I'm starting to freak out about this dream. Is that how the meeting is going to turn out? They're going to pull out a gun on us, and maybe blow us away?" Tony suddenly was looking very scared.

"Sometimes when we have strong fears, we create fearful dreams about what is to come," continued Don Emilio. "Boys, let me say again, that there is one main truth about the way the Universe works, and that is: *You Get What You Focus On*, and in that way, *You Create Your Own Reality*. If you focus on getting beat up or shot, that will be what you bring about in your life. If you carry that negative fear into this meeting, you could reinforce the negative fears of some of those guys.

"You need to trust in this process we have been going through, and trust in the positive things about your life. You and the other boys have lived through some negative experiences. But most of the time, you and they live in a good place, with laughter, good times, and good friendship. You don't need to let the little negative stuff, and the fear, control your lives. You can go into that meeting knowing that this is the first step to a better life for all. You can leave there feeling good about your life and about your contribution to their lives, knowing that you found a way to share this learning with your homies, and that you *did not* abandon them."

"Yeah, well, that's what Tony and I decided we were going to do, and I still want to do that. I just hope it turns out that way. You know, maybe there was some information for us in that dream. The old man said not to worry about those guys."

"Trust your own insights," said Don Emilio. "Trust that those spirits who are with you and guiding you through this life experience will help you with this one as well. Do not just hope. Rather, believe and trust that it will work out in a way that is consistent with the direction in which the two of you have focused your thoughts and your energy. That is the other side of creating your own reality--belief that what you focus on will come about."

"Well, I'm ready to believe that it will go like we originally planned," Tony said, no longer sounding afraid. "I've been looking forward to staying involved with our homies, and teaching them karate classes and eventually other things as well. That's what we've been saying we want, and that's where I have been putting my energy and my focus. So let's get going."

"Where are you meeting them?" Don Emilio asked.

"I'm glad you asked," I said. "The clubhouse is over on Logan Avenue, across from the tortilleria. You gonna be there, or nearby?" I asked, hoping he would say that he'd be near.

He didn't answer right away. He just stood there looking at each of us.

"There is no reason for me to be there," he said finally. "You guys go on now. Be positive and believe in the power of your own energy."

After we walked out of the house, Tony said, "Big Mike asked me to come by to be sure he didn't need any more help today."

Gulp! I started to get real nervous. "You mean you might not be able to go over to the clubhouse with me?" I asked with surprise and fear in my voice.

"Jeeze, don't get so excited. It's late in the day, so it's not like there's gonna be a semi-truck unloading. I shouldn't have much, if anything, to do."

When we turned the corner and saw the truck outside the store, my heart started pounding. "Oh hell, this is gonna turn out like my dream, Tony!"

"Hold your horses man! Don't jump to conclusions. Everything will be fine. Trust yourself!" Tony went into the store and talked to Mr. Amador, then came back to the front door where I waited for him. He came back looking a little frustrated.

"They're almost finished unloading, but I have to put the price tags on, and shelve them. Shouldn't take me more than fifteen minutes...."

"Oh God! It's just like in my dream!" I blurted out again.

"....if I have someone to help me," he continued. "I'll print out the tags and show you where to put them. We should be done quickly and get over there just a few minutes late."

"Okay then, let's do it!" I responded with some forced enthusiasm. This little change in the script made me feel better. I could feel the fear go away, and a feeling of confidence taking over.

Tony showed me where to put the price tags as he made them up, and I just pasted away. I was suddenly in a good mood and got so into the work that I started to whistle the tune, *Whistle While You Work*.

"Boy, you sure switched gears here," Tony remarked. "First you were freaking out, now you are acting like you don't have any concerns in the world."

"No, you know what it is? I set aside my fears. I stopped letting fear take over. As Don Emilio was telling us to do, I began again to trust that what we set out to do would happen. I mean that's the direction all our efforts have been headed towards. I guess I chose to trust that, rather than to build up the fear. It felt like when I let go of the fear, I could feel everything else falling into place. And suddenly it made sense to just focus on what was in front of me—putting on price tags. Being in the moment, as Don Emilio would say. And by being in the moment fully, I could feel a shift, maybe a little opening into another level of awareness, and I sorta felt an assurance, a knowing, that everything will go well. I felt so good, I just started whistling."

"Right on, homie. If it works for you, well..." and Tony started whistling the same tune, with a big gleam in his eye and his head bouncing around as he worked, as if to try to show me a smile while his lips were puckered to whistle.

He was right, it really didn't take much time, and before long we were done and on our way through Chicano Park and walking along Logan Avenue toward the clubhouse.

Tony insisted that he be the one to make the proposal about the karate classes, because he was really into it and had been itching to get started with these classes. For the past few weeks, after karate classes he had been talking about the instructor's teaching approach rather than just focusing on learning and practicing the moves being taught.

So I agreed to let him do the talking. In my dream, I didn't convince but a few guys to let us do these classes. I figured that was a clear message to let Tony do it. Similar to what we had learned from Don Emilio, Tony was directing lots of energy and enthusiasm into this concept of karate and energy classes for the guys and getting more excited and animated in his talking as we got closer. He seemed to literally be a bursting ball of energy by the time we got to the clubhouse door. I decided that the best thing for me was to support him by channeling my energy to him.

We walked in the door and it seemed like *deja vu* all over again. It was like I was repeating my dream, except that Tony was added to the picture. They started shouting like before, getting meaner and meaner. But Tony seemed to somehow rise above it all. He ignored the negative comments and the verbal threats and just laughed and joked with the guys as if they weren't serious. But then things settled down to business.

"Shut the hell up, Tony!" Manuel yelled. "Shut up, all of you," he yelled again. "We got some serious business to deal with here."

"Damn straight, it's serious business." Tony jumped right back into it. "Vincent and I have been working our asses off learning important stuff from the *brujo*, stuff that's going to help all of you and help our barrio. We've been learning how to increase our power, our energy. We've been learning how to tap into the power of the Universe and to use it to make things happen that will benefit us all. The first step in tapping into that energy was learning how to increase it and move it through our bodies. Part of that was learning karate and Toltec energy movements. Just learning those energy movements could help you sissies from getting the crap beat out of you."

"Oh damn, Tony!" I whispered to him. I knew that was going to get them going again. Guys were yelling at Tony for calling them sissies and implying that anyone could whip them. Why in the hell did he challenge them like that? I thought we were done for. But Tony stood his ground and kept his smile. I was surprised that he challenged them so directly. But he acted like he knew what he was doing, so I just sucked it up and stood my ground too. I decided again that I would just continue sending energy Tony's way to help him through this.

"Vincent and I have been so busy with school, work, and the *brujo* that we can't hang out with you guys like before. But we've learned a lot, and we want to share it with you."

All the while he was talking, Carlos and Flaco kept on a constant countering dialogue.

"We don't need no help from them bastards."

"All we need is to kick their ass."

"Right on, bro. Don't nobody skip out on our homies."

"Yeah. They gotta pay."

The other guys were listening to them and to Tony. Tony just ignored them and continued.

"So we've got a proposal. We think it's time for us to give back to the barrio and to you guys. We want to change our roles. Rather than finally joining as regular members, we propose that we be your personal instructors. And we'll start off with Toltec energy movements and karate lessons. And later, if you want, we can add in other stuff we've learned from the *brujo*, like...."

"Like mind reading," yelled Pablito. "I wanna learn how you do that!"

"We don't need none of that," yelled Carlos.

Flaco, who along with Carlos had been talking the whole time and challenging Tony jumped toward the front of the room. "I don't need none of this bull. And I don't need no karate to kick your ass!"

Flaco moved toward Tony, and when no one jumped in to stop him, he decided to go for it. Flaco, who wasn't so *flaco* anymore, must have outweighed Tony by forty pounds and was four to five inches taller. He reared back his right fist and sent it right at Tony's face as he charged toward Tony.

In a classic karate movement, Tony deflected the blow, stepped aside, and used the force of the charging body to help him flip Flaco onto his back. He hit the floor with a loud thud. The room fell silent as Flaco just laid there on his back, totally stunned. He even started to laugh softly at his own surprise that he ended up on the floor.

"How did you do that?" Flaco asked as he stared up at the ceiling.

Then the noise started up again, with guys yelling at each other and at Tony.

"*Pinche cabrón!* What a move, Tony!"

"Yeah, what a move, Tony," someone said sarcastically, then added "Get up Flaco and kick his ass!"

"Hey Tony, teach me how to do that," Flaco said, still staring up at the ceiling.

"Come on, Flaco, get up. Get him."

"Hey man, let's don't wait for Flaco to get up. We're here to whip both their asses. Let's get it on."

"I'm ready, let's go!"

Suddenly Manuel pounded his fist on the table, and again yelled, "Shut the hell up! Shut up, dammit! We're gonna cut out all this crap right now, once and for all."

My jaw dropped. He had on that loose Pendleton shirt. Just like in my dream, he reached around behind the shirt....

"Oh God, no," I thought to myself, "it can't be...."

...and he pulled out his bandana headband. He put it on his head, jumped into a karate pose, and said to Tony, "Come on homie, let's get started with these lessons. You don't got no time to waste."

We both stood there frozen from the shock.

Manuel stared at Tony, then at me, then back at Tony.

"Hey, what's wrong man? You *vatos* look like you seen a ghost."

"I...we thought you were gonna pull out a gun," I answered.

"Hell, you guys think I'm crazy? First of all, I don't own a gun. Second, it would be stupid for me to walk down the street and into this place carrying a gun. What if I got stopped by a cop and he frisked me? And third, you don't never pull no gun on your homies. If anyone ever did that, they'd be kicked out of here, right after I hit him over the head with it."

"But a lot of the guys were yelling and screaming for us to get beat up," said Tony, "and for someone to pop us."

Most of the guys were laughing now.

"They were yelling all that stuff just to scare you guys. It was Pablito's idea."

"I wanted to see if you guys could read our minds," said Pablito as he walked up with a big grin on his face. "Got you back, *ese*," he said as he lightly punched Tony on the shoulder.

"Since that day at Eddie's house," Manuel continued, "when I first heard about the *brujo* being here, I been checking you out, and been hearing from the guys about how you been doing, workin' with him and stuff. I even talked with my grandfather about it. At first he said it was just someone teaching you about old magic, and it didn't mean nothin'. He said lots of people get sucked into that and just waste their time or cause problems for themselves. But later, I told him I heard what the *Brujo* was teaching had really helped you guys, and that you were trying to find a way to help the rest of us learn about it. He seemed really pleased about that, and said this must be a good man and a good *Brujo*. He asked me to watch out for you and the *Brujo*, and to help you if I could."

Manuel jumped back into the karate stance and moved his hands back and forth like he was ready to practice some moves. "So," he said, "after we finish these karate lessons, are you guys gonna teach us some of the other stuff the *Brujo's* been teaching you?"

"Uh...well...I...." Tony stammered. At first, he didn't know what to say. The question was a complete surprise. This is what we had been hoping for, but we were willing to settle for just doing karate classes, and then see what happens next.

"Well, at least start with a little bit, the easy stuff," Manuel urged, "so we can kinda get to know what it's all about, okay?"

Tony and I looked at each other. The shock on Tony's face faded as we both broke out into big smiles and started nodding our heads.

"Well, sure, of course." answered Tony. "Okay!"

"Well then, like I said, homies, let's get on with it!"

34

Honoring Don Emilio

*"You are a creator. You create with your every thought.
Anything you can imagine is yours to be or do or have."*

Abraham (Esther Hicks)

The next day Tony and I met with Don Emilio and excitedly told him about our amazing experience at the showdown with the guys, and our surprise at the outcome. Don Emilio, of course, seemed not at all surprised that our friends were so supportive of our studies with him, and that they had an interest in learning some of it too. He said this usually happens wherever he teaches young people. Their friends find out about it and want to know more. Young people, he said, seem to have a thirst for this hidden knowledge, and are more open to it than those of previous generations who may carry remnants of the taboos against "the old ways."

"What do you think were the main things you learned from yesterday's experience?" asked Don Emilio, trying to focus our rambling chatter.

"Don't pre-judge people," I said. "I thought the thugs in that group really wanted to bash our heads in, but they were just playing along with Pablito's trick. It reminded me that the guys who like to act tough are really just boys who like to laugh and have fun like the rest of us."

"I think I learned that we really can control the outcomes in our lives," said Tony. "We don't have to expect bad things to happen just because it looks like that's what is going to happen, especially if this negative viewpoint is coming from our own personal fears. I think our own fears colored our perception of the situation, and when we realized that maybe we didn't have accept those fears, we were able to put new positive energy into the situation and turn it around."

"That's true for our dreams too," I said. "I had that negative dream, but it came out of my own fears. We don't have to accept dreams based on fear. We can filter out the parts that may be colored by our fears and change the dreams or ignore them, and change the outcomes in our life to positive."

Don Emilio sat there with a big grin on his face, happy with what he was hearing.

"Your experience yesterday, your dreams about it before hand, and your ability to process all that information now and find your own insights make up one of the major learning experiences you have had during our time together," said Don Emilio. "You have done well. I am proud of you." Don Emilio closed his eyes and took a few deep breaths. Tony and I did the same.

In the quiet, the thought came to me. We had come to the end—for now anyway. I knew there was much more to learn, but it would come later. Don Emilio had said we were nearing the end of the first part, and it certainly felt like we had arrived. He sat there quietly, eyes closed, looking like he had just finished a long journey. And he had. He had taken us from feeling helpless about what was going on around us, to an amazing place we couldn't have even dreamed of. Not that we had felt completely helpless, but with friends like Pablito, who thought he'd be dead by age 25, and Arturo, part of a drug dealing family, we weren't giving ourselves much of a chance for a decent future. We didn't think it was a big deal, but Tata saw us repeating the mistakes his sons had made. So he had called for help.

I never gave Tata credit for knowing just what kind of help he called in. It took a while for me to realize that Tata was also studying the secrets of the ancestors. If he hadn't known about this stuff and talked to his cousin Emilio over the years, he never would have asked him to come help. And my life and Tony's would be much different right now.

I remember saying I didn't need no brujo to straighten me out, that I didn't need some relative I'd never heard of to teach me about "old ways" that people didn't even like to talk about. Don Emilio not only talked about it, he told us the secrets of the "old ways," the secret to creating a new and better life. He showed us the path—at least the first steps to making it happen, and assured us that we really had the power to make our own wishes come true. He had us talking to trees, using x-ray vision, and calling in eagles.

We were just beginning to scratch the surface, learning to drop old habits, and taking on new habits that were helping us to keep our energy up and raise our energy vibration. And that was helping us to hear messages from our higher self and the spirit guides around us. Before Don Emilio, we hadn't even known there was help like that available to us.

So, I could see an ending coming. I thought it would be better to acknowledge that fact rather than wait for Don Emilio to break the news. I knew he would appreciate hearing that we got the message without him having to voice it. I turned to Tony.

"Do you know...that this is it?"

"The end?" he asked, and nodded in agreement. "I've been expecting it for the past few sessions, but there was always more for next time."

Don Emilio was looking at us, listening and nodding his head.

"That is what I was thinking," he said. "We have reached our stopping point. You must have been reading my mind. Hey, how did you do that?"

Tony and I laughed, because we didn't expect it. Months ago, we were using that phrase all the time. Now we knew how he could just know things, like we were doing now.

"We have come to the end," Don Emilio continued, "the end of the first part. You have both learned the basics, and you have learned them well. I am so very proud of your accomplishments and the growing awareness that shows in your words and actions. We are complete for now. I didn't even have to tell you. We have come to the place where you take over. Continue your practice. Live what you have learned. As you live it, you will learn more, and the knowledge will shift from your head to your whole being.

"From this point on, at least for now, no one can be your teacher in these matters. You must now go deeper, on your own, and allow your own awareness, the knowledge of your higher self, to emerge. That is your new task as you move forward. As you practice quieting your mind and allowing your full self to emerge, you will be guided internally to live your life to the fullest, in joy and happiness, creating and experiencing all that you can dream and desire. Your world is ready for you to call it forth.

"Your awareness will expand much greater than you can imagine as you grow into greater alignment with your higher self, and become your higher self. But there will come a day when it will be time for us to sit down together again, and explore a second level of ancient teachings, for which you may need some guidance or direction."

You could tell it was a very special occasion. Most of the family was gathered at Nana and Tata's for this feast—my mother's sisters and brothers, and their kids. This time it looked like all the tíos and tías were involved in the cooking. The guys had set up the big grill they used for large family gatherings. They were making carne asada and pollo asado. As the heat seared the chicken skins, the deliciously sweet, pungent and smoky aromas of the marinade began to disrupt some of the many conversations, and people started to move closer to the grill and the tables in the patio.

Inside the house my mother, her sisters, and Nana were busy preparing the rest of the afternoon meal. My guess was that they were working on big pots of the standard rice and beans, and probably a salad. Because there were too many people for hand-made tortillas, Nana had sent me to Porkyland earlier in the day to buy a few dozen of both corn and flour tortillas.

The family was honoring Don Emilio as he prepared to go back to Mexico. Quite a difference from when he arrived. In all the turmoil of those first few days, I wasn't sure they were going to let him stay. Some, like my mother, welcomed him because he was a relative, but didn't really want anything to do with him, and didn't want him to have anything to do with me. Today, they were gathered to thank him and say goodbye.

Don Emilio had won over those who had distrusted him, not so much by what he said, but by what he had accomplished. Tata had asked him to come here to "straighten me out." I hated that term, but now I didn't care. He *had* straightened me out, and Tony too. He had turned our lives around. Those who initially objected to his being here didn't know what he taught us, but rather were happy for the change they saw in us, and especially for the fact that we were not locked up.

"I told you guys it would work itself out," said Tío Pancho, standing next to sizzling thin strips of steak. "I told you he would outgrow this teenage mischief if you just left him alone and quit coming down so hard on him."

"Yeah, we just didn't know if he would outgrow it at home, or in prison, like your brothers," said Tía Paula as she set a big bowl of salad on one of the tables.

"Easy now," Tío Marcos responded. "Don't get so worked up over this. Look, I'm fine. Juan's fine. And Vincent seems to be doing fine since he's been spending time with Emilio."

"*Orale, pues,*" said Tío Pancho, with a big grin, "we got these *fine* men in the family!"

My mother overheard what they were saying, so she came outside and sat with them.

"You're right, Marcos," she said, smiling, trying to ignore Tío Pancho's joking. "I didn't want to admit it, because I was concerned about *brujos* and what I've heard about them. I didn't know what *brujo* things Emilio would be teaching my son, but now that doesn't even matter. We see how he's much more sure of himself, and not following along after those neighborhood friends. He's thinking for himself, and spending more time with his school homework. And Emilio has given him assignments to do every day."

Turning to me, she said smiling, "Now you're too busy to get into trouble, aren't you?" She didn't wait for an answer. "But I'm not worried about that anymore. I'm so glad he and Tony..." she paused as her voice cracked and tears came to her eyes, "I'm glad they had the opportunity to study with Emilio."

Just then, Don Emilio and Tata walked by. She stood up and reached out and gave Don Emilio a big long hug.

"I want everyone to know," she said loudly, so all could hear, "I am so grateful for all that Emilio has done for us, and especially for Vincent and Tony. Emilio spent a lot of time with them, coming down from his work in Los Angeles. I didn't agree with my father about this, but he insisted. I am glad he did. And I am glad to know our cousin Emilio better, after all these years."

Tío Pancho stood and offered a toast, and they all gave Don Emilio a round of applause, and then hugs all around. It was certainly a different story than before. I guess we had all changed. Even Doña Rosa.

Tony came to the celebration with his grandmother and grandfather. Shortly after everyone acknowledged Don Emilio, Tony came over to me, anxious to give me some news.

"Hey, man," he said pulling me aside, "did you know that Doña Rosa and Gloria arrived a little while ago? They're still out in the front yard talking to one of your relatives. Anyway, Doña Rosa came into the store a few days ago." He paused and changed his voice to almost a whisper so others could not overhear. "She and Big Mike talked about the sessions we've had with Don Emilio. I was working that day and I heard most of their conversation. Big Mike made a point of telling Doña Rosa about the changes he saw in me, and in you. She seemed pretty pleased with what she heard. She said she got reports from Gloria about us, like we seemed to be doing better in school, and weren't hanging out with the wrong crowd much anymore. Pretty cool, huh? I figured you'd want to hear that before she said anything to you today. Sorry I didn't tell you sooner, but this was the first chance I've had."

"Hey, that's really good news. I'll find out from Gloria what she's heard."

Tony and I were standing in the side yard away from everybody. We stopped our conversation when we saw Doña Rosa and Gloria coming toward us. Not surprisingly, Don Emilio came walking up from the back yard just as Gloria and her Nana reached us. As everyone greeted each other, Gloria looked at me and smiled a little more warmly than usual. With a little coaxing from Gloria, Doña Rosa got right to the point.

"Don Emilio," she said addressing him directly, "you probably know from Julia that I originally had concerns about a brujo coming to our neighborhood and teaching young men about the old ways that my family had rejected long ago. But our conversation in Amador's market a couple of months ago, and one I had with him in the store a few days ago, along with reports from my granddaughter have opened my eyes. They have allowed me to judge on results, rather than on my preconceived notions. I want you to know that I think you have done a wonderful job with these two."

Turning to face Tony and me, she said, "I understand that you boys want to share with your friends what you have learned from Don Emilio. My granddaughters Gloria and Linda want to participate in that when you are ready. I want you both, and Don Emilio, to know I give my consent to having them join you for those classes."

"Wow, that's great news!" I said, excitedly, looking at Gloria, and giving Doña Rosa and Don Emilio big hugs. I really didn't expect that, even with what Tony just told me.

"And are you going to help with the classes for their friends?" Doña Rosa asked Don Emilio.

"The boys and I have not discussed this yet in detail, but I offered to help." Then turning to us, he said, "Vicente and Antonio, if you would like, I will be available to advise you on these classes, and perhaps even come occasionally and participate with you."

Tony and I nodded in agreement. "That would be great having you help us," I said, "especially with the harder stuff."

Don Emilio reached out and shook hands with Tony and me, sort of to seal the deal. I think his agreement, right in front of Doña Rosa, to continue to work with us helped put to rest any lingering concerns about sorcerer's apprentices gone wild.

Gloria looked at me in a funny way. I could tell she had something to say, so I just looked back at her and waited. She smiled, and it turned into a big grin.

"My Nana has one other thing to say which might be of interest to you," she said as she turned to her Nana and waited. As Doña Rosa began to speak, Gloria drifted away a few feet. Doña Rosa cleared her throat, like she was about to make a major statement. Not speaking to anyone directly, she turned her head up slightly and made an announcement to the air.

"If a certain young man were to ask my granddaughter to the junior prom, I would give my permission. And I would see to it that her parents gave their approval as well. But, this certain young man has not asked yet, so she can't say much more about it."

I could feel my heart beating faster, and I was sure my ears were getting red. I didn't know what to say, but I had a big grin on my face. Don Emilio came to the rescue.

"Before I leave," he said smiling, "I will have a talk with a certain young man to be sure the asking requirements are handled."

I was a little embarrassed that Don Emilio and Doña Rosa got involved in the Junior Prom, but if that was what it took to be able to go with Gloria, I was so okay with it.

We could see that the rest of the family was getting seated and digging into the feast, so we moved in that direction to join them.

35

CHANGES

"Synchronicity happens when we align with the flow of the universe rather than insisting the universe flow our way."

AKEMI G, *WHY WE ARE BORN*

I had just come out of City Hall after getting information about a student internship when I heard a familiar voice.

"Hey, homie, need a lift?"

I turned and saw Pablito standing next to their family car, parked about four car lengths from where I stood at the traffic light.

"Hey, Pablito," I called as I walked over, "what are you doing here?"

"Came to pick up my mom from work. Check it out, man. She's working here at the Grant Hotel, and look where I'm parked. Right in front of the place! I swear, when I have to come get her, I always find a space within a block of here. I got this thing about parking spaces now. I been working on keeping my energy up, and focusing on making parking spaces show up when I come downtown."

"That's what you use your energy work for?" I asked. "To get parking spaces?"

"Hey man, I know it's just a little thing, but I use it to keep reminding me that this stuff works, that I can make things happen in my life. I'm not ready to work on getting a high paying job or a beautiful babe just yet. Hey, I'm just learning, you know."

Pablito attended the sessions that Tony and I were teaching. The sessions were an outgrowth of the karate and energy movement lessons we conducted for about a year. Eleven guys started those lessons and eight finished that first set. Five of them continued to work with us, and have attended sessions two times a month that we called *Creating Your Life*. This second set of sessions, which also included four of the girls (after separate karate sessions), are based on what Don Emilio taught us about increasing our energy and creating our own reality. The sessions have gone much slower than when we studied with Don Emilio. With so many people, there have been lots of questions, and some good discussions. But it has taken a long time to get through the topics, about nine months so far. But that was okay though, as no one was in a rush, and they all remained very interested and actively involved. I was pleased to hear that Pablito had found a useful reward for his efforts.

"I think that's pretty cool. I know it's always pretty hard to find a parking space downtown. At least for the rest of us it is. You should tell the other guys about this. Any success like this can help reinforce their efforts."

"Hey, I don't want them to laugh. I mean, it's just parking spaces."

"*Just* parking spaces. People fight over parking spaces, anywhere, not just right in front of where they are going. This is pretty amazing."

"So, do you need a ride?" he asked.

"No, thanks. I drove over here. I had to park about four blocks away though. Hey, how do you do that?"

We both laughed, remembering very well how Pablito used to ask that of me and Tony, just like we used to ask that of Don Emilio.

"What were you doing here?" he asked. "Were you over there, in City Hall?"

"Yeah. I have to do an internship for a class at State, so I thought I'd see what's available in the City Planning department. I think I'll also go talk to some of the community groups that are doing neighborhood economic development and housing and see what I can do there. Well, I better get going. Take it easy. See you Saturday?"

"Yeah, I'll be there," he called to me as I walked toward Broadway.

As I walked away I thought about how far we had come—me, Tony, Pablito, Arturo and the guys. From the brink of disaster to this place where we were working on creating what we want in our own lives. That was the power that Don Emilio was telling us about. The simple powerful truth of our ancient Mexican culture—which is, everything in the Universe is made up of energy, and energy helps us to create our own reality if we focus on increasing our energy, and allow that energy to make magical connections to people, things, and events.

Before he left to go back to Mexico, Don Emilio told us that the best way to learn was to teach. And he was right. By trying to teach, we relearned everything. We had to understand it better in order to try and talk about it. Tony and I have been forced to do research, talk to people, call Don Emilio, read books, or whatever was necessary to try to stay ahead of the others. Just talking to Tony about how we would present something helped to make it sink in better for my own use. And we have had local teachers come in to talk about certain topics on occasion. Don Emilio even stopped in a couple of times. While I am not entirely comfortable with my understanding of everything he tried to teach us, I know it is coming together as we share with the others.

My big regret however, remained the fact that I had not been able to tell Tata about what I had learned. Not just the language issue. He had been sick a lot, and recently had another stroke. He was in a coma for a time, and when he came out of it, he still occasionally slipped back into a deep sleep for long periods. When my mother called me with an urgent message to get over to Tata's house, I was afraid I might not have the chance to tell him.

36
—

PASSING

"At the center of your being, you have the answer."

L A O T Z U

On my way to Tata's house, all kinds of thoughts were going through my head. I couldn't believe we could be about to lose him. Mom's voice on the phone sounded especially upset. He'd been down before, had previous strokes. She took those all in her usual strong, chin up, no emotions showing but caring way. Concerned, but not wigged out the way Tía Paula gets.

But this time she sounded different. This most recent stroke was really bad. She said he couldn't talk and had very little movement from the right side, and none on the left. When I asked why he wasn't in the hospital, she said they couldn't do anything else for him, and the doctor's advice was just to take him home and make him comfortable. They thought he might slip away at any time.

It was Tata that got me started on this path. He wrote to Don Emilio and asked him to come up.... No, it was even before that. Tata and my parents took me down to Mexico right after I was born to introduce Gracie and me to his family. That was my first encounter with the eagle.

Tata started out as a rancher, close to the earth, growing crops and raising cows and pigs. He felt the power of the earth. He knew there was something more, just on the other side. But the part of his culture that turned its back on that knowledge kept him from opening up, from letting it in. I think the reason he kept in close

▸ 273 ◂

touch with his cousin Emilio was that he didn't want to let go of that side completely. Once he had learned basic information from his talks with Don Emilio, and he learned the strange connection that I had to Don Emilio, he made sure that I was given the opportunity to choose—and hoped that I would not make the same choice he did.

After getting over the shock of finding out that he was interested in this stuff and that he knew a lot about it, I watched him talk with Don Emilio. I knew he was trying to absorb as much as he could. I knew he had practiced the focused attention exercises, and some of the tai chi energy movements. But he felt that he didn't have the strength or sufficient time left in his life to make a commitment to really get into it. But he really wanted me to take advantage of having a teacher like Don Emilio available to help me.

As I drove up, I could see a lot of cars in front of the house and lots of cousins outside, sitting on the front porch, in Tata's favorite spot. I hesitated a little before I got out of the car. I had this feeling that Tata would have wanted me to do something special for him at this time, related to the spiritual work I had been doing. But it wasn't clear to me what I should do.

Gracie came out of the house just as I was getting out of the car. She walked down to the gate and held it open for me as I walked up the stairs.

"How is he?" I asked.

"He's getting worse and worse," she said with a very worried tone. "He's been passing in and out of consciousness. I don't think he has much time left. Most of the family has been in there visiting with him for the last few hours, but mostly there has been no response from him. Most of the family just sat down to eat dinner. Come in and let's sit with Tata for a while."

I followed Gracie into the house, waving a brief and somber hello to the guys on the porch eating their dinner. I did the same to the crowd of family inside the house as we made a quick turn from the *sala* into Tata's bedroom. Mom was just walking out. I gave her a hug and kissed her hello. Then she quietly continued out of the room, saying nothing. Tía Paula was sitting in a corner of the bedroom, sniffling into a pink handkerchief. She motioned for the two of us to go up to the bed. Gracie and I sat down in two chairs that were placed next to Tata. She was close to his head; I was close to his hands.

"Hola, Tata," she said to him quietly. *"Ya viene Vincent. Está aquí conmigo."*

He wasn't moving at all. His right hand was at his side. They had placed his left hand on his stomach. I took his right hand in mine.

"Hola, Tata. Estoy aquí." He seemed to be asleep. But I was surprised to feel a twinge of movement in his hand, and distinctly felt him try to squeeze my hand. Then he relaxed his hand and seemed to drift back to that other place, while still taking slow, shallow breaths. Then it struck me. I remembered. I knew what to do.

I closed my eyes, took three very deep breaths, and let the air out slowly and completely. While still holding Tata's hand, I relaxed my entire body. Putting my attention on the light energy raining down on me and filling me up, I asked for the assistance of my higher self and my guides.

I could sense that Tía Paula had left the room. Only Gracie was in the room with Tata and me. I was glad she was here. She would be able to help, whether she was aware of it or not. I knew she was praying. Gracie lived close to God. She would have already called in all of her saints and guides.

Losing awareness of anything but a point of light in the middle of my head, I willingly slipped down to another level of consciousness. I continued to drift lower and lower, willing myself to go further, into the trance state. I could see the lines of energy coming from me, connecting with the weak lines of energy coming from Tata. I followed those energy lines into another place, a beautiful bright golden room where I was sitting with Tata. Tata's helpers and guides were here, and Gracie's too. I could feel a wash of emotion pass over me, a strong feeling of love and support. Then I saw him. He looked the same as in my dream, and I knew this was Tata's father. So my grandfather's father was one of Tata's guides! And my great-grandmother was here too. My grandfather's mother was one of Gracie's guides! Although I had never met them in physical life, I knew who they were in this crowd of spirit helpers. Soon I saw my own guides come into the room, my circle of elders who have come to me on other occasions.

I began, silently, in my head: "Tata, in the beginning was the light. We are all a part of that light. We are all spiritual beings of light. We are all connected to each other, to all things on this Earth, and to that source of light, to which we will return. We are the warriors of the light, the seekers of spiritual power. Our job is to increase our spiritual energy, our light, and thereby increase our connection with God and the power of the Universe in order to use that power to improve our own lives and the lives of others...."

He smiled at me and reached out to take my hand. Meanwhile my physical body felt his hands move in mine. I continued, for I had much to tell him, and all the time in the world to tell him, for in this place there was no time. And so I shared with him, in much detail, all that I had learned over the past few years. He beamed with what I knew to be both amusement and joy. Then I realized that not only was there no time in this place, there was no language. Although I thought for a while that I was talking, I realized instead that I was sharing thoughts and visual images with him. Tata therefore could understand me and I could understand him perfectly.

Soon we were moving from place to place, so he could see examples and experience the main teachings. I was able to guide us to these places by means of my intent, and at times by his intent he moved us more in-depth in an area that he wanted to explore. There was nothing linear about this exploration into the teachings. Each piece showed up out of my intent and enthusiasm to share with him what I had learned.

In the process, I forgot all about my own self-doubt, my own feelings of not having quite learned all that I needed to learn, my feelings of having forgotten some of the information I was taught, or not remembering key pieces when I tried to recall them. This time it just all flowed while we were there in that other space, that other level of consciousness.

That was what Don Emilio had tried to tell me, to reassure me. He had said, "All that you have learned is information which comes from another place, another level of consciousness. You will be able to access it when you are connected with the source.

"I am teaching," he had said, "and you are learning. But this information is in your cells, and in your genes. You have already learned it in other lifetimes. We are simply going through a process of helping you to recall it, and relearning how to get to that place where you can access anything you want to know."

And here I was, bringing it all forward to show to my grandfather before he passed on to the other side––where he would have been able to access it all anyway, come to think of it. Then it struck me. This was for me! Tata didn't really need to know. He wanted *me* to know that I knew. I looked at him with this new realization, and he knew what I was thinking. He was smiling at me. He knew that I finally got it. And he was pleased.

Now that we had finished, we were back in the beautiful gold room. My guides came forward at this point to acknowledge this long-sought accomplishment.

"But," one of them said, "please try not to forget what was accomplished here. Try to remember that you *do* know this ancient knowledge. It is difficult to carry it back into the usual conscious state, but you must keep trying. We are here to help you remember, and you can access our help anytime. Know also that your Tata will now join this circle to help guide you in your work."

The room then began to get brighter and brighter. Tata's guides and mine thanked me for him, and said it was time for me to go. They said they had to take Tata to the next level. Upon hearing that, I heard and felt a swoosh as I traveled back on those lines of energy, back into Tata's bedroom. I opened my eyes and was looking right into Gracie's.

"Are you okay?" she asked. "You haven't moved a muscle for over ten minutes. I wasn't even sure you were breathing."

"I'm fine," I said, "but Tata is leaving us now. Call in the others." I bent over and kissed him on his forehead, then slowly got up out of the chair, taking one last look at him lying there motionless, barely breathing, knowing that most of him was already in another place, moving on to where God and his guides wanted him to be next.

"Thank you Tata," I said to him for one last time. "Thank you for making it possible for me to learn about the ancient spiritual power of our culture. I promise to use this knowledge, this power, to help make this little corner of our world a better place for all."

I turned and walked away from his bed, and walked out onto his porch to allow room for the rest of his *familia* to be with him as the final strands of his consciousness slipped away.

AFTERWORD

The story about how this book came to be is perhaps as out of the ordinary as the story itself, yet is very much a part of the message in the book. It began when I saw the Edward Olmos movie *American Me*. I thought it was a great movie, but at the same time, a horrible movie. It left viewers with a terrible impression of Latino people and our culture, because of what it showed about Latino prison gangs, and especially because of the last scene, in which a young teenage gang member does a totally random drive-by killing. As Olmos stated later at an *Alma Awards* presentation, the scene sadly showed a very horrible development within our culture–that some of our youth were now killing people for no reason.

Latinos are very proud of our people and our culture, and obviously know we are so much more than prison gangs and drive by shootings. For months after seeing that movie, the thought came to me over and over that, because *American Me* showed such a terrible side of our culture, we need to see stories focused on the positive aspects of our culture.

Be careful what you ask for. I was attending a retreat in a wilderness area in northern New Mexico, accessible only by twelve miles of a bumpy and sometimes one-lane dirt road, with no electricity, phones, TV, or computers––a real get-away-from-it-all retreat. I took many books to read, but never opened even one, because after two days of unwinding from the pressures of the work I had left 1,000 miles away, a movie started playing in my head. I took out a pad of paper and, as fast as I could, started writing what I saw and heard. I had to keep rewinding the movie in my head so my hand could catch up.

So began the book, coming from someplace, I was not sure where. But I knew I wasn't making it up. It seemed more like it was being dictated to me, visually. I kept thinking I knew someone needed to write the positive story, but why me? I came to New Mexico to relax and unwind my stress. Writing a book didn't seem like relaxation. But I loved the story. I enjoyed getting inside the characters and listening for what they would say next, and discovering where the story was going. After sharing my progress on the book with a friend I was asked what happens next. My response was, "I don't know, I haven't read that far." I realized I was along for the ride.

I quickly discovered, however, that when I went from the idyllic wilderness environment back to the busy city and the stressful job, I could no longer hear the audio or see the images. I plodded along, finding time to go to the mountains to get away occasionally on weekends to write, even taking a month-long break two years later at a retreat in Montana. Eventually I learned what writers learn–you have to establish your creative environment where you are. I had to do what it takes to get into that space where I could again hear the messages and see the continuation of the movie. However, I also realized I had a lot of work to do, as the dictation sometimes gave me information, but not all the details required for a written story. And this other source was other times so wordy that my first draft was much too long. An agent suggested cutting it way back.

I came to learn the answer to the question, Why me? I was burdened (and gifted) with this task because, as a result of the sacrifices of my grandparents and parents, I was able to receive a quality education, and developed good language and writing skills. In addition, my experiences growing up in an inner-city barrio and an unquenchable thirst for knowledge about shamanism and native spirituality seemed to make me an appropriate candidate to take on the task of helping to get this particular material out to readers.

This book came to be a truly collaborative effort, with my research and writing, combined with ongoing insight and inspiration coming from my own guidance and from the original source of the material. It took a lot longer to write this story than I anticipated, because I was not ready to simply accept what was given to me. I needed to truly understand the material. It had to move from intellectual knowledge in my head, to a true knowingness in my gut or in my Being. As the teacher in the story says, I had to get to that place where I remembered again what I already knew. In addition, the research confirmed that the material was consistent with what others had taught.

Even though the material is presented as fiction, the story is about the two boys going through the process of learning real ancient spiritual knowledge, which really has been passed down by our ancestors for many, many generations. The elders who have hidden this information, for the reasons stated in the story, are now making an effort to share it with the world. This book is one of those efforts.

I make no pretense that this is new information. Others are sharing similar material in their own way, through lectures, and written fiction and nonfiction. This book is an effort to share it in a manner that will resonate with young people, and with their parents and other adults interested in its slant toward Latino culture and shamanism.

Finally, I would like to say that my own personal spiritual learning experiences are woven into the fictional narrative. So I know the material and the experiences are true and possible. The story line is fiction, but the setting, Barrio Logan in San Diego, is a real neighborhood. Other than that, any resemblance to real persons and places is purely "coincidental."

RECOMMENDED READING

Dance of Power: A Shamanic Journey, Dr. Susan Greg, Llewellyn Publications. 1993.

E²: Nine Do It Yourself Energy Experiments That Prove Your Thoughts Create Your Reality, Pam Groat, Hay House Insights. 2012.

Just Ask The Universe: A No Nonsense Guide to Manifesting Your Dreams, Michael Samuels. 2011.

Miracles, Stuart Wilde, White Dove International, Inc. 1983.

No Ordinary Moments, Dan Millman, H J Kramer, Inc. 1992.

Personal Power Through Awareness, Sanaya Roman, H J Kramer, Inc. 1986.

Spiritual Growth: Being Your Higher Self, Sanaya Roman, H J Kramer, Inc. 1989.

The Complete Idiot's Guide to Toltec Wisdom, Sheri A. Rosenthal, DPM, Alpha Books-Penguin Group Inc. 2005.

The Force, Stuart Wilde, Wisdom Books Inc. 1984.

The Nature of Personal Reality: A Seth Book, Jane Roberts, New World Library. 1994.

The Science Behind Miracles: Unveiling the Huna Tradition of the Ancient Polynesians, Max Freedom Long, DeVorss & Company. 1948.

The Science of Getting Rich, Wallace Wattles, Elizabeth Towne Company. 1910.

The Teachings of Don Juan: A Yaqui Way of Knowledge, Touchstone Books/Simon & Schuster, New York, NY. 1968.

ACKNOWLEDGMENTS

To start at the beginning, I want to thank Grove Burnett and Linda Velarde, co-founders of Vallecitos Mountain Ranch, Wilderness Learning and Retreat Center, located in the Carson National Forest in northern New Mexico. Thanks to their efforts and the generosity of their funders I was able to attend a 10-day retreat where I began writing the story. Later, I was selected to attend Windcall, a month-long retreat in Bozeman, Montana, where I was able to continue the writing, thanks to the generosity of Susan and Albert Wells, founders of the Windcall Institute Residency Program.

The most significant contribution to the book came from Corinn Codye who edited the manuscript, many times. Corinn is very familiar with much of the subject matter of the story, so in addition to editing for grammar and typos, she was able to make invaluable suggestions on wording and presentation of certain material. Another significant contribution came from Jeanie Lemaire, a healer, counselor and spiritual intuitive. Over the years, more than anyone in my life, she has helped me grow personally and spiritually. I very much appreciated her support and encouragement for the book and for me.

I also want to thank the following for reviewing the manuscript and providing much needed edits, questions, and suggestions: Bonnie Horrigan, Olivia Puentes Reynolds, Miguel Castro Jr., Robert Hernandez, Rebecca Mobley, CJ Mobley, Carolyn Juarez, Carolina Juarez, Joan Martin, Heather Valencia, and Robert Ames. Thanks to Liz Shear for the eagle trip, and to Maria Pini for the Spanish translations.

Special thanks to Annie Lane, Anna Daniels, Brent Beltrán, and the family of editors at the **San Diego Free Press** for selecting *Tío Emilio and the Secrets of the Ancestors* to appear in their publication.

ABOUT THE AUTHOR

Tío Emilio and the Secrets of the Ancestors is set in the Logan Heights/Barrio Logan community of San Diego. Richard Juarez grew up there and in the adjacent community of Southeast San Diego. His experiences living there influenced his decisions to study city planning and community development, and to focus his work efforts in planning, community economic development and revitalization in inner-city communities, with a slight diversion to head up a state of California office dealing with US-Mexico border issues, and a stint as chief of staff to a San Diego City Councilman.

Throughout that time, and as he continues to work on community development and revitalization efforts, he has also been following an inner drive to learn more about and to share the hidden spiritual knowledge of his ancestors and others who have taught the ancient secrets of the life force energy that flows throughout the Universe, how we are all connected to it, to each other, and to all things in the Universe.

He read books, took classes, attended workshops, participated in ceremonies, and talked with individual teachers, covering a range of paths to spiritual growth, including the one most closely connected to his Mexican ancestry, the Toltec path. His spiritual quest led him to find similarities in the spiritual practices of North American (Sioux, Hopi, Maya) and South American (Inca) tribes, the ancient Huna practices of Hawaii and Polynesia, the Sangoma (shaman) practitioners of South Africa, and the channeled teachings of Seth, Orin, Abraham, and others. He preferred immersing himself in this wide range of spiritual teachings to studying one path under one teacher.

It was when this information from books, classes, workshops and channeled information shifted from mental knowledge to an internalized knowingness that he was able to finish the book. It is set in an old Latino neighborhood so that others, especially teenage youth, could relate to the story, find out about these secrets of the ancestors, and learn the basics of this ancient knowledge by way of a semi-autobiographical, partially fiction novel.

The author can be contacted at richjuarez1@me.com.